THE WINDS OF
DUNE

BRIAN HERBERT
& KEVIN J. ANDERSON

SIMON &
SCHUSTER

London · New York · Sydney · Toronto

A CBS COMPANY

First published in Great Britain by Simon & Schuster UK Ltd, 2009
A CBS COMPANY

1 3 5 7 9 10 8 6 4 2

Simon & Schuster UK Ltd
1st Floor
222 Gray's Inn Road
London WC1X 8HB

www.simonandschuster.co.uk

Simon & Schuster Australia
Sydney

A CIP catalogue record for this book is available
from the British Library

Hardback ISBN: 978-1-84737-724-1
Trade Paperback ISBN: 978-1-84737-423-3

Printed in the UK by CPI Mackays, Chatham ME5 8TD

*It is difficult to be married to an author, more challenging
in many ways than the writing task itself. For their sacrifices,
for their unconditional love and patience, this book,
like others, is dedicated to our remarkable wives,*
JANET HERBERT *and*
REBECCA MOESTA ANDERSON.

ACKNOWLEDGMENTS

While we are busy writing new novels in the incredible Dune universe, many other people contribute to what the reader sees on the printed page. We would like to thank Tor Books, Simon & Schuster U.K., WordFire Inc., the Frank Herbert family, Trident Media Group, New Amsterdam Entertainment, and Misher Films for their contributions and support. As always, we are especially grateful to Frank Herbert, who left the most remarkable literary legacy in all of science fiction, and to Beverly Herbert, who devoted so much of her own talents and energy to the success of the series.

To the Fremen, he is the Messiah;
To the vanquished, he is the Tyrant;
To the Bene Gesserit, he is the Kwisatz Haderach;
But Paul is my son and always will be, no matter how far he falls.

—LADY JESSICA, Duchess of Caladan

The Emperor Paul-Muad'Dib survived a major assassination attempt when a stone-burner robbed him of his eyesight. Though blind, he could see the cracks in his empire, the political stresses and long-festering wounds that threatened to tear his rule apart. Ultimately he knew—whether through prescience or Mentat analysis—that the problems were insurmountable.

With his beloved Chani dead in childbirth and his newborn twins helpless, Muad'Dib turned his back on humanity and his children and walked into the desert, leaving the empire to his sixteen-year-old sister, Alia. Thus, he abandoned everything he had worked to create.

Even the most careful historian can never know the reason for this.

—BRONSO OF IX, Analysis of History: Muad'Dib

Though he is gone, Muad'Dib never ceases to test us. Who are we to doubt his choices? Wherever he is, in life or death, Muad'Dib continues to watch over his people. That is why we must pray to him for guidance.

—PRINCESS IRULAN, The Legacy of Muad'Dib

PART I

10,207 AG

After the overthrow of Shaddam IV, the reign of Paul-Muad'Dib
lasted fourteen years. He established his new capital in Arrakeen
on the sacred desert planet, Dune. Though Muad'Dib's Jihad is
over at long last, conflicts continue to flare up.

Paul's mother, the Lady Jessica, has withdrawn from the constant
battles and political schemes and returned to the Atreides
ancestral home of Caladan to serve there as Duchess.

In my private life on Caladan, I receive few reports of my son's Jihad, not because I choose to be ignorant, but because the news is rarely anything I wish to hear.

—LADY JESSICA, Duchess of Caladan

The unscheduled ship loomed in orbit over Caladan, a former Guild Heighliner pressed into service as a Jihad transport.

A young boy from the fishing village, apprenticed to the Castle as a page, rushed into the garden courtyard. Looking awkward in his formal clothing, he blurted, "It's a military-equipped vessel, my Lady. Fully armed!"

Kneeling beside a rosemary bush, Jessica snipped off fragrant twigs for the kitchens. Here in her private garden, she maintained flowers, herbs, and shrubs in a perfect combination of order and chaos, useful flora and pretty pleasantries. In the peace and stillness just after dawn, Jessica liked to work and meditate here, nourishing her plants and uprooting the persistent weeds that tried to ruin the careful balance.

Unruffled by the boy's panic, she inhaled deeply of the aromatic evergreen oils released by her touch. Jessica rose to her feet and brushed dirt off her knees. "Have they sent any messages?"

"Only that they are dispatching a group of Qizarate emissaries, my Lady. They demand to speak with you on an urgent matter."

"They *demand?*"

The young man quailed at her expression. "I'm sure they meant it as a request, my Lady. After all, would they dare to make *demands* of the Duchess of Caladan—and the mother of Muad'Dib? Still, it must be important news indeed, to warrant a vessel like that!" The young man fidgeted like an eel washed up on shore.

She straightened her garment. "Well, I'm sure the *emissary* considers it important. Probably just another request for me to increase the limits on the number of pilgrims allowed to come here."

Caladan, the seat of House Atreides for more than twenty generations, had escaped the ravages of the Jihad, primarily because of Jessica's refusal to let too many outsiders swarm in. Caladan's self-sufficient people preferred to be left alone. They would gladly have accepted their Duke Leto back, but he had been murdered through treachery at high levels; now the people had his son Paul-Muad'Dib instead, the Emperor of the Known Universe.

Despite Jessica's best efforts, Caladan could never be completely isolated from the outside storms in the galaxy. Though Paul paid little attention to his home planet anymore, he had been christened and raised here; the people could never escape the shadow cast by her son.

After all the years of Paul's Jihad, a weary and wounded peace had settled over the Imperium like a cold winter fog. Looking at the young messenger now, she realized that he had been born after Paul became Emperor. The boy had never known anything but the looming Jihad and the harsher side of her son's nature. . . .

She left the courtyard gardens, shouting to the boy. "Summon Gurney Halleck. He and I will meet the delegation in the main hall of Castle Caladan."

Jessica changed out of her gardening clothes into a sea-green gown of state. She lifted her ash-bronze hair and draped a pendant bearing a golden Atreides hawk crest around her neck. She refused to hurry. The more she thought about it, the more she wondered what news the ship might bring. Perhaps it wasn't a trivial matter after all. . . .

Gurney was waiting for her in the main hall. He had been out running his gaze hounds, and his face was still flushed from the exercise. "According to the spaceport, the emissary is a high-ranking member of the Qizarate, bringing an army of retainers and honor guards from Arrakis. Says he has a message of the utmost importance."

She pretended a disinterest she did not truly feel. "By my count, this is the ninth 'urgent message' they've delivered since the Jihad ended two years ago."

"Even so, my Lady, this one feels different."

Gurney had aged well, though he was not, and never would be, a handsome man with that inkvine scar on his jaw and those haunted eyes. In his youth he'd been ground under the Harkonnen boot, but years of brave service had shaped him into one of House Atreides's greatest assets.

She lowered herself into the chair that her beloved Duke Leto had once used. While scurrying castle servants prepared for the emissary and his entourage, the director of the kitchen staff asked Jessica about appropriate refreshments. She answered in a cool tone, "Just water. Serve them water."

"Nothing else, my Lady? Is that not an insult to such an important personage?"

Gurney chuckled. "They're from Dune. They'll consider it an honor."

The foyer's oaken castle doors were flung open to the damp breeze, and the honor guard marched in with a great commotion. Fifteen men, former soldiers from Paul's Jihad, carried green banners with highlights of black or white. The members of this unruly entourage wore imitation stillsuits as if they were uniforms, though stillsuits were completely unnecessary in Caladan's moist air. Glistening droplets covered the group from the light drizzle that had begun to fall outside; the visitors seemed to consider it a sign from God.

The front ranks of the entourage shifted aside so that a Qizara, a yellow-robed priest of the Jihad, could step forward. The priest lowered his damp hood to show his bald scalp, and his eyes glittered with awe, completely blue from addiction to the spice melange. "I am Isbar, and I present myself to the mother of Muad'Dib." He bowed, then continued the bow all the way to the floor until he had prostrated himself.

"Enough of this. Everyone here knows who I am."

Even when Isbar stood, he kept his head bowed and his eyes averted. "Seeing the bounty of water on Caladan, we more fully understand Muad'Dib's sacrifice in coming to Dune as the savior of the Fremen."

Jessica's voice had enough of an edge to show that she did not wish to waste time on ceremony. "You have come a long way. What is the urgency this time?"

Isbar seemed to wrestle with his message as if it were a living thing, and Jessica sensed the depth of his dread. The members of the honor guard remained silent as statues.

"Out with it, man!" Gurney ordered.

The priest blurted, "Muad'Dib is dead, my Lady. Your son has gone to Shai-Hulud."

Jessica felt as though she had been struck with a cudgel.

Gurney groaned. "Oh no. No . . . not Paul!"

Isbar continued, anxious to purge himself of his words. "Forsaking his rule, the holy Muad'Dib walked out into the desert and vanished into the sands."

It took all of Jessica's Bene Gesserit training to erect a thick wall around herself, to give herself time to think. The shutdown of her emotions was automatic, ingrained. She forced herself not to cry out, kept her voice quiet and steady. "Tell me everything, priest."

The Qizara's words stung like sand pellets blown by a harsh wind. "You know of the recent plot by traitors among his own Fedaykin. Even though blinded by a stone-burner, the blessed Muad'Dib viewed the world with divine eyes, not the artificial Tleilaxu ones that he purchased for his injured soldiers."

Yes, Jessica knew all of that. Because of her son's dangerous decisions, and backlash from the Jihad, he'd always faced the very real threat of assassination. "But Paul survived the plot that blinded him. Was there another one?"

"An extension of the same conspiracy, Great Lady. A Guild Steersman was implicated, as well as the Reverend Mother Gaius Helen Mohiam." He added, as an afterthought, "By order of the Imperial Regent Alia, both have now been executed along with Korba the Panegyrist, architect of the cabal against your son."

Too many facts clamored at her at once. Mohiam, *executed*? That news shook her to the core. Jessica's relationship with the old Reverend Mother had been tumultuous, love and hate cycling like the tides.

Alia . . . Regent now? Not Irulan? Of course, it was appropriate. But if *Alia* was the ruler . . . "What of Chani, my son's beloved? What of Princess Irulan, his wife?"

"Irulan has been imprisoned in Arrakeen until her involvement in the plot can be measured. Regent Alia would not allow her to be executed with the others, but it is known that Irulan associated with the traitors." The priest swallowed hard. "As for Chani . . . she did not survive the birth of the twins."

"Twins?" Jessica shot to her feet. "I have grandchildren?"

"A boy and a girl. Paul's children are healthy, and—"

Her calm façade slipped dangerously. "You did not think to inform me of this immediately?" She struggled to organize her thoughts. "Tell me *all* that I need to know, without delay."

The Qizara fumbled with his story. "You know of the ghola who was a gift to Muad'Dib from the Tleilaxu and the Guild? He turned out to be a weapon, an assassination tool created from the slain body of a faithful Atreides retainer."

Jessica had heard of the ghola grown from Duncan Idaho's dead cells, but had always assumed him to be some sort of exotic performer or Jongleur mimic.

"Hayt had the appearance and mannerisms of Duncan Idaho, but not the memories," the priest continued. "Though programmed to kill Muad'Dib, his true personality surfaced and defeated the alter ego, and through that crisis he became the true Duncan Idaho again. Now he aids the Imperial Regent Alia."

At first, the idea amazed her—Duncan, truly alive and aware again?—then her focus returned to the most pressing question. "Enough distractions, Isbar. I need more details about what happened to my son."

The priest kept his head bowed, which muffled his voice. "They say that through prescience, Muad'Dib *knew* the tragedies that would befall him, but could do nothing to prevent what he called his 'terrible purpose.' That knowledge destroyed him. Some say that at the end he was truly blind, without any future sight, and he could no longer bear the grief." The Qizara paused, then spoke with greater confidence. "But I believe, as do many others, that Muad'Dib knew it was his time, that he felt the call of Shai-Hulud. His spirit is still out there on the sands, forever intertwined with the desert."

Gurney wrestled with his sorrow and anger, clenching and unclenching his fists. "And you all just *let* him walk off into the dunes, blind?"

"That's what blind Fremen are compelled to do, Gurney," Jessica said.

Isbar straightened. "One does not 'let' Muad'Dib do a thing, Gurney Halleck. He knows the will of God. It is not for us to understand what he chooses to do."

Gurney would not let the matter drop so easily. "And were searches made? Did you attempt to find him? Was his body recovered?"

"Many 'thopters flew over the desert, and many searchers probed the sands. Alas, Muad'Dib has vanished." Isbar bowed reverently.

Gurney's eyes were shining as he turned to Jessica. "Given his skills in the desert, my Lady, he *might* have survived. Paul could have found a way."

"Not if he didn't want to survive." She shook her head, then looked sharply at the priest. "What of Stilgar? What is his part in this?"

"Stilgar's loyalty is beyond question. The Bene Gesserit witch, Korba, and the Steersman died by his hand. He remains on Dune as liaison to the Fremen."

Jessica tried to imagine the uproar that would occur across the Imperium. "And when did all this happen? When was Paul last seen?"

"Twenty-seven days ago," Isbar said.

Gurney roared in astonishment. "Almost a month! By the infinite hells, what took you so long to get here?"

The priest backed away from the man's anger, bumping into members of the entourage. "We needed to make the proper arrangements and gather a party of appropriate importance. It was necessary to obtain a sufficiently impressive Guild ship to bring this terrible news."

Jessica felt pummeled by blow after blow. Twenty-seven days—and she hadn't known, hadn't guessed. How had she not sensed the loss of her son?

"There is one more thing, my Lady, and we are all disturbed by it," Isbar added. "Bronso of Ix continues to spread lies and heresy. He was captured once while Muad'Dib was alive, but he escaped from his death cell. Now the news of your son's death has emboldened him. His blasphemous writings demean the sacred memory of the Messiah. He distributes treatises and manifestos, seeking to strip Muad'Dib of his greatness. We must stop him, my Lady. As the mother of the Holy Emperor, you—"

Jessica cut him off. "My son is dead, Isbar. Bronso has been producing his tracts for seven years and you haven't been able to stop him—so his complaints are hardly news. I have no time for trivial conversation." She rose abruptly. "This audience is at an end."

Scenting prey, the gaze hounds bayed, and Gurney ran with them. The cool air of that afternoon burned his lungs as he crashed through the underbrush, subconsciously trying to run from the devastating news.

The muscular gaze hounds, with gold-green eyes, wide set and bright, had vision as acute as an eagle's, and a keen sense of smell. Protected by thick coats of russet and gray fur, the beasts splashed across brackish puddles, ripped through pampas grass, and howled like a choir performing for the tone deaf. The joy of the hunt was palpable in their actions.

Gurney loved his hounds. Years ago, he had kept another six dogs, but had been forced to put them down when they contracted the bloodfire virus. Jessica herself had given him these puppies to raise, and he resisted placing himself in a risky emotional position again, resolving not to become attached, considering the pain of losing all those other dogs.

That old grief was nothing compared to what he felt now. Paul Atreides, the young Master, was dead. . . .

Gurney stumbled as he lagged behind the hounds. He paused to catch his breath, closed his eyes for just a moment, then ran on after the baying dogs. He had no real interest in the hunt, but he needed to get away from the castle, from Jessica, and especially from Isbar and his Qizarate cronies. He could not risk losing control in front of others.

Gurney Halleck had served House Atreides for most of his life. He had helped to overthrow the Tleilaxu and reclaim Ix for House Vernius, before Paul's birth; later he'd fought at Duke Leto's side against Viscount Moritani during the War of Assassins; he had tried to protect the Atreides against Harkonnen treachery on Arrakis; and he had served Paul throughout the years of his recent Jihad, until retiring from the fight and coming here to Caladan. He should have known the difficulties were not over.

Now Paul was gone. The young Master had walked into the desert . . . blind and alone. Gurney had not been there for him. He wished he had remained on Dune, despite his antipathy toward the constant slaughter. So selfish of him to abandon the Jihad and his own responsibilities! Paul Atreides, Duke Leto's son, had needed him in the epic struggle, and Gurney turned his back on that need.

How can I ever forget that, or overcome the shame?

Splashing through sodden clumps of swamp grasses, he abruptly came upon the gaze hounds barking and yelping where a gray-furred marsh hare had wedged its bristly body into a crack under a mossy limestone overhang. The seven dogs sat back on their haunches, waiting for Gurney, fixated on where the terrified hare huddled, out of reach but unable to escape.

Gurney withdrew his hunting pistol and killed the hare instantly and painlessly with one shot to the head. He reached in and pulled out the warm, twitching carcass. The perfectly behaved gaze hounds observed him, their topaz eyes gleaming with alert fascination. Gurney tossed the animal to the ground and, when he gave a signal, the dogs fell upon the fresh kill, snapping at the flesh as if they had not eaten in days. A quick, predatory violence.

A flash of one of the bloody battlefields of the Jihad crossed Gurney's memory vision, and he blinked it away, relegating those sights to the past, where they belonged.

But there were other memories he could not suppress, the things he would miss about Paul, and he felt his warrior self breaking down, crumbling. Paul, who had been such a huge, irreplaceable part of his life, had faded into the expanse of desert, like a Fremen raider evading Harkonnens. This time, Paul would not be coming back.

As he watched the gaze hounds tear the meat apart, Gurney felt as if parts of himself had been torn away, leaving raw and gaping wounds.

THAT NIGHT, WHEN Castle Caladan lay dark and quiet, the servants retired, leaving Jessica to mourn in private. But she could not sleep, could not find peace in an empty bedchamber that echoed with cold silence.

She felt off balance, adrift. Due to her Bene Gesserit training, the valves of her emotions had been rusted shut with disuse, especially after Leto's death, after she had turned her back on Arrakis and returned here.

But Paul was her son!

With a silent tread, Jessica glided down the castle's corridors to the doorway of Gurney's private chambers. She paused, wanting someone to talk to. She and Gurney could relate their common loss and consider what to do now, how to help Alia hold the already strained empire together until Paul's children came of age. What sort of future could they create for those infant twins? The winds of Dune—the politics and desert storms—could strip a person's flesh down to the bone.

Before she knocked at the heavy door, Jessica was surprised to hear strange sounds coming from within—wordless animal noises. She realized with a start that Gurney was sobbing. Alone and in private, the stoic troubadour warrior unleashed his sorrow with an unsettling abandon.

Jessica was even more disturbed to realize that her own grief was not nearly so deep or uncontrolled: It was somewhere far away, out of her reach. The lump inside her was hard and heavy. And numb. She didn't know how to access the emotions beneath. The very idea upset her. *Why can't I feel it the way he does?*

Hearing Gurney's private sorrow, Jessica wanted to go in and offer comfort, but she knew that would shame him. The troubadour warrior would never want her to see his naked sentiments. He would consider it a weakness. So she withdrew, leaving him to his own grief.

Unsteady on her feet, Jessica searched within herself, but encountered only hardened barriers that surrounded her sadness and prevented a real emotional release. *Paul was my son!*

As she returned to her chambers in the dead of night, Jessica quietly cursed the Bene Gesserit Sisterhood. Damn them! They had stripped away a mother's ability to feel the proper anguish at losing her child.

The beginning of a reign, or a regency, is a fragile time. Alliances shift, and people circle like carrion birds, hunting for the new leader's weaknesses. Sycophants tell leaders what they wish to hear, not what they need to hear. The beginning is a time for clarity and hard decisions, because those decisions set the tone for the entire reign.

—ST. ALIA OF THE KNIFE

The envoy from Shaddam IV arrived less than a month after Paul vanished into the desert. Alia was astonished at how swiftly the exiled Corrino Emperor acted.

Because the representative was so rushed, however, he had only a sketchy knowledge of the situation. The man knew that the twins had been born, that Chani had died in childbirth, that Paul had surrendered to his blindness and vanished into the sandy wastelands. But he was unaware of the many dire decisions Alia had made since then. He did not know that the Steersman Edric and Reverend Mother Mohiam had both been executed, along with Korba the Panegyrist. The envoy did not know that Shaddam's daughter Irulan was being held in a death cell, her fate undecided.

Alia chose to receive the man in an interior chamber with walls of thick plasmeld. Bright glowglobes flooded the room with garish yellow illumination, not unlike the lighting in an interrogation chamber. She had asked Duncan and Stilgar to sit on either side of her; the long table's veneer of blue obsidian made its polished surface look like a window into the depths of a distant ocean.

Stilgar growled, "We have not even announced formal plans for

Muad'Dib's funeral, and this lackey comes like a vulture drawn to fresh meat. Official Landsraad representatives haven't arrived from Kaitain yet."

"It's been a month. " Alia adjusted the sheathed crysknife that she always kept hanging on a thong around her neck. "And the Landsraad has never moved quickly."

"I don't know why Muad'Dib bothered to keep them in the first place. We don't need their meetings and memoranda."

"They are a vestige of the old government, Stilgar. The forms must be obeyed." She herself hadn't decided how much of a role, if any, she would let the Landsraad nobles have in her Regency. Paul had not actually tried to eliminate them, but he had paid them little attention. "The main question is—considering the travel times, and the fact that we did not dispatch any notice whatsoever to Salusa Secundus—how did their emissary get here so swiftly? Some spy must have rushed off within the first few days. How could Shaddam have already put a plan in place . . . if it is a plan?"

Brow furrowed with thought, Duncan Idaho sat upright in his chair as if he had forgotten how to relax. The man's dark curly hair and wide face had become so familiar to Alia, who remembered him with a double vision—the old Duncan from the memories she'd obtained from her mother, superimposed over Alia's own experiences with the ghola named Hayt. His metal, artificial eyes—a jangling, discordant note on his otherwise human features—served to remind her of the new Duncan's dual origin.

The Tleilaxu had made their ghola into a Mentat, and now Duncan drew upon those cerebral abilities to offer a summation. "The conclusion is obvious: Someone in the exiled Corrino court—perhaps Count Hasimir Fenring—was *already prepared to act* on the assumption that the original assassination plot would succeed. Although the conspiracy failed, Paul Atreides is still gone. The Corrinos acted swiftly to fill the perceived power vacuum."

"Shaddam will try to snatch back his throne. We should have killed him here when we had him prisoner after the Battle of Arrakeen," Stilgar said. "We must be ready when he makes his move."

Alia sniffed. "Maybe I'll have the envoy take Irulan's head back to her father. *That* message would never be misconstrued." Even so, she knew that Paul would never have sanctioned Irulan's execution, despite her clear, if peripheral, role in the conspiracy.

"Such an act would have grave, far-reaching consequences," Duncan warned.

"You disagree?"

Duncan raised his eyebrows, exposing more of the eerie eyes. "I did not say that."

"I would take satisfaction in throttling that fine Imperial neck," Stilgar admitted. "Irulan has never been our friend, though she now insists she truly loved Muad'Dib. She may be saying that just to save her body's water."

Alia shook her head. "In that she speaks the truth—Irulan reeks of it. She did love my brother. The question is whether to keep her as a tool whose worth has not yet been proven, or to waste her on a symbolic gesture that we cannot retract."

"Maybe we should wait and hear what the envoy has to say?" Duncan suggested.

Alia nodded and her imposing amazon guards led a statuesque and self-important man named Rivato through the winding passages of the fortress citadel to the brightly lit meeting room. Though the route was direct, the sheer length of the walk had confused and flustered him. Shutting him inside the thick-walled chamber with Alia and her two companions, the female guards stationed themselves outside in the dusty passageway.

Composing himself with an effort, the Salusan envoy bowed deeply. "Emperor Shaddam wishes to express his sorrow at the death of Paul-Muad'Dib Atreides. They were rivals, yes, but Paul was also his son-in-law, wed to his eldest daughter." Rivato glanced around. "I had hoped Princess Irulan might join us for this discussion?"

"She is otherwise occupied." Alia briefly considered throwing this man into the same death cell. "Why are you here?"

They had placed no empty chair on the opposite side of the blue obsidian table—an intentional oversight that forced Rivato to remain on his feet as he faced the three inquisitors, and kept him off balance and uncomfortable. He bowed again to hide the flicker of unease that crossed his face. "The Emperor dispatched me instantly upon learning the news, because the entire Imperium faces a crisis."

"Shaddam is not the Emperor," Duncan pointed out. "Stop referring to him as such."

"Your pardon. Since I serve in his court on Salusa Secundus, I tend to forget." Regaining his momentum, Rivato forged ahead. "Despite the sad events, we have a tremendous opportunity to restore order. Since the . . . fall of Shaddam IV, the Imperium has faced extreme turmoil and bloodshed. The Jihad was driven by a man of great charisma—no one denies that—but with Muad'Dib gone, we can now return much-needed stability to the Imperium."

Alia interrupted him. "The Imperium will stabilize under my regency. Paul's Jihad ended almost two years ago, and our armies remain strong. We face fewer and fewer rebellious worlds."

The envoy tried to give a reassuring smile. "But there are still places that require, shall we say, considerably more *diplomacy* to settle things down. A restoration of the Corrino presence would calm the waters by providing continuity."

Alia regarded him coldly. "Muad'Dib has two children by his concubine Chani, and these are his imperial heirs. The line of succession is clear—we have no further need of Corrinos."

Rivato raised his hands in a placating gesture. "When he took Princess Irulan as his wife, Paul-Muad'Dib recognized the need to maintain ties with the former Imperial House. The long tradition of Corrino rule dates back to the end of the Butlerian Jihad. If we strengthen those ties, it would benefit all humanity."

Stilgar pounced on the remarks. "You suggest that Muad'Dib's reign did not benefit humanity?"

"Ah, now, that is for historians to decide, and I am no historian."

Duncan folded his hands on the table. "What are you, then?"

"I offer solutions to problems. After consulting with the Padishah—I mean, with Shaddam—we wanted to suggest ways to face this transition of rule."

"Suggestions, such as?" Alia prodded.

"Rejoining the bloodlines, in whatever manner, would eliminate much of the turmoil, heal the wounds. There are many possible avenues to accomplish this. For instance, you, Lady Alia, might marry Shaddam—in name only, of course. It has been well established that Muad'Dib took Princess Irulan as his wife in name only. There is an obvious precedent."

Alia bristled. "Shaddam's wives have not had a high survival rate."

"That is in the past, and he has been unmarried for years."

"Nevertheless, the offer is unacceptable to the Regent." Duncan's voice carried a slight undercurrent of jealousy, Alia thought.

"Tell us what other marriages you suggest," Stilgar said, "so that we may scoff at those as well."

Unruffled, Rivato sorted through his fallback plans. "Shaddam has three surviving daughters—Wensicia, Chalice, and Josifa—and Muad'Dib has a young son. Perhaps the Atreides boy could be betrothed to a Corrino daughter? The difference in ages is not so significant, considering the geriatric effects of melange." Seeing their scowls, Rivato continued quickly. "Similarly, the Emperor's grandson, Farad'n, by his daughter Wensicia, could be betrothed to the daughter of Muad'Dib. They are close enough in age."

Alia rose to her feet, a sixteen-year-old girl among grim men, yet she was obviously the one who wielded the power. "Rivato, we need time to consider what you've said." If she let him continue to speak, she might order his execution after all, and then she would probably regret it. "I must attend to many pressing matters, including the state funeral for my brother."

"And a Fremen funeral for Chani," Stilgar added in a low voice.

She gave Rivato a cold smile. "Return to Salusa and await our answer. You are dismissed."

With a hurried bow, the unsettled man withdrew and the amazon guards marched him away. As soon as the door closed again, Duncan said, "His suggestions are not entirely without merit."

"Oh? You would have me wed old Shaddam?" The ghola remained impassive, and Alia wondered if he felt nothing for her after all. Or did he just hide it well? "I will hear no more of these dynastic absurdities." With a brisk gesture, she cut off further discussion. "Duncan, there's something else I need you to do for me."

THE FOLLOWING DAY, Alia peered into the death cell through a hidden spy-eye. Princess Irulan sat on a hard bench, looking at nothing in particular, showing no sign of impatience. Her demeanor exuded sadness rather than fear. *Not terrified for her life, that one.* It was difficult to accept that she was truly mourning the loss of Paul, but Alia knew it to be true.

Bored with the game, she left the surveillance screen and instructed one of the yellow-robed Qizara guards to unseal the door. As the Regent entered, Irulan rose to her feet. "Have you come to inform me of my execution date? Will you kill me, after all?" She seemed more interested in the answer than afraid of it.

"I have not yet decided your fate."

"The priests have, and their mobs howl for my blood."

"But I am the Imperial Regent, and *I* make the decision." Alia gave her a thin, mysterious smile. "And I am not yet ready to reveal it to you."

Irulan sat back down with a long sigh. "Then what do you want from me? Why did you come here?"

Alia smiled sweetly. "An envoy from Salusa Secundus came to see me. Through him, your father suggested outrageous marriages into House Corrino as a way to solve most of the Imperium's problems."

"I considered that myself, but you no longer listen to my counsel, despite the respect you had for me when you were younger," Irulan said evenly. "What answer did you give him?"

"Late yesterday, the envoy boarded a small shuttle to take him back to a Heighliner in orbit. Unfortunately, his shuttle experienced inexplicable engine failure and fell out of the sky from a high altitude. I'm afraid there were no survivors." Alia shook her head. "Some people suspect sabotage, and we will mount a full investigation . . . as soon as we have time."

Irulan gazed at her in horror. "Did Duncan Idaho sabotage the engines? Stilgar?"

Alia tried to maintain her implacable expression, but she softened, remembering when she and the Princess had been rather close. This was not a black or white situation. Grayness surrounded Irulan. "With my brother gone, conspirators and usurpers will come at me from all directions. I need to show my strength and mettle, or everything Muad'Dib worked for will be lost."

Irulan said, "But what else will you lose along the way?"

"Perhaps you, Princess. It would take only a flick of my finger."

"Oh? Then who would raise Paul's children? Who would love them?"

"Harah is quite competent in that regard." Alia left the death cell, and the Qizara guards sealed the door again, leaving the Princess alone with her unanswered questions.

No contemporary can decide the worth of my son's actions. Muad'Dib's legacy will be judged on a scale that extends longer than a single lifetime. The future makes its own decisions about the past.

        —LADY JESSICA, Duchess of Caladan

K nowing that Alia now faced the turbulent aftermath of Paul's death, Jessica decided to depart for Dune—to be with her daughter and help in any way she could. She sent a formal message to the Qizara Isbar, telling him that she and Gurney Halleck intended to leave Caladan as quickly as possible. The priest's delegation scrambled to accommodate her wishes.

The military-augmented Guildship remained in orbit, and Gurney arranged for them to ride in a lavish old Atreides frigate from the private spaceport hangar. This ornamented workhorse vessel had been put into service by Old Duke Paulus, and Jessica remembered that Leto had used it during their initial journey to Arrakis. *Everything we do brings the baggage of history with it,* she thought.

As Gurney issued curt instructions to the pilot, the obsequious priest appeared in the empty bay, bowing deeply. "The Heighliner crew awaits your pleasure, my Lady. In Muad'Dib's name, we already diverted the vessel to Caladan so that we could deliver our sad news to you. The needs of the delayed passengers are not more pressing than yours."

"Passengers? I had assumed this was a special military ship commandeered by the Qizarate."

"Now that the Jihad has been declared over, many of the military vessels have been placed back into service as passenger ships. We took the first available vessel after Regent Alia instructed me to bring you word of Muad'Dib's death. What other business can possibly be so important? All those other people can wait."

Gurney dropped a heavy pack on the frigate's ramp, muttering to himself. Though not surprised by the offhanded show of power, Jessica was alarmed that Isbar would simply divert an entire ship with a crowded cargo hold and a full roster of passengers. "Well, let us be quick about it."

Isbar stepped closer, and Jessica could see the hunger in his eyes, the blind awe. "May I ride with you in the frigate, my Lady? As the mother of Muad'Dib, you can teach me much. I would be your rapt pupil."

But she had no need of sycophants. She didn't want this priest as her pupil, rapt or otherwise. "Please travel with your own party. I require solitude for my prayers."

Disappointed, Isbar gave a solemn nod and backed out of the hangar, still bowing, as Jessica and Gurney climbed aboard the frigate. The ornate hatch sealed them inside. Gurney said, "Paul would have despised that man."

"Isbar is no different from the other priests that have formed a power structure around Muad'Dib, and around his legacy. My son was trapped by his own mythos. As the years went by, it became apparent to me—and to him—how much had slipped out of his control."

"We removed ourselves from the equation, my Lady," Gurney said, then quoted a familiar saying, "'Those who do nothing but observe from the shadows cannot complain about the brightness of the sun.' Perhaps we can make amends now, if Alia is inclined to permit it."

During the flight up to the Heighliner, Jessica tried to relax while Gurney took out his baliset and began to strum softly. She feared he had already composed a memorial hymn for Paul, and she wasn't ready to hear that. To her relief, he merely played a familiar tune that he knew was one of her favorites.

She looked at his craggy face, the patchy blond hair that was going gray, the prominent inkvine scar. "Gurney, you always know the right piece to perform."

"From practice, my Lady."

ONCE DOCKED ABOARD the Heighliner, Jessica and Gurney left the comfort of the frigate and went out into the common areas. In nondescript clothing, they drew no attention to themselves as they entered the promenade. Isbar had already told her his version of Muad'Dib's death; Jessica wanted to hear what the people were saying.

Some passengers never left their private vessels inside the great hold, but many of those who faced long passages with many stopovers and roundabout routes busied themselves in the Heighliner's communal decks, visiting restaurants, drinking establishments, and shops.

She and Gurney crossed the vast open decks, looking at the wares for sale from numerous planets. Some vendors had already created items to commemorate the reign and death of Muad'Dib; she found it disturbing, and Gurney pulled her away. He led her to a brightly lit drinking establishment that was all plaz, crystal, and chrome, crowded with noisy patrons. Arrayed on the wall were colorful liquors, specialties from countless planets.

"This is the best place to eavesdrop," Gurney said. "We'll take seats and let the conversations come to us." With a glass of black wine for herself and a frothy, bitter beer for him, they sat facing each other, comfortable in their closeness. And listened.

A race of itinerant people, the Wayku, served as staff aboard all Guildships; they were a silent, oddly homogeneous race, well known for impersonal solicitousness. Barely noticed, dark-uniformed Wayku stewards walked about among the patrons, clearing tables, delivering drinks.

The main topic of conversation involved the death of Muad'Dib. Debates raged at table after table about whether Jessica's son had been savior or monster, whether the corrupt and decadent Corrino rule was preferable to the pure but violent reign of Paul-Muad'Dib.

They don't understand what he was doing, she thought to herself. *They can never understand why he had to make the decisions he did.*

At one table, a heated argument degenerated into shouts and threats. Chairs were cast aside and two men rose, red-faced, yelling insults. One hurled a knife, while the other activated a personal shield— and the fight continued until the man with the shield lay dead from a slow thrust. The crowd in the bar had watched without attempting to intervene. Afterward, Guild security men came to remove the body and to arrest the befuddled-looking murderer, who could not seem to believe what his rage had led him to do.

While others were focused on the commotion, Jessica watched the silent Wayku stewards circle the tables. She saw one of them surreptitiously deposit printed sheets on several empty tables, then glide away. The move was so smooth that if she hadn't been paying close attention, she never would have spotted it.

"Gurney." She gestured, and he slid his chair back to retrieve one of the documents. He'd seen the same thing, brought it back. The title said, *The Truth About Muad'Dib.*

His expression darkened. "Another one of those scurrilous propaganda leaflets, my Lady."

Jessica skimmed the flyer. Some statements were so outrageous as to be laughable, but others pointed out the excesses that Paul had allowed in his Jihad, emphasizing the corruption in Muad'Dib's government. These had the ring of truth. Bronso of Ix had been a thorny problem for years, and the man was so very good at what he did that he'd become a veritable legend.

Jessica knew that neither Paul's worst critics nor his most ardent admirers fully understood her son. Here in the bar, a man had just been killed for adhering to his beliefs, thinking that *he* understood Paul's motives and intentions. Muad'Dib's calling was infinitely complex, his goal too tangled, subtle, and long-term for anyone, even her, to comprehend fully. She accepted that now.

Gurney crumpled the leaflet, threw it aside in disgust, while Jessica shook her head, wishing it could have all been different. Still, Bronso served his purpose, as did they all.

Subakh ul kuhar, *Muad'Dib! Are you well? Are you out there?*
—Fremen chant to wind and sand

He needed the desert, the vast ocean without water that covered most of the planet. Too much time in the city with its priests and Landsraad members arguing over plans for Muad'Dib's funeral had been wearing on Stilgar. And those noisy pilgrims from other worlds! They were everywhere, clamoring and pushing, giving him no space or time to think.

Finally, after the envoy from Shaddam IV suffered his tragic accident, Stilgar decided to depart for Sietch Tabr, to immerse himself in the purity of Fremen life. He hoped it would cleanse his mental palate and make him feel *real* again, a Naib instead of a robed ornament in Alia's court. He made the journey alone, leaving his wife Harah back at the Citadel to watch the Atreides twins.

At Sietch Tabr, however, he found many changes that disappointed him. It was like the slow fall of sand grains down a slipface, each grain too small to be noticed, but cumulatively causing a significant change. After so many years of Jihad, offworld influences had diluted the Fremen. Their hardships had eased, and their lives were no longer the difficult struggle they once had been. And with comforts came weakness. Stilgar knew the signs. He had watched the changes, and the sietch could no longer offer him the purity he sought. In the end he stayed only one night.

Early the next morning, he was out on the open sand, riding a powerful worm. As the behemoth carried him back toward the Shield Wall and Arrakeen, he wondered if the mother of Muad'Dib would return for her son's funeral. Jessica was a Sayyadina in her own right, and Stilgar felt that Dune had lost part of its soul when she'd chosen to go back to her water world instead of remaining here. How good it would be to see her again, though he was sure even Jessica must have changed.

As a precaution, he would gather his best Fedaykin in Arrakeen, where they could stand guard with Alia's soldiers to welcome the mother of the Messiah—if she chose to return. Jessica didn't need the pomp and ceremony, but she might need his protection.

Stilgar found his solo ride across the desert invigorating and cleansing. Sitting high on the gray-tan segments of the sandworm, he listened to the hiss of grains as the enormous sinuous body glided along. The hot desert winds caressed Stilgar's face, winds that would easily erase the tracks of the worm behind them, winds that would make the desert pristine again. This experience made him feel whole once more— planting his own thumper, mounting the worm with his hooks and spreaders, guiding the monster to his will.

Ever since Muad'Dib had gone out to face his fate, the superstitious Fremen and the people of pan and graben claimed that he had joined Shai-Hulud—literally and spiritually. Some villagers had taken to placing empty pots on shelves or in windows to symbolize the fact that Muad'Dib's water had never been found, that he had mingled with the sands, with the deity Shai-Hulud. . . .

Only hours after Muad'Dib had walked out onto the sand, sweet and bereaved Alia had asked Stilgar to follow orders that he knew were contrary to Paul's direct wishes. She tapped into the Naib's core beliefs and his need for revenge until he convinced himself that Muad'Dib's contradictory intent was merely a test. After so much pain and death, Stilgar had *wanted* to feel blood on his hands. As a Naib he had killed many men, and as a fighter in Muad'Dib's Jihad, he had slaughtered countless others.

A night of killing had ensued, as the details of the complex conspiracy began to unfold. Korba, a brave Fedaykin who had let himself become too important in the priesthood, was the first implicated, his guilt plain to a council of Fremen Naibs. His execution at Stilgar's hands had been easy, necessary, and bloody.

But Stilgar had never before killed a Guild Steersman, nor had he ever killed a Reverend Mother of the Bene Gesserit. Yet, when Alia gave the command, he'd committed the acts without question.

The captive Steersman Edric had wielded the power of the Spacing Guild and carried the political weight of an appointed ambassador, but his safety depended on civilized restraints that meant nothing to Stilgar. Smashing the tank had been simple. When the spice gas drained away and the Steersman flopped about like a spindly aquatic creature cast up on a hostile shore, Stilgar had gripped the mutant's rubbery flesh and snapped the cartilaginous neck. He had taken no great pleasure in it.

The Bene Gesserit witch Mohiam was another matter entirely. Though Stilgar was a great Fremen fighter, this old woman had powers he did not understand, fearsome ways that could have rendered an attack against her very difficult, had he not had the advantage of surprise. He succeeded in killing her only because Mohiam never believed he would actually disobey Paul's orders that she was not to be harmed.

To accomplish the task he had used a clever subterfuge to have her gagged so that she could not use the power of Voice against him, and the old witch had submitted. Had she suspected that her life was threatened, she would have fought tenaciously. Stilgar had not wanted a battle; he wanted an execution.

With the gag firmly set over her mouth, and her hands tied to the chair, Stilgar had stood before the old woman. "Chani—daughter of Liet and beloved of Muad'Dib—is dead after giving birth to twin children." Mohiam's bright eyes widened; he could see she wanted to say something, but was unable. "The ghola Hayt has broken his indoctrination and refused to kill Paul-Muad'Dib." The witch's expression had been a thunderstorm of activity as thoughts flashed through her mind. "Nevertheless, Muad'Dib has given himself to Shai-Hulud, as a blind Fremen is expected to do."

Stilgar withdrew the crysknife from his belt. "Now true justice falls to me. We know your part in the conspiracy." Mohiam began to struggle against her bonds. "The Guild Steersman is already dead, and Korba, too. Princess Irulan has been imprisoned in a death cell."

There was a sound of snapping bonds . . . or perhaps it was the sound of wrist bones breaking. Regardless, Mohiam freed one of her hands. It flashed to the gag over her mouth, but Stilgar's crysknife was faster. He stabbed her chest, knowing it to be a mortal wound, but the Reverend Mother kept moving, forcing her hand to pull the gag free.

Stilgar struck again, puncturing her larynx and slashing her throat, causing her to slump. He kicked the chair and body over, then looked at his sticky fingers. As he wiped the milky blade on the Reverend Mother's dark robes, he realized that the blood of the witch looked and smelled the same as any other blood. . . .

Those had not been the only killings ordered by Alia. It had been a long and difficult night.

Now, as the great worm approached the gap that had been blasted through the Shield Wall by Paul's atomics, Stilgar saw a barricade of water-filled qanats that no worm could cross—especially a tired one like this. Better to release the beast here, out on the open sand. He had ridden and released so many sandworms that he had lost count. As a Fremen, guiding the sacred creatures over the dunes had always been dangerous, but not to be feared. If you followed the proper protocol.

Short of the gap, he set the creature in motion, slipped down the pebbled rings, and tumbled off onto the sand. Then he rose to his feet and remained motionless, so that the worm would not detect his presence. Sandworms had no eyes, simply sensed vibrations.

But the creature paused and turned his way as soon as Stilgar released it. Usually, a worm set free of its rider would lurch away into the desert, or bury itself under the sand and sulk. But this one remained where it was, looming, intimidating. It raised its giant head high, facing down, toward him. Its mouth was a round cave bristling with tiny crystalline knives.

Stilgar froze in the enormous presence of the creature. It knew he was there, yet it did not move toward him, did not attack. Trembling slightly, the Naib could not forget the whispered rumors that Muad'Dib, having trekked out on the sands, had become one with Shai-Hulud. The sandworm's eyeless head had an eerie, sightless gaze . . . making him think of Muad'Dib. Though blinded, the great man had been able to see Stilgar through prescience.

He felt a sudden chill. Something was different. He breathed slowly, forming the words in his thoughts but with barely a sound passing across his dry lips. "Muad'Dib, are you there?"

It seemed foolish, but he could not escape the feeling. In an instant, the sandworm could dive down and devour him, but it did not.

After several long, tense moments, the enormous creature turned and glided off into the sands, leaving Stilgar standing there, shaking. He watched as the creature drifted off and burrowed itself deep, leaving barely a ripple to mark its passage.

Tingling with awe, wondering what exactly he had just experienced, Stilgar sprinted with a well-practiced stutter-step across the dunes toward the Shield Wall and the great city beyond.

There is a rule about surprises: Most of them are not good.

—ANONYMOUS, of Old Terra

Jessica had been a long time away from the desert, from the Fremen, and from the mind-set that permeated Arrakis. *Dune.* She drew a deep breath, sure that the air inside the passenger cabin already felt dryer.

As the showy political transport descended from orbit, she stared down at the sprawling city beyond the spaceport, picking out familiar Arrakeen landmarks, noting swaths of new construction. The immense Citadel of Muad'Dib dominated the north side of the city, though many additional new structures vied for attention on the skyline. Numerous government buildings shouldered up against enormous temples to Muad'Dib and even to Alia.

With her knowledge of Bene Gesserit methods for controlling impressions, manipulating history, and herding large populations, Jessica saw exactly what Paul—or, more accurately, his bureaucracy—intended to do. Much of government was about creating perceptions and moods. Long ago, the Bene Gesserit had unleashed their Missionaria Protectiva here on Arrakis to plant legends and prime the people for a myth. Under Paul-Muad'Dib, those seeds had come to fruition, but not in the way the Sisterhood had anticipated. . . .

The transport settled on a demarcated area reserved for important visitors. Swirls of sand obscured Jessica's view through the porthole.

When the exit doors opened, she smelled dust in the air, heard the susurration of a waiting crowd. The mobs had already gathered, a sea of dirty robes and covered faces. It was late afternoon by local time, and the white sun cast long shadows. She saw hundreds of people in brown and gray desert garb intermixed with those who wore city clothing in a variety of colors.

All had come to see her. Still inside the transport, Jessica hesitated. "I wasn't anxious to return here, Gurney. Not at all."

For a long moment, he remained silent in an unsuccessful attempt to hide his emotions, his uneasiness, maybe even his dread of facing the wailing masses. Finally, he said, "What is this place without Paul? It isn't Arrakis."

"*Dune*, Gurney. It will always be Dune."

Though Jessica still could not grieve—with those feelings locked down, or trapped, inside of her—now she felt moistness in her eyes, a stinging hint of the release she wanted and needed. But she didn't allow a single tear. *Dune* did not permit her to give water to the dead, not even for her son—and the Sisterhood discouraged emotions, except as a means of manipulating outsiders. Thus, both disciplines—Fremen and Bene Gesserit—prevented her from letting the tears flow.

Jessica stepped toward the open hatch and the bright sunlight. "Did I retire from this place, Gurney, or did I *retreat?*" She had hoped to spend the rest of her life on Caladan, never setting foot on this world again. "Think of what this planet has done to us. Dune took my Duke and my son and shattered all our hopes and dreams as a family. It *swallows* people."

"'Each person makes his own paradise, or his own hell.'" Gurney extended his arm, and she reluctantly took it. He activated his body shield before they stepped out into the open. "I recommend you do the same, my Lady. With a mob this size, they can't all be searched for weapons." Jessica did as he suggested, but even the shimmering field did not make her feel entirely safe.

Flanked by six big Fedaykin guards, Stilgar appeared at the shuttle ramp to escort her. He looked weathered, dusty, and grim—as always.

The same old Stilgar. She was reassured to see the Naib again. "Sayya-dina, I am here to ensure your safety." It was both a greeting and a promise; he did not allow himself to show any overt joy at seeing her again after so many years. "I will take you directly to Regent Alia."

"I am in your care, Stilgar." Though he was all business now, she expected they would share spice coffee later and talk, after he and Gurney got her away from the throng.

More Fremen warriors waited at the base of the shuttle ramp, form-ing a cordon to clear a way through the crowd for the Mother of Muad'Dib, as if sheltering her from the winds of a sandstorm. Stilgar led the visitors forward.

Overlapping voices in the crowd called out her name, shouting, chanting, cheering, begging for blessings from Muad'Dib. The people wore grimy clothes of green, the color of Fremen mourning. Some had scratched at their eyes until blood ran down their cheeks in some kind of eerie homage to Paul's blindness.

With her heightened attention, Jessica perceived a thread of ani-mosity woven into the tapestry of voices, calling out from every direc-tion. They wanted, they needed, they demanded and grieved, but could not crystallize their feelings. The loss of Paul had left an immense void in society.

Stilgar hurried her along. "We must not delay. There is danger here today."

There is always danger here, she thought.

As the Fedaykin guards pushed at the crowd, she heard a clatter of metal and a scream. Behind them, two of the guards threw themselves to the ground, covering something with their own bodies. Gurney put himself between them and Jessica, further protecting her with his body shield.

An explosion tore the two guards into bloody fragments that splat-tered back into the crowd. Stunned by the shock wave, some people touched the red wetness, marveling at the moisture that had suddenly appeared on their clothes.

Stilgar pulled Jessica toward the terminal building, hurting her arm. "Hurry," he said, "there may be other assassins." He did not look back at the fallen guards.

With the shrieks and shouts rising to a roar of vengeance and anger,

Jessica moved quickly into the guarded structure. Gurney and the remaining Fedaykin closed a heavy door behind them, greatly diminishing the crowd noise.

The cavernous building had been swept and cleared for her arrival, and now it echoed with emptiness. "What happened, Stilgar? Who wants me dead?"

"Some people wish only to cause harm, and any target will do. They want to hurt others as they have been hurt." His voice was dark with disapproval. "Even when Muad'Dib was alive, there was much turmoil, resentment, and discontent. People are weak, and do not understand."

Gurney looked carefully at Jessica to make certain she was not injured. "Angry people lash out wildly—and some will blame you, as the mother of Muad'Dib."

"That's who I am, for good or ill."

The terminal building looked brighter than she remembered, but not much different: a fresh coat of paint and more decorations, perhaps. She didn't recall seeing so many Atreides hawks on the walls the last time—Paul's doing, or Alia's? New alcoves displayed statues of Muad'Dib in various heroic poses.

Stilgar led them up a staircase to the rooftop landing platform, where a gray armored ornithopter sat waiting for them. "This will take you to the protection of the Citadel. You are in good hands now." Without further words, Stilgar hurried away, anxious to get back to the crowds to investigate the explosion.

A man strode toward them dressed in a stillsuit marked with Atreides green and black; the face mask hung loose. A chill of amazed recognition ran down her spine. "Lady Jessica, welcome back to Dune. Much has happened since the time I died here."

Gurney shouted his own disbelief. "Gods below—Duncan?"

The man was almost an exact duplicate of Duncan Idaho. Even his voice was perfect; only the gray, metallic eyes distinguished him from the original. "In the flesh, Gurney Halleck—ghola flesh, but the memories are mine."

He extended his right hand, but Gurney hesitated. "Or are you the one the Tleilaxu call Hayt?"

"Hayt was a ghola without his memories, a biological machine programmed to destroy Paul Atreides. I am no longer that one. I'm

Duncan again—the same old Duncan. The boy who worked in the Old Duke's bull stables on Caladan, the young man who trained on Ginaz to become a Swordmaster, the man who protected Paul from House Moritani assassins and fought to liberate Ix from the Tleilaxu." He offered Jessica a sheepish smile. "And, yes, the man who got drunk on spice beer and blurted to everyone awake in the Arrakeen Residency that you were a Harkonnen traitor, my Lady."

Jessica met his strange eyes. "You also gave your life so Paul and I could escape after Dr. Kynes's base was raided." She could not drive away the memory of the original Duncan falling under a flurry of Sardaukar dressed in Harkonnen uniforms. Seeing the ghola gave her an unsettled feeling, as if time had folded in on itself.

Now this Duncan gestured toward the 'thopter, inviting them to climb aboard. Despite its thick armor, the large aircraft had a luxurious interior.

When she entered the passenger compartment, Jessica was startled to see Alia seated, facing her direction. "Thank you for coming, Mother. I need you here." Seemingly embarrassed by the admission, she added, "We all do." The teenager's coppery hair was long, and her face thinner than before, making her blue-within-blue eyes look larger.

"Of course I came." Jessica took a seat beside her daughter. "I came for Paul, for you, and for my new grandchildren."

"'Tragedy brings us together, when convenience fails to do so,'" Gurney recited.

No one is ever completely forced into his position in life. We all have opportunities to take different paths.

    —*Conversations with Muad'Dib* by the PRINCESS IRULAN

Inside the 'thopter, Jessica was surprised when Duncan sat close to Alia, rather than taking the pilot's controls, leaving that particular task to a Fremen guard. Smiling, Alia touched his arm with genuine warmth, an obvious romantic bond. So much had changed on Dune, and in House Atreides. . . .

"Of course, you will want to see that the twins are safe, Mother." Alia turned to Duncan. "Tell the pilot to use the west landing pad. We'll go directly to the creche."

The boy and girl, Paul's children, would never know their father. The twins were the heirs of Muad'Dib, the next step in a new dynasty, political pawns. Her *grandchildren*. "Have they been named yet? Did Paul . . . ?"

"My brother gave them names as one of his last acts, before he . . . left. The boy is Leto, named after our father. The girl is called Ghanima."

"Ghanima?" Gurney sat back with a frown, recognizing the Fremen term. "A spoil of war?"

"Paul insisted. Harah was there with Chani at the end, and now she watches the newborn babies. Since Harah was Muad'Dib's *ghanima* after he killed Jamis, maybe he meant it to honor her. We'll never know."

The 'thopter flew over the huddled rooftops of Arrakeen, the hive-like homes of a disorganized, passionate, desperate throng: pilgrims, opportunists, beggars, veterans of the Jihad, dreamers, and those who had no place else to go.

Alia spoke loudly over the thrum of the engines and the whir of moving wings. She seemed energetic, frenetic. "Now that you're here, Mother, we can proceed with Paul's funeral. It is a thing that must be done with a grandeur appropriate to Muad'Dib's greatness—enough to awe the whole Imperium."

Jessica kept her expression neutral. "It is a funeral, not a Jongleur performance."

"Oh, but even a Jongleur performance would be fitting, given Paul's past, don't you think?" Alia chuckled; it was clear she already had her mind set. "Besides, it is necessary, not just for my brother's memory, but for Imperial stability. The force of Paul's personality held our government together—without him, I've got to do whatever I can to strengthen our institutions. It's a time for showmanship, bravura. How can Muad'Dib's funeral be any less spectacular than one of the Old Duke's bullfighting spectacles?" When the girl smiled, Jessica saw a familiar echo of Leto in her daughter's face. "We also have Chani's water, and when it best suits us, we will conduct a ceremony for her as well, another great spectacle."

"Wouldn't Chani have preferred a private Fremen funeral?"

"Stilgar says the same thing, but that would be a wasted opportunity. Chani would have wanted to assist me in any way possible—for Paul's sake, if nothing else. I was hoping I could count on you to help me, Mother."

"I am here." Jessica looked at her daughter and felt complexities of sadness whisper through her. *But you are not Paul.*

She also knew things that her daughter did not, some of Paul's carefully guarded secrets and aspirations, especially how he viewed history and his place in it. Though Paul might have taken himself off the stage, history would not release its hold so easily.

With a slow flutter of wings and the roar of jets, the 'thopter landed on a flat rooftop of the extraordinary citadel complex. Disembarking, Alia strode with confidence and grace to a moisture-sealed door. Jessica and Gurney followed her into an elegant enclosed conservatory with soaring clearplaz panels.

Inside, the sudden humidity made Jessica catch her breath, but Alia seemed not to notice the miniature jungle of moist, exotic plants that overhung the walkway. Tossing her long hair, she glanced back at her mother. "This is the most secure area of the Citadel, so we converted it into the nursery."

Two Qizaras armed with long kindjals guarded an arched doorway, but the priests stepped aside without a word to let the party pass. Inside the main chamber, three Fedaykin stood ready and alert.

Female attendants in traditional Fremen garments bustled back and forth. Harah, who had once been nursemaid and companion to Alia, stood like an attentive mother over the twins, as if they were hers. She looked up at Alia, then flashed a nod of recognition to Jessica.

Jessica stepped forward to look down at Leto and Ghanima, surprised by how the two children struck her with a sense of awe. They seemed so flawless, so young and helpless, barely a month old. She realized she was trembling a little. Jessica set aside all thoughts of the Empire-shaking news she had received in the last few days.

As if they were linked, both babies turned their faces toward her simultaneously, opened their wide-set blue eyes, and stared with an awareness that startled Jessica. Alia had looked that alert when she was just a baby. . . .

"They are under close observation for their behavior and interactions," Alia said. "More than anyone else, I understand the difficulties they might face."

Harah was forceful. "We do our best to care for them as Chani, and Usul, would have wanted."

Kneeling, Jessica reached out to stroke the small, delicate faces. The babies looked at her, then locked gazes with each other, and something indefinable passed between them.

To the Sisterhood, babies were just genetic products, links in a long chain of bloodlines. Among the Bene Gesserit, children were raised without any emotional connection to their mothers, often without any knowledge of their parentage. Jessica herself, a ward of the Mother School on Wallach IX, had not been told that her father was the Baron

Harkonnen and her mother Gaius Helen Mohiam. Though her own upbringing among the emotionally stifled Bene Gesserit had been less than ideal, her heart went out to her grandchildren, as she contemplated the turbulent lives that undoubtedly lay ahead of them.

Again, Jessica thought of poor Chani. One life in exchange for two . . . She'd grown to respect the Fremen woman for her wisdom and her intense loyalty to Paul. How could he not have foreseen such a terrible blow as the loss of his beloved? Or *had* he known, but could do nothing about it? Such paralysis in the face of fate could have driven any man mad. . . .

"Would you like to hold them?" Harah asked.

It had been a long time since she'd held a baby. "Later. I just . . . just want to look at them right now."

Alia remained caught up in her visions of ceremonies and spectacles. "It is a very busy time, Mother. We need to do so much to give the people hope, now that Muad'Dib has gone. In addition to the two funerals, we will soon have a christening. Each such spectacle is designed to remind the people of how much they love us."

"They are children, not tools of statecraft," Jessica said, but she knew better. The Bene Gesserit had taught her that every person had potential uses—as a tool, or a weapon.

"Oh, Mother, you used to be so much more pragmatic."

Jessica stroked little Leto's face and drew a deep breath, but found no words to speak aloud. No doubt, political machinations were already occurring around these children.

Sourly, she thought of what the Bene Gesserits had done to her and to so many others like her, including the particularly harsh treatment they had inflicted on Tessia, the wife of the cyborg prince Rhombur Vernius. . . .

The Bene Gesserit always had their reasons, their justifications, their rationalizations.

I write what is true about Muad'Dib, or what should be true. Some critics accuse me of distorting the facts and writing shameless misinformation. But I write with the blood of fallen heroes, painted on the enduring stone of Muad'Dib's empire! Let these critics return in a thousand years and look at history; then see if they dismiss my work as mere propaganda.

—PRINCESS IRULAN, "The Legacy of Muad'Dib,"
draft manuscript

T*he quality of a government can be measured by counting the number of its prison cells built to hold dissidents.'*" Jessica recalled the political maxim she had been taught in the Bene Gesserit school. During her years of indoctrination, the Sisters had filled her mind with many questionable beliefs, but that statement, at least, was true.

On the day after her arrival in Arrakeen, she tracked down where Princess Irulan was being held. During her search of the detention records, Jessica was astonished to discover just how much of her son's sprawling fortress was devoted to prison blocks, interrogation chambers, and death cells. The list of crimes that warranted the ultimate penalty had grown substantially over the last few years.

Had Paul known about that? Had he approved?

It was probably wise that Reverend Mother Mohiam had been killed without a drawn-out trial, which would have allowed the Bene Gesserit to disrupt the government. And Jessica did not doubt that the old Reverend Mother was truly guilty.

But Irulan remained locked away, her fate undecided. Having reviewed the evidence herself, Jessica knew that Shaddam's daughter had been involved in the conspiracy, though her exact role was not clear. The Princess languished in one of the death cells operated by the Qizarate, but so far, Alia had refused to sign the death warrant.

During her first month as Regent, the girl had already caused enough of an uproar, offended many potential allies, provoked numerous possible enemies. There were larger issues to consider. Alia was wise to delay her decision.

Jessica had first met the Emperor's eldest daughter on Kaitain in the last months before giving birth to Paul. Since the downfall of Shaddam, Irulan had done much for, and some things against, Paul. But how much against him? Now, however, Jessica hoped she could stop the execution, for reasons both political and personal.

She marched down to the prison levels without an escort, having memorized the route from charts. Standing before the metal door of Irulan's sealed cell, she scrutinized strange markings on the wall, mystical symbols modeled after the writings of the vanished Muadru race. Paul's priesthood had apparently adopted the ancient runes for their own purposes.

Outside Irulan's cell stood two fiercely loyal Qizara guards, implacable priests who had advanced through the religious power structure that had sprung up around Paul, a structure that Alia intended to preserve or even expand. While these men would never defy the direct orders of the Regent, they also viewed Jessica with dread and reverence, and she could use that.

With squared shoulders, Jessica stepped up to them. "Stand aside. I wish to see my son's wife."

She expected an argument, or at least resistance, but the priestly guards did not think to question her command. If she had asked them to fall upon their crysknives, she wondered, would they have done that, too? With simultaneous bows, they unsealed the cell door and allowed her to enter.

Inside the dim and stifling room, the blonde Princess rose quickly from the bench on which she sat. She composed herself and straightened her rumpled clothes, even managing a slight bow. "Lady Jessica. I expected you would come to Arrakis as soon as you heard what had happened. I'm glad you arrived before my execution."

Despite the shadows of the cell, Jessica could see the haunted, resigned look in the Princess's once green eyes, which were now spice-

THE WINDS OF DUNE

indigo. Even Bene Gesserit calming techniques could not assuage the persistent wasting of fear and tension.

"There will be no execution." Without hesitating, Jessica turned to the priest guards. "Princess Irulan is to be released at once and returned to her former rooms. She is the daughter of Emperor Shaddam IV and the wife of Muad'Dib, as well as his official biographer. These quarters are unacceptable."

The two guards were taken aback. One of the priests made a warding sign against evil. "Regent Alia has ordered Irulan's incarceration, pending her conviction."

"And I order this." Jessica's voice was neither flippant nor threatening; she was simply stating a fact, filled with confidence. All other questions hung unanswered in the air, leaving the guards intimidated at the prospect of defying her wishes.

With all the elegance she could muster, Irulan took three steps to meet Jessica at the cell door, but did not cross the threshold. Despite her great stake in the outcome of this small power struggle, her patrician face betrayed no relief, only a distant expression of interest.

As the guards shuffled, neither of them willing to commit to a decision, Jessica continued in a reasonable tone. "There is nothing to fear. Do you believe she would attempt to escape? That a Corrino princess would run into the desert with a Fremkit and try to survive? Irulan will remain here in the Citadel, under house arrest, until Alia can issue a formal pardon."

Taking advantage of the guards' hesitation, the Princess stepped out of her cell to stand beside Jessica. "I thank you for your courtesy and your faith in me."

Jessica remained cool. "I will withhold judgment until I learn more about what role you had in my son's death."

They walked briskly away from the priest guards until they were alone and unobserved. Irulan drew a shuddering breath, and Jessica heard the truth in her words when she spoke. "In that cell I've had much time to contemplate. Although I did not try to kill Paul . . . in a way I did cause his death. I am at least partly responsible for what happened."

Jessica was surprised by the easy admission. "Because you failed to expose the conspiracy when you had the chance?"

"And because I was jealous of his love for that Fremen woman. *I* wanted to be the mother of his heirs, so I secretly added contraceptives to Chani's food. Over the long term, those drugs damaged her, and when she did become pregnant, the delivery killed her." She looked intensely at Jessica, her indigo eyes intense. "I did not know she would die!"

Jessica's training automatically damped down her anger, just as it had kept her from expressing her true grief. Now she understood more about what had driven her son, and Irulan. "And in his despair Paul chose to walk out into the desert. He had nothing to hold him back, no loving companion. He didn't care enough for any person to make him want to live. So that is your fault."

Irulan skewered Jessica with her desperate gaze. "Now you know the truth. If you want me to return to the death cell, I'll go willingly, so long as the punishment you decree is honest and swift."

Jessica found it hard to maintain her composure. "Maybe we'll exile you to Salusa Secundus with your father . . . or maybe you should stay here, where you can be watched."

"I can watch over Paul's children. That is what I want, and need."

Jessica wasn't convinced that this woman should be allowed near the twins. "That will be decided later—if you survive." She guided the Princess out of the prison levels. "Enjoy your freedom. I can't guarantee how long it will last."

THOUGH FURIOUS, ALIA had the presence of mind to confront Jessica in private, thus avoiding a spectacle. "You forced the guards to disobey me, Mother. In this time of crisis, you made me look *weak*, and you cast doubt on an aspect of my rule."

They stood in a large, well-appointed chamber, just the two of them. Yellow-tinted sunlight passed through a filtered skylight over their heads, but patterns of dust on the panes cast cloudy shadows. Jessica was surprised that Alia hadn't summoned Duncan Idaho, or Stilgar, or her amazon guards to be there at her side for authority. Apparently Alia really did want to have a candid, if uncomfortable, discussion.

Jessica replied in an even voice, "Frankly, your orders concerning the Princess were poorly conceived. I only hope I acted quickly enough to prevent further damage."

"Why do you stir up trouble? After being gone for years, you sweep in here, release an important prisoner, and disrupt the legitimate workings of my government. Is that why you've come to Dune, to undermine my Regency, and take it over?" Looking young and forlorn, Alia sat down at the long, empty table. "Be careful—I have half a mind to give it to you."

Jessica detected an unexpected note of pleading in her daughter's voice. Some part of Alia, however small, *wanted* to surrender rule to her mother, wanted to give up the pressure and responsibility. That sad agony was a part of leadership—whether one ruled a city, a planet, or an empire.

Jessica took a seat across the table from Alia and took care to soften her words. "You don't need to worry about that. I've had enough of power games from the Bene Gesserit, and I have no interest in leading an empire. I am here as your mother and the grandmother of Paul's children. I'll stay for a month or two, then return to Caladan. That's where I belong." She straightened, made her voice harder. "But in the meantime I will protect you from your decisions, when I must. Executing Irulan would have been a titanic mistake."

"I don't need you to protect me, Mother. I contemplate my decisions, I make them, and I stand by them." With a little shrug, changing her mood with surprising swiftness, Alia admitted, "Don't worry, I would have let the Princess out sooner or later. The mob demanded as many scapegoats as I could give them, and they howled for her blood in particular. Irulan's incarceration was for her own protection, as well as to make her face her own conscience, because of the mistakes *she* made. Irulan has very important uses, once she is properly controlled."

Jessica stared at her. "You hope to control Irulan?"

"She is the official source of knowledge about Muad'Dib, his own official biographer, appointed by him. If we executed her as a traitor, that would cast doubt on everything she's written. I'm not that stupid." Alia studied an imagined speck at the end of one fingernail. "Now that she has been sufficiently chastised, we need her to counter the heresies of Bronso of Ix."

"Is Paul's legacy so fragile that it can't withstand a bit of criticism?

You worry too much about Bronso. Perhaps the people need to hear the truth, not myths. My son was great enough as a man. He doesn't need to be turned into a messiah."

Alia shook her head, letting Jessica see her vulnerability. Her shoulders trembled, her voice hitched. "What was he *thinking*, Mother? How could Paul just walk off like that and leave us?" The waves of sudden grief coming from Alia surprised her, this girl showing naked emotions that Jessica herself had not been able to express. "Chani's body not even in the deathstill, two newborn children, and he abandoned us all! How could Paul be so selfish, so . . . *blind?*"

Jessica wanted to hold her daughter and reassure her, but held back. Her own walls remained too rigid. "Grief can do terrible things to a person, chasing away all hope and logic. I doubt Paul was thinking beyond just running away from the pain."

Squaring her shoulders, Alia summoned inner strength. "Well, I won't run away. This Regency is a big problem Paul dumped in my lap, and I refuse to do the same thing he did. *I* won't leave others to clean up the mess. *I* won't turn my back on humanity, on the future."

"I know you won't." Jessica hesitated, lowered her gaze. "I should have consulted you first about Irulan. I acted . . . impulsively."

Alia looked at her, long and hard. "We can fix this. Provided I have your cooperation, my ministers will announce that *I* issued the orders to release Irulan, and you simply carried them out."

Jessica smiled. The end result was the same, and the news would not be seen as a conflict between mother and daughter. "Thank you, Alia. I see that you're learning the art of statecraft already. That is a good decision."

Crucial events from my first life stand at the forefront of my mind: the murder of Old Duke Paulus in the bull ring, the War of Assassins between Ecaz and Grumman, young Paul running off to join the Jongleurs, that terrible night in Arrakeen when the Harkonnens came . . . my own death at the hands of the attacking Sardaukar in the stronghold of Dr. Kynes. The details remain vivid.

—DUNCAN IDAHO, as put to paper by Alia Atreides

Dawn light touched the surface of the desert and the rock escarpments as a lone ornithopter flew high enough that its vibrations would not disturb the great worms. Duncan Idaho piloted the craft.

Like old times, Gurney thought. *And yet completely different.* For sixteen years he had known that his friend was dead, but death wasn't always a permanent condition, thanks to the axlotl tanks of the Tleilaxu.

Ahead, flashing in the low-angled sunlight, they could see the silvery rooftops and bastions of a ground-based scanner facility. "There's our destination," Duncan said. "A typical base. It will tell us much about our general security status before the funeral ceremony. Tens of thousands of ships are arriving for the event from countless worlds. We have to be ready."

While preparations for the grand spectacle continued, a stream of mourners arrived on Dune, from diplomats hoping to curry favor with the Regency to the lowliest paupers who had sacrificed everything to pay for space passage. Gurney was not sure the planetary defenses could handle the extra influx and constant turmoil.

The evening before, he had asked Duncan about the state of the defensive facilities on the outskirts of Arrakeen. Still feeling out their new/old friendship, the two men sat at a worn table in the Citadel's commissary levels, drinking outrageously expensive spice beers, hardly caring about the cost.

Taking a long sip, Duncan had said, "I intended to inspect those sites in due course, but other duties kept me away. Now you and I can do it together."

"The death of an emperor certainly wreaks havoc with schedules," Gurney said bitterly.

Duncan's previously sociable nature had been supplanted by Mentat mysticism programmed into him by the Tleilaxu, but he began to open up by the second spice beer, and Gurney's heart felt both heavy and happy to see glimmers of his old friend. Still wary, though, he said, as a test, "I could sing us a song. I have my baliset back in my quarters—it's the same old instrument I bought on Chusuk, when the two of us went with Thufir Hawat to search for Paul after he ran away from Ix."

Duncan responded with a thin smile. "Thufir did not go with us. It was just you and me."

Gurney chuckled. "Just making sure you really have all your memories."

"I do."

Now, as the 'thopter approached the perimeter outpost, Gurney recognized it as one of the old Harkonnen scanner stations dotted around the Plain of Arrakeen. What had once been a moderately armed facility now sported new battlements and utility structures, its multiple roofs and high walls studded with powerful ion cannons capable of destroying vessels in orbit—even Guild Heighliners, should the situation demand it.

"Because Arrakis was always a target, Paul expanded planetary defenses during the Jihad. Now that he is gone, Alia wants me to make certain we are ready to stand against opportunists."

"Shaddam is still alive and in exile on Salusa Secundus," Gurney pointed out. "Is that what you're worried about?"

"I worry about many things, and try to be prepared for all of them." He transmitted their identification signal as he circled the 'thopter in toward the outpost's landing pad, retracting the wing thrusters. "I'd never turn down your assistance, Gurney. Paul would have wanted us to work together."

Paul, Gurney thought with a wave of sadness. Though it was how the real Duncan Idaho would have remembered him, that Atreides name was a remnant of Caladan, a historical artifact. Here on Dune, Paul had become *Muad'Dib*, a far different person from the Duke's son.

With a roar of jets and a masterful dance of subtle stabilizers, Duncan landed the ornithopter on a fused stone apron inside the outpost's fortified walls. The pair disembarked and made their way to a central mustering area, where soldiers hurried through a nearby portico for the unannounced inspection.

With Gurney at his side, Duncan proceeded methodically from one station to another, chastising the soldiers for sloppy conditions. He pointed out unpolished and uncalibrated guns, dust in the tracking mechanisms, wrinkled uniforms, even the boozy odor of spice beer in the morning air.

Gurney couldn't blame him for being displeased with the level of disarray, but he also remembered the faltering morale among Atreides troops after Duke Leto had arrived on Arrakis. "With Paul gone, these men are adrift and uncertain. 'A soldier will always fight, but he fights hardest when he fights *for something*.' Isn't that one of your Swordmaster sayings?"

"We are both masters of the sword, Gurney Halleck, even if you didn't do your own training on Ginaz. I taught you a few things, you know." Looking at the men, Duncan had made his own Mentat analysis. "They will adjust. Alia needs to be made aware of this sloppiness. After Paul's funeral, I will implement a thorough crackdown on her behalf, punishing the worst offenders harshly to shake up the others."

The statement made Gurney uneasy, because the Atreides had not historically ruled through fear. But all of that had changed when Paul Atreides became a messianic Fremen and ascended to the throne of Dune, ruling an empire with thousands of restless worlds.

"I wish you could do it some other way," he said.

The ghola turned to him with his metal eyes, and in that moment he did not look at all like Duncan. "You must think of realities, my old comrade. If Alia shows weakness now, it could lead to our downfall. I must protect her."

From a high battlement, Gurney gazed out into the rugged distance at a rock escarpment that partially framed the expanse of desert. He knew Duncan was right, but there seemed no end to the governmental brutality.

"I noted subtle weaknesses in the eyes of the soldiers, and I heard it in the voice of their station commander." Duncan glanced at his companion. "I have learned how to read the most minute details, for there are always messages beneath the surface. I even see them in your face at this very moment, the way you look at me. I am not an alien creature."

Gurney took a moment to consider his response. "I was a friend of Duncan Idaho's, that's true, and I lamented his death. Such a brave, loyal warrior. You look and act like him, though you're a bit more reserved. But a ghola is . . . beyond my comprehension. What was it like?"

Duncan had a distant gaze as he stared away into the past. "I remember my first moment of awareness, huddled afraid and confused in a pool of liquid on a hard floor. The Tleilaxu said I had been a friend of the Emperor Paul-Muad'Dib, and that I was to ingratiate myself so that I could destroy him. They gave me subconscious programming . . . and ultimately I found it *unbearable*. In refusing to follow the fundamental commands they imposed upon me, I shattered that artificial psyche, and in that moment I became Duncan Idaho again. It's me, Gurney. Really, I'm back."

Gurney's voice was a low growl, more of a promise than a threat, and he held his hand on the hilt of his sheathed knife. "If I ever suspect that you intend to harm the Atreides family, I'll kill you."

"And if that were truly the case, then I would let you." Duncan lifted his chin, tilted his head back. "Draw your dagger, Gurney Halleck. Here, I bare my throat to you now, if you feel this is the time."

A long moment passed, and Gurney did not move. Finally, he removed his hand from the hilt of his weapon. "The real Duncan would offer his life like that. I'll accept you, for now . . . and accept that I'll never be able to understand what you've been through."

Duncan shook his head as they went down the steep, winding staircase to the landing field and the waiting 'thopter. "One day you'll die, and then you'll be halfway to understanding."

True forgiveness is a rarer thing than melange.

—Fremen wisdom

The crowd surrounding Alia's Fane surged with an energy of humanity. So many lives, so many minds, all in a single mood. . . .

Standing on the balcony of the temple high over the blur of population, Jessica knew what Paul must have felt as Emperor, what Alia now felt daily. With the white sun of Arrakis high overhead, the Fane's tower became a gnomon, casting a shadow blade across the sundial of humanity.

"Thank you for doing this, Alia," Princess Irulan said, standing proud and cool, but not bothering to cover her sincere gratitude and relief.

Alia looked back at her. "I do it out of necessity. My mother has spoken to me on your behalf, and she made good sense. Besides, this is what Paul would have wanted."

Next to the Princess, Jessica folded her hands together. "It is an open wound that needs to be healed."

"But there are conditions," Alia added.

Irulan's gaze didn't waver. "There are always conditions. I understand."

"Good, then it's time." Without further delay, Alia stepped forth into the bright glare of the open sunlight. When the people below noticed the movement, their voices thundered upward like a physical force. Alia stood facing the throng, a smile fixed on her countenance, her hair loose, feral.

"My father was never greeted like that when he addressed the people in Kaitain," Irulan whispered to Jessica.

"After Muad'Dib, the people will never again look upon their leaders the same way." Jessica understood how perilous, how seductive that power could be; she also understood that Paul had unleashed the Jihad intentionally, knowing what he did. And it got out of his control.

Long ago, in a Fremen cave, she had greatly feared his choice of touching a flame to the religion-soaked kindling of desert traditions. It was a dangerous path, and it had proved to be as treacherous as she'd feared. How could he think he could just shut it away when its usefulness was over? Jessica feared now for Alia in that storm, and for the flotsam and jetsam of humanity, as well.

Alia spoke, her amplified voice echoing across the great square. The crowd dropped into a hushed silence, absorbing her words. "My people, we have been through a difficult and dangerous time. The Bene Gesserit Sisterhood teaches that we must adapt. The Fremen say that we must avenge. And *I* say that we must *heal*.

"The conspirators against Muad'Dib, those responsible for the plot against him, were punished. I ordered their executions, and we have taken back their water." She turned and extended her hand into the tower chamber, summoning Irulan. "But there is another wound we must heal."

The Princess squared her shoulders and emerged into the sunlight beside Alia.

"You may have heard rumors that Princess Irulan had some involvement in the conspiracy. A few of you wonder how much she is to blame."

Now the murmur grew like a low, synchronous growl. Out of sight in the chamber, Jessica clenched her hands. She had convinced Alia what she must do, and her daughter decided on this wise course of action. But right now—with a single word, with all these people under her thrall—Alia could change her mind and command Irulan's death, and no force in the universe could stop it. They would break into the tower and rip her apart.

"Let there be no further doubts," Alia said, and Jessica let out a long, slow sigh of relief. "Irulan was my brother's wife. She loved him. Therefore, it is out of my own love for my brother, for Muad'Dib, that I proclaim her to be innocent."

Now Jessica stepped into view, so that the three powerful women, the three *surviving* women who had so influenced the life of Paul-Muad'Dib, stood together. "And as the mother of Muad'Dib, I shall write and seal a document that completely exonerates Princess Irulan of any crimes of which she has been accused. Let her be guiltless before your eyes."

Alia lifted her arms into the air. "Irulan is the official biographer of Muad'Dib, anointed by him. She will write the truth so that all can discover the true nature of Muad'Dib. Blessed be his name throughout the annals of time."

The automatic rumbling response came back from below: "Blessed be his name throughout the annals of time."

The three women stood for an extended moment and clasped hands, so that the people could see their harmony—mother, sister, and wife.

The Princess said quietly to Alia, "Again, I am indebted to you."

"You have always been indebted to me, Irulan. And now that we have passed this troublesome distraction, we'll see how best we can put you to use."

Muad'Dib was never born and never died. He is eternal, like the stars, the moons, and the heavens.

—The Rite of Arrakeen

N o mother should have to attend the funeral of her son.

In a private box overlooking Arrakeen's central square, Jessica and Gurney stood beside Alia, Duncan, Stilgar, and the newly pardoned Princess Irulan. A funeral coach approached them, draped in black and pulled by two Harmonthep lions. Irulan had suggested this touch of Corrino symbolism, a tradition that had accompanied the mourning of emperors for centuries.

Jessica knew that this would be nothing like a traditional Fremen funeral. Alia had planned the ceremony, insisting that the carefully crafted—and continuously growing—legend of Muad'Dib demanded it. The whole Plain of Arrakeen, it seemed, could not hold the millions who had come to mourn Muad'Dib.

Just past sunset, the sky was awash with pastels; long shadows stretched across the city. Numerous observation craft flew overhead, some at high altitude. As the sky began to darken, dozens of commissioned Guildships streaked through the atmosphere releasing plumes of ionized metal gases, pumping up the debris in the magnetic field lines to ignite a wondrous aurora show. A blizzard of tiny pellets sprinkled into low, swiftly decaying orbits that created an almost constant meteor shower, as if the heavens were shedding fiery tears for the death of such a great man.

Seven days of pageantry would reach a climax this evening in a celebration of Muad'Dib's life, rites meant to chronicle and praise Paul's greatness. As Jessica watched, she felt that the overblown display was more of a reminder of the *excesses* committed in his name.

An hour earlier, Jessica had watched two Fedaykin place the large funeral urn inside the coach, an ornate jar that should have contained Muad'Dib's water from the deathstill. But the vessel was empty, because Paul's body had never been found, despite exhaustive searches. The hungry sands had swallowed him without a trace, as was fitting.

By leaving no body, Paul had enlarged upon his own mythos, and set new rumors in motion. Some people fervently believed he was not actually dead; for years to come, they would no doubt report seeing mysterious blind men who might be Muad'Dib.

She felt a chill as she recalled the report of Tandis, the last Fremen who had seen Paul alive before her son left Sietch Tabr and wandered into the hostile vastness. Paul's last words, which he'd called back into the night, were, "Now I am free."

Jessica also remembered a time when Paul was only fifteen, immediately after his ordeal with Reverend Mother Mohiam's gom jabbar. "Why do you test for humans?" he had asked the old woman.

"To set you free," Mohiam had said.

Now I am free!

Had Paul, in the end, seen his unorthodox exit as a means to return to his *human* nature and attempt to leave deification behind?

From the observation platform, she gazed toward the high Shield Wall splashed with fiery bronze light in the last glimmers of dusk. That was the place where Muad'Dib and his fanatical Fremen army had broken through in their great victory against the Corrino Emperor.

Jessica recalled Paul at various ages, from a bright child to a dutiful young nobleman, to the Emperor of the Known Universe and the leader of a Jihad that swept across the galaxy. *You may have become Fremen,* she thought, *but I am still your mother. I will always love you, no matter where you have gone, or what path you took to get there.*

As the plodding lions pulled the coach toward the viewing stand, a cadre of uniformed Fedaykin and yellow-robed priests marched alongside. Ahead of them, two heroes of the Jihad led the procession with fluttering green-and-black Atreides banners. The immense, murmurous crowd parted for the coach's passage.

The throngs were beyond anyone's ability to count, millions and millions of people crowded into the city and into camps outside, Fremen as well as offworlders. The water softness of the new arrivals was readily apparent, not only in their smooth, unweathered flesh, but in their colorful raiment, faux stillsuits, or outlandish outfits that had been made especially for this occasion. Even those who tried to dress like natives were obviously unauthentic. It was a dangerous time and place for the unwary. There had been killings of outsiders who purportedly did not show the proper respect for the Emperor Muad'Dib.

Jessica fell into a particular category of offworlder: one that had adapted. Upon first arriving on Arrakis sixteen years earlier, she and her family had been softer than they'd realized, but time spent here had hardened them physically and mentally. While taking refuge from Harkonnen treachery, Jessica and her son had lived closer to the Fremen than virtually any other offworlder ever had. They had genuinely become part of the desert, harmonious with it.

Paul had consumed the Water of Life and nearly died, but in the process he gained unfettered access to the sheltered Fremen world. Thus, he not only became one of them, he became *them* in totality. Muad'Dib was not merely one individual; he encompassed all Fremen who had ever been born and ever would exist. He was their Messiah, the chosen one sent by Shai-Hulud to show them the path to eternal glory. And now, having walked off into the desert, he made the place even more sacred than before. He embodied the desert and its ways, and the winds would spread his spirit across all of human existence.

The funeral coach came to a stop in front of the viewing stand. The robed Fremen driver sat high on top. Showing no outward grief, Alia issued a command to her aides.

Attendants removed the black drapes from the coach, while others unhitched the pair of lions and led them away. The driver climbed down, bowed reverently to the idea of what it contained, then backed into the crowd.

A glow brightened inside the ornate coach, and its sides began to open like the broad petals of a flower, revealing Muad'Dib's urn inside on a plush purple platform. The urn began to glow as if from an inner sun, shining light onto the surrounding square in the thickening dusk. Some in the crowd fell to their knees attempting to prostrate themselves, but there was not much room for them to move.

"Even in death, my brother inspires his people," Alia said to her mother. "'Muad'Dib, the One Who Points the Way.'"

Jessica comforted herself with the knowledge that Paul would live forever in the memories, stories, and traditions passed on from generation to generation, from planet to planet. Still, deep inside, she could not accept that Paul was dead. He was too strong, too vibrant, too much a force of nature. But his own prescience, his own immensity of grief over what he'd done, had defeated him.

Here, at his funeral, Jessica saw distraught, sorrow-struck people everywhere . . . and felt uncomfortably hollow inside.

Billions and billions of people had died in the name of Muad'Dib and his Jihad. All told, he had sterilized *ninety planets*, wiping them clean of life. But she knew it had been necessary, made inevitable by his prescience. It had taken her a long time to understand, to *believe*, that Paul had truly known the righteousness of his actions. Jessica had doubted him, almost turned against him with tragic consequences . . . but she'd eventually learned the truth. She accepted the reality that her son was correct in his assertion that more of humanity would die if he had not taken such a difficult course.

Now, all of the deaths focused into one: Paul Orestes Atreides.

As the urn glowed, Jessica grappled with her feelings of love and loss: alien concepts to the Bene Gesserit Sisterhood, but she didn't care. *This is the funeral for my son.* She would gladly have let the people see her sadness. But she still could not openly grieve.

Jessica knew what would come next. Upon reaching its maximum brightness, the empty urn would rise on suspensors over the plaza and cast brilliant light over the enthralled crowds below, like the sun of Muad'Dib's existence, until it rose out of sight into the night sky, symbolically ascending to heaven. Ostentatious, perhaps, but the crowds would view it with awe. It was as grand a show as Rheinvar the Magnificent himself would have put on, and Alia had planned the ceremony with a disturbing intensity and passion.

Now, as the bodiless urn continued to brighten, Jessica heard heavy engines and flapping ornithopter wings overhead. Looking up into the darkening sky that shimmered with artificial auroras and shooting stars, she saw a group of flying craft in a tight formation spewing clouds of dense vapors, coagulating gases that spilled and swirled like a congealing thundercloud. An unexpected addition to the show? With a sound like shattering rocks, a sharp thunderclap rang out above the crowd in the square, followed by a low, menacing rumble.

The people turned away from the funeral urn, sure that this was also part of the ceremony, but Jessica knew it had *not* been part of the plan. Alarmed, she whispered to Alia, "What is this?"

The young woman whirled, her eyes flashing. "Duncan, find out what's going on."

Before the ghola could move, a massive, scowling face appeared on the underside of the cloud, a projection that shone through the rolling knot of vapors. Jessica recognized the countenance instantly: Bronso of Ix.

From the fading rumble of thunder emerged a voice that boomed across the plaza. "Turn away from this circus sham and realize that Muad'Dib was just a man, not a god! He was the son of a Landsraad duke, and no more. Do not confuse him with God—for that dishonors both. Open your eyes to these foolish delusions."

As the crowd howled in outrage, the glow from the funeral urn sputtered and went out, the suspensors failing so that the urn fizzled and crashed into the square. Mourners cursed the sky, demanding the blood of the man who had disrupted their sacred ceremony.

Overhead, the projected face broke into fragments as evening breezes dispersed the artificial thunderhead. The linked 'thopters simultaneously dropped out of the sky and crashed in multiple fireballs onto the rooftops of the sprawling government buildings that ringed the square.

The screaming crowd ran in all directions, trampling each other. Emergency sirens sounded, while police and medics rushed forth, shifting electronic containment barriers. Alia barked orders and sent zealous priests out into the crowd, ostensibly to calm them but also to search for any accomplices of Bronso.

On their observation stand, Jessica stood her ground. From her vantage, the injuries looked minimal, and she hoped there were no deaths.

She grudgingly admired Bronso's cleverness, knowing he had used Ixian technology to produce his own show. Jessica knew full well, too, that he was skilled enough to elude capture. Bronso himself would be nowhere close to Arrakeen.

Water is life. To say that one drop of water is insignificant is to say that one life is insignificant. That is a thing I cannot accept.

—*The Stilgar Commentaries*

To Alia, Bronso's disruptive actions seemed more an insult directed at *her,* rather than mud thrown at the memory of Paul. She dispatched searchers and spies to locate the perpetrators, rounding up hundreds of suspects in due course.

While Jessica could not approve of what Bronso had done to ruin the solemn ceremony, she did not reject his underlying motives. In fact, she suspected that Paul himself would have disliked the ostentatious nature of the funeral itself. Though her son had voluntarily cultivated a demigod's image, he had realized his mistake, had tried to alter course in any way he knew how.

On the morning after the funeral ceremony, Jessica found Stilgar at the edge of the Arrakeen Spaceport, supervising the removal of Fremen clan banners, flags of Landsraad Houses, and pennants from conquered worlds.

Jessica tilted her head back to watch a descending water-ship appear like a bright spot of reflected sunlight high above, dropping in a rippling plume of exhaust and ionized air, flanked by armed military craft to defend the cargo. A crackle and boom split the sky with a familiar non-thunder sound as the decelerating ship braked against the atmosphere above the small landing area.

Other vessels had landed at the spaceport, the air rippling with heat around the hulls. Egress doors opened with a hiss of equalizing pressures. A steward checked the ramp and tromped down to hand documents to one of the spaceport administrators who wore the yellow robe of a Qizara. Fuel technicians rushed forward to hook charge linkages to the suspensor engines.

All around, more shuttles, cargo haulers, and frigates were landing, one of them with a bone-jarring shriek of maladjusted engines. Ground-cars whirred up to cargo doors; manual laborers lined up for their shifts and invoked the blessings of Muad'Dib before performing their tasks.

Jessica stood next to Stilgar, who kept his voice low, his gaze straight ahead at all the spaceport activity. "I wanted to attend a farewell ceremony for my friend Usul from Sietch Tabr. But that *funeral* was not a Fremen thing." He gestured to the still-milling crowds, the work crews, the heavy equipment. Souvenir vendors still hawked their trinkets, some of them reducing their prices to get rid of leftover merchandise, others raising prices because such items were now more rare and meaningful.

"Your daughter wants to organize a water ceremony for Chani, too." The stern and conservative Naib shook his head. "After seeing what the Regent arranged for Muad'Dib, I have my concerns that Chani will be honored properly, in the way that she and her tribe would have wished."

"The situation has been out of control for some time, Stilgar. Paul created and encouraged it himself."

"But *Chani* did not, Sayyadina. She was a member of my troop and the daughter of Liet, a Fremen—not a mere symbol, as Alia wants her to be. We Fremen do not have funerals."

Jessica turned to him, narrowing her eyes. "Maybe it's time to impose reality again. Chani's water means more to the Fremen than to any other spectators. The flesh belongs to the person, the water to the tribe. No part of her belongs to an Imperial political show. A true Fremen would make sure that her water is not wasted."

Stilgar's expression darkened. "Who can oppose what the Regent has decided?"

"You can, and so can we. If we are careful. It's what we are obligated to do."

Stilgar arched his eyebrows and turned his leathery face toward her. "You ask me to defy the wishes of Alia?"

Jessica shrugged. "The water belongs to the tribe. And the *Fremen* are Chani's tribe, not the entire Imperium. If we take Chani's water, we can do the thing right. Let me deal with my daughter. There may be a way for us all to be satisfied. Right now, Alia is engrossed in her search for Bronso and any of his associates. Now is the time to take Chani's water—for safekeeping."

Water-sellers walked down the streets chanting their eerie calls. Beggars and pilgrims milled around the workers who removed funeral pennants from high posts. Jessica saw that the orange-garbed foremen were tearing the cloth into scraps and selling the swatches as souvenirs from Muad'Dib's memorial. A spice lighter came down to the space-port, filling the air with a loud roar, but Jessica and the Naib existed in a small universe of their own.

Stilgar looked at her with his blue-within-blue eyes. "I know how."

AT NIGHT, LISTENING to the daily hordes of wailing mourners, seeing the pilgrims continue to swarm in from offworld after the death of Muad'Dib (and knowing the Spacing Guild was reaping great profits from each passage), Stilgar concluded that such shameful excesses were decidedly non-Fremen.

He had been a friend of Paul Atreides from the moment the young man took his sietch name of Usul. He'd seen Paul kill his first man— the hotheaded Jamis, who would have been forgotten by the tribe, ex- cept that dying at the right time and by the right hand had given him a certain historical immortality.

But *this*, Stilgar thought, as he stood on a crowded Arrakeen street, wearing a well-fitted stillsuit (unlike most of these offworlders, who never learned or understood proper water discipline)—*this* was not the Dune he remembered.

Stilgar had never liked Arrakeen, nor any city for that matter: the shuffle and press of ill-prepared pilgrims, the dark-alley crime, the garbage, noise, and strange odors. Although life in the crowded sietches had changed, it was still more pure than the city. Out there, people didn't pretend to be something they were not, or they would not survive long. The desert sorted the faithful from imposters, but the city did not seem to know the difference, and actually rewarded the impure.

Hiding his disgust behind noseplugs and a filterscarf, Stilgar walked the streets, listening to atonal music that wafted from a small gathering area where a group of pilgrims from the same planet shared cultural memories. Gutters stank from piled rubbish: The crowds left so much refuse behind that there was no place to put it—even the open desert couldn't swallow it all. Bad smells were an evil omen to the Fremen, because rotting odors implied wasted moisture. He fitted his noseplugs more tightly.

In busy Arrakeen, the only place a man could be alone was inside himself. No one paid any attention to the disguised Naib as he made his way toward the Citadel of Muad'Dib. Only when he reached the gates did he reveal his identity and give the countersign. The guards stepped back with a sudden snap of respect, as if they were clockwork mechanisms in tightly wound thumpers.

For what Stilgar intended, it would have been better if his presence had remained unnoticed, yet without the unwavering authority Muad'Dib had conferred on him, he could never achieve what Jessica had asked of him. Stilgar was breaking supposed rules, following the course of honor instead of someone else's law. He had to do this quietly and secretly, even if it required several trips, several secret nighttime missions.

Muad'Dib was not the only one who had died. At least Stilgar and Jessica remembered that. . . .

He reached the oppressively silent quarters where Usul had lived with his beloved concubine. Sooner or later, members of the Qizarate would convert this wing of the palace into a shrine, but for now the people regarded the rooms with religious awe and left them untouched.

Atop a sand-etched stone slab, an ornate canopic jar held Chani's water. Rendered down from her small body by a huanui deathstill after the difficult and bloody birth of the twins, only twenty-two liters of water had been recovered from her body.

She'd been the daughter of Liet-Kynes before becoming the woman of Muad'Dib. A true Fremen warrior on Dune, she had fought many battles as a member of Stilgar's troop. With callused fingers, he traced the intricate markings on the outside of the jar. A tremor of superstitious fear ran down his spine. Water was just water . . . but could it be that Chani's ruh-spirit still lingered here?

Her father Liet, the Imperial planetologist murdered by Harkonnens, had been the son of Pardot Kynes, who had inspired the Fremen dream of climate change on Dune. Stilgar's comrade against Harkonnen excesses, Liet had died because he'd dared to help Paul Atreides and his mother.

As Emperor, Muad'Dib had ensured that the dreams of Dr. Kynes endured. By his command, he had accelerated the terraforming process and established a new School of Planetology. If Muad'Dib was indeed the Lisan al-Gaib, the Shortening of the Way, then Liet-Kynes was the catalyst.

And Chani was his daughter.

The Regent and her amazon guards would curse him for what he was about to do, but Stilgar already had the blood of the Reverend Mother Mohiam on his hands, and the blood of others. He would do this.

Unstopping the heavy jar, he drained some of the liquid into literjon containers that were easier to handle and hide under his cloak. In order to take it all, he would need to do this at least two more times, but as captain of the guard, Stilgar had ways of avoiding detection. With his precious burden, he slipped out of Muad'Dib's quarters.

"WHY WOULD ANYONE do such a thing?" Alia was at first genuinely baffled, but that swiftly changed. Jessica watched the emotions sweep across her daughter's face, one after another—confusion, then outrage, then a hint of fear. "Who could have gotten into my brother's quarters?"

Ziarenka Valefor, the amazon guard reporting to them now, was a head taller than Alia, but she was so rattled by her accidental discovery that she looked to the young Regent for strength. Alia snapped an order to her guard. "Send for Duncan." With a quick bow, Ziarenka slipped away.

Shaking her head, Alia looked at her mother. "This must be another outrage committed by Bronso of Ix. After what he did at Paul's funeral, now he wants to ruin Chani's water ceremony, too. I'll denounce him! When the people learn—"

Jessica cut her off. "Better that you speak to no one of this, Alia."

Alia blinked, eased herself back down. "Chani's water has been stolen. How can we just ignore it? And what can they possibly want? When a question has no obvious answer, I suspect the worst."

Jessica had already worked through the possibilities in her mind, choosing the best way to defuse an overreaction, and for Stilgar and the Fremen to get what they needed—what Chani needed—and what Alia needed.

"I didn't say to ignore the matter, but you can completely defuse it. Whoever committed this crime—one of Bronso's cronies or some other perpetrator—probably intends to cause panic and unrest. Do they want to ransom it? Threaten to profane the water in some way? Regardless, they'll *expect* you to create an uproar over it, but don't give them the satisfaction. Don't call attention to what has happened."

The suggestion did not sit well with Alia. "We've got to thwart their plans, whatever they are. Chani's water is gone. How are we to hold her memorial service now?"

Jessica remained calm, unconcerned. "It was water. Refill the container, and no one will ever know. If Bronso claims to have Chani's water, how can he prove it?" She didn't consider the suggestion to be devious or dishonorable. It was a solution that even the Bene Gesserit would have considered acceptable. *We both get what we want.* "Water is water, and you can hold your memorial service as planned."

And the Fremen would have their own ceremony to honor Chani in their own way. Stilgar would be satisfied, too. As would Paul, who would know even after his own death that the right thing was being done.

Alia considered, then nodded. "That is an acceptable solution. It renders any threat impotent."

We have reports of arms merchants attempting to sell stone-burners, even after one blinded Muad'Dib and such weapons were declared illegal. The fires of a stone-burner shall be as nothing compared to the avenging spirit of Muad'Dib.

—ZIARENKA VALEFOR, chief of Alia's guardian amazons

After the funeral debacle, hapless detainees faced various forms of interrogation, guided by Alia's most aggressive priests. The late (and unlamented) Korba had called the process "customized terror." Large groups might unite in common cause, filled with grand dreams and righteous delusions, but alone and fearful in a shadowy chamber, individuals behaved quite differently. Each one had a key weakness that the inquisitors used expert methods to discover.

And Alia needed to find answers.

During Paul's reign, he had not been innocent of such tactics himself, but had looked the other way as his surrogates conducted brutal interrogations. The criminal Bronso of Ix had been arrested and questioned then, and—against all odds—had escaped! Alia had never been able to shake her suspicion that Paul himself might have had a hand in the Ixian's release, though she couldn't understand why. Paul had not wanted to watch the interrogation of Bronso in his death cell, even though the Ixian spewed hateful rhetoric against him.

With all the billions who died in his far-reaching Jihad, why didn't her brother have the stomach for smaller unpleasantries? Having learned from Paul's mistakes, however, Alia routinely, and clandestinely, watched during key interrogations. With her own powers of observation, she sometimes picked up things that others missed.

So far, despite the most rigorous questioning of the suspects, the sessions had yielded no valid information. Either Bronso and his allies had a superhuman level of cleverness and luck in concealing their tracks, or the Ixian was acting alone. She refused to accept either answer.

On a more positive note, Alia had used the funeral episode with Bronso as a catalyst to ferret out other affronts against Muad'Dib or House Atreides. In the dark of night, Qizara police forces spread through Arrakeen, Carthag, and countless villages, knocking down doors and arresting alleged arms merchants who had been trying to sell stone-burners like the one that had blinded Paul in a pillar of fire.

When the questionable merchants were brought in, they in turn provided customer lists, and the offending weapons were rounded up and delivered to Arrakeen—for Alia's own stockpile. In these dangerous and delicate months of her fledgling Regency, Alia Atreides needed to consolidate her power and control the manufacture, distribution, and use of significant weaponry.

"Names provide names," said Valefor.

At a session of her Regent's Council, by unilateral decree, Alia amended the long-standing rules of the Great Convention that applied to atomics. Previously, Great Houses had been permitted to keep their warheads, which could be used only under strictly defined defensive circumstances. Henceforth, as a temporary emergency measure, no one except the Imperial Regent herself could possess such weaponry.

But how to pry the dangerous warheads from entrenched Landsraad families? To begin with, she set up an exchange program, under which noble houses could trade their family atomics for large rewards of spice, voting shares in CHOAM, or other perquisites. In the weeks following the Regent's decree, many Great Houses dutifully surrendered their atomics, hungry for cash and spice after the hardships of the Jihad. Atomics hadn't been openly used in warfare against rival families in millennia anyway.

But some Landsraad families held out, hoarding their ancient warheads . . . to no good purpose, she knew. As her priests and bureaucrats carefully noted the arrival of the weapons and stored them for "appropriate use," it soon became apparent that certain noble Houses were not quite so forthcoming.

Using that as a starting point, Alia asked Duncan to maintain a list of potentially troublesome Houses. She submitted their names to the reconstituted (and ineffective) Landsraad that had reconvened on Kaitain, and she demanded exhaustive investigations and complete disclosure of their activities during the Jihad. Alia would not be caught by surprise.

Armed with information, she would first try economic reprisals against the passively recalcitrant worlds, but she did not rule out any options, even the application of atomics in particularly stubborn cases. After all, Paul had sterilized ninety worlds over the course of the Jihad, so what was the loss of a few more planets?

BACK ON CALADAN, Jessica had fallen into a routine of tending her courtyard garden alone each morning for an hour or two, to contemplate the day's obligations. Now, under a daybreak sky colored beige with dust and the canary yellow of the brightening sunrise, Jessica visited one of the sealed dry-climate gardens within the Citadel of Muad'Dib. The plants required very little water—some through natural selection, others by intentional hybridization. They had grown twisted hard branches, thick-skinned leaves, sharp spines, and thorns, impenetrable defenses against the harshness of the environment.

Upon hearing of Paul's death, she had rushed to Dune, but her thoughts had been about more than the loss of her son. An entire empire was at stake, a government that would survive or fall depending on the decisions Alia made. In all the times Jessica had thought about Paul's legacy, and how his actions and words were being distorted by popular belief, she had not pondered what might happen to the Imperium *without Paul*. What was the legacy of House Atreides for the children, Leto and Ghanima?

Her thoughts were interrupted when three men and a woman entered the dry-climate garden, seeking her out. They were an odd mix: Each wore a strikingly different outfit, and their facial features and skin tones left no doubt that they came from four different worlds, races, and cultures. They bore the look of governmental delegates.

Jessica rose, standing beside a modified cholla cactus whose bent limbs looked as if they had frozen in the act of flailing. The cactus provided a shield as she faced her visitors, though surely they had passed through stringent security measures to get this far.

"We apologize for arriving unannounced, my Lady, but we hoped for privacy and candor," said the delicately built woman with porcelain white skin; blue-black hair hung to her shoulders. She seemed as stiff and formal as her diction. Jessica knew her: Nalla Tur from the Tupile Alliance. "We come to speak to you not only as the mother of Muad'Dib and the mother of the Imperial Regent, but also as the Duchess of Caladan."

The tall, gaunt man next to her had rich brown skin, red beads in his hair, and dull rounded gems set into the flesh of his cheeks. He spoke in a deep baritone voice. "We must talk to you of Landsraad matters. I am Hyron Baha from Midea. Regent Alia has ignored our many messages, but we hope that you can make our words heard."

Jessica massaged a soreness on the back of her own neck as she spoke cautiously. "Even if I agreed to speak on your behalf, you think too much of my power. I have no formal position here. I merely came for the funeral of my son, and I will go back to Caladan as soon as I can."

Nalla Tur answered in a brisk voice, "You are still a member of the Landsraad, by virtue of your rulership of Caladan. Whether or not you choose to attend Landsraad meetings in the new hall on Kaitain, you have legal responsibilities to the reconstituted Houses."

"I have many responsibilities. What is it you ask—and on whose behalf?"

The third speaker was a squat and solid man who seemed to be made entirely of muscle adapted to a high-gravity world. Andaur, she guessed, from the man's accent. "We four are members of formerly exiled noble Houses who took refuge behind Guild shields on Tupile. During the last year of Paul-Muad'Dib's reign, he signed a treaty that effectively granted us amnesty and allowed us to return to the government without fear of trial or execution."

"Now the entire Landsraad—or what's left of it—is shut out," said the dark-haired woman.

Hyron Baha crossed his arms over his chest, tossed his bead-studded strands of hair. "We have been in session on Kaitain with the representatives of ninety-eight other Houses, but the Regent grants the Landsraad no real power. And now she has demanded that we surrender our atomics. Clearly, she means to disarm us all."

"What if we need to defend ourselves against an outside enemy? The Landsraad families are entitled to their atomics!" said the fourth representative, an obese, olive-skinned man with a shrill voice. Jessica didn't recognize him, nor did he introduce himself.

She made a placating sound. "There has been no outside enemy for ten thousand years. Maybe my daughter is more worried about intransigent Houses. Atomics haven't been used against populations for centuries, so of what use are they to you? Given the past conspiracies against my son, Alia has legitimate concerns about having atomics turned against her."

The shrill-voiced man said, "And is it better to place them in the hands of unruly Fremen fanatics? Look at the damage already done in the Jihad!"

Jessica could not dispute that, but there were things she could not say to this group. She showed no reaction, though they looked for one in her.

"We are talking about the Landsraad." Nalla Tur sounded impatient. "For millennia, we provided checks and balances against supreme Corrino rule. By virtue of our rights and long-standing tradition, we *must* be part of the current government. Even Muad'Dib knew the wisdom in letting the Landsraad continue. The Regent Alia should not rule without us."

Jessica didn't accept all of their arguments. "Muad'Dib has been gone only a month. You expect the entire government to change back to the way it was so swiftly?"

The stocky man from the high-gravity planet sounded conciliatory. Yes, his accent was definitely from Andaur. "Your son paid only lip service to the reconstituted Landsraad, and the Regent is even less receptive to shared governmental responsibilities. We need your help. We cannot allow Alia to become a tyrant."

Jessica scowled. "A tyrant? You should choose your words carefully in my presence." She made a warning gesture and accidentally bumped her hand against the spines of the enhanced cholla cactus, drawing blood from her palm.

"Apologies, great Lady, but we only seek the best for all concerned, and we need your help desperately."

"I will speak with my daughter when the opportunity arises, as both her mother and—as you say—as a Landsraad representative. But she is the Regent, and I can't guarantee that she will listen to either."

Hyron Baha bowed formally, letting the red beads in his hair dangle in front of his face. "We've all been affected by the Jihad, Lady Jessica. We all know the human race will be generations recovering from the last few years. We should not let it grow worse."

Jessica glanced down at her hand, then at the cactus. *For every move I make, there will be sharp hazards*, she thought, *and caution cannot protect me from all of them.*

Paul was a reflection of our father, Duke Leto the Just. I, however, am not a reflection of only our mother, Jessica, but of all the mothers before me. From that vast repository of Other Memories, I am the beneficiary of great wisdom.

—ST. ALIA OF THE KNIFE

Jessica felt she needed to pay her respects to Paul in a more private manner; it was neither a Bene Gesserit nor a political need, but the need of a mother to say goodbye to her son. Thanks to Stilgar, she would also soon attend a traditional, solemn, and secret Fremen memorial ceremony for Chani . . . but Alia did not know about that.

After breakfast, Jessica told her daughter that she wanted to go out to Sietch Tabr to visit the place from which Paul had walked off into the dunes, releasing his body to the desert planet, while leaving his memory firmly ensconced in legend.

Alia smiled at her uncertainly, her expression that of a daughter longing for acceptance from her mother. Despite possessing wisdom beyond her years, Alia was physically a teenager, growing into her body, discovering the world with her own senses. "I'll go with you, Mother. It is a pilgrimage we should make together . . . for Paul."

Jessica realized that she had been thinking primarily of herself and her son, giving inadequate consideration to Alia. *Have I always brushed my daughter aside, without realizing it?* Jessica had lost Duke Leto, and now Paul—leaving her with only Alia. Jessica chastised herself for the slight, then said, "I'd be glad to have you accompany me."

They made quick preparations for an informal journey out to the sietch, neither of them wanting to make this into a grand procession of sycophants and wailing priests. Now that the public funeral was over, Alia seemed to understand her mother's need for privacy; maybe the girl felt it herself as well.

The pair dressed in the simple garb of pilgrims so they could walk to the public landing areas without anyone remarking on their presence. Duncan would meet them at the pad, where he had readied an ornithopter for the flight across the desert.

Moving through the Arrakeen streets, Jessica immersed herself in the sights and sounds, sensing the clamoring energy of the populace: all those minds and souls generating a collective power that drove the human race forward. Here she and Alia were merely another mother and daughter, indistinguishable from others in the crowd. She wondered how many of those parents felt awkward around their children. Other teenage girls had entirely different troubles than the ones that weighed so heavily on Alia's mind.

"When I learned you were coming here," the girl said suddenly, "I looked forward to talking with you, hearing your advice. Paul valued your opinion, Mother, and *I* value you as well. But I know you don't approve of some of my initial decisions as Regent. I am only doing what I believe is necessary and what Paul would have wanted."

Jessica's reply was noncommittal. "Paul made many decisions that troubled me, too." Despite her second-guessing of her son's leadership, she had come to realize that he did indeed see a much larger picture, a vast landscape of time and destiny with only a very faint and treacherous path through it. He had a terrible purpose that few others could grasp. He had been *right* and knew it so firmly that his mother's disapproval had not swayed him in the least. In retrospect, Jessica realized that Paul had done some of the same things for which she now resented Alia. Maybe she had a blind spot where her daughter was concerned. "I'm worried, both as a mother and as a human being. I can't help but fear that you are about to slide off the edge of a precipice."

Alia's response was filled with confidence. "My footing is sure, and I'm pragmatic."

"And I have no interest in ruling the Imperium. There doesn't need to be friction between us."

Alia laughed, touched her mother's sleeve. "Of course there is friction between us, for we are too much alike. I have all your memories within me."

"Only my memories up to the moment of your birth. I've learned and changed much since then."

"And so have I, Mother. So have I."

At the edge of the spaceport, they passed a bazaar that had sprung up as a temporary camp of vendors and their wares. Over the course of decades, it had grown and evolved into a permanent fixture in Arrakeen. Polymer tarps formed artificial ceilings to shield pilgrims and curiosity seekers alike from the unrelenting sun. Large intake fans sucked in air and filtered out every drop of wasted moisture.

Fortune-tellers sat at booths, staring at ornate and colorful cards, doing readings from the enhanced Dune Tarot, with illustrations drawn to include recent events and the tragic loss of Muad'Dib; the artwork on the card of the Blind Man was particularly eerie. Most of the merchants, Jessica saw, offered religious icons, holy relics, and other "sacred" paraphernalia—all sorts of garbage—to which they had applied dubious "authentications" of their significance.

"This cloak was worn by Muad'Dib himself!" a man shouted, then named a price astronomical enough to "prove" the item's provenance. Half a dozen vendors claimed to possess the original Atreides signet ring and accused one another of being liars. Alia, of course, had the genuine ring locked away back at the fortress citadel. Other salespeople hawked items supposedly touched by Muad'Dib or blessed by him or—for the bargain-conscious—merely glimpsed by him, as if his gaze imparted some sort of residual holiness.

The sheer tonnage of material in the bazaar was absurd, and this was only one shopping complex. Hundreds more were scattered throughout Arrakeen, and similar markets had sprung up on countless planets. Jessica stared in dismay. "My son has become a tourist attraction. Fodder for charlatans taking advantage of customers who are easily—and willingly—duped."

A flash of anger crossed Alia's face. "They are liars, all liars. How can they prove any of their claims? They are a disgrace to my brother's name."

"Similar men did this on Caladan while Paul was alive, during the worst years of his Jihad. When I could no longer tolerate it, Gurney and I evicted them."

"Then I should do the same here. The Dune Tarot has always made me uneasy." Wheels seemed to be turning in Alia's mind, and she brooded for a moment. "Might you offer me your advice about how to accomplish it?"

The fact that her daughter would ask so openly for her help lightened Jessica's mood. "Yes, but later. Right now, we are off to the desert to say farewell to my son and your brother. This isn't a time for politics."

They walked in silence the rest of the way to the landing pad, where Duncan waited beside an ornithopter, young and healthy in a crisp uniform that made him look as if he had leapfrogged across years from the past.

AFTER THEY LANDED at the distant sietch, Jessica stood outside the entrance and gazed out upon the desert. "This is where my grandchildren were born. And where Chani died."

Duncan had a strange, disturbed look about him, but not the far-off expression of a Mentat engrossed in calculations. "Sietch Tabr is also the place where I tried to kill Paul."

"And where the ghola Hayt became Duncan Idaho again." Alia turned, wrapped her arms around him.

Without asking them to accompany her, Jessica followed the winding path out of the rocks and picked her way down to the edge of the sweeping vista of open dunes, the undulating crests and slopes of golden sand. The wind had picked up, a breeze the Fremen named *pastaza*, strong enough to stir sand and dust but presaging no storm.

Jessica walked out onto the soft warm dunes, leaving prominent footprints as she crested the nearest rise. She gazed past the arid horizon and envisioned the unbroken landscape stretching on forever. She stared at the pristine sands until her eyes ached from the glare, searching for signs of Paul, as if a silhouetted figure might stride back out of the dunes, returning from his sacred journey, his own hajj to Shai-Hulud.

But the winds and the sands of time had erased his footprints, leaving no sign of his passing. The desert was empty without him.

I know what you are thinking. I know what you are doing.
Most of all, I know what I am doing.

—ST. ALIA OF THE KNIFE

U npredictability.

Sitting in the nearly empty audience chamber, Alia smiled to herself as she let the word float through her mind. Unpredictability was far more than a word; it was a useful tool and a powerful weapon. It worked not only on her closest aides and advisers, and on the Qizarate, but also on the masses she ruled. No one knew how she thought or why she made her choices as Regent. And that kept others off guard and unsettled, making them wonder what she might do next, what she was capable of.

Her unpredictability would make the worst jackals hesitate, for now, and she hoped it gave her the time she needed to secure her hold and gather her strength, before any usurpers could try to rock the seat of government. But she had to be swift, and firm.

Dressed in a black aba with the red Atreides hawk on one shoulder, Alia waited impatiently. It was midmorning in the second week after Paul's funeral, and a team of workers were shifting the position of the heavy Hagar emerald throne. "Turn it around. I want my back to the delegation from the Ixian Confederacy as they enter."

The workers paused, confused. One man said, "But then you will not be able to see the delegation, my Lady."

"No, they will not have the honor of seeing *me*. I'm not pleased with them."

Though the technocrats insisted—as they had for years—that Ix had severed all ties with Bronso, she did not entirely believe them. Too many suspicions and questions, too many convenient explanations. While Paul had a certain affinity for Ix, thanks to his childhood memories, Alia did not suffer from such sentimentality. The technocrats would find that Muad'Dib's sister was a different sort of ruler. Alia needed to keep the Ixian Confederacy unbalanced; it was easier to control power structures when they remained on unsteady ground.

She had considered this carefully.

Even when she was alone, Alia frequently chose to spend time pondering the consequences of her decisions. She knew that her mother had much wisdom to impart, but often Jessica's advice seemed one-sided or limited. Today, at least, Alia would not ask her mother's opinion. Caladan was known to make people soft and take away their edge.

Alia had additional advisers as well—Other Memories that unfolded like fractal patterns inside her consciousness in a cacophony of conflicting advice. Often in her private chambers she would consume great amounts of spice, inducing a trance so that she could journey into that Bene Gesserit archive of memories, and stir them up. She did not have the skill to pick and choose among them or locate any particular person as if she were querying a library. The memories came and went, with some presences shouting more loudly than others.

She let them assail her now, while she brooded about the Ixians' arrival. Listening to the clamor, she heard one of those past lives rise above the others, a sharp-tongued voice in the archive. A wise old woman who was familiar with many of the challenges that Alia faced. She had, after all, been the Truthsayer to Emperor Shaddam IV . . . Reverend Mother Gaius Helen Mohiam.

Alia spoke to her in a taunting mental tone. *Do you still call me "Abomination," Grandmother, even when you are one of the voices inside of me?*

Mohiam sounded dry and tart. *By allowing me to advise you, child, you demonstrate wisdom, not weakness.*

Why should I trust the voice of a woman who wanted to kill me?

Ah, but you were the one who ordered my death, child.

What of it? I also killed my grandfather, the Baron, because he needed killing. How could I do any less for you? Aren't we taught to ignore or even despise emotional attachments?

Mohiam sounded pleased. *Perhaps with maturity you have learned from your mistakes. I am willing to help.*

Have you learned from your mistakes, Grandmother?

Mistakes? The dry rasp of a laugh echoed in Alia's head. *If you believe me so fallible, why ask me for advice?*

Asking for advice is not the same as heeding it, Grandmother. What do you think I should do with these Ixians?

I think you should make them squirm.

Because they continue to secretly support Bronso?

I doubt very much if they've had any knowledge of that renegade for years now. However, they will be so eager to prove it that you can gain many concessions from them. The more fear and guilt you make them feel, the more they will want to appease you. I suggest you use this as a lever against them.

Alia made no further reply as she heard Mohiam's presence fall back into the buzz of the background voices. Considering what Alia had done to the witch, could she trust her advice? Perhaps. Something about what she said, and the way she said it, rang of truth.

Meanwhile, the sweating workers threw themselves into the labor of turning the throne around. They could have attached suspensors to move the enormous blue-green seat with the nudge of a finger, but instead they grunted, strained, and pushed. It was their way of serving her.

Three black bees hummed over the heads of the workers, particularly irritating a swarthy offworld man who had a dark bristle of beard. The stinging insects darted around the sweat of his forehead. He released his hold to swat at them, while the other workers squared the heavy chair into position on the dais. The annoyed man knocked a bee out of the air and onto an arm of the throne, where he then crushed the insect with his fist and casually wiped it away.

Alia startled him. "Who gave you permission to smash a bee on the Imperial throne?"

Astonished at what he had done on impulse, the man turned, suddenly trembling, his face flushed, his eyes downcast and guilty. "N-no one, my Lady. I meant no affront."

Alia drew her crysknife from its sheath at her neck and said in a measured tone, "With Muad'Dib gone, all the lives in his empire have been left to my stewardship. Including yours. And even a life as insignificant as that of an insect."

The worker closed his eyes, resigned to his fate. "Yes, my Lady."

"Extend the offending hand, palm up!"

Shaking, the worker did so. With a deft move, Alia slashed with the crysknife's razor edge, neatly shaving a thin slice of flesh from the man's palm, the portion that had killed the bee and touched the throne. He hissed in pain and surprise, but did not draw back, did not beg for mercy.

Good enough, she thought. He had learned his lesson, as had the other workers. Alia wiped the milky blade on the man's shirt and resheathed the weapon. "They called my father Leto the Just. Perhaps I have some of him in me."

Unpredictability.

WHEN THE IXIAN delegation arrived, Alia sat dwarfed on the great crystalline throne and stared at the orange hangings that covered the wall behind the dais. Her coppery hair was secured with golden water rings, pieces of tallying metal that announced to everyone that she, like her brother, considered herself Fremen. Though she heard the commotion as the technocrats entered, she did not turn to see the men. Duncan would have told her never to sit with her back to a door, but Alia considered it symbolic of her disdain for these men.

From behind her, the chamberlain announced the Ixians, and she heard the approaching footsteps. Their shoes made sharp sounds on the hard, polished floor, because by her orders the workers had not laid out a royal carpet. She heard an unevenness—uncertainty?—in their gait.

A standing audience in the huge hall murmured, then grew quiet, curious as to what Alia would do next. Her amazon guards were stationed as usual, and ever alert. She did not know the name of the delegation leader, nor did she care. All technocrats were the same. Since the fall of the ruling House Vernius seven years earlier—when

Bronso, the last heir, had gone into hiding to promote his sedition—the planet Ix had increased its research and industrial production, with little interest in the politics of the reconstituted Landsraad.

She heard the men stop at the base of the dais and shuffle uncomfortably. A clearing throat, the rustle of clothing, and a hint of annoyance in a male voice. "Lady Alia, we have come as you requested."

Alia spoke straight ahead to the wall. "And do you know why I *summoned* you?"

A different voice, cooler, more logical. "We can postulate. An Ixian has affronted the Imperial household. You hope that our Confederacy has information on the whereabouts of Bronso of Ix."

The first voice: "We condemn the actions of the Vernius exile!"

Alia hardened her tone. "Bronso Vernius used Ixian technology to bring disaster to my brother's funeral. What other tricks might he use? What technologies have you given him that he intends to turn against me?"

"None, my Lady! I guarantee that the Technocrat Council had nothing to do with it." She detected no falsehood in his voice.

The second voice: "We respectfully ask you to remember that Ix was once a close friend to House Atreides. We hope to reestablish that beneficial alliance."

"The Atreides alliance was not with the Technocrat Council," she said, "but with House Vernius. Bronso himself severed those ties when he was young."

"So, you see, my Lady—Bronso has been making unwise decisions for years. He does not represent the best interests of Ix. He is an unwanted remnant of an old time and obsolete ways."

Old and obsolete, Alia thought. *There was a time when my father and Rhombur Vernius were fast friends, when Ix served the needs of honor, not just commerce and industry. These men have forgotten so much from the days when House Atreides helped restore Vernius to power after the Tleilaxu takeover.*

"Even so, you must earn your way back into my good graces." She tapped her fingers on the arm of the throne. "Have your representatives bring me new technologies, devices that are not available to anyone else. Duncan Idaho will inspect them for me and decide which can be used to strengthen our Regency. When those choices are made, you must grant me exclusive use of the technologies. After you've impressed me, we will see about restoring Ix's standing in my eyes."

A slight hesitation, perhaps a silent consultation among the men, and finally the logical voice said, "The Technocrat Council sincerely appreciates the opportunity, Great Lady."

Memories and lies are painful. But my memories are not lies.
—BRONSO OF IX, transcript of death-cell interview

Inside the Heighliner's layered decks of public areas and service corridors, the Wayku always provided a place for Bronso to hide. Feeling an affinity for him, the gypsylike people who served as Guildship stewards had secretly helped Bronso since he started his strange quest to destroy the myth surrounding Paul Atreides.

Bronso switched his location from day to day and port to port, taking up temporary residence in unclaimed staterooms or tiny cabins. Always alert and wary, he kept his power usage to a minimum so that Guild watchdogs would find nothing amiss. He had been on the run for seven years, ever since he began distributing his writings.

Sometimes he took advantage of well-appointed suites that reminded him of his days in the Grand Palais of Ix, as the heir of House Vernius. Even so, Bronso did not for a moment regret losing his comforts and riches. He had rejected them voluntarily, in order to follow a more important calling. The Technocrat Council had corrupted everything that was good and noble on his home world. Now Bronso was performing vital work . . . history-making work.

In the turmoil that continued to ripple across the uncertain worlds following the death of Muad'Dib, most Guildships were overbooked, and wealthy noble family members fought over the available cabins. On this particular passage, Ennzyn—one of Bronso's Wayku allies—had relegated him to a tiny crew cabin that was not listed in any brochure.

He didn't complain, since his requirements were few: He needed only a light and a private place to sit while writing his latest condemnations. His struggle against the fanaticism that muddied Paul's legacy always seemed impossible, but he had accepted the task. He was the only man brave enough to criticize Muad'Dib so openly. Bronso might have been reckless, but he had never been a coward.

His Wayku friends sheltered, protected, and aided him. As an itinerant class of workers, solicitous, unnoticed and unassuming, they possessed no real identity as far as the Imperium was concerned. When he and young Paul Atreides had first met these wayfarers nineteen years ago, Bronso had not expected to enlist them as such dedicated allies. Now, they quietly secreted his "heretical" tracts among the belongings of random travelers, so that the publications appeared on other planets, seemingly without any point of origin.

People needed to know the truth, needed skepticism to counterbalance the nonsense that Irulan had put forth as *The Life of Muad'Dib*. To him had fallen the task of swinging the pendulum in the opposite direction. To accomplish that, he had to commit the words to paper. His statements needed to be infuriating, irrefutable, and compelling.

Throughout the bloody Jihad and Alia's recent crackdowns, the people accepted repression in the name of orthodoxy because Paul had allowed—*allowed!*—his Fremen bureaucracy to become a ravenous cancer. Bronso recognized that Paul had, at times, made attempts to rein in the excesses, but the warfare and fanaticism, like the mythology that deified him, had taken on a life of its own.

Exhausted, frightened people forgot the truth so easily. Paul's apologists rewrote history and expunged the direst events from the official record: the horrific battles, the sterilization of entire planets, the mass murder of monks in the Lankiveil monastery. With so much privation and such a scattering of peoples, who would question histories kept by the "official" purveyors of truth? Who would gainsay a source as unimpeachable as the Princess Irulan herself, wife of Muad'Dib? Surely, her accounts must be the true version, the way history had actually occurred.

But it was not so, and Bronso had to continue the attempt to correct the record. It was a matter of honor, and he had given his word.

His Wayku companion had brought him food, but Bronso was not hungry. In his cramped cabin, he sat on an uncomfortable metal bench, leveled the writing surface, and sank into his memories. By the light of a low-power glowglobe, he laid crime after crime at Muad'Dib's feet. Each damning line was like the crack of a flagellant's whip.

Only by stripping away the softening untruths, only by laying bare the callous acts committed in the name of Muad'Dib, only by making the human race aware of the appalling crimes that Paul had unleashed, could Bronso accomplish what was necessary to preserve the future of mankind.

May God save us from a messiah of our own making!

As he wrote, the images of those events screamed behind his eyes. "Oh, Paul, my friend . . ." He continued to write, and tears streamed down his face.

*Once, when Muad'Dib was walking in the desert, he came upon a
kangaroo mouse, a muad'dib, perched in the shadows of a rock.
"Tell me your story, little one," he said. "Tell me of your life."*

*The mouse was shy. "No one wants to know about me, for I
am small and insignificant. Tell me of your life."*

*To which Muad'Dib replied, "Then no one wants to know
about me either, for I am just a man and equally insignificant."*

—*A Child's History of Muad'Dib* by the PRINCESS IRULAN

W hen Alia commanded Irulan to accompany her to the Arrakeen warehouse quarter, the Princess had no choice but to
obey. Though she had been freed from her death cell, and a formal pardon had been signed and stamped, Irulan knew that the Regent could
easily exile her to Salusa, or worse.

They went together with a security contingent and entered a small
warehouse. Inside, workers moved about like insects in a hive, busily
packaging small books, stacking them into containers, preparing them
for wide distribution across the Imperium. Irulan smelled spice-based
plastic and paper dust in the air, along with the ubiquitous musk of
sweat and the metal tang of machinery.

As she watched them work, Irulan recognized the volumes. *The Life
of Muad'Dib.* "That's my book."

Alia smiled, delivering good news. "A revised edition."

Irulan picked up a copy and thumbed through the thin, indestruc-
tible pages, the densely printed text. "What do you mean, revised?"
She skimmed paragraphs and tried to identify sections that had been
changed, added, or deleted.

"A better version of the truth, edited for the benefit of the masses,
taking into account changes in our political situation."

Duncan Idaho, silent and uneasily threatening, stood beside the confident Regent. From his placid expression, Irulan could not tell if he approved, disapproved, or did not care.

Alia tossed her hair back and explained. "My brother was a tolerant, confident man. While your treatises were positive for the most part, he did allow you to write some critical passages that questioned his decisions, painted him in a slightly uncomplimentary light. I don't know why he permitted this, but I am not my brother. I do not have Muad'Dib's force of will. I am just the Regent."

Irulan fought the annoyance in her voice. "Modesty and self-deprecation don't suit you, Alia."

"These are precarious times! With the future of the Empire in doubt, I am tiptoeing across drumsand. Anything that diminishes the worth of Paul's memory will weaken my position. Bronso's manifestos are like borer worms chewing away at our foundation, so I shall control what I can control."

In the warehouse, workers piled boxes of the revised biography onto suspensor pallets and moved them out to waiting groundcars that took them to cargo ships. Nearly a billion of Irulan's books had already been distributed to the planets Paul had conquered in his Jihad.

"Your purpose in my government is to be Bronso's counterpoint. Given the governmentally subsidized distribution, your books will have a much broader platform than the traitor's seditious publications can ever receive. Your official histories will easily overwhelm his lies, by brute force if necessary."

Irulan wasn't a coward who trembled at any threat made on her life, but she did feel an obligation to Paul, and she had to consider the welfare of her husband's twins. "And what is it exactly that you want from me?"

"Imperial security depends upon the reverence the people still hold for my brother. From now on, your writings shall serve a specific purpose. Publish only good things about Paul, positive aspects of his rule, even if you have to distort the truth." Alia gave her a girlish smile, looking like the child that Irulan had helped raise in the first years of Paul's reign. "If you do that, you have absolutely nothing to fear."

OVER THE ENSUING weeks, Irulan returned to her writings with a passion and enthusiasm that took Jessica by surprise. The Princess seemed intent on preserving—and exaggerating—the memory of Paul. In a creative fervor, she wrote chapters that expanded the glorious legend of Muad'Dib, taking even more liberties than she had during Paul's lifetime.

Finding it alarming and distasteful, Jessica decided to speak with Irulan. For Paul's sake.

In her private wing of the immense citadel, the Princess had selected the décor and worked with craftsmen and artisans to create an echo of the Corrino palace on Kaitain, where she had grown up. Irulan had her own courtyards and glassed-in greenhouses, dry fountains and wind-scoured obelisks. She kept to herself on the Citadel grounds and did not often venture out in public.

Making her way without escort or criers, Jessica found the Princess in a courtyard gazebo, scribing words onto crystal sheets. The younger woman glanced up, and tucked a loose strand of gold hair behind her ear. "Lady Jessica, this is an unexpected pleasure." She gestured toward an empty seat beside her at the writing table. "Join me. I'm always happy to talk with you."

"You haven't yet heard what I have to say."

The words elicited a frown. "Have I done something to displease you?"

Taking the offered seat, Jessica did not mince words. "Paul deserves better than shameless propaganda. You've always shaded the truth one way or the other, Irulan, and most of the time I could not fault you for it, because you came close to representing my son accurately. But now, when I compare your histories with known and irrefutable facts, I find them far from the mark. The new revisions to *The Life of Muad'Dib* are very disturbing."

"Alia's revisions." Irulan tried to cover her embarrassment. "In any case, who can know every fact? My purpose is not to memorialize dry data, but to aid our government in these uncertain times, for the sake of Imperial security. You know the way of it. We were both trained by the Sisterhood."

"I know what Alia wants, and I understand the necessity for propaganda, but now . . . nothing negative at all? Not the tiniest thing? Even starry-eyed pilgrims can see your obvious slant."

"In Alia's view, the slant itself provides balance." Irulan straightened her back. "She's right, actually. Bronso's constant unflattering revelations are doing a great deal of damage, and I find them personally reprehensible. They weaken the Regency at its most fragile, unstable moment, when it's just getting under way. So, if my writings are overly favorable toward Muad'Dib in portraying historical events, it is only to counter the slander." The emotion in Irulan's voice surprised Jessica. "History is in *my* hands—Paul himself told me that. I can't let Bronso's seditious tracts go unchallenged."

Jessica let out a long sigh. She had kept Paul's secret for many years, but now she decided that Irulan needed to know. "There's a key point you don't understand."

Irulan set down her stylus and pushed the crystal sheets away. She seemed stiff and overly formal. "Then enlighten me. What is it, exactly, that I am missing?"

"That Bronso was once *Paul's friend*."

Irulan frowned. "I studied Paul's youth, so I know of his contacts with House Vernius."

"And you know as well that there was a falling out between the Atreides and the Ixians."

"Yes, but the historical record is sketchy and vague. It was not a subject that Paul wanted to discuss, though I did ask him about it."

Jessica lowered her voice, concerned that someone might be eavesdropping, although these events were common knowledge to a person willing to dig into old Imperial records. "The two Houses once had strong ties, and Paul met Bronso when the Vernius family went to Caladan for Duke Leto's wedding. Later, when Paul was twelve, he traveled to Ix to study with Bronso—just as my Leto went to study with Rhombur Vernius when he was young. Duke Leto felt it was important for Paul's training, to make him the next leader of Caladan. The boys became the best of friends—blood brothers sworn to guard each other's life. Until everything changed."

With the comment hanging between them, Jessica met the other woman's inquisitive gaze. Then Jessica proceeded to tell the story.

PART II

10,188 AG

Paul Atreides, age twelve, six months after the end of the War of Assassins between House Ecaz and House Moritani

Three years before House Atreides leaves Caladan for Arrakis

I do not regret any of the challenges of my youth. Each experience shaped me into what I am today. If you want to understand me and my motivations, look backward.

—Conversations with Muad'Dib *by the* PRINCESS IRULAN

Disembarking from the Heighliner at Ix, the Lady Jessica rode with young Paul, Duncan, and Gurney on one of the many shuttles to the surface, whereupon they descended through the crust to the cavern city of Vernii.

Jessica saw her son gazing at the immense enclosed space, fascinated by the artificial sky, graceful support girders, and glittering columns that extended from cavern floor to ceiling. The open area pulsed with activity, whirred with the sound of smoothly functioning machinery, and Paul said, "My father told me of his time studying here with House Vernius, but his descriptions did not do justice to this place."

Gurney struggled not to show how impressed he was by the view. "You will find it time well spent, young Master. A worthy tradition—like father, like son."

Duncan stood rigid, perhaps remembering when he had come to Ix in the battle to restore Rhombur to the throne. "Your invitation here demonstrates to everyone that House Vernius has restored normalcy to Ix after the Tleilaxu invaders were ousted."

Jessica took her son by the arm. "As for me, I'm looking forward to seeing Bronso's mother again. Tessia has written me often to tell me how much she misses Caladan."

"Then we should get to the Grand Palais," Paul said. "It would be rude to keep Bronso and his family waiting for us." He was barely able to restrain his eagerness to begin his new adventure.

The past year's experiences had dramatically matured Paul: his first trip offworld to Ecaz, his first taste of battle during the War of Assassins on Caladan and Grumman. Duke Leto had commented on the boy's early transition to manhood, and Jessica could not help but agree. Whenever she guided him through prana-bindu exercises, pushing the boundaries of his mental and muscular abilities, she had begun to see him as an adult. Even at age twelve, Paul was more prepared for the hazards of his life than many of the Landsraad nobles she had met. Jessica thought Paul's eyes looked wiser now than they had even half a year ago.

With businessmen, CHOAM representatives, and industrialists arriving and departing in a constant flow of shuttles, the city of Vernii was a bustling blur of activity. The small Atreides group made their way from the shuttle arrival area toward the inverted palace structure that glittered amidst the other industrial buildings. From the gliding tram that whisked them along the ceiling, they could see a dizzying view of diamond lattice columns that supported the ceiling, as well as the skeleton of an immense Heighliner being built on the wide cavern floor. The Spacing Guild constantly needed new ships, and construction continued at a furious pace.

When they reached the expansive portico station of the Grand Palais, Paul pointed to a tall, red-haired boy, whom he knew to be eleven years old. "There's Bronso!" Overhead, crystal chandeliers glittered with myriad prisms, while hidden sonic vibrators in the walls played recorded Ixian folk songs.

Among the arrival party, Jessica was glad to see her old friend Tessia, a fellow Bene Gesserit concubine sent from Wallach IX as a partner to the exiled Prince Rhombur after the temporary overthrow of House Vernius by the Tleilaxu. Rhombur had taken sanctuary on Caladan for years, until he rallied enough of his people to oust the invaders and return Ix to normal rule.

As the Earl of Ix now, Rhombur Vernius was by far the most distinctive in the group greeting Jessica, a patchwork man made of artificial limbs and cyborg systems, reassembled by the Suk doctor Wellington

Yueh after a horrific skyclipper explosion. Dr. Yueh himself, Rhombur's personal physician, also accompanied the welcoming party. Jessica remembered him from his years on Caladan, when he tended the recovering Rhombur.

Earl Vernius moved with an uneven, strained gait, as if his synthetic muscles were no longer coordinated. "Welcome! Welcome, my Atreides friends." He lurched forward, his eyes—one real and one artificial—fixed on Paul. "The son of my dear Leto. And Jessica . . . Duncan Idaho, Gurney Halleck! How pleased I am to see you all again."

Bronso looked at his father, then joked. "He's also pleased because this gave him an excuse to skip the Technocrat Council meeting."

The cyborg Earl straightened. "Uh, *this* is much more important. Friends and family. I promised Duke Leto that his son would feel at home here."

Paul bowed formally. "I present myself to the noble family of Ix. Thank you for hosting me, and providing me with this experience."

Tessia extended her hand for Paul to take in formal greeting, then gave him a quick hug. "There are always things to learn. We'll have plenty of time together—and Jessica, I look forward to renewed conversations with you. It's been a very long time." She looked at her husband. "But the Earl really should be getting back to the Council meeting. What would Bolig Avati do without you, my dear?"

Rhombur made a rude grunt. "They do what they like, no matter what I say." He leaned forward, speaking conspiratorially to Paul and Jessica. "Four times in the past two years, they've tried to stage accidents to get rid of me, but I haven't been able to prove anything." When Duncan and Gurney reacted with alarm, the cyborg nobleman merely grinned. "Uh, not to worry. I've promised Duke Leto that you'll be safe here."

"And my father made me promise to keep Bronso safe," Paul said.

The other boy flushed. "I thought I was supposed to watch out for *you.*"

Rhombur gave a sober nod. "Exactly. You both gave your word to your fathers. Now you are bound to watch out for each other, guarding and supporting each other in all possible ways. That is the bond between Vernius and Atreides. A pledge between friends is more binding than any legal document."

The cyborg man tried to reassure Jessica, Gurney, and Duncan. "Don't worry—I know who my friends and enemies are. Still, the way the technocrats keep whittling away at my responsibilities, I'm becoming a mere figurehead. Soon enough, I won't be worth the trouble for them to make an assassination attempt."

"Then we should stand up to what they're doing!" Bronso said. "I'm going to be Earl someday."

Rhombur swiveled his head. "Wait your time, my son, before getting your hands dirty. Be patient, and learn everything you can."

As they stood among the crowds in the portico station, a lift came down through the ceiling from the surface, and three black-robed women emerged. Jessica spotted the delegation, and some instinct warned her not to draw their attention. The stern-looking Bene Gesserits, two of them Reverend Mothers, glided like self-important crows through the people in the reception foyer as additional trams docked.

Next to her, Tessia also stiffened, then reacted with clear alarm. "What are they doing here?"

Seeing the three Bene Gesserits, Paul lowered his voice. "Why don't you want those women to see you?"

"I'd rather not have to answer their questions. They would want to know why we're here."

Paul remained perplexed. "It's no secret, Mother. You came to see Bronso's mother. You and Tessia were friends, and I'm here for offworld training. Why should that raise questions?"

"The Sisterhood always raises questions, lad," Gurney said. "Your mother is right."

Tessia watched the three Sisters carefully. "I don't think this is about you at all. The tall, wrinkled one in front is Reverend Mother Stokiah. I met her once at the Mother School, and it was not pleasant. I had to recite the Litany Against Fear every night for a week just to get to sleep. Be on your guard."

"In that case, I bet they didn't come to purchase new technology for the laundries on Wallach IX," Paul said.

Rhombur gave a loud laugh. "Vermillion Hells, even a twelve-year-old boy is suspicious about why they're here!"

Yueh frowned deeply. "Unanswered questions don't always signify sinister dealings." He stared fixedly at one of the arriving Bene Gesserits, his sallow face turning pale and troubled. But he did not explain why the strange woman so captivated his attention.

Tessia tried hard to pretend that she wasn't bothered, but she kept her voice low. "We should go inside the Grand Palais. The Sisters will tell us what they want soon enough. For now, we've got more important business. Bronso, kindly show our guests to their quarters. And Jessica . . . I will speak with you later."

Bronso led them into the main building, devoting most of his attention and excitement to Paul. "You'll be staying with me. I promise, we'll get along famously, just as our fathers did."

An obligation without honor is worthless.
—THUFIR HAWAT, Mentat and Weapons Master
of House Atreides

While Paul settled in and got to know Bronso better, Jessica met with Rhombur's wife in the woman's royal apartment as the artificial night began to fall. Jessica had looked forward to a peaceful, social visit before returning to Caladan and leaving her son here to study. But seeing the three Bene Gesserits had changed the tone of their reunion.

Soon enough, the Sisterhood's delegation would reveal their true purpose in coming to Ix. Jessica didn't imagine for a moment that this was a social call. They wanted something. The Sisterhood *always* wanted something, and often it had to do with control. Maybe they would challenge her about Paul.

Jessica was not a clinging, doting mother, but she did encourage her son to study subjects that went far beyond politics. Since he had no other dedicated tutor, she shared subtleties of her own Bene Gesserit training. Because the Sisterhood had never wanted her to bear a son in the first place, she was sure those women would disapprove of her methods.

Let them disapprove, she decided. She had been making decisions independent of the Sisterhood for some time now.

Jessica made herself smile, trying to shake her mood. "I'm glad Paul is here. He needs a friend, too, since he has no playmates his own age on Caladan—Leto considers it too dangerous."

"The boys will take care of each other." Looking tense, Tessia seemed unable to relax. "Times are much more stable than when Leto and Rhombur were young. Without the Tleilaxu, our industries are burgeoning, our exports tripling annually." Her voice became troubled. "Rhombur has had to appoint more and more lieutenants. Business subsidiaries run the manufacturing centers, and the Technocrat Council has been swiftly and silently stealing power from him. I fear that House Vernius is becoming obsolete."

From the broad windows in Tessia's quarters, Jessica looked out at the enormous cavern, with its swirling factories and industrial lights, the bustle of workers. One nobleman could not oversee it all without a cadre of loyal administrators, and with profits growing and growing, no one would want the production to slow down.

"Despite the political problems on Ix, I have so much in my life now, Jessica—a family, a place . . . and *love*, though no Bene Gesserit would recognize, or even understand, that."

Love, Jessica thought. There were certain things the Sisterhood simply didn't understand. "Yet they will always have a hold on us, even after we draw our last breaths and slip into Other Memory."

Without making a sound, the trio of women appeared like a flock of shadows at the doorway. Tessia met the gaze of stern Reverend Mother Stokiah, feigned casualness, and sat back in her chair. "Tell us why you're here." The women did not introduce themselves.

Still standing, Stokiah spoke only to Tessia, not deigning to notice Jessica. "The Sisterhood has new orders for you."

Tessia did not invite them to sit. "I'm no longer certain that the Sisterhood's *orders* are in my best interests."

The two other visitors stiffened visibly, while old Stokiah scowled. "That is not, and never has been, our concern. Orders are orders."

Jessica moved closer to her friend. "Maybe you should explain what you want from her."

Undercurrents of acid flowed through the Reverend Mother's voice. "We know who you are, Jessica—and you are no shining example of following the Sisterhood's instructions." Without bothering to look at Jessica's reaction, Stokiah turned to Tessia. "After inspecting the bloodlines in our breeding index, we require various permutations of your genes. You are hereby recalled to Wallach IX so that you may bear certain children."

Jessica noted how well Stokiah maintained her calm. In contrast, Tessia reddened. "My womb isn't a tool for you to borrow whenever you like. I love Rhombur. He is my husband, and I will not be a brood mare for you."

One of the other Reverend Mothers in the entourage, the smallest of the trio, tried to sound conciliatory. "It will not be an extraordinary commitment—three daughters, no more, with different fathers." She sounded so reasonable, as if she were asking Tessia to do nothing more than change a garment. "Rhombur knew you were a Bene Gesserit when he chose you as a concubine. He will understand, and we have asked so little of you in your lifetime."

Jessica felt she had to come to her friend's defense. She quoted the Bene Gesserit motto with stern sarcasm. "'We live to serve.'"

Tessia rose to her feet. "I have other obligations now. I am also a wife and mother, and I will not turn my back on all that. If you can't understand why, then you're ill-informed about human nature. I shall accept no other lover than Rhombur. That is not a subject for negotiation."

For a woman who should have been in perfect mastery of her emotions, Stokiah allowed a hint of her anger to show. The other two Sisters seemed more confused than upset by Tessia's response, turning as pale as limestone. "*Sister* Tessia," Stokiah emphasized the title, "it seems you both have forgotten a great deal. You defy the Bene Gesserit at your peril."

"Nevertheless, I refuse. You have your answer. Now please leave."

Startling them all, Rhombur appeared at the door, his powerful augmented body primed for use, like a loaded weapon. "Vermillion Hells, you are upsetting my wife, so you're no longer welcome on Ix. If the next Heighliner has no available staterooms, I'm sure we can find a cargo container to accommodate all three of you."

Stokiah slipped into a fighting stance, and the other two women stood coiled beside her. Then, unexpectedly, she gave an abbreviated bow. "As you wish. We have nothing further to discuss here."

"No, you do not."

Departing like shadows fleeing the light, Stokiah and her two companions slipped away. Jessica was left feeling angry and unsettled. "I'm sorry you had to endure that."

"The Sisterhood taught us to be strong, if nothing else." Tessia pressed herself against her husband and said in a hoarse voice, "I love you so much, Rhombur."

He folded her within his powerful cyborg arms. "Oh, I never had any doubt of that."

AS A SUK practitioner, Dr. Wellington Yueh had learned to control his feelings; he was cool and logical, sincere but not vulnerable. His personality made him a perfect match for his Bene Gesserit wife Wanna, who was equally adept at compartmentalizing her thoughts and feelings, at least in public.

Yet when he saw the three Sisters arrive at the Grand Palais—and recognized one of them as *Wanna,* the first time he had seen her after such a long separation—his heart lurched. The barriers almost melted away. Almost. During his diligent service as Rhombur's private physician, he often tried to forget how much he missed her, convincing himself that their relationship was as solid as stone, no matter how long they were separated.

And now she had arrived on Ix. Her presence with the Bene Gesserits, here and now, could not possibly be a coincidence. But he didn't reveal this to Earl Rhombur, not until he learned more about why she was here. He longed to think that she had come to see him . . . but he did not dare believe it.

When Wanna appeared at the door to his private quarters that evening, Yueh simply stared at her narrow but lovely face, feeling like a complete, helpless fool. Though she stood right there, she seemed untouchable in her Bene Gesserit facade, but he could see a flicker behind her brown eyes, a spark that he knew represented much brighter flames. "I am pleased to see you, Wellington."

His response took a moment to emerge from his throat; it did not carry the weight of the real emotions he felt. "I have missed you."

Wanna smiled, and the awkward wall between them seemed to

crumble. She stepped closer, her presence radiating tension and bottled feelings. "It's been much too long, my dear husband. When my Sisters announced their trip to Ix, I filed a petition with the Mother Superior. I can't tell you how much I wanted to see you!"

When they embraced at last, *at last* after so many years, he thought she felt warm and comfortable in his arms. So many years, so much distance between them . . . yet so much still binding them together. He didn't have to hide his feelings here. No one could see them.

When they had married on Richese, he was a well-respected but unremarkable physician, and Wanna had been the appropriate choice for him. Before long, he'd been surprised by the depths of his feelings for her, and she seemed to share that love, although he could not be entirely certain—no one could ever be certain with one of the witches.

Yueh considered himself a solitary man, not a mooncalf romantic, yet the love he discovered inside himself had no analytical answer. Because they shared their thoughts and hearts, he had convinced himself that he and Wanna didn't need a close day-to-day companionship. When she had left him years ago to study at the Mother School, it was a sad parting, but her talents were needed on Wallach IX.

"How are your meditations progressing? Your studies?" He didn't know what else to say. He remembered times they had shared on a wooded Richesian lakeshore, whispered promises in the dark, shared laughter at private jokes. He wondered what the Sisters had done to change her in the intervening years.

Primly, Wanna walked over to a comfortable well-lit spot near the outer wall, folding her hands in front of her. "The human psyche is complex, Wellington. Understanding it takes a long time." She had short auburn hair, a small mouth, and thin lips that could quirk into a rare but radiant smile. "I'd like to ask you about Rhombur and Tessia Vernius. Since you are the Earl's personal physician, you would know the answers."

Yueh rubbed fingers along his drooping mustache, pursed his dark lips into a faint frown. "Is this your own curiosity, Wanna, or something the Sisterhood asks? Is that why the Sisters came here?"

"Oh, Wellington, my own curiosity benefits my Sisters."

He tried not to sound defeated. "What is it you need to know?" Inside, he could already feel his walls rebuilding.

"Earl Rhombur's cyborg enhancements are functioning properly? His life is relatively normal now?"

"As normal as it can be. Considering the amount of surviving cellular material I had to work with after the accident, Rhombur's components function remarkably well."

She continued, as if she had memorized a list of questions. "And what about the Lady Tessia? Bronso was born almost a dozen years ago, well after Rhombur's accident. Can they have more children?"

"Tessia has no desire to, and Rhombur isn't capable."

"She is still fertile, but Rhombur is sterile?"

Yueh heard himself talking, the words escaping in a rush from his mouth. He longed to restore his intimate connection with her. "Bronso is not Rhombur's biological son. Genetically, the father is his half brother, Tyros Reffa—the bastard son of old Emperor Elrood IX and Lady Shando Balut. Rhombur and Reffa had the same mother." Unable to keep the alarm from his voice, Yueh added quickly, "The boy doesn't know. We've kept the matter private. You know the prejudice against any artificial means of conception."

Why did I reveal that to her? His expression hardened. "It's much like the prejudice against repairing damaged body parts with my cyborg components. The repairs I made to *you* demonstrated the potential of my work." He felt the hurt growing inside him again. "You should have been able to conceive a child."

Wanna sounded like a stranger as she said to him now, "Some things are not to be, Wellington. Be satisfied with what we have."

He had always wanted a family, but early in their marriage Wanna had suffered a severe accident that damaged her reproductive organs. As she healed, Yueh had succeeded in replacing her injured tissue and organs so that she *was* capable of bearing children—in theory. But it had never happened. . . .

Now, sudden questions appeared in his mind. He wasn't sure he wanted to know the answers, but he spoke before he could stop himself. "Tell me the truth. Did the Sisters *instruct* you not to conceive?"

Wanna retained her calm demeanor for a moment longer, before it crumbled. Despite their years apart, he knew her well enough to read the subtle changes, the flickers of her expression. "Oh, I *conceived*, Wellington. I have delivered four children—offspring that the Bene

Gesserit demanded of me, important bloodlines, necessary genetic combinations." Her body shuddered, and he held her woodenly, afraid to move, startled by her revelations. He couldn't even express his disbelief . . . but he knew with a sinking sensation that she was telling the truth.

"My replacement parts functioned perfectly . . . but your bloodline, my love, did not fit into the Sisterhood's plans." She looked at him with anguished eyes. "I am so sorry. I could not . . ."

He knew she wanted him to pretend that he understood and accepted the realities of being married to a Bene Gesserit. But he froze, wrestling with the shock. "You've had . . . four children?"

"They were taken away from me as soon as they were born. I never stopped thinking of you, but I had to block off my feelings, shield myself. That is how the Bene Gesserit trained me to handle emotions, and now . . . I don't know if I even remember what I once felt for you." Leaving him speechless, stiffly trying to regain her composure, Wanna tried to pull away. "I should go."

Shaken and nervous, he clutched her tightly. "So soon?"

Wanna looked at him, and her expression melted again. "No, not just yet. I can stay with you tonight."

*Of course we take substantial risks. That is how we live. Alas, that
is also how we die.*

—EARL DOMINIC VERNIUS OF IX

From his mother, Paul had learned how to concentrate on his body,
from the tiniest muscles to his whole being, aware of every nerve,
isolating the smallest sensations. He could meditate and focus his
attention on a problem for as long as it took to solve it.

Bronso Vernius, though, was unable to sit still for more than a few
minutes. His interest shifted repeatedly. He had never done well in controlled study atmospheres with filmbooks or dreary instructors; rather, the
eleven-year-old preferred to learn by asking questions of his father inside
the Grand Palais. In that manner he learned of poisonings and murders
and artificial spice manufacturing, of the Tleilaxu takeover on Ix and
Prince Rhombur seeking sanctuary on Caladan . . . of his father's horrific
injuries and how Dr. Yueh had reassembled him with cyborg parts.

Paul had first met the copper-haired young Bronso when the
Vernius party came to attend Duke Leto's disastrous wedding to Ilesa
Ecaz. The other boy was intense and interesting, and perhaps a bit odd.
Though Paul had come to Ix to study, as well as to experience, a new
culture, his companion had an entirely different agenda. "Are you ready
to be scared, Paul? Really scared?"

"How?" He knew Gurney and Duncan would try to stop him if he
exposed himself to danger. And he had only just arrived.

Bronso rose from the study table inside his quarters, pushed aside filmbooks listing summaries and statistics of the numerous planets in the Imperium. "By climbing the buildings—from the outside. Are you ready?"

"I've climbed sea cliffs on the Caladan coast." Paul paused. "Do you bother with harnesses and equipment, or should we do it freehand?"

The other boy laughed. "I like you, Paul Atreides! Sea cliffs! You'll be crying like an infant when I get done with you." From his personal equipment locker, he retrieved a set of traction pads and a suspensor harness, which he tossed to Paul. "Here, take mine. They're already broken in." He rummaged around until he found a new set for himself and unsealed the packaging.

Paul followed his friend through corridors and passages to an open balcony so high up on the cavern ceiling that air currents whistled around them. With an extended finger, Bronso traced their route to a support beam, then to an adjacent walkway, and then onto a dangling roof. "See the line we can take, from there, to there, and if you've got the stamina for it we'll circle back to the Grand Palais."

As the other boy donned his equipment, Paul studied the traction pads that Bronso had used frequently. Some of the seams looked freshly split, as if from the delicate touch of a vibrating blade. Though unfamiliar with the equipment, his instinct told him to look more closely. "Something isn't right here." He tugged at a seam, and it easily ripped away. "Look, this would have failed as soon as I got out onto a rock face!"

Bronso scowled at the pad. "I climb with that equipment almost every day. It's always been reliable before." He poked at it. "This was tampered with."

"Is someone trying to kill you?" Though the question seemed melodramatic, Paul had been caught up in other deadly feuds and rivalries.

Bronso laughed—a bit too loudly. "The Technocrat Council would be very happy if the only Vernius heir suffered an 'accident.' They've tried to arrange something unpleasant for my father, but they've never targeted me before."

"We've got to report this." Paul remembered the careful training he had undergone from Thufir Hawat, Gurney Halleck, Duncan Idaho. Poison snoopers, personal shields, guards . . . it was a way of life for noble families in the Landsraad.

"I'll show this to my father, but Bolig Avati is too clever to leave any proof. Still, this is an escalation that will not make my parents happy."

Paul said with great confidence, "Thufir Hawat told me that once you're aware of a threat, you have done half the work of defeating it."

A human being can become a terrible weapon. But all weapons can backfire.

—*Bene Gesserit Acolytes' Manual*

Tessia often spent the darkest, quietest hours of night alone in their private chambers, because Rhombur needed little sleep, and the restless cyborg leader spent his nights walking through the ceiling tunnels of Vernii, and across the transparent walkways that connected the stalactite structures.

She awoke out of a troubled sleep to a deep, foreboding darkness, and a sensation that something was wrong. As she blinked, Tessia was startled to realize that someone stood near her—an intruder! Her dark-adapted pupils widened as she opened her mouth, sucked in a breath to shout.

A command uttered with the perfect precision of Voice chopped across her consciousness like an axe blade. A female voice. *"Silence!"*

Tessia's larynx shut down, her vocal cords locked. Even her lungs refused to exhale. As a Bene Gesserit, she'd been taught how to resist Voice, but this aural blow had been delivered by a powerful expert, someone who had gauged Tessia, measured her, and knew her precise weak points.

As her eyes adjusted, she discerned the looming form of Reverend Mother Stokiah. Tessia felt like an insect specimen pinned to a mounting board by a long needle. She wanted badly to scream, but her voluntary muscles had shut down.

Stokiah leaned closer, her breath soft as a whisper. "You have been deluded into believing that you have freedom of choice. *Stand.*"

Tessia's body swung itself out of her bed, like a puppet. Her legs straightened, and her knees locked as she stood before the Reverend Mother.

"The Sisterhood's rules countermand the wishes of the individual. You have always accepted this. You need to be reminded of your important, yet minuscule, place in our world . . . the *Bene Gesserit* world."

Tessia managed to rasp, surprising herself with her own strength, "*Refuse.*"

"You cannot refuse. I already made that clear." The wrinkles on Stokiah's face were a map of black fissures in the gloom. "You have always had a purpose to serve, but now I have another use for you. The Sisterhood cannot allow open defiance without consequences. Therefore everyone must see your guilt, and you must *feel* it. You must *know* it." Her papery lips formed a smile. "The Sisterhood has developed a new weapon, a technique that combines both psychological and Jongleur training. I am one of the first, and most powerful, Bene Gesserit guilt-casters, and you *will* obey."

Guilt-casters . . . women able to manipulate thoughts and emotions to magnify a person's own doubts and regrets and reflect them back like a lasbeam ricocheting off a mirror. Tessia had thought them only a frightening rumor leaked by the proctors in order to compel unruly acolytes.

"You must feel so sorry about what you have done." Stokiah's voice was slippery and poisonous, not at all compassionate. "So sorry, and so terribly guilty."

Tessia felt the psychic waves. Her heart hammered, and her conscience became a palpable weight. She could hardly breathe.

"How could you betray the Sisterhood, after all we have done for you? All we've taught you?" Stokiah's insidious tone unlocked floodgates of memories and regrets in Tessia's mind. "We gave you a mission, and now you have let us down." Each word scratched across her nerves like a sharpened steel nail. "You turned your back on us. You failed us. Worst of all, you succumbed to love."

Tessia wanted to shrink away, desperate to avoid each accusation, but she couldn't move. The weight thrummed around her, made her head throb, dulled her thoughts.

"You betrayed your son, too. Does Bronso know that Rhombur is not his real father? You allowed yourself to be impregnated with another man's sperm, for love—yet you refuse to do it for *us?*"

Though Stokiah's voice did not change, the volume of the words inside Tessia's head grew louder and louder. Each phrase became a scream. She closed her eyes, shuddered, tried to withdraw into a corner. Stokiah wielded her power like a Master Jongleur who could manipulate every audience member, stopping hearts with terror or wringing tears from their eyes.

The tiny rational corner that remained in Tessia's mind insisted that the words were an exaggeration, that they had no merit. She clung to her confidence, her love for Rhombur, for Bronso. And she failed miserably.

Thick oppression wrapped itself around Tessia, strangling her like a black ghost as she collapsed to the floor. She couldn't hear anymore, but the remembered words continued to echo in her mind. She couldn't move her body, couldn't run, couldn't scream. She tried to retreat, to find a zone of refuge inside her head, convinced she could survive no more of this.

But it continued . . . and continued.

A flicker of respite surprised her then, and she could see again. Stokiah stood at her doorway, ready to depart. "Never forget that you belong to the Sisterhood—heart, mind, soul, and flesh. You exist to serve. Contemplate that in your personal hell." With a dismissive gesture and an uttered syllable, Stokiah slammed the curtains of guilt back down around Tessia.

With mental screams, she fell deeper and deeper into herself, hiding inside a single black dot of consciousness. But even there, Tessia was not safe. Not even close.

WHEN HE RETURNED to their quarters, Rhombur found his wife lying on the floor, conscious but unresponsive. Tessia's eyes were glazed and unseeing; her skin twitched and trembled as if her nerves were firing in random patterns. He shook her, called out her name, but received no response.

She had folded into herself like a dying butterfly. Lifting her back onto the bed, Rhombur called for emergency medical help. He ordered the immediate shutdown of the Grand Palais and sent teams to look for assassins, fearing that she had been poisoned.

Dr. Yueh rushed in, used his medical kit to check her pulse and brain activity. He ran blood samples through a scanner to detect drugs or toxins. "I see no obvious cause for this, my Lord. No head injury, no telltale marks of a needle or any other known poison-delivery system."

Rhombur was like an overheated engine about to explode. "Vermillion Hells, something caused it!"

As the alarms continued to sound, Vernius guards rushed to the royal chambers. Gurney Halleck arrived with Duncan Idaho, swiftly followed by a very concerned looking Jessica. Bronso came running into the room with Paul Atreides beside him, the two boys sagging with worry and confusion as they saw Tessia, her jaws clenched together, her eyelids twitching and trembling.

Frightened and angry, Bronso jumped to conclusions. "The technocrats couldn't kill me, so they attacked my mother instead?"

Rhombur had seen how the climbing equipment had been sabotaged, presumably by agents working for the Technocrat Council. "Is this another attempt to strike at me—through my wife?"

Yueh looked up from his portable diagnostic instrument, looked at the readings from the blood sample, shook his head, and repeated, "No detectable poison."

"What else could have put her in a state like this?" Duncan asked.

Paul spoke up. "Some kind of stunner, or neural scrambler? Does Ix have any new weapon that could account for this?"

Rhombur felt as if his artificial systems were about to collapse. "I can't know every project my scientists undertake. I see only the results when a device is ready for marketing. It's . . . possible, I admit." He increased the volume of his voice until the windowplates rattled. "Summon Bolig Avati! Tell him his Earl demands his presence—it is not a request."

Rhombur turned to Jessica. "And what about those three Bene Gesserits? They were here to demand that Tessia become a breeding mistress. Could *they* have done this? Do they have such powers?"

Jessica paused long enough to be certain of her answer. "I've never heard of any such skills."

Seeking answers, he called for the three Bene Gesserits, and the women were ushered in so swiftly that they nearly tripped on the hems of their robes. They did not seem overly upset as they regarded Tessia, who lay curled up, shivering, lost in some inner maze of pain.

Rhombur demanded, "Well? Are you responsible for this?"

Stokiah raised her chin haughtily. "We have seen this before—it is peculiar to members of our order, very rare. The conflicting pressures of your demands upon Tessia and her obligations to the Bene Gesserit order were too much. But we have ways of treating her on Wallach IX."

The youngest of the Bene Gesserit trio spoke to Yueh. "Your medicine can treat diseases or poisons, Wellington, but this . . . this appears to be a condition of the mind. Yes, I am aware of similar collapses among the Bene Gesserit. The mind ties itself into a Gordian knot, and it requires a skillful sword to cut apart the twisted strands without destroying the mind." She turned to the cyborg leader. "Earl Vernius, as Reverend Mother Stokiah suggests, let us take her back to Wallach IX. Only the Sisterhood has ways of treating this."

"I will not leave her side! If she goes there to be treated, then I go with her."

"You are not welcome on Wallach IX, Rhombur Vernius," Stokiah said. "Release Tessia to our care. There is no telling how long our treatment might require, and no guarantee of success. But you cannot cure her here. If you love this woman, as you claim, then give us an opportunity to work on her."

The Suk doctor remained at a loss. "I'll continue to run tests, my Lord, but I suspect my diagnosis will not change. If there's a chance, and time is of the essence . . ."

"Don't worry, Rhombur. *I* can go see her as the treatment progresses," Jessica offered. "The Sisterhood takes care of its own."

Bronso knelt beside Tessia, his reddish hair tousled with sweat. "Mother, come back to us! I don't want them to take you." But she did not respond.

Rhombur realized that he had already lost. He felt cast adrift, a man floating in space with no lifeline and no oxygen tank. "Keep trying, Yueh. I will give you two more days. If you can't do anything to save her by then, then I'll have to trust the witches."

Everyone lies, every day of his life. The effect of such untruths is a matter of degree, of purpose, and of benefit. Falsehoods are more numerous than the organisms in all the seas in the galaxy. Why then are we Tleilaxu perceived as being deceptive and untrustworthy, while others are not?

—RAKKEEL IBAMAN, the oldest living Tleilaxu Master

Bronso watched helplessly as his father allowed the witches to take Tessia away to their far-off world. After two seemingly unending, painful days had passed, there was no better option. Though he had attempted every esoteric Suk treatment, Dr. Yueh had been unable to penetrate her mindless state.

Tessia was clearly in pain, in terror, in misery, and she would not wake up. And the Bene Gesserits claimed they could help.

Bronso knew where to place the blame. The technocrats had done something to her mind, he was sure of it. In the past several years, the bureaucratic bastards had tried repeatedly and unsuccessfully to get rid of Bronso's father. They had sabotaged Bronso's own climbing gear only a few days ago, in hopes of killing him. Now the enemies of House Vernius had found a way to make his mother vulnerable and strike her down. . . .

The interrogation of an indignant Bolig Avati revealed nothing useful, though the technocrat leader did admit that if Ix were to be "unencumbered by archaic noble traditions," business would proceed more smoothly. But there was no proof to link him to any of the sabotages or assassination attempts.

While Yueh tried in vain to revive Tessia, a distraught Rhombur gave full investigative authority to Duncan Idaho and Gurney Halleck. Along with loyal House Vernius guards, they searched the Ixian research facilities, studied the test records and prototype apparatus being developed by Ixian research teams, broke down doors to high-security areas—and found one researcher dead.

A man named Talba Hur, a solitary genius with an abrasive personality, lay in his locked lab with a broken neck and his skull crudely bashed in, dead among the cinders of research papers and diagrams. According to the only known records of his work, Talba Hur had been developing a technological means to erase or disrupt the human mind. Such a device might explain what had happened to Tessia.

Rhombur had no proof, no direct suspects . . . and no doubts. But even that didn't help cure his wife. The damage had been done, and Yueh was unable to do anything to aid her.

Only the Bene Gesserits offered a slender hope, though they seemed to be without compassion. Distraught, Bronso stared as the three dark-robed Sisters whisked his mother away as if she were some sort of package to be delivered. He hated their attitude. The young man had already said goodbye to her, struggling to contain his tears. The Bene Gesserits merely brushed him aside, hurrying her along. Bronso thought he saw a knowing look in their eyes, which he presumed meant they had a particular treatment in mind.

But he wondered if he could truly trust them.

Bolig Avati stood among the party, wearing an expression of studied grief. "My Lord Vernius, perhaps it would be best if you withdrew from public life for a time." Avati sounded drippingly sincere. "Rest and spend time with your son."

Bronso wanted to strike the leader of the Technocrat Council. How could the man seize this opportunity to make Earl Vernius loosen his hold even further? Rhombur stood looking lost, devastated, speechless— he did not know what else to do, couldn't conceive of any alternative. Not bothering to answer Avati, Bronso's father stared in disbelief as the shuttle's doors sealed and the vessel withdrew, rising up to the launching area.

Jessica and Paul both watched, keeping their distance but ready to show their support if Rhombur needed them. In light of the turmoil and tragedy, Jessica had suggested that it would be best if Paul returned to Caladan, leaving Bronso alone with his father and their shared grief.

No one could do anything to help. All of Bronso's preconceptions and assumptions were crumbling. Throughout his life, he had expected his father to solve all problems, to be a decisive leader. Right now, he should have forced the technocrats to confess, or at the very least extract promises from the witches for the treatment they proposed. When could they visit Tessia? When would they know something about the treatment? How would the Sisters take care of her?

But Rhombur remained paralyzed and ineffective—and Bronso seethed at his failure. And now his mother was gone, with no guarantees that he would ever see her again. The young man spent the rest of the day in misery and anger, locked in his quarters, refusing even to see Paul.

When Bronso couldn't stand it anymore, he burst into his father's private office to find the patchwork man sitting on a reinforced chair. Rhombur's scarred face did not easily show a full range of emotions, but he wiped a tear from his natural eye. "Bronso!"

When he saw his father in such despair, most of his anger and frustration dissipated. Just looking at the tapestry of scars and artificial limbs, the oddly matched melding of polymer skin with human flesh— everything reminded Bronso of how much physical and mental pain his father had already suffered.

Bronso faltered, but he still had something to say, and his frustrations overtook all compassion. Over the past year, he had noticed the decline in respect with which influential members of Ixian society regarded his father. At one time, according to the glorious stories, Prince Rhombur had shown uncanny daring and persistence, fleeing into exile while continuing to fight against the Tleilaxu invaders. Or were those merely stories? Now Bronso felt only scorn. Rhombur was no longer a hero in his eyes.

He lashed out. "People walk all over you, don't they? I've seen it with my own eyes."

Rhombur's synthetic voice made an unusual sound, a humming in his throat. He seemed too weary to move. "The Sisters said they could help. What else could I do?"

"They said what you wanted to hear—and you believed them!"

"Bronso, you don't understand."

"I understand that you're weak and ineffective. Will there be anything left when it's time for me to be Earl? Or will the technocrats murder both of us first? Why don't you arrest them? You know Avati's guilty, but you let him just walk away."

Rhombur half rose from his seat, scowled angrily. "You're upset, but you have no idea what you're saying." Daunted, he locked his hands together, kneading them, making the artificial material strain. He hesitated, as if afraid to speak further, and finally said, "Uh, there's something else I've been meaning to tell you, but your mother and I never found the right time. I'm sorry I kept it from you. Now you're all I've got left—until your mother gets better."

Feeling a sense of foreboding, Bronso lashed out in a clumsy attempt to protect his own feelings. "What? What else don't I know?"

Rhombur sagged further into his reinforced chair. "After my body was nearly destroyed, I could never father children, could never hope for an heir to House Vernius. Tessia might have returned to the Sisterhood and become a concubine for some other noble." His voice hitched. "But she stayed with me and insisted on marriage, even when I had nothing to offer. We managed to overthrow the Tleilaxu and regain control of Ix, but I still needed an heir, or House Vernius would vanish after all. And so we—"

He stopped, willing the rest of the words to come. "You see, I had a half brother, a child that my mother bore a long time ago when she was a court concubine to Emperor Elrood IX, before she married your grandfather. At least he had half of my bloodline, so Tessia . . . she obtained, uh, genetic samples. And with my approval she used them."

"Used them? What are you talking about?" Why couldn't his father just speak plainly?

"That is how you were conceived. I could not contribute the . . . the sperm, but I could grant my blessing. Artificial insemination."

Bronso heard thunder in the back of his head. "You're saying that you aren't my real father. Why would you say that? And why tell me now?"

"It doesn't matter, because you are my heir. Through my mother, Lady Shando Balut, you still have my bloodline. My love for you is the same as if—"

Bronso reeled. First, he'd lost his mother, and now this! "You lied to me!"

"I didn't lie. I am your true father in every way that matters. You're only eleven. Your mother and I were looking for the right time—"

"And she's not here. She may never come back, may never recover. And now I learn that you're not even my father!" His voice was as sharp as a dagger. He turned his back on Rhombur and stormed out of the apartment.

"Bronso, you *are* my son! Wait!"

But he kept going, without looking back.

FUMING AND UNABLE to concentrate, Bronso grabbed his climbing gear and strapped on new traction pads and a suspensor harness. He wanted to run away, but had no destination in mind. Breathing heavily, fighting the clamor in his head, he went to an upper floor of the Grand Palais and opened the slanted plates of transparent plaz. Not caring about anything but movement, he wormed his body through the gap as the processed wind drifted in. Barely bothering to look where he was going, Bronso vaulted out into the vastness of the chamber and scrambled up the sheer wall. He had no fear, nothing to lose.

"Bronso, what are you doing!"

He looked down to the window he'd left open and saw Paul Atreides sticking his head out, looking up. He ignored his friend, kept climbing the wall. He didn't think he could ever get far enough away.

Moments later, however, he saw Paul ascending with his own set of traction pads and harness, moving awkwardly but making surprising speed. Annoyed, Bronso shouted, "You don't have the skills for this. One mistake, and you'll fall."

"Then I won't make a mistake. If *you* stay out here, then I'm staying with you." As Bronso hung there, Paul caught up with him, panting. "Just like climbing sea cliffs."

"What are you doing here? I don't want you with me. I need to be alone."

"I promised to keep you safe. Our bond, remember?"

Dangling there on the rock wall, Paul looked at him so earnestly that Bronso surrendered and agreed to accompany him slowly, and safely, back to his rooms. "Well, you'll be free of that promise. You're going back to Caladan soon—and I'll still be here with nothing but lies."

Paul regarded him with calm seriousness. "Then we'd better talk now, while we still can."

With emotions building up in him, but unwilling to admit his confusion and shame, Bronso said, "On your honor, swear that you will tell no one else what I'm about to say to you. I need to know I can trust you."

"You should know about Atreides honor." Paul gave his word, and after they returned to Bronso's private chambers, with the entrance sealed, they sat together for a long time afterward. Far from anyone else, Bronso explained what Rhombur had told him. Caught up in distant thoughts, the redheaded boy stared out at the twinkling cavern city. "So here we are. My mother is gone, and my incompetent father isn't really my father. I'm not even truly a Vernius! Ix has nothing to do with me anymore. I don't belong here." He ratcheted up his courage. "I'm running away from home, and no one can stop me—not Rhombur, not his guards, no one."

Paul groaned. "I wish you hadn't told me what you're going to do."

"Why? Are you going to stop me? You swore to keep this secret!"

Backed into a corner of responsibilities, Paul reached the best solution he could. "My promise to you is clear—I won't turn you in or reveal what you're doing. But I also made a promise to my father that I would watch out for you. I can't have you getting yourself lost or killed, so I'm going with you. Now tell me, where are we going?"

"As far away from Ix as we can get."

Each breath carries the risk that there may not be another one to follow.

—ancient saying

After slipping out of the cavern city and emerging into the starlight near a subsidiary spaceport, Paul followed Bronso toward a large, silent cargo ship on the landing field, its hold open and waiting. "Up the ramp and look for a hiding place aboard! After they finish loading in the morning, this thing will take off and enter the hold of a Heighliner—bound for points unknown."

Paul wrestled with his friend's impetuous decision, but he saw no honorable way to abandon him or report his intentions. Duncan and Gurney would never suspect that Paul intended to do something so foolhardy. He couldn't say goodbye to them, or to his mother. If he saw her, Jessica would instantly sense the change. . . .

Hidden among hard, sharp-edged containers, the boys snatched a few hours of restless sleep until noises woke them: clanging, voices and men moving about, engines humming, loaders stacking cargo.

"Don't worry, they've already loaded this compartment," Bronso said in a loud whisper. "They've got no reason to come here. Nothing to worry about." Paul listened to the tone of the voices, but detected no hint of hunters, no determined search teams. These were just men at work.

Two hours later, the hold was full, the heavy hatches sealed, the chambers pressurized. The engines surged on, undamped by baffles or insulation, and since the sealed hold had no windowports, the ride to orbit was long, loud, and nerve-wracking. Finally, after a series of heavy clangs, a shudder through the deck and bulkheads, and a sharp hissing of equalizing atmospheres, the cargo ship went absolutely still and silent.

"I think we're inside a Heighliner hold," Paul said.

Bronso stretched and looked around in the dim light of emergency strips mounted to the bulkheads. "Let's go. There are more interesting places to be aboard a Guildship."

When Bronso found that the access doors had been locked from the outside, he crept up a ladder, pushed open a hatch in the ceiling of the cargo ship, and motioned for Paul to follow. The two of them crawled out onto the main deck. Paul had been aboard Atreides cargo ships and recognized the same general layout. From here, knowing the docking configuration, they could slip off the ship and go out into the layered decks of the immense Guildship.

Bronso marched toward an exit hatch, but Paul grabbed his arm. "Once we make our way to the passenger decks, how do we prove we paid for passage? Maybe we should stay in our safe hiding place."

The Ixian boy glanced dismissively back at the hold. "Do you want to hide in the cargo ship all the way to its destination, or would you rather ride the Heighliner from system to system? I want to see the Imperium, not just the home world of one Ixian customer."

Paul relented, and they passed through the cargo ship's connecting doors into the receiving decks. Other people milled around, disembarking from the hundreds of vessels in the great ship's hold. Acting as if they had business, the two young men walked briskly away.

Bronso rummaged in his pack for a crystal pad projector and led the way to a quieter alcove. He called up schematics, which he projected in the air for Paul to see. "This Heighliner was built in an Ixian shipyard. I think we're *here*, and the levels we want"—he pointed toward a zigzag of ramps on a bulkhead in the hold—"should be in that direction."

They blended in with other passengers, and followed them up ramps into crowded public promenades that seemed as vast as the cavern city of Vernii. Bronso pointed to a lavishly decorated lounge, where people filled their plates with food from a sumptuous buffet. Paul realized his stomach was growling, and his companion didn't hesitate. They boldly followed two gentlemen through the door of the lounge, then headed straight to the food-laden table. Trying to act casual, the two filled their plates, then found an unoccupied table.

Almost immediately a thin Wayku attendant approached, his eyes shielded behind dark, opaque glasses. He sported a black goatee on a very pale face; a headset blocked his ears, and Paul heard loud noises—music? voices?—wafting from the earpieces. The steward said tersely, "This food is for a private CHOAM party. You are not members of that party."

Bronso grabbed another bite before he rose to his feet. "We didn't realize. Should we return the food to the buffet? We haven't touched much of it."

"You're stowaways." They could not read his eyes behind the Wayku's dark lenses.

"No," Bronso said. "We're paying passengers."

"It is my profession to spot anything out of the ordinary. You must have been very clever to get aboard the Heighliner."

Bronso looked angry, as if the steward had insulted him. "Come on, Paul. Let's go."

The deck vibrated and hummed, and a faint ripple of disorientation passed through them. The set of the Wayku man's expression changed, and he let out a resigned sigh. "Those were the Holtzman engines. We have already left the system, so there would be little point in sending you back to Ix. My job is to keep the passengers satisfied and maintain uninterrupted service."

"We won't cause any trouble," Paul promised.

"No, you won't, provided you pay attention and follow certain rules. I don't intend to turn you in. I am Ennzyn, one of the chief stewards, and I have jobs for both of you. We're somewhat understaffed." He lifted his dark glasses to reveal pale blue eyes. His tone suggested that they had no choice. "I need help with the cleanup duties."

Paul and Bronso exchanged glances and nods of acceptance.

"Finish your meals first." Ennzyn motioned them back to their seats. "I abhor waste. When you're done, I'll show you where to stow your gear."

Is it better to remain blissfully ignorant of a tragedy, or to know all the details even when you can do nothing about it? That question is not easy to answer.

—DUKE LETO ATREIDES

When Rhombur Vernius approached Jessica on an enclosed balcony in the Grand Palais, the cyborg Earl opened his mouth, but no words came forth. She knew immediately that something terrible had happened. "Tell me—what is it?"

"It's the boys . . . Bronso and Paul. They're gone!" He explained in a rush, but as he finished, the confusion passed from his demeanor like mist blown on a wind, and he drew himself taller. "I promised Leto to keep your son safe. If an enemy has abducted them, or *harmed* them—!"

Jessica forced herself to rally, to speak in a calm, matter-of-fact voice that helped focus Rhombur. "There are several possibilities. It seems most likely that someone has taken them, they're lost or injured, or they've run away. How long have they been gone? The first few hours are the most critical." When his expression flickered, then fell, Jessica realized he had not told her everything. "Now is not a time for secrets, Rhombur—our sons are missing!"

With deep regret, the cyborg Prince described how he had revealed the boy's true parentage—and Bronso's angry, distraught reaction to the news. Bronso's voice shook with tension. After the loss of his wife, Jessica didn't know how much more the rebuilt man could bear.

Back inside the Grand Palais, in the lower exhibition chamber surrounded by transparent plaz walls, Jessica helped Rhombur establish an emergency center. Gurney and Duncan came running at her summons, and both vowed to find the boys at all costs. Gurney paced across the checkerboard floor and doubled back. "Call that Avati in here again. I still think he had something to do with what happened to Tessia, and the boys would be his next likely target. 'Suspicion is like a foul odor, tainting all and slow to disperse.'"

"Even if they are innocent, the technocrats will rejoice to hear about another problem I have to face," Rhombur groaned. "Another Vernius blunder."

Jessica's voice was hard as she called up projected maps of the sub-terranean city complex. "What if they've left the planet? Could they have fled or been taken to the surface? Gotten aboard a ship?"

"Uh, we have security systems. I have already asked teams to check the imagers, but they saw no record of—" His shoulders sagged again. "But it would have been child's play for Bronso to bypass them. He had access to any number of scramblers. He used them as toys, but now . . . I don't know."

"Let's have a look at your spaceport records, to find out how many ships have come and gone since the boys went missing."

"Dozens," Rhombur said. "Shipping is quite active, with vessels coming and going at all hours. We've had three Heighliners since yesterday—"

Jessica cut him off. She would not allow Rhombur to drown in his doubts, but urged him to pursue every possibility. "Then we will also ob-tain Spacing Guild records. We'll study the routes of those three Heighlin-ers, and determine which ships the boys could have gotten on—willingly or unwillingly—and plot a matrix of destinations where they might be."

Rhombur was moving now, ready to gather the information. He looked stronger and more determined, and Jessica was relieved. She had helped him out of his malaise, and now he was ready to charge ahead. "You're right, Jessica. If they ran away, Paul or Bronso must have left some trace. They're just boys, after all."

Jessica didn't contradict him, though she knew that Paul was not just a boy. Next she turned to her own difficult task, mentally compos-ing a message to be given to the next Guild courier to depart from Ix.

She had to tell Duke Leto the bad news.

Prescience cannot be a random thing. It must be by design. The question is, whose design?

—comment, Intergalactic Commission on Spirituality

For several days, as the two boys settled into their new circumstances aboard the Guildship, the Wayku steward showed them around the service decks. Exclusive side passages allowed employees to move about without mingling with the passengers.

Paul and Bronso wore common work clothes, and Ennzyn assigned them to jobs that even the Wayku found unpleasant. Because the boys had no better option, they worked without complaint. The man showed a remarkable lack of curiosity, not even bothering to ask their full names. Wayku seemed to respect secrets and privacy.

Paul and Bronso stood with him on a wide landing surrounded by exposed pipes, power conduits, and harsh glowglobes. Ennzyn warned, "Beware of Guild officials or Heighliner inspectors. They are the greatest hazard on this ship: Don't let them notice you. If anyone asks to see your employment documentation, send them to me. We Wayku have a certain amount of influence."

Paul noted his odd attire. "Your people seem to be everywhere on Guildships, but where's your home world? Where do the Wayku come from?"

"By Imperial decree, all of our planets were destroyed in the Third

Coalsack War—ages ago. Our descendants have no home, and we are forbidden from ever setting foot on a planetary surface."

Paul could not imagine the level of vindictiveness that would lead to the obliteration of entire planetary populations. "For what offense?"

"When a few militant commanders committed war crimes, my entire race was held accountable for the atrocities." Ennzyn pushed his dark glasses up, clicked them into his headset, and regarded the boys with his blue eyes. "The Wayku backed the wrong side against a powerful emperor, and he sent his armies to annihilate us. But the Spacing Guild granted us sanctuary aboard their ships, where our people have worked for many generations.

"We are space gypsies and survive as best we can, without riches or a homeworld. So much time has passed that not many people remember. In fact, I could probably slip off a Guildship if I truly wanted to." He clicked his glasses back into place over his eyes. "But why would I want to? The Guild pays us well, and we make our homes in their midst."

He motioned both boys to step out of the way as they heard approaching voices. Moving briskly, a contingent of officials dressed in gray marched past them and up the metal stairs, speaking in an arcane tongue. The men passed through a hatch and onto the brightly lit main decks, wasting not so much as a glance on the steward or his young companions.

When they were gone, Ennzyn said, "The powerful are often blind to those they believe to be insignificant. We Wayku are invisible, unless we do something to call attention to ourselves."

TWO WEEKS LATER, inside the small interior cabin they shared aboard the Heighliner, Paul scowled at Bronso. The pair had just completed a food service shift in one of the passenger lounges, and Bronso combed his hair, wiped his hands on a towel. "Neither of us has ever seen a Navigator! This could be our only chance."

The redheaded boy sometimes tested the limits and put both of them at risk, to the consternation of their mentor Ennzyn. "You're trying to get us thrown off the ship," Paul said. Then, he thought, at least they could go home. How much longer did Bronso want them to remain on the run? He knew many people must be terribly worried about them by now. Knowing he wouldn't convince his friend, he suggested, "We should find a way to send a message to Ix or Caladan, just to let our parents know we're all right."

Bronso stiffened. "Parents? My mother is in a coma and being held by the Bene Gesserit, and I never met my real father."

"You're being unfair to Rhombur. He tried—"

"He should have been honest with me."

"Still, there has to be a way for us to get back home. We're both noble heirs, future leaders of our Great Houses. We shouldn't have run away."

"*I* ran away. *You* just came along to keep me safe." He tossed the used towel onto the floor next to his discarded work clothes. "Are you going with me to see the Navigator, or not?" Using his projected schematics of the Ixian-built Heighliner, Bronso had already plotted a way for the two of them to sneak onto the navigation deck. "I want to find out for myself if they're mutated monsters, or human just like us. Why else would the Guild keep them so secret?"

Paul frowned, but had to admit he was intrigued. One of the reasons his father had sent him from Caladan was to have new experiences. "When I'm Duke, I'll have dealings with the Spacing Guild. I suppose the information might be useful."

"I know I can get us inside." Bronso searched among his belongings and withdrew two Ixian gadgets, bypass keys he could use on the Heighliner's security systems. "You worry too much." He sealed his pack and stood. "Ready?"

"I haven't agreed to go." Stalling, Paul stepped out of his soiled work coveralls, hung them in a small closet, and reached for a clean pair of trousers.

"If you're afraid, just wait here. When I get back I'll tell you about the experience." Without another word, Bronso darted out into the corridor.

Torn between keeping himself out of trouble and watching out for his friend, Paul struggled into his clothes. By the time he ran after Bronso, the boy was nowhere in sight, but Paul knew where he must be headed. He ran up four flights of back-deck stairs and crossed a connecting walkway to a secure lift. An override security code took him to the restricted navigation levels.

Worried about his friend's impulsive decision, Paul moved cautiously toward where they suspected the Navigator was located. Ahead, shouts came from the opposite side of a sealed hatch. Abruptly, the door burst open and two uniformed Guildsmen stumbled out, each rubbing their eyes and cursing. A yellowish mist hung in the air. As the blinded men careened past without seeing him, Paul smelled the gas, but it wasn't the cinnamon odor of melange. A sulfurous burn irritated his nostrils, and he staggered back.

Two more Guild security men wrestled someone—Bronso—out of the chamber. "Let go of me!" The boy kicked one man in the shin and wrenched free, but the other seized him. Ixian devices clattered out of his pockets onto the deck. More guards rushed toward them, and Paul, rubbing his stinging eyes, saw no way to avoid them. He refused to abandon Bronso to his fate, but he didn't see how he could help.

A sour-faced Guild administrator arrived in a huff, inspecting the scene with distaste. Through the open door and the swirling, yellowish gas, Paul caught a glimpse of a large, clearplaz chamber that enclosed thicker smoke of a rust-brown color, and a shadowy shape visible inside. The Navigator? Abruptly, the doors sealed shut again, cutting off the foul defensive gas.

"Remove these boys to a secure area!" The administrator picked up Bronso's scattered devices from the floor, looked them over. "They are obviously spies or saboteurs."

Paul's captors held his arms behind his back, and he struggled, unable to break free. Remembering what the steward had said, he blurted, "We aren't spies. We work for the Wayku. Ennzyn will verify it."

HE AND BRONSO stood behind the electronic containment barrier of a holding cell. Waiting. The Guild had already done full identification scans on them, and soon enough somebody would figure out who they really were.

From the other side of the pale yellow barrier, Ennzyn's voice was the embodiment of a sigh. "You can give someone advice, but you cannot force them to listen." At the Wayku's command, a guard dropped the security barrier so that the boys could step out. Ennzyn barely even looked disturbed. "I knew it would only be a matter of time before I had to come here. Fortunately, you two were so predictable that I had the forethought to make a contingency plan."

The steward was accompanied by a tall, elderly man in a white suit with long tails and an eccentric, old-fashioned top hat; every item of clothing, even his shoes, sparkled with tiny ice diamonds. He carried himself with an air of success and elegance.

"Rheinvar the Magnificent has agreed to take you off my hands," Ennzyn said. "You'll disembark with his Jongleur troupe at the next planetary stop. I used all my influence just to prevent the Guildsmen from tossing you both into space. It just so happens that my good friend Rheinvar has offered to provide you with probationary positions to assist him. Besides, he owes me a favor."

"We're joining a Jongleur troupe?" Bronso sounded excited now. Paul had sensed that his companion was already growing bored with his menial duties aboard the Guildship.

Rheinvar the Magnificent doffed his stylish hat with a flourish. His blue eyes twinkled, and Bronso noticed happy creases on his face, seemingly from a lifetime of practiced smiling for audiences. "Welcome to the life of a Jongleur."

"Thank you, Ennzyn," Paul said. "Thank you for everything."

Ennzyn was already walking away, accompanied by the two sour-looking guards. "I enjoyed the experience as well. And now, I leave you in Rheinvar's capable hands. Learn something from him."

The Bene Gesserit Sisterhood is a well-connected network, with eyes and ears in every level of government and responsibility. Someone in their organization will know the answer to almost any question that might be posed.

But do not expect this knowledge to be free of cost, or the Sisters to be altruistic.

—CHOAM Analysis of the Bene Gesserit, Report #7

While Duncan and Gurney searched Guild records and transportation manifests from the subsidiary Ixian spaceports, Rhombur sent repeated requests to the technocrats, since their commercial connections extended across the Imperium; he even made a direct plea to Bolig Avati, although the Council leader was less than sympathetic after all the accusations leveled against him.

So far, none of the investigations had borne any fruit.

Jessica, though, had a different set of resources, avenues that even a Landsraad nobleman did not possess. While Leto was on his way to Ix, she composed a message to her old teacher on Wallach IX, Reverend Mother Gaius Helen Mohiam. With all of the Sisterhood's observers across the Imperium, *someone* must have seen Paul or Bronso.

Careful to expunge any hint of desperation from her message, Jessica outlined everything she knew about the boys' disappearance. She pointed out the very real possibility that the two might be hostages, pawns in some dangerous political game played by the Harkonnens against House Atreides, the Tleilaxu or the technocrats against House Vernius, or as-yet-unknown enemies. Paul was missing; that was all Jessica needed to know.

A day later, Leto arrived on an express Guild transport generally reserved for cargo, but he had paid an exorbitant amount for swift passage. When he stalked into the Grand Palais, he was filled with a simmering energy to *do something* immediately. Jessica embraced him, drawing comfort and also showing her strength. "We've already begun the search, Leto. Earl Rhombur has rallied all the resources of Ix."

Leto's gray eyes held storm clouds. "Any ransom demand or threat?"

Gurney said, "There is a strong possibility that the boys fled voluntarily."

Duncan and Gurney bowed formally before the Duke. Duncan spoke first, "We failed you, my Lord. We let the boys slip through our fingers."

"I am the one who failed," Rhombur said. He plodded forward until he stood facing the Duke. "You are my friend, Leto. You entrusted your son to me, and I let you down. I gave my word that I would keep Paul safe, and for my failure I am deeply sorry. In the end, I am responsible for the foolish things that Bronso does, if indeed he ran away because of the . . . unwelcome things I told him about his parentage. You cannot forgive me. Nevertheless, I'm truly sorry. I, uh, let myself be distracted with other tragedies."

For a moment Leto glared at Rhombur, then he took a deep breath and looked at his friend with compassion. "Paul isn't some weak-willed boy who can easily be talked into doing something foolish. No matter what Bronso may have done, my son makes his own decisions."

"But my situation has put him into danger," Rhombur said.

"*Our* situation. A long time ago, you and I found ourselves in the middle of the Ixian revolt that turned your family renegade. My father didn't blame yours for what happened then. I can't blame you now." He reached out to clasp Rhombur's prosthetic hand in the traditional half-handshake. "My God, Rhombur—your wife, your son . . . For all our sakes, we must not let this turn into a greater tragedy."

The Ixian leader looked as though he might break down. "Leto, how do I deserve you as a friend?"

"By being the same kind of friend to me."

JESSICA SCOURED THE manifests of each arriving Guildship, hoping that some visitor would arrive with a message from the Bene

Gesserit, but she felt her hopes slipping as time passed. If Paul had indeed left voluntarily, she could not grasp why. Paul wasn't a flighty, impulsive boy, and running off with Bronso Vernius didn't make sense.

Finally, an officious but poorly dressed man arrived to see Lady Jessica, handing her a sealed message cylinder. "I was told to deliver this to you." He shuffled his feet, tugged at his sleeves. "There was some discussion of a reward for service?" After she paid the man and sent him away, Jessica activated the opening mechanism. Hope began to build in her heart.

Mohiam had written a terse, impersonal message in one of the numerous Bene Gesserit codes. The answer was not an admission of failure, nor an expression of knowledge about the boys, or lack of it; instead, she attacked Jessica for her concerns. The blunt sentences oozed with a surprising bitterness.

"Why worry so much about this boy-child whom you never should have conceived in the first place? If he is gone, then he is gone. Now you can concentrate on your duty to the Sisterhood. This is your chance for redemption. Go back to your Duke and bear us the daughter we have always demanded of you. Your purpose is to serve the Sisterhood."

As Jessica read and reread the message, she felt the sting of tears, then a burn of shame that she would allow the old woman's curt response to affect her so. She had been taught better than this—by Mohiam herself. With great force of will, she blocked off her emotions.

"As for the condition of Tessia Vernius," the Reverend Mother added as a postscript, "she has never been any concern of yours. Remember your place, for once. She is in safe hands in the Mother School."

It was not just the logic, but the venom that made her reel. Yes, Jessica had been told to bear a daughter by Duke Leto, but after the death of little Victor in the skyclipper crash, Leto had been crippled by grief, paralyzed by the loss. Out of her sheer love for him, Jessica had let herself conceive a son instead of a daughter. The Bene Gesserits, and Mohiam in particular, were appalled by Jessica's disobedience. Now they felt the need to punish her. They would always need to punish her.

And Paul would have to pay the price. She knew now that the Bene Gesserits, even with all of their resources and information, would never offer assistance in this matter.

Jessica tried to tear the message into pieces, but the instroy paper was too durable. Frustrated, she crumpled it up and fed it into an Ixian incinerator, watching her private hopes for a quick resolution vanish in the flames. Help would have to come from another quarter.

SEASONED GUILDSMEN AVOIDED setting foot on solid ground, claiming that gravity unsettled them. When a Guild official presented himself to Rhombur Vernius in the Grand Palais, accompanied by two silent and unnaturally large companions, Jessica was both intrigued and wary.

All three men wore gray uniforms with the infinity symbol of the Guild on the lapels. The hairless lead representative seemed displeased by the riotous work in all the bustling factories filling the cavern floor, as if he preferred activities to be more controlled. He took small shuffling steps, as though unfamiliar with the weight of his own body.

Rhombur strode forward. "You come with word of my son? And Paul?"

The man regarded him with oddly unfocused eyes. "The Spacing Guild is aware of your situation. We have located Paul Atreides and Bronso Vernius."

Jessica felt sudden relief after so many days of uncertainty. "They're alive and safe?"

"At last report." The man's aloof demeanor signaled either disdain for the two noblemen or simply a lack of social skills. "They stowed aboard a Heighliner and posed as workers amongst the Wayku. But they were careless, and we caught them."

Jessica let out an audible sigh of relief, but Leto remained suspicious. "So, where are they? Are you returning them to us?"

The Guildsman blinked in confusion. His two burly companions remained silent, staring straight ahead. "We did not come here for that purpose. We came to collect the fee for their passage. Your sons traveled great distances without paying for transport. House Atreides and House Vernius owe the Spacing Guild a significant sum."

In a tone of disgust, Leto muttered a curse. Jessica pressed, "Will you at least tell us where the boys are?"

"I do not have that knowledge."

"Vermillion Hells, you already said you caught the boys!" Rhombur took an ominous step forward, but the two muscular companions did not flinch.

"The boys were put off-ship, according to Guild policy, at one of our stops."

"Which stop?" Leto was growing more and more exasperated.

"We pride ourselves on confidentiality, and do not discuss the movements of our passengers."

Leto called his bluff. "In that case, we have no proof of their travels, and we refuse to pay for their passage."

The Guildsman was startled. "Those are separate matters."

"To you, perhaps, but not to me. Tell me where my son is, if you want to be paid."

The representative deferred to his massive companions, who consulted each other in quiet tones before nodding. Jessica wondered who was really in charge. "Payment first," the man said.

"No. Location first," Rhombur countered.

Leto fumed. "Enough of this! House Atreides guarantees payment to the Guild. If you tell us what we need to know, I'll release the solaris immediately."

The representative gave the slightest bow. "Very well. Bronso Vernius and Paul Atreides were granted sanctuary among a Jongleur troupe that disembarked on Chusuk four days ago."

There is a natural compatibility between our two groups, don't you think? Your "gypsy" Wayku and my Jongleurs are both inveterate space travelers, and in a sense we are both performers—my people put on spectacular shows, while yours perform tasks so efficiently that passengers hardly notice they're being served.

—RHEINVAR THE MAGNIFICENT, from a letter
to his Wayku friend Ennzyn

When the shuttle dumped the Jongleur troupe on Chusuk, Bronso shouldered closer to Paul, eager to drink in all the details at once. "A Jongleur's life is full of such things. If we stay with Rheinvar's troupe, we'll see a new planet every week."

"We just joined the troupe." They hadn't even met the other performers yet. Still, Paul was glad to see his friend enthusiastic again, because Bronso had been so bitter for weeks.

"Yes, but we're on Chusuk!"

Gurney Halleck had told stories and sung many songs about the planet Chusuk, renowned for its fine balisets. Paul doubted Gurney had ever been here before, though he talked like an expert. The thought of the big, lumpish man made Paul miss Caladan. He was sure his parents would be greatly concerned about him, though he hoped his mother and father had sufficient faith in his resourcefulness. Maybe he could find a way to at least send a reassuring message home, so long as he did not reveal too much. . . .

Rheinvar sauntered up to them, dressed in his sparkling white suit. "You two have to earn your keep. A favor for Ennzyn only goes so far."

"I've always wanted to work with Jongleurs," Bronso said.

The troupe leader let out a loud snort. "You don't know the first thing about Jongleurs. Rumors, embellished stories, superstitions—hah! I'll bet you think we're sorcerers living in the hills who can use telepathy to manipulate audiences."

"Exactly. And your performances are so emotionally powerful that audiences can die from the experience."

"That wouldn't help us get repeat customers, now would it? Those are just tall tales and rumors, ridiculous exaggerations. We're professional showmen, acrobats, entertainers." Rheinvar leaned closer, and his eyes twinkled. "The powerful skills you mention are only used by *Master* Jongleurs."

"And are you a Master Jongleur?" Paul asked.

"Of course! But using my powers would be strictly against Imperial law." Paul couldn't tell if the man was serious or not. "Ages ago, House Jongleur founded an ancient school of storytelling, employing clever showmanship and performing skills . . . but some of us had an extra gift, mental abilities that let us share emotions—strictly for entertainment purposes, you understand—to enhance the experience and increase the fear, romance, and excitement."

He let out a booming chuckle. "Or so the stories say. My people from the planet Jongleur used to be the best troubadours in the Imperium. We traveled from House to House, entertaining the great families, but some Master Jongleurs made the mistake of getting involved in intrigues with inter-House feuds, spying and the like . . . and ever since, we've been shunned by the Landsraad." Rheinvar's eyes glinted playfully. "As a result of our disgrace, some say there are no true Master Jongleurs left."

"But you just told us you're one of them yourself," Paul said.

"You believe everything I say? Good! In truth, I think the audiences come to watch because they *hope* I might demonstrate some supernatural powers."

"And do you?" Bronso asked.

Rheinvar waggled his finger. "The most important rule you need to learn is that a showman never divulges his secrets." The other troupe members began to move across the Chusuk field, and Rheinvar shooed the boys along. "Enough storytelling. I hope you two can do more than take up space and breathe the air. Tend the birds and lizards, haul crates, set up, tear down, clean up, run errands, and do the dirty work that no one else wants to do."

"We'll do the work, sir," Paul said. "We're not lazy."

"Prove it. If you can't find something to do on your own, then you're either blind, helpless, or stupid." He strode down the ramp, already looking like a showman. "I'm off to set up the performance venue. We start our practice shows tomorrow."

WITH ASTONISHING SPEED, the troupe members erected, fitted, powered, and furnished the stage inside the largest available theater in Sonance, the capital of Chusuk. The performers, roustabouts, and stagehands—Paul had trouble telling them apart—worked together like the well-coordinated components of an Ixian clock. He and Bronso did their best to help, while not getting in the way.

Rheinvar the Magnificent began promoting the show by going into the city to meet with family-league representatives, taking with him a few of the dancers, who demonstrated some of their more complicated moves.

Paul and Bronso did their chores without complaint, feeding the animals, cleaning equipment, helping move things into proper positions. At every opportunity, however, they gazed restlessly out at the city, wanting to explore.

When the frenetic work had died down, one of the performers came up to the boys, a lithe young male in black trousers and blouse. "I have business in Sonance, and you two are welcome to join me." He smiled at them. "My name is Sielto, and part of my job is to observe the leading locals so that I can glean specific details for use in the show."

Bronso and Paul did not need to consult each other before agreeing. Leaving the Jongleur encampment, the trio went out to explore Sonance. They wandered down narrow streets lined with shops, where artisans worked thin strips of golden harmonywood: planing, carving, and laminating the layers into graceful mathematical arcs and perfect shapes. Their companion gave a dry explanation: "Harmonywood comes from a special stunted tree that grows on the windswept high-lands. That wood is the key to the sophisticated characteristics of Chusuk balisets."

While the three proceeded from shop to shop, craftsmen glanced up at them from their workbenches. The smells of potent lacquers, col-orful paints, and sawdust filled the air. As soon as the artisans judged that they were mere curiosity seekers rather than actual customers, they turned back to their work.

"As the harmonywood grows," Sielto continued, "the trees are in-fested with tiny borer beetles, which create honeycombs in the wood. No tree is the same as any other, so no two instruments sound exactly the same. That special wood gives Chusuk instruments their sweet, rich sound and complexity of resonance." Through various doorways he indicated different coats of arms, varying colors and designs displayed outside the craftsman shops. "Each family league grows its own strain of the trees."

"They're not very innovative, though," Bronso said, "just using the old methods over and over." He bent over to inspect a basket of loose, polished multipicks for the balisets. The shopkeeper watched them closely, suspiciously.

Still wearing a contented smile, Sielto glanced around the work-shops. "You may not notice it, but this is an industry undergoing a great deal of turmoil. The Ollic League recently developed a synthetic vari-ety of harmonywood, you see, and it greatly offended the traditional-ists. Arsonists burned many of the new arbors to the ground." He looked around warily, as if expecting a mob to appear out of the streets and al-leys.

"But what's so special about those trees, and why would somebody want to destroy them?" Paul asked.

"Only a few years ago, the Ollic family was a minor player among har-monywood growers. They had fallen upon extraordinarily hard times, until the patriarch, Ombar Ollic, took a daring chance that offended all the other Chusuk leagues, using Tleilaxu engineers to genetically modify his strains. What would have taken ten years to grow, now matured in a single year. And thanks to the Tleilaxu modifications, clonewood trees have a *natural* honeycombed structure, so there's no need for the time-consuming borer beetles."

Noting that the shopkeeper was paying far too much attention to them, Sielto led the boys back out into the streets. "Many objective critics say that clonewood balisets sound even sweeter than originals, and such an idea appalls the Chusuk purists. That's why other families wish to destroy the Ollic League."

Despite his natural antipathy toward the Tleilaxu, who had greatly damaged Ix, Bronso sounded surprised, even offended. "But anyone who creates more efficient production methods *deserves* to get more business."

"You're thinking like an Ixian. From your manner of speech, I can tell you are from Ix, correct?" Sielto seemed to be probing for information, but Bronso avoided answering. He turned to Paul. "And you? I have not yet determined your homeworld, though there are a number of options."

Paul smiled calmly. "We're space gypsies, not unlike Wayku, or Jongleurs." For years, his tutors had drilled an understanding of consequences into him, explaining the complexities of commerce, government, alliances, and trade—all the things a Duke would need to know. "If Ollic clonewood sounds the same and grows faster, then their family's profits are increased at the expense of other leagues. No wonder the rival families hate them so and burned their arbors."

"Progress won't be stopped by a few instances of petty arson." Bronso's nostrils flared. "If the artificial clonewood is better, faster, and cheaper to produce, why don't the other families just adopt it in their own arbors, so they can be competitive again?"

"Maybe they should . . . but they will not. They are far too proud."

JUST BEFORE NOON the following day, Paul and Bronso stood beside Rheinvar in a vault-ceilinged wing of the gilded theater for the first rehearsals. Overhead, magnificent frescoes depicted colorful dancers, actors, and masked performers.

The Jongleur leader had arranged an appropriate time to launch their grand performance, but the troupe needed to practice before the big event. Each planet had its differences in gravity, sunlight, and atmospheric content.

With a skeptical eye, Rheinvar observed a troupe of dancers going through graceful, athletic movements on the stage. The music was quick and uplifting, with stunning harmonics. Above them, a pair of immense Gorun birds, their wings wide and powerful, clung to suspensor bars.

Though this was merely a setup and practice show, Rheinvar allowed a crowd of curiosity seekers to watch. "Their word of mouth is better advertising than all the announcements I could possibly make," he told Paul.

Bronso's eyes sparkled as he took in the elaborate routine of the dancers, all of whom wore pale blue leotards and tight feather caps in a variety of colors. A dozen dancers—ten men and two women—performed backflips and jumped high in the air; at exactly the right moment the Gorun birds spread their wings to provide a place for the dancers to land. Instantly, the enormous birds lifted into the air with slow, powerful sweeps of their wings and six dancers poised on top of them like daredevils, circling the theater and landing back on the stage. Finally, the dancers alighted onto the floor and took a bow as cheers filled the theater.

While the performers peeled away and vanished backstage, Rheinvar motioned to the lithe lead dancer in a red-feather headcap, and the man hurried over. "Outstanding practice performance. Have you met our new roustabouts?"

"Of course I have." The man removed his cap to reveal a bald head that glistened with perspiration. Something looked familiar about him, but Paul was sure he hadn't been among the workers setting up the stage. "How could I forget them? *Their* features don't change."

Rheinvar winked at the man, then led him and the boys backstage. Once they were out of sight of the crowd of onlookers, the dancer's face shifted, changed as he twitched muscles, adjusted his appearance all the way down to the bone structure. Paul's eyes widened as the performer became *Sielto*.

The man's features altered again, taking on the appearance of someone else whom Paul remembered from their communal meal the previous night. The countenance shifted again, and finally returned to the appearance of the lithe man who had performed onstage. "I'm much more than a dancer, as you can see—I am a Face Dancer."

Paul had heard of the exotic mimics before, and now he remembered that performance troupes often employed shape-shifters.

"A Face Dancer of the *Tleilaxu*," Bronso said with a clear growl in the back of his words, but he was unable to reveal the reasons for his aversion to the loathsome race without exposing his connection to House Vernius.

Sielto took no offense at his tone. "Is there any other kind?" He gestured to the other performers backstage, who now looked entirely different from their stage appearances. "Most of the troupe is made up of Face Dancers."

Rheinvar brushed imaginary dust from the sparkles on his top hat and placed it back on his head. "The audiences love it when the performers suddenly look like local political figures or recognizable heroes."

"And our Master Jongleur has tricks of his own." Sielto made a comical face. "Go sit out in the audience for the next routine, young roustabouts. Rheinvar, demonstrate what a Master Jongleur can truly do."

"Well, I do need to keep in practice . . . and it is just a rehearsal." As the Face Dancer bounded away, Rheinvar directed Paul and Bronso to empty seats in the main theater. "It's the grand finale. Watch it from the front step. You've never seen anything like this."

Dressed in his sparkling white suit under the intense lights, the Jongleur leader stepped to the center of the stage. Paul watched Rheinvar's stiff movements, the deep breaths and trancelike concentration as he seemed to prepare himself for a great exertion.

When he spoke, the man's voice carried throughout the great hall. "For our most spectacular event yet, we will attempt a dangerous routine that has been forbidden on seven planets—but have no fear, there is very little risk to any *individual* audience member."

Uneasy laughter rippled through the stands. Bronso nudged Paul in the ribs and rolled his eyes.

Rheinvar stood like a stone at the center of the stage, where he drew a deep breath and closed his eyes. Paul felt a strange flicker pass in front of his vision, a crawling sensation on the surface of his skin, but he shook it off. He felt dizzy, but focused his thoughts as his mother had taught him to do, trying to identify what Rheinvar was attempting. Presently, he focused his vision—and everything seemed normal again.

Sielto and the Face Dancers stepped casually onto the stage behind Rheinvar. They remained motionless except for their eyes, gazing around the audience, to the deepest reaches of the old theater. It all seemed very sedate.

Beside Paul, however, Bronso shuddered and blinked, and his expression took on an odd, dreamy look. The audience sucked in amazed breaths in unison. Groups of people gasped and moved in waves, as if something invisible was darting among them. But Paul didn't see anything.

On the stage, neither Rheinvar nor the Face Dancers had moved.

Audience members clapped and cheered; many did gyrations in their seats as though trying to avoid things that weren't really there. Even Bronso whistled his approval. "But they aren't doing anything!" Paul said, baffled.

Bronso pointed. "See there—oh! I've never seen so much leaping and twirling as the troupe goes out into the audience. Look how clever, the pinpoint landings, and the way they contort their faces to look like monsters. They're amazing! The audience is sure to have nightmares."

Paul, though, merely saw Rheinvar in deep concentration and the group of dancers behind him, standing casual and patient. "But . . . everyone is just standing on the stage. They're doing nothing."

"Are you blind and deaf?" Bronso clapped again and shot to his feet. "Bravo! Bravo!"

Finally, the Jongleur leader raised his head and opened his eyes. The Face Dancers bounded to the front of the stage and took a bow to the thunderous approval of the audience.

Then Paul understood. "It's mass hypnosis on the audience. I thought it was just a legend."

The Jongleur leader called the boys over to him, and doffed his top hat. "What did you see and hear? Were you impressed?" He looked from one boy to the other.

"We were both impressed," Paul said. "But for different reasons."

Bronso gushed about what he had seen, but Paul regarded the elegant old man with a measuring expression and said, "You played the audience like a musical instrument. Generating illusions, hypnotizing them. They saw exactly what you wanted them to see."

Rheinvar was taken aback by Paul's statement, but then he chuckled.

"You saw that? Well, it seems we have an unusual specimen here, more interesting even than a shape-shifter." He slapped Paul on the back. "Yes, a very small number of people have a kind of mental immunity. Jongleurs use a resonance-hypnosis technique similar to what the Bene Gesserit use, except these players merely use it to enhance their performances."

Bronso regarded his friend with clear astonishment. "You were serious? You really didn't see anything?"

"He *is* a Master Jongleur. You were the one seeing things that weren't there."

As Jessica continued to tell her story in the Princess's private wing of the Citadel, Irulan looked at her with obvious impatience and skepticism. "Paul told you all these things?"

"Yes, he did. He felt it was important for me to understand, just as it's important for you. Otherwise you can't write the truth."

"I admit it's interesting, but I still don't see the point of all this, or why you considered it so urgent to tell me. I've already had enough trouble with Fremen traditionalists who believe that your son's past has no bearing, that before he became Muad'Dib, there was nothing worth remembering." A flush infused her smooth cheeks. "Paul said it himself after his first sandworm ride, and the Fremen quote it often—'And I am a Fremen born this day on the Habbanya erg. I have had no life before this day. I was as a child until this day.'"

Jessica pressed her lips together into a thin line. "Paul said many things to the Fremen, but he did not come to Arrakis as a newborn. Without the first fifteen years of his life, he could never have become Muad'Dib."

Irulan turned her back and toyed with a ringlet of her golden hair as an idea occurred to her. "I've been considering adding a companion volume to my biographies, one tailored to a younger audience. A Child's History of Muad'Dib, perhaps. Alia says that it's necessary to indoctrinate the youth, so that children grow to revere and respect the memory of Muad'Dib." Disapproval hung heavy in her words. "Yes, the adventure of Paul and Bronso could be included in that book . . . and it is entertaining. It's good to see Paul doing heroic things, acting as a dedicated and honorable friend." She frowned. "But I don't see how it's relevant to the Imperial Regency that is the legacy of Paul's government and his Jihad. That is what's important."

Jessica lifted her chin and lowered her voice to a whisper, suddenly worried again that unseen spies might be recording their conversation. "Haven't you understood what I just told you? Where do you think Paul learned how to manipulate populations, to cast the power of his personality across large crowds? He applied Jongleur techniques not just to an audience for a performance, but to the Fremen, and then to the population of the entire Imperium!"

"But—"

Lady Jessica lifted a finger to emphasize her point. "And now it appears that Bronso of Ix is applying his own experience to spread the opposite message." Despite Irulan's obvious surprise, Jessica pressed on. "Be patient. Listen to the rest of the story."

Our most effective costumes are the assumptions and preconceptions the audience has about us.

—RHEINVAR THE MAGNIFICENT

Two days later, after the grand final performance, the Chusuk audience dwindled away from the theater into the night. Rheinvar did not take time to socialize with prominent baliset craftsmen or members of the various harmonywood leagues. Immediately after the performance was over, the troupe leader became a stern taskmaster. "Time to go—not a minute to waste. We've got new venues to play, new planets to visit, but we can't get *there* until we leave *here*."

Still wearing his glittering white jacket and top hat, Rheinvar directed Paul and Bronso to help tear down the props and holoprojectors, secure the animals, pack up the costumes, and load suspensor pallets for delivery to the spaceport. He had paid a substantial bribe to hold the last cargo shuttle of the evening, so they could make the Heighliner in orbit before it departed in a few hours.

Stepping out of the way as six large men slid a heavy cage onto a wide flatbed, Paul asked Bronso, "Have you seen Sielto? Or any of the Face Dancers since the performance?"

"How can you tell, one way or the other? They could be any of these people."

Paul didn't think so. "By now I recognize the other workers, for the most part. I haven't seen the dancers since they took their bows and ran back into the tent."

"Maybe Rheinvar gave them another job to do."

The troupe leader shouted at the two boys. "Hurry up! Chat all you want aboard the Heighliner, but if we don't make that cargo shuttle by departure time, the pilot charges me a hundred solaris for every extra minute. I'll take it out of your wages!"

"You're not even paying us wages," Bronso countered.

"Then I'll find some other way to take it out of you!"

The boys hustled to their tasks, though they kept an eye out for the Face Dancers. When the last groundcars and wheeled platforms were loaded, boxes and packs piled high, Paul and Bronso scrambled to the top of one carrier stack and rode there as a wheeled engine pulled them out to the Sonance spaceport. A dirty old cargo ship waited for them there, bathed in white launching lights. Small figures scurried about, stowing the last of the troupe's belongings.

But Paul still hadn't seen any sign of Sielto, and they were about to depart. He followed Rheinvar up the boarding ramp behind the last of the suspensor platforms. "Excuse me, sir. The Face Dancers . . ."

Bronso added, "If they don't get here in time, we won't have much of a performance troupe left."

Rheinvar didn't seem the least bit troubled as he ducked inside the ship. "They have their own schedules. Don't worry—they're professionals."

Taking one last glance at the edge of the illuminated spaceport, Paul spotted a group of identical men running toward the ship at a distance-eating pace. They burst into the light of the landing field and raced across the armorpave surface.

The shuttle's engines began to hum and throb as the pilot completed his systems check, and a hiss of exhaust gases spat from outflow pipes. Paul paused at the hatch, motioning for the group to hurry, and all the Face Dancers ran up the ramp, unruffled. Bronso looked at them as they passed. "I can't tell which one's Sielto, but he must be among them."

"I am the one you call Sielto." The speaker stopped while the other shape-shifters passed without pause, disappearing into the cargo vessel's gloomy interior. Two of them smelled of thick smoke.

A sheen of sweat glistened on Sielto's pale skin; Paul noticed that his hands were covered with blood, and spatters of scarlet ran up his sleeves. "Did you hurt yourself?"

"It is not my blood."

When the cargo ramp retracted, the hatch door automatically closed, forcing them to retreat into the ship. The rest of the Face Dancers had already vanished into the corridors without bothering to speak to the boys; only Sielto lingered. "We had another performance, you see—an obligation to fulfill."

Seeing the blood, smelling the smoke, putting the pieces together, Bronso blurted the conclusion that Paul had hesitated to voice: "You murdered someone, didn't you?"

Sielto's expression remained bland. "By the professional definition under which we operate, a necessary assassination is not murder. It is merely a political tool."

The deck began to rumble, and Paul caught the bulkhead for support. Unlike passenger transports, where everyone had to find safe and comfortable seats and buckle themselves into restraints, the cargo ship didn't bother with such niceties. As the vessel lurched off the ground, Paul focused on what Sielto had said. "Political tool? What's a 'necessary' assassination? You . . . you're a Tleilaxu Face Dancer—I thought you had no political interests."

"Correct, we have no political interests of our own. We are actors playing roles. We perform services."

"They're hired assassins," Bronso said with a wry smile. "Mercenaries."

"*Performers*," Sielto corrected. "You might say that we are playing our roles as assassins—real-life roles. There is always a need to eliminate troublesome people, and we simply fill that need."

"But whom did you kill? Who hired you, and why?" Paul asked.

"Ah, I cannot reveal any names or details. The reasons for the assignment are irrelevant, and we don't take sides."

Sielto showed neither conscience nor regret for having killed, and his revelations deeply disturbed Paul. His own grandfather, Duke Paulus, had been assassinated in the bull ring on Caladan. Paul also remembered the traumatic attacks by Viscount Hundro Moritani during his father's wedding ceremony, and the subsequent War of Assassins that caused so much bloodshed for Ecaz, Caladan, and Grumman. "Assassination isn't just a political tool—it's a bludgeon, not a precise instrument. There's too much collateral damage."

"Nevertheless, it is part of the Landsraad system. The practice has been condoned, at least implicitly, for countless generations." Sielto flexed his sticky fingers and regarded the mess as he walked down the shuttle's narrow corridor toward the crew quarters. "If you wish to do away with assassinations, young man, you'll have to change the face of the Imperium."

Paul raised his chin. "Perhaps one day I will."

It is said that one can neither play nor hear the true beauty of music without first having experienced considerable pain. Alas, that may be why I find music to be so sweet.

—GURNEY HALLECK, *Unfinished Songs*

Though they took the swiftest passage from Ix, Gurney Halleck and Duncan Idaho arrived on Chusuk three days too late to intercept the Jongleur troupe.

When the Heighliner reached orbit, the planet was in a state of upheaval. Sonance Spaceport had been locked down for two days, and new security measures delayed their transport to the surface by six hours. Something big had happened down there.

Before being allowed to board a shuttle, each passenger underwent intense Guild questioning about their business on Chusuk. Since Duncan and Gurney had letters of marque from Duke Atreides and Earl Vernius, they passed with comparative ease; other travelers, though, suffered indignities, and several simply returned to their staterooms to wait for the next planetfall.

"Gods below, is it a revolution?" No one would answer Gurney.

"One fundamental principle every Swordmaster learns is that security should be proactive, not reactive," Duncan said. "Unfortunately, most governments don't realize that until it's too late."

When the two men finally reached the capital city, anxious to find Paul and Bronso, they observed numerous paramilitary operations, with competing militias that enforced security for different family leagues.

The rival harmonywood growers regarded each other with as much suspicion as they did offworlders. In the distant fields and arbors surrounding the capital city, crooked plumes of black smoke marked scattered cropland fires. Half of the harvest was in flames.

The news was everywhere, some accounts more titillating than others: Three nights before, Ombar Ollic and all the members of his family had been murdered in their homes. The Ollic League arbors had been set afire, destroying most of the genetically modified harmonywood. Recriminations were numerous, but evidence minimal. Almost every family league had much to gain by removing the fast-growing clonewood from the market. Fingers were pointed, and the leagues began attacking each other.

Not interested in local politics, Gurney asked about the Jongleur troupe. Many people had attended the recent performance, but when Duncan displayed images of Paul and Bronso, no one recognized the boys, although a few said the pair might have been among the troupe as ragamuffin stage workers.

Gurney pressed one middle-aged woman who headed toward the town market with three children in tow. "Do you know where the troupe went after the performance? Are they still on Chusuk?"

She hurried away, leery of strangers. "Who cares about entertainment when such a heinous crime happened right under our noses?" Her children stared over their shoulders at the two men as she yanked them along.

While Duncan left to talk to the spaceport master about how many vessels had departed from Chusuk in recent days, Gurney surveyed the rows of workshops that lined the narrow, winding streets of the old town. Noblemen might not notice minor stagehands in a traveling show, but craftsmen paid more attention to details. Someone here might have seen something.

As Gurney strode down the streets, a sound like stringed songbirds filled the air, a clash of different melodies played all at once. He heard it drifting through open doorways, saw street musicians performing.

He smelled fine sawdust and the clinging odor of sweet shellac. One baliset maker used tuning pegs carved from obsidian; another advertised strings of silk braided around a thin thread of precious metal. A flamboyantly dressed man boasted that his frets and cavilers were made of human bone, authentic splinters from the skeleton of a great musician who had offered his body for such a remarkable purpose so that he could keep creating music long after his death.

Walking along, Gurney listened with appreciative nods, but he did not buy. Vendors could see that he was no idle curiosity seeker, though, and suggested that he try their balisets himself. They demonstrated the purported superior qualities of their harmonywood strains, how the resonance and purity of tone could not be matched. Testing the instruments, Gurney wrung beautiful melodies from some, jarring off-key tunes from others.

When he raised the subject of the recent Jongleur show, their attitudes changed swiftly. "Well, some Jongleurs may know how to play music, but that doesn't make them musicians," drawled one baliset maker. "They're just actors, manipulating their audiences. House Jongleur should have remained in exile. I don't know why Emperor Shaddam lets them keep performing, after that assassination attempt by his half brother, oh, a dozen years ago."

Gurney recalled that Tyros Reffa's foiled strike against Shaddam IV had occurred during a Jongleur performance. And now the entire Ollic League had been murdered. "Assassinations seem to accompany Jongleur shows."

And Paul was in a Jongleur troupe?

One street in particular was in turmoil. Instrument-makers' stalls were shuttered. Only one shop had open awnings and wares spread out on display, but the pieces carried excessive prices. The proprietor was tall and thin with an oddly puffy face. "These balisets are made from the clonewood grown by the Ollic League! Exquisite wood with perfect resonance."

"I've heard the opposite claims from many other merchants today," Gurney said.

"I don't doubt it, good sir." He leaned over the wooden display table, lowering his voice. "But ask yourself—if Ollic clonewood wasn't so superior, why did someone burn their arbors and murder the whole family?"

Gurney hefted one of the instruments and ran his fingers across the strings. The man had a point. He set the wheel in motion so that the gyroscopic tone cylinder made the wood vibrate. When he began to use the multipick, music seemed to flow out of his fingers. He had played nine-string models before, but it wasn't his usual instrument.

"Nine strings are what you need, my friend. One for each note of an octave, and another to enhance."

Gurney's fingers strummed a beautiful chord. The wood certainly seemed equivalent, and perhaps even superior, to the instruments he'd tested in the past hour. "My baliset is old and in need of repair. It's my fourth one."

"You're hard on your instruments."

"Life's been hard on me." His fingers kept playing, then he plucked out a more ambitious tune. The sound was pleasing.

The craftsman saw Gurney forming an attachment to the instrument. "They say balisets choose their players, not the other way around."

Setting the instrument back on the table, Gurney reached into his pocket and displayed the images of Paul and Bronso. "To be honest, I'm not just in the market for a baliset. I'm searching for these two young men. One is the son of my master." He stroked the curve of the baliset enticingly. "I'd be in a position to reward you with a sale and a generous bonus, if you help me find them."

The craftsman looked at the images, but shook his head. "Everyone around here has an apprentice. They all look the same to me."

"These boys weren't apprentices. They're with a Jongleur troupe."

"Oh yes, I heard about their performance. The same night Master Ombar Ollic was killed." Seeing another passerby, he lifted a chunk of his polished wood and called out, "Balisets made with Ollic clonewood! Now's your last chance—with the Ollics killed and their arbors burned, these will be the only such instruments ever made." As the passerby continued on his way, uninterested, the vendor lowered his voice once more to Gurney, conspiratorial now. "Hence the reason for the high prices. These instruments are sure to become a rarity, my friend. You may never be able to buy another baliset like it."

While the craftsman regarded the image of the boys again, Gurney continued to caress the instrument. "And does the Jongleur troupe have any other performances scheduled here?"

"Oh, they're long gone from Chusuk. After the murders, nobody's in the mood around here to see Jongleurs."

Gurney furrowed his brow. He would have to find out which ships left that particular night before the murders were discovered, since Chusuk security had locked down the spaceports immediately afterward. How could Paul and Bronso be involved with assassins?

"I'll buy the baliset." Though he had no idea where the Jongleur troupe would go next, at least the music would keep him company during their travels.

INSIDE THE BUSINESS offices of House Vernius, Rhombur seemed deflated and unsure of what to do. Jessica and Leto remained with him, waiting. After more than a month of intense searching for the boys, every lead had gone nowhere; every sighting proved false; every rumor was just that. Jessica felt her hopes slipping as time passed. Paul had still sent no message, no signal of any kind.

Accompanied by a silent aide, Bolig Avati bustled over to the Grand Palais, carrying a sheaf of papers, the Technocrat Council's weekly report to Earl Vernius. A supercilious man, Jessica thought; Avati's body language suggested that he didn't think Rhombur needed to be consulted about anything. "We have been managing everything in your time of difficulty, my Lord. Please attend to these documents as soon as possible, so as not to impede the progress of new developments." As an afterthought, he turned. "Oh, yes, a message cylinder arrived this morning, a communiqué from two House Atreides men." He waved a hand casually, and his aide stepped forth to present a cylinder.

"I would have preferred this information the moment it arrived," Rhombur snapped, grabbing the message. "Vermillion Hells! This could be vital—"

Avati demurred with no sincerity whatsoever. "Apologies. We had other pressing business." He left without further ado.

Rhombur unsealed the cylinder so quickly with his cyborg hand that he broke the cap. As he scanned the lines of the instroy document, his prosthetic shoulders sagged. "Your men arrived on Chusuk too late. The Jongleur troupe gave a performance and then departed immediately on another Guildship. No information on where they went afterward."

"We can ask the Guild," Leto said. "An inspector is due this afternoon."

"We can *ask*," Jessica agreed, "but they weren't very cooperative the last time."

BEFORE HE COULD proceed to the Heighliner construction site, the Guild inspector was intercepted by Rhombur's household guard and escorted to the Vernius administrative office. He was annoyed by the disruption in his plans. "My schedule does not allow for interruptions."

"We request information," said Rhombur and explained what they needed to know.

The inspector was unimpressed. "Information is not gratis, nor is it readily available. The only reason we spoke with you earlier about your sons is because of the fees they owed for passage. Such discussions are over, because confidentiality is a hallmark of the Spacing Guild."

Rhombur's scarred face darkened. "Then let me pose the question in a way you can better understand. Effective immediately, I shall order that all construction work cease on your Heighliner. My crews will not lift a hull plate or install a single rivet until you give us answers."

Jessica felt a warm satisfaction in her chest. Leto's hard grin showed he was proud of the position Rhombur was taking.

The Guild inspector was startled. "That makes no commercial sense. I shall protest."

"Protest all you like. I am House Vernius, and my commands rule here."

Jessica stepped closer to the Guildsman. "You don't have any children, do you, sir?"

He seemed to see her for the first time. "Why is that relevant?"

"It explains your complete ignorance and lack of humanity."

With heavy footfalls, Rhombur crossed to a wall-comm and contacted the construction crew chief on the grotto floor. "Stop all operations immediately. Perform no further work on the Heighliner until I give the word. Tell your crews to take a break—it might be a long one." He switched off the speaker and turned to the inspector. "You may as well go back to your Heighliner and discuss the matter with your superiors. I'll be here when you return."

Thrown off balance, the Guildsman hurried out of the administrative office. Jessica looked through the transparent windows to the construction floor, where tiny figures rode suspensor platforms down from the superstructure as they exited the Heighliner framework. Workers milled about like busy insects on the wide cavern floor, not knowing what else to do.

INSTEAD OF DEPARTING for his Heighliner, the inspector demanded a special meeting with the technocrats. The Council members reacted with astonishment to hear what Rhombur had done, then showered the Guildsman with apologies.

Avati's voice was soothing. "This is just a misunderstanding. Earl Rhombur is preoccupied with personal concerns and isn't thinking lucidly. Obviously, his decision is not in the best interests of the Ixian economy."

In an emergency session, the Council members unanimously invoked an obscure clause of the Ixian Charter: Because Rhombur's brash decision could cause irreparable harm to Ix's reputation, they voted to countermand his order and called for work to recommence at once. As a show of good faith, they reaffirmed the delivery date, promising to release the Heighliner as planned.

Rhombur could protest, but with his power base diminishing day by day, he could do nothing about it.

There are countless definitions and interpretations of a life well spent, and of the opposite. There are often widely divergent biographies of a particular person. The same individual can be either demon or saint, and even shades of both.

—from *The Wisdom of Muad'Dib* by the PRINCESS IRULAN

Aboard the Heighliner, Rheinvar gathered his troupe in a large, echoing compartment that the Wayku had provided for them to relax in together. Their belongings had been containerized and placed in a cargo hold of the great ship. The Jongleur leader strutted back and forth, smiling. "Balut is our next venue. For the first time ever, we play the famed Theater of Shards!"

Though the Face Dancers showed neither enthusiasm nor disappointment, the other troupe members murmured with excitement. Bronso perked up and whispered to Paul. "My grandmother was from Balut. Lady Shando—"

Paul nudged him. Though they had provided their first names, neither boy had revealed much about their identities. Bronso fell silent, but one of the Face Dancers—Sielto?—leaned closer. "Your family comes from there, young man?"

Paul said in a hard voice, "Do Face Dancers have unusually acute hearing? And no respect for personal privacy?"

The shape-shifter smiled. "Old Emperor Elrood had a concubine named Shando, and she was from Balut."

"Shando is a common name there, especially after the Emperor's concubine," Bronso said. "Many families fantasized that their own daughters might go off to join the Imperial court."

"I see." The Face Dancer was maddeningly unreadable. "That certainly explains the coincidence."

Before they reached Balut, Rheinvar held several private sessions with Paul and Bronso. "If you two are going to be part of this troupe, I should teach you simple techniques that Jongleurs use to generate enthusiasm in the audience, to enhance emotions and make the people love you, cheer for you, follow your lead. Won't there be times in your lives that you need to convince others? Maybe even large crowds?"

"But we're not Master Jongleurs," Paul said.

"No mass hypnosis, no telepathic techniques, or complex tricks—those things are not necessary for you to know. But at the very least, you both need to be competent orators in order to spread the word on various planets about our upcoming shows. Let me show you how to mesmerize the listeners!"

Rheinvar leaned closer, striking a pose with an utterly sincere and captivating smile. "You see, much of the technique of convincing people, of selling them, involves the careful use of voice and facial expressions. Once you master the subtle art of manipulating people—either one at a time, or in great numbers—you will always be able to achieve your goals."

As the two boys sat down to listen and Rheinvar began his instruction, Paul was reminded of some of the lessons his mother had taught him about Bene Gesserit techniques and manipulations.

He frowned, having second thoughts. "If you have to trick people into cooperating with you, then you are not an honorable person." It went against everything Duke Leto had taught him, but he recalled seeing a harder side of his father when it came to political realities.

"Honor or dishonor depends on how you *employ* your talents, not the nature of the talents themselves. Surely there's nothing wrong with encouraging people to attend an entertaining show?"

AS THE PASSENGERS filed off into the Balut terminal building, Paul was surprised to see so much security. Hypervigilant red-uniformed soldiers monitored all exits, all lines of people.

"More internal troubles?" he said to Bronso.

"Every Great and Minor House feuds with other noble families, I suppose."

Joining them on the deck, Sielto grinned at Paul. "The more arguments, the more *customers* for us. Balut is a cesspool of saboteurs and agents for each side." Now that the boys knew their secret, the Face Dancers were oddly casual about their secondary profession.

"You've wasted no time doing your research on local tensions, I see," Bronso said.

Sielto acted nonthreatening, even trustworthy. "It is an important part of my job. The ruling Kio family has entered into an alliance with House Heiron, a wealthy but minor offworld family. House Heiron has only been on Balut for a couple of decades, and already they control the most exquisitely talented crystal carvers, glassmakers, and etchers. Now the Heirons have worked their way into Governor Kio's inner power circle."

"And some of the old-guard families don't like it," Paul said with a sigh. "Naturally." He scanned the crowd as people milled around. The arriving passengers lined up to pass through a series of checkpoints.

"They don't want Balut tainted by outsiders." The Face Dancer smiled.

At the security checkpoints, all of the troupe's cargo cases, prop wardrobes, and animal cages received an intense examination. Neither Paul nor Bronso carried identity documents, nor did many of the troupe members, so they passed through secondary screening, where they were thoroughly catalogued.

Ahead of Paul in line, Bronso pressed his hand against an identity plate, and a silvery scanner light bathed him. Unlike the previous passengers, Bronso remained under the glow for a long moment. Paul held his breath, sure that they had been caught.

A suspicious, red-uniformed officer told Bronso to stand still as he checked the readings. Paul swallowed hard as the line backed up behind them, and a guard diverted him to a second scanner, where he was sure he'd trigger a security alert as well. He swallowed hard as he went through the identification process—but he passed without anyone giving him a second glance.

Paul glanced over to where the uniformed officer looked Bronso up and down, scowling. "Scanner says you're a member of the former Balut noble family." The redheaded boy was disheveled, his clothes stained and threadbare, a roustabout scamp traveling with a Jongleur troupe.

"Yeah, I get confused with royalty all the time," Bronso said with bold sarcasm. The guard glanced at his companion, and both let out loud guffaws. They pushed him through and called the next person forward. Bronso joined Paul, wiping perspiration from his forehead. Sielto followed close behind.

Sometimes the best way to search is to be found.

—Zensunni postulate

A week later, in their small stateroom aboard another Heighliner, Gurney strummed his new baliset, experimenting with melodies and humming tunes in his head.

Now that they had left Chusuk with no particular destination in mind, Duncan pored over the charts of star routes, trying to imagine where the Jongleur troupe might have gone. So far, they had spent many fruitless days. "I'd have to be a Mentat to figure this out. We should have brought Hawat along, after all. Paul and Bronso could have gotten off almost anywhere. There are too many possible locations for us to search them all."

Gurney plucked a wrong note. "Neither of us is going to give up. We promised the Duke."

Duncan pushed the papers aside. "Yes, and we owe it to the young Master as well. Paul has gotten in over his head, but he's never seemed like the type who needs rescuing."

"We all need to be rescued at one time or another." It wasn't a familiar quote, but a nugget of his own wisdom. Gurney toyed with a new tune.

A Wayku steward appeared at the stateroom door, bearing a tray of food. Duncan looked up at him suspiciously. "We didn't order meals in our quarters."

"You are correct, but I needed some reason to come here." The Wayku man had a black goatee and impenetrable glasses over his eyes. "We've all heard about the search for the missing sons of Duke Atreides and Earl Vernius. Paul and Bronso are their names, correct?"

Gurney rose to his feet, setting the baliset aside. "Do you have any leads on the boys?"

"I have facts. My name is Ennzyn. I did know two boys that matched the descriptions I've read, and their names were Paul and Bronso."

"Where?" Duncan asked. "And when did you last see them?"

"They worked with me for a time on a Heighliner, but when the Guild discovered that they were stowaways, they were put off at Chusuk. They joined a Jongleur troupe."

Gurney's shoulders slumped with disappointment. "We've already tracked them that far. We lost their trail after that."

"There is more. A certain member of that same Jongleur troupe dispatched a message to us, from Balut. It seems that when Rheinvar's group arrived there, a security scan identified the genetic markers of the former noble family, House Balut, in one of the young roustabouts."

Duncan put the pieces together. "Bronso's grandmother was Lady Shando of Balut."

"Did they detain the boys?" Gurney pressed.

"No. Security had no record of—nor any particular interest in—a missing member of the Balut family. Fortunately, my source takes interest in a great many matters." The Wayku steward stepped inside and rested the food tray on a small table, then removed the coverings to reveal an unappetizing-looking meal. "The dinner comes free with the information."

"And what do we owe you for the information itself?" Duncan said.

Ennzyn gave a faint smile. "I developed a fondness for the boys. After I researched your situation in greater detail, I became concerned about them. Though Bronso and Paul both struck me as flexible, intelligent, and resourceful young men, they don't belong on their own, traveling as they do. It would be sufficient reward for me to help you bring them home."

"And why would a member of the Jongleur troupe have sent you this news?" Gurney was suspicious at the Wayku's lack of any demands.

"Wayku and Jongleurs have much in common, traveling as we do through the various regions of space. Our peoples yearn to see new places, have new experiences, and so we've developed a natural affinity for one another. Shared information is sometimes mutually beneficial."

"And are the boys still on Balut?"

"As far as I know. But who can know all the movements of a Jongleur troupe?"

Duncan hauled out the star charts again. "We've got to get to Balut as soon as possible, Gurney."

"Unfortunately, this vessel does not go there," Ennzyn said. "You'll have to take an alternate route from the next hub. I would be happy to help you plot the best course."

"Where's the next hub stop?" Gurney wished his sense of urgency could make the Heighliner arrive faster.

"Ix," Ennzyn replied.

Gurney glanced sharply at Duncan. "That'll do just fine."

THE TWO MEN burst into the Grand Palais, surprising Jessica and Leto. Gurney got the words out first, "We have a new lead on the boys, my Lords! 'Those who search long enough, and with great faith, shall be rewarded.'"

Duncan added, "But we need to leave immediately, before they move on again. I've checked the Spacing Guild schedules—we can get to Balut within three or four days. I wish it could be sooner, but we can't change Heighliner schedules."

Rhombur summoned his Suk doctor. "Yueh, you're coming with us. If anything's happened to either of the boys, I need you there to help them."

After calling on Ixian officials to arrange for immediate transport on the next Guildship bound for Balut, the cyborg Earl grudgingly sent a message to Bolig Avati. "I have to let him know that I'll be away from Ix."

Leto did not try to hide his concern or skepticism. "I don't trust that man, Rhombur."

"Vermillion Hells, I don't trust the whole damned Technocrat Council! But when I'm away from Ix, Avati's the de facto administrator here."

"If they hadn't ruined your bargaining position with the Guild inspector," Jessica pointed out, "we could have had a clear answer days ago."

"Uh, I'm more worried about what they might do while I'm gone. The technocrats could take over Ix with a few pen strokes, and a lot less bloodshed than the Tleilaxu did."

"Then maybe we should take some preemptive action," Leto said.

When he arrived, the Council leader sketched a sloppy bow. "Preparing to leave again, my Lord Vernius? I understand completely! Family matters must take priority over running a planet. Ix will be in good hands in your absence."

Leto spoke up in a crisp tone, as if Avati were not there. "Rhombur, I can offer to station House Atreides troops here during your absence, to help maintain stability. With your blessing, we'll leave Duncan and Gurney here to arrange it. That way, Vernii will remain in good shape while we're gone—and your enemies will not perceive any weakness."

Avati showed clear alarm. "There is no need for an offworlder army. Ix has no instabilities! And no enemies."

"It's better to be sure," Rhombur said with a smile. "The Duke is correct—without me here, there's only a proxy Council to monitor administrative details. Other Houses may see Ix as an undefended prize. Certainly you remember how easily the Tleilaxu took over when we weren't prepared? Who knows what might happen in my absence?" He was pleased to twist the knife. "Gurney Halleck and Duncan Idaho are renowned throughout the Landsraad for their bravery and strength. Yes, Leto, have your men send word to Caladan. A battalion or two should suffice."

"A battalion?" Avati cried.

Gurney did not look keen to be left behind. "But, my Lord, shouldn't we accompany you to see that the boys are safe?"

"If my son and Bronso are indeed on Balut, we'll retrieve them without any trouble. You and Duncan can do more here . . . for my friend Rhombur."

The Earl could not hide his obvious relief. "Thank you, Leto! And

Counselor Avati, you are to give your full cooperation to the Duke's representatives and welcome his troops when they arrive."

The technocrat squirmed, but nodded.

Leto issued crisp orders. "Duncan and Gurney, send a high-priority courier to Caladan and have Thufir Hawat dispatch a security force as soon as he receives the message. Ix will be safe, if I have anything to do with it. That's what friends are for."

Everyone has a history. The question is, how much of that history
really occurred the way it is documented?
—from *The Life of Muad'Dib, Volume 2*, by the PRINCESS IRULAN

Balut's Theater of Shards was so stunning that the architecture threatened to overshadow the performance. Paul and Bronso stood outside the fluted gates, dizzied by the sight of millions of reflecting prisms. In such a breathtaking venue, who would want to look at mere acrobats and dancers? With its soaring crystalline towers, angled planes, and intersecting mirrors and lenses, the building seemed more optical illusion than physical structure. Paul thought he could *smell* the light in the air.

Settling in on the planet, having worked out all the details for their main performance on Balut in a week's time, the Jongleur leader got down to business. Rather than being awed by the celebrated Theater of Shards, Rheinvar worried about possible snags in the complex stage assembly, lighting problems posed by the nonperpendicular planes of the walls, complications caused by tall turrets that would either magnify or attenuate the normal acoustics. He needed to see the inside for himself.

With a terse all-business demeanor, Governor Alra Kio opened the crystalline gates to give Rheinvar full access to the theater. "I intend to make the formal announcement of my betrothal to Preto Heiron at your performance, when I have a large audience. I ask only that your performance be perfect," she said with a hint of a smile. "Make sure your troupe gives the most impeccable show of their careers."

"That's all?" Rheinvar asked, half amused.

"That's all." Though plump and known to be of a mature age, Governor Kio had a youthful body and complexion, undoubtedly retained through heavy, and costly, consumption of melange. Her fiancé was much younger.

The Jongleur leader removed his sparkling white top hat. "What the dance troupe does is in my purview, but I leave the politics to you, Madam Governor."

She swept away, returning to her offices and leaving Rheinvar, Paul, and Bronso to walk the venue and assess what adjustments might need to be made. As the Jongleur leader moved along, he carried a crystalpad projector that displayed blueprints and acoustical projections of the performing area so he could map the arrangement of his great stage.

The three entered the core of the arena, where the beauty surpassed even that of the ornate exterior. Governor Kio and her young fiancé would occupy seats on a sweeping, separate balcony at the focal point of the reflected light projectors and sound-wave generators.

"It's not often you find a place whose real substance meets or exceeds stories of its flash and dazzle." With quick, deft motions, Rheinvar made notations on the crystalpad, marking where mirrors needed to be installed, along with the correct positioning for laser projectors and amplifiers.

"This Theater of Shards was designed and built some fifty years ago by a famous architect . . . whose name I forget now. One of Balut's wealthiest ruling families bankrolled the entire project, and the details were kept highly confidential. No one but the architect himself had the complete blueprints."

Rheinvar lowered his voice and used now-familiar Jongleur tricks to draw the boys into his story. "But *then*, on the night of the grand opening, the wealthy patriarch of the ruling family was found murdered at the hands of the architect. A day later, the architect also died mysteriously, said to have been the victim of angry members of the noble family."

"Quite the drama," Bronso chuckled. "Sounds like fodder for another play."

Rheinvar continued in his rich professional voice. "Some say that this Theater of Shards contains a powerful secret known only to the nobleman and the architect. That's the story, anyway. I can't say whether or not it's true—but it should be."

Paul looked around the arena, studying the angles, planes, prisms, and magnifiers. He gestalted and analyzed each detail, as his mother had taught him to do. The Theater was a monumental experiment in physics, optics, and harmonics.

Bronso stared all around. "The engineers of Ix would have a grand time deconstructing the angles and focal points here."

Rheinvar finished making notations and handed Paul his crystalpad projector. "Here's the plan, boys. You have traction pads, hooks, adhesives, and guidance calipers. I need you to hang enhancement mirrors there, there, and there. Once you're finished, run a tracer beam to make sure the surfaces are aligned, then set up secondary stations at the five points noted on the pad."

While Bronso seemed excited by the responsibility, Paul said, "Don't you want more seasoned stage technicians to take care of this?"

"Others may be more seasoned, but you two are agile and fearless."

"I am, at least." Bronso sent a teasing look toward Paul.

"I'm the accurate and meticulous one," Paul countered. "So we make a good team. Between the two of us, we'll get it done, sir."

Hatred should not be so easy, nor forgiveness so difficult.
—EARL RHOMBUR VERNIUS

The groundcar sped from the starport toward Balut's capital city. In the backseat, Jessica could only hope that they would arrive in time. If Paul and Bronso had slipped away again, if the information turned out to be a false lead, she would feel crushed . . . and she knew what it would do to Leto.

Beside her, the Duke kept his outward emotions tightly in check, but long familiarity allowed her to read his concerns. He was a rigid man who had endured many tragedies that covered his emotions with hard scars, like those on the body of a seasoned warrior.

Jessica spoke gently. "Once we see Paul, we can find out what he did, and why."

In Leto's reply, she heard the undertone of anger that masked his worry. "I will be interested to hear his explanation."

Leto did not often show overt warmth toward Paul, maintaining what he considered to be a seemly distance, so that his son could better prepare to be Caladan's next Duke. But the formality did not fool Jessica. Ever since Bronso and Paul had run away, Leto had been worried sick, distraught even to consider what he would do if he lost his son. Only those closest to the Duke could see the anger—much less look past it to his fear.

Earl Rhombur hunched his cyborg body on a wide seat across from them with Dr. Yueh squeezed in next to him. Rhombur felt an intense anxiety, with an added layer of guilt, since he was sure that his own words had driven Bronso away.

As Leto stared impatiently ahead, the cyborg Earl said, "Don't scold your boy too much, Leto. Vermillion Hells, I'd bet that Paul did it out of a sense of honor, to protect Bronso. We did make them swear to watch out for each other. You would have done the same for me, when we were younger."

"We weren't so foolish as those two."

Rhombur chuckled. "Oh, we had our moments."

The vehicle took them directly to a grassy park expanse lined with Balutian maples and oaks. A number of military vehicles encircled an area where large tents had been set up, and uniformed soldiers strutted about, carrying their weapons. Behind the cordon, restless Jongleur performers stood around, worried about all the fuss.

"Governor Kio has really taken this seriously," Leto said.

"When I communicated with her, I had only to say that my mother was from the Balut noble family. Lady Shando is still revered here." His scarred face held an anxious smile. "The Governor promised to prevent *any* members of the Jongleur troupe from slipping away."

Jessica stepped out with her companions and saw a plump brunette woman followed by an entourage of formally dressed men. Alra Kio was all smiles, pleased to earn the goodwill of two Great Houses. "Duke Leto, Earl Rhombur—your sons are safe. Rheinvar was quite astonished when we revealed the true identities of his two roustabouts."

Rhombur was ready to surge ahead. "Where are the boys?"

A tent flap rustled behind the group of military men, and Paul emerged from one of the tents, dressed in a white tunic and dark trousers. His black hair was tousled, and a smear of dirt crossed his forehead. Seeing his parents, he lit up and ran to them without any hesitation. "I'm so glad to see you. How did you find us?"

Unabashed, he embraced his father first, but the Duke pulled back awkwardly and coolly shook the boy's hand. Jessica could see the joy and relief nearly bursting from Leto, but he locked it all inside. "I am happy you're unharmed, son. That was a foolish risk you took, jeopardizing House Atreides and completely disregarding your responsibilities. You could have—"

Jessica squeezed Paul in a crushing hug. "We were so worried about you!"

Paul saw his mother wrinkle her nose at the thick, unpleasant odors from his perspiration-damp clothes. "Bronso and I work with animals and do other odd jobs. I've got so much to tell you both."

Leto remained stern, and Jessica understood why he felt he needed to be so harsh. "Yes, you do."

"I didn't disregard my responsibilities, sir. I—"

With much more hesitation than Paul had shown, another boy appeared at the tent opening. Rhombur lumbered toward him, followed closely by Dr. Yueh. "Bronso!"

The redheaded boy folded his arms across his chest and glared at the cyborg prince. Puffed up with anger and resentment, he struggled to maintain his hard façade, but words were already spilling out of Rhombur's mouth. "Oh, Bronso. I know I handled our situation badly. I'm sorry. Please forgive me—I can't lose both Tessia and you! We had a good relationship before—uh, can't we go back to that and talk about what happened between us?"

Bronso's voice was as cold as the plazcrete gray of his eyes; he had been holding the words inside for some time, had probably even rehearsed them for an imagined confrontation with Rhombur. "You want me to forget that you lied to me all of my life? That you're not my real father?"

Rhombur refused to accept that guilt. "A *real* father is the one who gives you a home and raises you, the one who trains and teaches and loves you no matter what. A *real* father would travel across the entire galaxy to find you, leaving everything else behind because nothing else matters as much."

Time seemed to have frozen around them, and Jessica longed to see the breach healed. She looked imploringly at Bronso. *Reach out to him, boy!*

An expression of remorse shaded the youth's face as he looked at Rhombur. Jessica wondered if he saw only a cyborg who was broken and deficient in so many ways. Bronso unfolded his arms, heaved a deep breath, and after a long silent moment, began to cry. "And my mother? Do the witches still have her?"

"They do." Rhombur pulled the boy against his artificial chest. "I promise, you and I will travel together to Wallach IX to see her. We'll go as soon as we leave here, and I don't care how the Sisters feel about it. I'd like to watch them stop me from seeing her." He stepped back, looking down at the boy. "Then, when we get back to Ix, we'll attend council meetings together. We'll stand firm against the technocrats as a united House Vernius. We can be strong enough to do anything."

THEY COULD NOT book passage to Caladan for three days. Pacing the floor inside the fine guest quarters that Governor Kio had provided, Duke Leto frowned at the printed transport schedule, then set it aside on a plaz-topped side table. "We won't be leaving Balut as soon as I'd hoped."

Paul was not disappointed in the least. Once home on Caladan, he would go back to being trained as a Landsraad nobleman, and Bronso would return to the technocracy on Ix, their carefree days over. "That means we'll be here for the performance. You can see the Jongleurs in action. Their Face Dancers are unlike anything you've—"

"I have no interest in acrobats or shape-shifters." For more than a day, Leto had maintained a veneer of displeasure at what Paul had done, though the Duke could not entirely hide his deep-seated relief.

Paul had admitted his culpability and apologized, though he could not deny the sense of honor he felt toward safeguarding Bronso. He had explained why he'd felt it necessary to stay with Rhombur's son, no matter what.

Now, he faced his father with a growing sense of confidence. "Sir, you sent me away to learn. Before that, you taught me about politics and leadership, while Thufir, Duncan, and Gurney showed me how to fight and defend myself. Rheinvar's troupe showed us how to affect great crowds, how to enhance emotions and reactions. Isn't that useful knowledge for a Duke to have?"

"You mean you learned how to trick and manipulate people."

Paul lowered his eyes, careful not to argue. "I believe there is a place for charismatic elocution in statecraft, sir."

Jessica interceded in a carefully controlled tone of voice. "The Bene Gesserit teach those things as well. Paul will face unexpected dangers and crises when he becomes Duke. Why object to any skill that might save him? He has the tools to use—now trust that he also has the honor and moral underpinnings to know when, and when not, to use them."

Leto remained stiff, didn't reply. . . .

Later that afternoon, Rhombur Vernius came to the doorway to speak on Paul's behalf. The cyborg prince knew full well that Bronso was the one who had instigated the brash flight from Ix. "*I* should have been there to protect the boys, Leto, even after what happened to Tessia. Paul did the honorable thing. I beg you, don't punish him. Without his courage, Bronso might very well be lost or dead."

Finally, Leto's sternness melted like frost on one of the castle windows on an autumn morning. He was forced to admit, "I did make Paul swear to watch over your son."

Nevertheless, the Duke was not quick to forget—and would not let his son forget, either. When the Balut governor invited them all to a banquet on the night before the scheduled Jongleur performance, Leto told Paul to take his meal alone and ponder the consequences of his foolish, shortsighted decision, no matter his good intentions toward Bronso Vernius.

Left by himself in their guest quarters, Paul considered how hard Rheinvar's troupe must be scrambling to assemble the rest of the stage and the complex special-effects mechanisms inside the Theater of Shards; the performers would be rehearsing repeatedly. Paul longed to be out there helping them.

But something troubled him. He had not told his parents that there were Face Dancer assassins in the Jongleur troupe. It was the sort of problem that he wished would just go away, because if he explained, his father would be even more upset with him and more critical of him. Paul didn't know how to phrase it, but knew he would have to find a way. Endorsing "necessary assassinations" was certainly not a House Atreides ideal.

A liveried Balut servant appeared at the doorway bearing a tray of dishes prepared by the Governor's finest chefs. The rich aromas wafting up from the covered plates made Paul's stomach rumble. The servant placed the tray on a table and removed the coverings with a showman's flourish. Paul thanked him distractedly, and the man straightened, meeting his gaze. "Don't thank me yet."

Instantly on his guard, Paul watched the plain features on the servant's face shift and revert to another familiar form. "Sielto?"

"You may call me that."

Paul didn't press him for a more definite answer. "What brings you here? Is Rheinvar all right?"

"Delivering a cautionary note is strictly against protocol, but . . ." The Face Dancer shrugged. "I decided to make an exception in this case, since I already chose to get involved—to interfere—when I informed the Wayku of your identity and whereabouts. That is how your family knew to come to Balut."

"*You* did that? Why?"

"Because you two boys dabble in this life, but do not belong here. You and your companion will both achieve great things, but not if you remain with a traveling Jongleur troupe."

Paul frowned. "I'm not sure why you're telling me this."

"Even a play may hold more drama than meets the eye."

"A play? You mean the performance tomorrow, or . . . ?"

"Everything is part of the performance, and no one has the complete script."

"A cautionary note? More drama than meets the eye? Is someone in danger?"

"Everyone is in danger, young man, every day. Danger can come from anywhere, and strike anyone. It can come in any form or package. Just remain vigilant, young friend, even though you are not in the script." Sielto's features resumed the appearance of a Balut servant, and he left without another word, though Paul had many more questions.

Sielto's cryptic words didn't rise quite to the level of a warning. To Paul, it sounded more philosophical. But Sielto had not come merely to philosophize with Paul. Something more had to be there. A script? Did that mean a plot?

Alone in his room, the young man looked at food that no longer tempted him. Thufir Hawat had told him never to lower his guard, and that habit had become second nature to Paul. He couldn't imagine how much more security Governor Kio could mount. Even without specifics, he decided he would have to tell his father, though he did not look forward to the conversation.

While an audience is captivated by the show, they must ask them-
selves: At whose expense is the entertainment derived?

—RHEINVAR THE MAGNIFICENT

When the grand Jongleur performance began inside the Theater of Shards, Paul was awash with emotions. Just a few days ago, he had expected to be part of this show behind the scenes, a nameless roustabout; now he found himself with his family high above the stage in a private balcony box, the son of a Landsraad nobleman occupying one of the best seats in the house, at the insistence of Governor Kio. He fidgeted on the Governor's Balcony, feeling like an outsider.

Beside him, his father sat in a formal black jacket emblazoned with the Atreides hawk crest, while the governor had provided Paul with a similar dark jacket. Jessica looked lovely in a dark green gown spangled with ice diamonds, much like those that adorned the costume of Rheinvar the Magnificent.

After Paul had delivered the mysterious and nonspecific warning from Sielto, revealing how the Face Dancers were sometimes involved in surreptitious assassinations, Duke Leto had scowled, then dispatched a message to Governor Kio to increase her security precautions.

But Leto had decided not to hide. "There are always threats against us, Paul, and we can't let them prevent us from going out in public. As the Old Duke used to tell me, 'If fear rules us, we don't deserve to rule.'"

Paul had sat quietly in his room, the food hardly touched on the table, his stomach roiling. He hated to have his father, whom he admired greatly, disappointed in him. "I'll do better, sir. I promise."

"See that you do." Duke Leto's features then softened. "Besides, I wouldn't want to miss the performance that is so important to you."

Remarkably, the Duke now looked fully at ease, afraid of nothing, which imparted similar feelings to Paul. When he and his family arrived at the theater, they immediately noticed the heightened security. Governor Kio's red-uniformed guards were on high alert, inspecting everyone who entered the premises, using scanners to search carefully for weapons, sending search teams into every corner of the building. Of course, Sielto and his Face Dancer cohorts were capable of looking like anyone, but at least Paul felt reassured that they would not be able to smuggle any weapons in.

Below them in the panoramic performance arena, the vivacious Jongleur leader bounded onto the stage as the lights rose, reflected, and were intensified into rainbows by the crystalline architecture. Rheinvar's voice boomed across the chamber crowded with thousands of spectators. "Every member of the audience is our friend. We welcome you all to celebrate Governor Kio's recent betrothal to Preto Heiron." He raised his arms to draw the onlookers' attention, as if he were a dominant source of gravity.

From her tall seat in the center of the special balcony, Alra Kio rose regally to her feet. She wore a tiara of gold threads over her dark hair, and her gown sparkled with thin folds of woven glass. She extended her left hand to take Preto's, raising the muscular young artist to his feet beside her. Her beau showed youthful enthusiasm, as well as a hint of shyness, as he bowed to the vast crowds.

When the audience applauded, Paul sensed that the cheering was not as exuberant as it should be. Governor Kio studiously did not show that she noticed anything amiss, but entire sections of the stands sounded muted.

Paul could not stop thinking about Sielto's odd comments. The Face Dancers' attuned senses would have alerted them to the disputes brewing in the local noble circles. Had they been hired to perform another "necessary assassination"? Or was there a different danger?

Earl Rhombur Vernius sat on the Governor's right in a reinforced seat. Formal robes of state and a loose sash covered the most obvious prosthetics, but his scars could not be hidden; the motors that drove his body hummed with well-contained power.

Attentive to his long-term patient, Dr. Wellington Yueh had a seat at the rear of the box, from which he could watch Rhombur more easily, albeit with a diminished view of the performance. Next to the Earl and across the balcony from Paul, Bronso eagerly waited for the performers to take the stage. He seemed fascinated by the illusory stage dressings and the dazzling lights he had helped to install.

Searching for subtleties of expression and body language, which his mother had taught him to identify, Paul could tell that Bronso and his father were both exhausted. Though he had not been privy to their discussions, Paul could imagine how drained they must both feel. Their father-son relationship had become a hurricane, the bonds spun and torn and then reassembled into a fragile construction that only time could strengthen.

After a glance at Paul, the redheaded boy looked away in apparent embarrassment and shame. Rhombur seemed more upset with Bronso because he had placed Duke Leto's son in danger, than because of the foolish risks the boy had taken for himself.

After the Jongleur leader finished his announcement, the Face Dancer performers ran onto the exhibition platform in enormous frilly costumes, ridiculous exaggerations of noble fashions, with hairdos that stood half again as tall as each wearer and open-mouthed sleeves voluminous enough to swaddle babies. The air shimmered, and the holo-sets solidified, creating a translucent illusion through which the bright reflections of crystalline facets penetrated.

A mist generator spewed clouds of billowy fog into the upper portion of the arena to simulate thunderclouds. Strobes and lasers flashed, ricocheting reflective lightning bolts from the mirrors into a beautiful tapestry of light. In a booming voice, Rheinvar bellowed to his performers, "What are you waiting for? On with the show!"

Spreading huge costume-feathered wings, two of the most agile performers leapt from high transparent shelves, buoyed by suspensors hidden in their suits. They swooped like hawks down to the stage, and then the winged performers swooped back up into the misty cloud, followed by a tangle of beams that sketched a net in the air. The crowd let out a gasp, then applauded loudly.

Admiring the technical aspects of the displays, Paul squinted at the arrangement of mirrors that he and Bronso had installed, followed the lines, and remembered the pattern he had tested many times. The webwork was complicated, composed of many strands of light, but he had been meticulous in setting up the grid, and he remembered every step of the process.

Gradually, though, he began to sense something subtly out of order. He and Bronso had followed Rheinvar's precise instructions: testing beam paths, aligning every mirror, checking and double-checking the reflections. He knew every strand of the pattern they had laid down, as well as the five amplifiers.

Though the remarkable tapestry of light was beautiful and dizzying, he saw that some of the angles were wrong. Several key intersections were *not* in the right places. No one else would have noticed, but Paul saw additional lines, out-of-place vertices. It was as if he had expected a five-pointed star, but instead saw a six-pointed star—only dozens of times more intricate than that. He tried to catch Bronso's attention, but his friend was on the opposite side of the balcony, engrossed in the performance.

His pulse quickening, Paul turned his attention back to the mirrors studded up and down the prismatic walls, in an effort to understand what had changed. Soon, one of the largest flashes was scheduled to take place, a fishnet of incandescent skeins of light, at a climactic point at the end of the first act.

He could find no other answer: Someone had climbed up there, moved the reflective surfaces, and added a substation that looked similar to the others . . . an amplifier. But who would have put an amplifier *there?*

Perhaps Rheinvar had asked other members of his stage crew to change the setup. Maybe the explanation was that simple and innocent.

Then again, Sielto had cautioned him. . . .

As the Face Dancer antics reached a crescendo, Paul edged forward in his seat. The simulated storm built, and the sonic rumble of thunder echoed inside the magnificent Theater of Shards.

Paul's gaze traced where the next network of beam paths would converge, and suddenly he *knew* that the added amplifier meant something was amiss, something that might use the architecture of the Theater itself for a dangerous purpose. He had no time to explain to his father—but he knew what he had to do.

The dramatic storm reached its climax, and the flying Face Dancers landed among the other costumed figures for a complex dance that would serve as the finale of the first half of the show.

Paul shouted at Alra Kio. "Governor, watch out!" She gave a dismissive gesture in the midst of a boom of simulated thunder, but Paul threw himself bodily onto the Governor, knocking her out of her chair and into Preto Heiron. They all tumbled to the floor.

A dance of hot threads, coherent light bouncing from mirror to mirror, pumped through the amplifier and converted into a bludgeon of energy. The blast of heat and ionized air vaporized the wobbling chair that had held the governor, spraying wooden fragments in all directions like flechette darts. Deflected by the prismatic balcony, secondary beams set fire to hanging pennants, a small buffet table, and a guard's red uniform.

The pulse lasted less than a second, and in the sudden blinding silence, the members of Rheinvar's troupe stumbled in their dance. The stunned audience hesitated with a collective indrawn breath, trying to fathom whether what they had just seen was part of the performance. A large black starburst in the Governor's Balcony showed where the deadly beam had struck.

Duke Leto grabbed his son's shoulder. "Paul, are you all right?"

The young man scrambled back to his feet, tried to compose himself. "She was in danger, sir. I saw what needed to be done."

The Governor looked at him in shock, then barked at her guards. "And you all missed something, despite the warning from this boy and his father! There will be a thorough review, and I want every guilty person arrested."

The Balut guards succeeded in extinguishing the fires and blocked the exits, as if expecting a full military assault on the private balcony. Dr. Yueh quickly checked Kio and Preto Heiron for injuries.

The terrified audience began to stream away from their seats, trying to escape, some pushing others out of the way in panic. Down below, ushers and security men commandeered the public address system and demanded that the performance be shut down and everyone remain in their seats. Few people heeded their calls for calm.

In the main arena, a frantic Rheinvar and his Face Dancers clustered together at center stage. The flying performers had stripped off their costume wings and now the whole troupe stood back to back, ready to fight for their lives if the crowd turned against them. As Paul looked at them, they rippled in his vision, and other audience members cried out, shouting toward the stage.

Paul saw what others did not, that Rheinvar had used his Master Jongleur powers to camouflage his troupe, making them vanish from the view of most of the audience. Were they part of the failed assassination attempt, or just protecting themselves from a mob?

"It's over now," Jessica said. "Paul, you saved the Governor's life, maybe all of your lives."

Guards began to flood the balcony, much too late to do anything, but they searched for other surreptitious assassins.

Leto was shaking his head while anger suffused his stormy expression. "How did you know, Paul? What did you see?"

Standing where the Governor's chair had been, Paul explained, trying to catch his breath. "The beam paths were changed, mirrors and an amplifier were added. With its architecture, the Theater itself became a weapon. If you study the performing-area blueprints, you'll see what I mean."

Rhombur strode forward, grinning at Paul. "Vermillion Hells, fine work, young man!"

Paul didn't want to take all the credit. "Bronso could have seen it, too."

The other boy crowded close, his face pale, eyes wide. "I should have figured it out earlier. Rheinvar told us about the original architect, the lost secret of the theater that died with him. The Theater of Shards was *designed* as a set of focusing lenses for exactly this sort of assassination. Apparently, the secret wasn't lost completely."

Rhombur clapped Paul on the shoulder, barely restraining the strength of his artificial limbs. "But it was *you*, young man. Leto, be proud of him!"

"Never doubt my pride in my son, Rhombur. He knows that."

Then the cyborg Earl paused, as if something tickled the back of his mind. A dozen guards poked around in the balcony seating area; others had already whisked the Governor away to safety. The shouts and turmoil made the background noise in the arena deafening, but Rhombur continued to concentrate, using his enhanced hearing. "Do you hear that vibration? A high-pitched tone?"

Alerted now, Paul felt the balcony's crystalline support structure thrumming like a tuning fork. "Some kind of resonance?" he asked. Suddenly he realized that the structure of the Theater of Shards was designed to reflect and intensify not only light but *sound*.

What if the lasers had merely been an opening salvo? A trigger to *set up* the vibration in all that layered crystal, reflecting the beams back and forth into a standing wave? The sound would continue to build, but the delay would be long enough to lure others closer. . . .

Rhombur moved with all the force and speed his cyborg body could manage. He knocked Bronso away as he pushed Paul to the other side of the balcony. "Move!"

But he couldn't get out of the way himself. The invisible but intense acoustic hammer slammed into Rhombur like two colliding Heighliners, smashed him between a pair of oncoming sonic walls.

He crumpled.

The echoes of the blast hurt Paul's ears, and made his skull ring. He pushed himself up to his hands and knees, looked around. His parents had both been knocked flat; Jessica reeled, disoriented, but not severely injured.

Paul was stunned, and the ringing remained in the back of his mind. A trap . . . a double trap. First the concentrated blast of the summed lasers, and moments later a second sonic onslaught. Killing blows of light and sound.

Three of Kio's guards nearby were crushed, dropping to the ground, killed instantly. But Rhombur. . . .

Even with his artificial reinforcements, polymer-lined torso, and prosthetic arms, the cyborg Earl's spine was bent as though someone had taken his shoulders and pelvis, then twisted him like the lid on a stubborn jar. His right prosthetic arm was folded back in on itself. Blood streamed out of his nose and eyes, and a wash of hemorrhages darkened his cheeks beneath pulped skin.

"Rhombur!" Leto threw himself down alongside his friend who had been at the center of the invisible blast. "Yueh, help him!"

The Suk doctor carried a minimal medical kit at all times, but nothing sufficient for this. Anguished, Yueh knelt beside the destroyed remnants of his most important patient.

Bronso was on his knees, sobbing over the fallen man. He touched the smashed shoulder. "Father . . . Father! Not now—I can't lead House Vernius without you! There's too much at stake, too much we still need to say to each other!"

Earl Rhombur Vernius opened his eyes, and a croak of unintelligible sound slid out of his throat. His artificial lungs were damaged, and he could barely breathe. Blood and nutrient liquids covered his face and leaked out onto the floor.

Leaning over him, Bronso continued, "I love you—I forgive you! I'm sorry for what I did, for leaving you, for denying—"

Rhombur twitched, rallied, and gathered a few last shreds of energy. He couldn't see anyone, barely managed to form his broken thoughts into words. Bronso leaned close, desperate to hear his father's final words.

Rhombur whispered, "Is *Paul* . . . safe?"

Then he shuddered, and died.

Bronso reeled back as if struck with a physical blow. Paul took a step closer to say how sorry he was, but Bronso flailed out at him, then fell weeping beside the mangled, lifeless body.

One sharp tragedy can erase years of friendship.
—THUFIR HAWAT, Weapons Master of House Atreides

In the days following the attack, Governor Kio launched a vigorous—some said excessive—investigation. The heirs of three old-guard noble families were soon implicated in the plot and, though evidence was thin, they were summarily executed in the dark of night. Afterward, Kio seized the assets of the guilty families and promptly married Preto Heiron.

Paul didn't care one bit about local politics. He'd been unable to sleep following the terrible tragedy in the Theater. In that critical moment, Rhombur had knocked Bronso aside, but his reactive movement had been to save Paul. During that instant, that flashpoint of a decision, he had not been thinking of his own son. And Bronso saw it all.

In the days while he waited for a Heighliner bound for Ix, Bronso Vernius isolated himself in his quarters, grieving. He ignored all company, refused to see Paul, and turned his back on everyone, shattered by what he had witnessed, feeling betrayed by Paul as well as his own father. "Is *Paul* safe?" The words were like the twist of a knife. Bronso would leave Balut as soon as possible, taking Rhombur's smashed patchwork body with him.

Duke Leto shook his head, sitting alone with Paul. "That young man is the sole survivor of House Vernius, the ruler of Ix, but he is soft and inexperienced. I fear the technocrats will take control and turn him into nothing more than a puppet."

"Why won't he talk with me?" Paul said. "We've been through so much together. I thought we would have done anything for each other."

Introspective now, Leto rarely left Paul's side, wistfully telling stories of how he and Rhombur had once gone diving for coral-gems and how the volatile stones had set their boat on fire. He talked about how Rhombur had saved a Guild Heighliner when the Navigator was incapacitated by tainted spice gas . . . how Atreides armies and loyal Vernius forces had fought side by side to recapture Ix from the Tleilaxu invaders. Paul had heard those legendary accounts many times before, but now he let his father talk, because the Duke needed to relive those memories.

Governor Kio hosted an impromptu celebration for Paul, during which she rewarded him for his clever and selfless actions in saving her from assassination. Paul had no interest in the rewards or accolades, and he felt that the show of appreciation was inappropriate after the death of poor Rhombur. The ceremony was just another slap in the face to the already hurting Bronso.

In the uproar following the attack, Rheinvar, his Face Dancers, the performers and members of his traveling crew were all arrested, separated, and placed in permanent cells. Even a Master Jongleur could not maintain his illusions and widespread hypnosis for so long, against so many people howling for their blood. They had been caught . . . and blamed.

Paul saw from the outset that the people of Balut—and Governor Kio herself—*needed* scapegoats, and that the troupe members would do nicely. However, because Paul had saved her life, because she offered to reward him with more than a mere medal, he pressed his advantage. At the appreciation ceremony in front of a large crowd, he asked her to grant his one request: that Rheinvar and his troupe be allowed to depart safely from Balut, on the condition that they never return. Though she grumbled, Kio reluctantly issued the command.

"They were my friends, Father," Paul explained. "They sheltered Bronso and me, kept us safe—and they taught me a great deal."

He would never forget his time among the Jongleurs, though he feared he would never see Bronso again.

TWO WEEKS AFTER they all returned to Caladan, unexpected shiploads of Atreides military forces arrived in the spaceport—the two battalions Leto had dispatched to help House Vernius. The uniformed soldiers marched off the numerous transports, but they did not appear happy to be home, at least not under these circumstances.

Duncan and Gurney emerged, both looking flustered and angry. Gurney issued his report. "We were ousted from Ix, my Lord. Bronso Vernius evicted us as soon as he returned to the Grand Palais. Gods below, he gave us three hours to pack up and get to a waiting Heighliner!"

"Three hours! After all we did for House Vernius." Duncan was incensed and not afraid to show it. "We did our duty, my Lord—exactly as you and Earl Rhombur asked of us. If we hadn't been there, Bolig Avati would've turned the Grand Palais into a factory."

"I was afraid Bronso would do something like that, sir," Paul said to his father. "He blames us."

"Misplaced blame, son—and he will realize it in time."

The last man to emerge from the military transport ship was not a soldier at all, but a slight-figured, sad-looking man with a thin face, sallow features, and long hair bound in a silver Suk ring. Dr. Wellington Yueh looked out of place, unsure of himself.

Yueh presented himself to the Duke with a careful bow. He drew a breath, pondered his words, and forged ahead. "Because I could not save Earl Rhombur from his grievous injuries, Bronso has no further need of my services. I am banished from Ix." Yueh's graying mustache drooped along the corners of his mouth as he bowed his head and spread his delicate hands. "By any chance . . . does House Atreides have use for a physician of my skills? Perhaps a tutor for the young Master, in matters other than fighting and military strategy?"

Leto did not take long to consider the man's offer. Even before Paul's birth, the Suk doctor had spent years on Caladan helping Prince Rhombur during his recovery, and he had been a wise, diligent, and loyal physician. "I've seen your work and valor over the years, Yueh. I know how hard you labored to save and repair Rhombur the first time. You added more than a dozen years onto his life, and because of that, he was able to be a good father to Bronso. The boy doesn't appreciate that yet, but I hope he will someday. Your loyalty is without question."

Jessica looked at Leto, then at the Suk practitioner. "You are welcome here on Caladan, Dr. Yueh. Any wise counsel you can offer Paul would be appreciated. His education on Ix was cut dramatically short, and it's not likely he'll go back to finish it."

Paul felt a heavy sadness inside and looked up at his parents. "This is a terrible rift between our Great Houses. How long do you think it will last?"

Leto merely shook his head. "It may never be healed."

PART III

10,207 AG

*Two months after the end of Muad'Dib's reign. Regent Alia
struggles to cement her control over the Imperium.*

What I write and what I know are not always the same thing. Muad'Dib placed a great responsibility on my shoulders, and I accept it as a duty that is holier and more compelling than anything the Sisterhood demands of me. I will continue to write as the needs of history require. My knowledge of true events, however, remains unchanged.

—PRINCESS IRULAN, response to Wallach IX demands

As Jessica finished her lengthy story, the restless but fascinated Irulan began to pace around the garden enclosure. She shook her head, as if to scatter the words that buzzed around her like biting flies. "So, more parts of Paul's past unfold. He never told me such things, never hinted—"

Jessica's throat was scratchy. "You already knew that he kept many things from you. You've had to rewrite your stories to incorporate new information. Paul understood exactly what he was doing." Suddenly leery of being overheard, she spoke quietly in one of the Bene Gesserit languages that no normal spy would ever understand. "Believe me, you do Paul no service by writing this sanitized, glorified version of him. You are sowing a minefield for the future of humanity."

Irulan rounded on her, speaking in the same language. "How do you know what he would have wanted? You left Paul and Arrakis, abandoned the Jihad. For most of your son's rule, during his worst stresses and challenges, you were on Caladan. I may have been his wife in name only, but at least I was at his side."

Jessica hesitated, not wanting to reveal all her secrets just yet. "I was still his mother. Even during his rule, Paul . . . trusted me with things he never told you."

The two reached a flagstoned contemplation area, where a pool of golden, mutated carp swam beneath a transparent moisture-seal dome. Irulan heaved a long sigh and spoke again in common Galach, not needing to hide her words. "I agree, philosophically, that it's important for the people to know what you have revealed to me. While the background material doesn't excuse Bronso's crimes, at least it explains his bitter grudge against Paul. It exposes his motivation for spreading destructive lies. His hatred is personal, obsessive, irrational."

Feeling sad, Jessica said, "You still don't see. As a Bene Gesserit, *you* of all people should understand that when one wheel turns, it turns another, and yet another." The Princess stiffened, looked insulted. While she stared down at the circling koi in the shielded pond, Jessica faced her evenly. "Listen to me, Irulan. You know only part of the story." Catching her glance, she moved her fingers in an even more secret Bene Gesserit coded language. "Bronso was, and is, doing *exactly what Paul wanted*."

Irulan crossed her arms in a closed, obstinate gesture, and she spoke defiantly out loud, still in Galach. "What Paul wanted? To defame his character? How can that possibly be? Nobody will believe that! Certainly, Alia will never believe it." Now, her fingers flickered as she added silently, "And she will never let me write what you're saying. It is ridiculous, and dangerous."

"It is indeed dangerous knowledge, Irulan. I realize that. You will have to be cautious—but let me tell you the rest, so that you can decide for yourself."

Irulan's expression became stony, and she erected a wall of denial around herself. Leaving the koi pond behind, she stopped at a doorway that led into cool interior shadows. "I'll tell you when I'm ready to continue this."

The greatest obligation of a mother is to support her children, to show them love and respect, and to accept them. Sometimes this is a most difficult task.

—LADY JESSICA, Duchess of Caladan

Stirring up so many memories from her past had exhausted Jessica, and she went to snatch a moment of quiet within the crèche where her grandchildren were held. Harah was still there watching over the infants, just as she had done with little Alia. Stilgar's wife had stood as a determined wall against all the mutterings and Fremen prejudices about Alia's strangenesses. Even as the girl matured into a powerful role, first as priestess and then as Regent, Jessica knew that Harah would always have a special place in her daughter's heart.

When the priest guards allowed Jessica to enter the lush conservatory, Harah bowed deferentially. Jessica touched the woman's chin and raised her face, saw the dark hair that swept back like raven's wings at the sides. "Come now, Harah, we've known each other too long for such formalities."

Harah stepped back so Jessica could peer down at the two silent and eerily alert babies. "Now would you like to hold your grandchildren?" Her voice held an undertone of disapproval that Jessica had taken so long to come.

Strangely reticent, Jessica bent down and picked up the girl. Ghanima settled into the crook of her grandmother's arm as if she belonged there, accepting this new person without fussing or crying. From the basket below, little Leto II watched with clear blue eyes wide open, as though to make sure his twin sister was all right. Given that their father was the Kwisatz Haderach, what kind of children might they grow up to be?

Alia burst into the crèche room with Duncan Idaho close beside her; she moved with an excitement, a cheerful energy that she had not shown since Jessica's arrival on Dune. Alia wore a broad smile. "I'd hoped to find you here, Mother. I wanted you to be the first to hear our announcement. Ah—and Harah, too! This is perfect." Alia folded her fingers around Duncan's, and the ghola stared with his eerie metal eyes.

Harah took the baby back from Jessica, replaced her in the small crib. Alia tossed her own coppery hair, making her announcement. "We have seen the need. After so much turmoil, the Imperium needs something to cheer, a pleasant spectacle that can show new hope for the future. Duncan and I have decided to move quickly. We have no doubts."

Jessica felt an unexpected knot in her stomach, instinctively wondering what her daughter had decided to do. Why wasn't the ghola saying anything?

In a bright voice that sounded like an imitation of joy rather than real happiness, Alia said, "Duncan and I are going to be married. We're a perfect match, and we love each other in ways that most people cannot understand."

Alia was barely sixteen, and Duncan was practically Jessica's age— the original Duncan at least. But Alia had been born with a panoply of adult memories; inside her mind, the girl had already experienced countless marriages, lifelong happy relationships, as well as those shattered by tragedy and strife.

And Duncan wasn't the same Duncan either.

Jessica tried to find the right thing to say. "This is . . . unexpected. Are you sure you aren't being too impulsive?"

Instantly, she regretted her own comment. All decisions didn't have to be the result of cold calculations—she wasn't a Mentat! Despite her Bene Gesserit training (and much to the Sisterhood's dismay), Jessica made decisions with her heart as well as her mind. She had done that when she'd chosen to conceive Paul in the first place. And Alia afterward . . .

Alia spoke with great surety. "Duncan is the right man, Mother, the man who can help me hold the Imperium together. I hope to have your support."

Jessica looked at her daughter. "As your mother, how could I offer anything else?" The smile and the sincerity, though, came much harder. "And who could ask for a braver, more loyal man than Duncan Idaho?"

The ghola spoke up for the first time, his words and voice sounding so familiar. "I realize this must be strange to you, Lady Jessica. I died for you and for your son. And now I love your daughter, who wasn't even born before my first life ended."

Jessica wondered why it was that she greeted this news with so little enthusiasm. *Am I just being selfish?* she thought. *My Duke loved me, but he never made me his wife. Paul loved Chani, but never made her his wife.*

And now Alia and Duncan. A strange pair, but oddly suited to each other.

Jessica reached out to place one hand on the ghola's arm and the other on Alia's. "Of course you have my blessing."

"Oh, child, I do hope you will be happy," Harah said. "You need strength. And if this man is the one to give it to you, then you two must be wed."

"Together, we will rule the Imperium and keep it strong." Alia glanced down at the babies. "Until Leto and Ghanima come of age, of course."

Bless the Maker and His water. Bless the coming and going of Him. May His passage cleanse the world. May He keep the world for His people.

—Fremen water ceremony

The excavated cave was a temporary camp, not an actual sietch, just a known stopping place for Fremen traveling across the desert. Located in Plaster Basin, the cave was far from the cultural amenities of Arrakeen: the shops, restaurants, and spaceport. And far from all the people.

Stilgar had chosen the perfect place for Chani's water ceremony, and Jessica approved of it. While Alia was beginning her wedding preparations, as well as responding to a new inflammatory document that Bronso of Ix had released, Jessica and the Naib had slipped away into the desert, to be among the Fremen again.

After so many years, Jessica knew she should feel like a stranger among these people, an interloper, but knew she belonged entirely. Stilgar had summoned the appropriate Fremen, arranged the ceremony, and Jessica felt a deep sense of reverence here, an intimacy. Yes, after the circus of Paul's funeral, this was how such things should be, much more like the private remembrance she had given Paul out at Sietch Tabr. She was sure Chani would have approved of this. And Alia's other ceremony for Chani, using ordinary water, was irrelevant to the true mourners.

The few habitable grottoes that remained in the Plaster Basin caves had once been part of a much larger complex used as a biological test area by Kynes-the-Umma, also known as Pardot Kynes, the father of Liet and grandfather of Chani. Until recent years, the elder Kynes was barely known in the Imperium, but because of the effect he had on Arrakis, his name was spoken of everywhere.

Pardot had been the instigator of terraforming activities on Dune, and a truly visionary man. Almost half a century ago, the elder Kynes had begun his work using materials gleaned from abandoned Imperial research stations. He had applied knowledge learned from formal Imperial ecological training as well as experiences gleaned from surviving on numerous harsh planets. Here, inside the deep caves of Plaster Basin, Pardot had created an underground oasis to prove that a garden could thrive on Dune. But over the years too much moisture had weakened the cave walls, causing a structural collapse that destroyed his oasis and killed the man.

But not his dreams. Never his dreams.

Dedicated followers of Kynes's vision had returned here to reestablish a few plantings of saguaro, mesquite, low prickly pear cactus, and even two water-greedy dwarf portyguls. Yes, Jessica thought, a fitting place to honor Chani in the Fremen way. It was not a spectacle for strangers.

Stilgar had learned a great deal about politics and human nature in the years since he began following Muad'Dib. Here, though, he was about to do something without politics for the young female member of his troop who had been his niece, and so much more to so many people.

Taking care not to spill a drop, Jessica and the Naib emptied the literjons of water that he had carefully smuggled out of the Citadel of Muad'Dib over the course of several weeks. They poured the liquid into a large communal basin that rested on a shelf of rock. Moisture seals had been closed across the cave entrance, so that the men and women could remove their noseplugs and face masks. The scent of water in the air made Jessica's blood flow faster.

As if she were a priestess, as Alia had become, Jessica turned to look upon the hundred gathered Fremen. Stilgar stood beside her like a pillar, gruff and respectful. Jessica had helped him choose each participant after careful consideration, men and women from Sietch Tabr who had traveled with Chani and Paul during the guerrilla struggles against Beast Rabban and the Harkonnens. Though years had passed, Jessica knew every face and name. Surprisingly, even Harah was here—Stilgar's wife, Chani's friend. But they had to keep this ceremony a secret from Alia.

These Fremen respected Chani as a *Fremen*, not just because of her connection to Paul. Jessica knew they were not religious sycophants, not self-important members of the Qizarate. They represented many tribes, and would take this memory back with them, and spread it among their people.

When all the observers stood silent, their voices quelled in pregnant anticipation, Stilgar deferred and Jessica began to speak. "We have gathered for Chani, beloved daughter of Liet, granddaughter of Kynes-the-Umma, and mother of Muad'Dib's children."

A murmur passed like a sunset breeze through the people. Jessica looked out and saw Harah's eyes shining, her earnest face bobbing up and down as she nodded.

Stilgar touched the edge of the basin, ran his finger along the ornate bas-relief designs. With a quick twist, he unsealed the access lid and removed it, so that the precious liquid could be dispensed. "The flesh belongs to the individual, but the water belongs to the tribe, and to the dreams of the tribe. Thus Chani returns her water to us."

"'The flesh belongs to the individual, but the water belongs to the tribe.'" The gathered witnesses repeated the phrase, intoning it like a prayer. Here in the confined cave chamber, Jessica could smell the heady overlapping mixture of moist odors that combined dust, dried sweat, and melange.

When Stilgar fell silent, she continued. "Though the Fremen have sipped and collected and stolen every drop for the green transformation of Arrakis, this place in Plaster Basin has a special significance to us all. These plantings are symbols, reminders of what Chani's grandfather and father envisioned for Dune. We now use Chani's water to help them thrive. Green is the color of mourning, but here it is also the color of hope."

Stilgar withdrew a demi-cup of water from the basin and walked to the nearest mesquite, whose warm multichord scent lifted like a whisper from its leaves and bark. "Chani was my friend. She was a member of my Fremen troop, a fighter, a boon companion. She was with me when we found a boy and his mother lost in the desert. She did not know it then, but she had already lost her father Liet to the Harkon-nens . . . and yet she found her true love." He poured the water at the base of the plant, letting it soak into the thirsty roots. "The strength of a woman can be boundless. In this manner, the sacred ruh-spirit of Chani, beloved companion of Paul-Muad 'Dib, remains an eternal part of Dune."

Jessica carried a second tiny cup of water to one of the struggling portyguls. The six hard, green fruits dangling from its branches would turn orange like a setting sun as they ripened. "Chani was my friend. She was the mother of my grandchildren, and she was my son's true love." It had been hard for her at first, but Jessica had indeed accepted Paul's Fremen woman, had told him that she loved Chani herself. She drew a breath now. "Even when all of humanity shouted his name, she made Paul remember that he was human."

Stilgar motioned for Harah to be next. His wife, normally so out-spoken, sounded nervous as she spoke. Jessica could see the emotions barely held in check by her set face. "Chani was my friend, a Fremen woman and a Fremen warrior. She was—" Harah's voice cracked. "As Usul was the base of the pillar, she was his base, *his* support."

The hundred guests came forward in a special type of communion, doling out sips of Chani's essence in a hushed and reverential ceremony. They took small measures of Chani's water for the plantings, while the remainder would be poured into the communal reservoir.

"It is said that Muad'Dib will never be found, but all men will find him," Stilgar announced as the final audience member emptied his demi-cup. "Chani's water will never be found, yet all Fremen in the tribes will find her."

Jessica added, "She did not wish to be deified. Chani, daughter of Liet, will be sacred to us in her own way. She needs nothing more, nor do we."

None of the Fremen here comprehended the vastness of Muad'Dib's empire or the underlying tangles of his Jihad, but they knew Chani, and understood what this ceremony meant for her identity as a Fremen.

When the somber gathering was over, Jessica whispered, "We did a good thing today, Stilgar."

"Yes, and now we can go back to Arrakeen and continue as before, but I feel rejuvenated. I must confess to you, Sayyadina Jessica, that I have long experienced a desire to withdraw from the government, to make myself remote from the wider and more unpleasant realities I've seen . . . just as Muad'Dib withdrew from his place in history by walking off into the desert."

"Sometimes it is a brave gesture to withdraw." Jessica remembered how she had turned her back during the heat of the Jihad, how she would soon return to Caladan to govern the people there. "And sometimes it is braver to stay."

He began fitting his stillsuit, twisted a noseplug into place, and brushed dust from his cloak. "I will continue to advise Regent Alia, and will watch over the children of Muad'Dib. In those duties, I shall always hold true to my Fremen self. Come, we must return to Arrakeen, before your daughter notices that we are gone."

My loyalty has always been to House Atreides, yet the needs of the various Atreides are often contradictory—Alia, Jessica, Paul, Duke Leto, even the newborn twins. That is where loyalty and honor become complicated and depend upon good judgment.

—GURNEY HALLECK

Though Bronso of Ix had been a wanted man for seven years already, Alia launched an even more vigorous hunt to find him and stop his never-ending character-assassination campaign against Paul Atreides. She felt his diatribes as personal affronts, and she wanted him captured before her wedding.

She placed Duncan Idaho in charge, with Gurney Halleck to offer any possible help—just like old times.

The ghola met with Gurney in a private room in a large and mostly empty wing of the Citadel. "Remember when we both went chasing after Rabban at the end of the military debacle on Grumman?" Gurney asked, taking a seat. "We ran him down, cornered him above a hydroelectric dam."

Duncan looked at him without amusement. "I see you're still testing me—it was at a waterfall in a steep canyon, not a dam. That was when I first blooded my own sword." He narrowed his artificial eyes. "Bronso is a far more devious man than Beast Rabban, and much more elusive. You should concentrate on hunting him, not on testing my memories."

Gurney made a low grunt. "You may have all your memories, my friend, but you don't seem to have your old sense of humor."

Duncan leaned forward, elbows on his knees in a surprisingly casual gesture. "We've got a job to do, and Bronso will not make it easy. Over the years, he's attempted to eliminate all images of himself from public records, and he's been so successful that he must have had help from influential sources—the Spacing Guild, perhaps, or the Bene Gesserit.

"Paul made powerful enemies. Therefore, Bronso has allies out in the Imperium, people who agree with his assessment of Muad'Dib's governmental excesses—disenfranchised members of the Landsraad, certainly the Guild and the Sisterhood, along with loyalists of the fallen Corrino Emperor."

Gurney frowned, scratched his chin. "But Bronso has also mortally offended many. I can't believe someone hasn't turned him in by now."

"The first time he was arrested, it did no good," Duncan said.

"Aye, but he wouldn't have gotten away if you or I had been in charge of security."

Three years earlier, during the final battles of the Jihad, Bronso Vernius had been thrown into a death cell and interrogated by ruthless Qizara inquisitors. According to the sketchy records Gurney could uncover about the embarrassing incident, the priests had kept Bronso there in secret, not even informing Muad'Dib . . . yet Bronso had escaped, and continued his seditious crusade.

Given the incredible security inside Muad'Dib's citadel, it did not seem possible that the renegade could have broken free without help—one rumor even suggested that Paul himself had a hand in it, although Gurney couldn't imagine why he would have done that. The Qizarate had tried to cover up the debacle, but word slipped out anyway, and the legend of Bronso of Ix grew. . . .

Now, after the Ixian's outrageous actions during Paul's funeral, Alia offered vast rewards of spice, and blessings in the name of Muad'Dib, for Bronso's arrest. But he was as mysterious and impossible to find as the outlaw Muad'Dib had been during his desert years. Having studied Paul so thoroughly—if only to criticize him—Bronso might be using similar techniques to elude capture.

"He couldn't have eliminated *all* images of himself," Gurney said. "Bronso was the heir to House Vernius. There must be Landsraad records?"

"They were either lost in the Jihad and the sacking of Kaitain, or intentionally deleted by cooperative Landsraad representatives. Paul made few friends there, and under Alia their power is slipping even further." Duncan fashioned a smile. "However, we've obtained images from the Ixian Confederation, who have no great love for him. They're still trying to buy themselves back into Alia's good graces. And I have a perfect memory of Bronso from when he was younger, when he was with Paul."

"He was just a boy then. This is a lot different from the last time you and I went hunting for him."

"But we will find him—as we did before." Duncan drew out a crystal-pad projector, called up an entry. "I followed the distribution of his new tracts. They seem to appear at random, all over the place, on world after world, involving people who have no obvious connection to each other, no political similarities, no apparent grudges against Paul. I believe Bronso has a Heighliner distribution network, using the Guild, possibly even without their knowledge."

Gurney scowled. "On our journey here, Jessica and I saw one of his manifestos left out in a public drinking establishment. At least some of the Wayku are involved. Bronso may have thousands of converts helping him, slipping publications to random travelers who inadvertently carry them to far-flung places, like a gaze hound transports ticks."

Duncan showed no surprise at the idea. "I've already developed a plan. I have recruited nine hundred trained Mentats. Each one has memorized Bronso's appearance from the images the Ixians provided, and they keep watch for him in spaceports, in cities, anywhere he is likely to appear."

"*Nine hundred* Mentats? Gods below, I didn't know you could gain access to so many."

"Nine hundred. If any one of them sees Bronso, he will be recognized and reported." Duncan stood up as if to adjourn the meeting. "I believe we should concentrate our efforts here on Arrakis. It's a gut feeling."

"A gut feeling? Now there's the old Duncan. You truly think he's here somewhere?"

"Specifically, in Arrakeen."

Gurney's brow furrowed. "Why would Bronso come here? He knows it's not safe. This would be the last place I'd expect to see him."

"That is precisely why I believe he's here, or soon will be. I've performed a detailed analysis of the movements and distributions of his publications. It fits his pattern. I can explain the Mentat derivation if you like, but it will take some time." Duncan raised his eyebrows.

"I trust your conclusions, whether or not I understand them. Meanwhile, I'll put the word out among my old smuggler contacts. There's a chance Bronso might seek their aid—his grandfather Dominic had quite a network among them." *Including me.* "We'll find him."

Duncan walked to the door. "Of course we will. We have resources he cannot match. And if you and I work together, no man can stand against us."

GURNEY HALLECK WAS always pleased when Jessica asked to see him. She called for him to meet her in the underground levels of the palace; the tunnels that had once been beneath the Arrakeen Residency were now access passages to huge buried cisterns that held water for daily use by the thousands of inhabitants. She had recently returned from the desert, but had been reluctant to tell him about it.

Normally, whenever the mother of Muad'Dib moved from chamber to chamber or went out into the city, a flock of functionaries followed her, but Jessica had brushed them aside under the pretense that she needed to inspect the palace's water supply without any interference. Gurney knew the real reason she had gone alone: She wanted a quiet, private place to speak with him.

He found her in a shadowy chamber lit by sparse glowglobes. A coolness hung in the stone-lined tunnels, and the shadows themselves seemed moist. Like music, Gurney could hear the background sounds of water dripping into the reservoirs, reclaimed moisture from the halls above.

Thanks to the long-term plans of Pardot Kynes and his son Liet, Fremen had been stockpiling enormous amounts of water for the eventual transformation of Arrakis. Even so, these huge polymer-lined reservoirs would have astonished inhabitants of the old Dune. Such a hoard proved the power and glory of Muad'Dib.

Jessica stood with her back to him. Her bronze hair was set in an intricate knot, her gown and demeanor an odd combination of Fremen practicality, sedate Bene Gesserit conservativism, and regal beauty.

It had been sixteen years since Leto's death, and in that time Gurney had struggled with his changing perception of Jessica. They had been close friends for a long time, and he could not stop his awakening feelings for her, though he tried to dispel them. He could not forget that when they were first reunited out in the desert—Gurney with his band of smugglers, Paul and Jessica with their Fremen—Gurney had tried to kill her, convinced she was a traitor to House Atreides. He had believed the lies spread by Harkonnens.

Gurney no longer doubted Jessica's integrity.

By the cistern, she turned to look at him, her face little changed despite the intervening years, but not through Bene Gesserit age-defying tricks. Jessica was simply beautiful, and she did not need chemicals or cellular adjustments to retain her stunning appearance.

He gave a formal bow. "My Lady, you summoned me?"

"I have a favor to ask, Gurney, something very important, and very private." She did not use Voice on him and applied no apparent Bene Gesserit techniques, but in that instant he would have done anything for her.

"It shall be done—or I will die in the attempt."

"I don't want you to die, Gurney. What I have in mind will require finesse and the utmost care, but I believe you are fully capable of it."

He knew he was flushing. "You honor me." He was not so foolish as to think that Jessica was unaware of his feelings for her, no matter how he struggled to maintain a placid demeanor and a respectable distance. Jessica was Bene Gesserit trained, a Reverend Mother in her own right; she could read his moods no matter how cleverly he covered them up.

But what *kind* of love did he feel for her? That was unclear even to Gurney. He loved her as his Duke's lady, and was loyal to her as Paul's mother. He was physically attracted to her; no doubt of that. Yet his sense of Atreides honor muddied all of his feelings. He had been her companion for so many years; they were friends and partners, and they ruled Caladan well together. Out of respect for Duke Leto, Gurney had always fought back his romantic feelings for her. But it had been so many years. He was lonely; she was lonely. They were perfect for each other.

Still, he didn't dare. . . .

She startled him out of his reverie. "Alia asked you and Duncan to track down Bronso of Ix."

"Yes, my Lady, and we will do our utmost. Bronso's writings promote chaos in this delicate time."

"That's what my daughter says, and that's exactly what she's forced Irulan to write." Troubled wrinkles creased Jessica's forehead. "But Alia doesn't understand everything. What I ask of you now, Gurney, I cannot explain, because I've made other promises."

"I don't need explanations, merely your instructions, my Lady. Tell me what you need."

She took a step closer to him, and he focused only on her. "I need you to *not* find Bronso, Gurney. It will be difficult, because Duncan is sure to throw all of his resources into the hunt. But I have my reasons. Bronso of Ix must be allowed to continue his work."

A storm of doubts swept into Gurney's mind, but he stopped himself from uttering them. "I gave you my word that I wouldn't ask questions. If that is all, my Lady?"

Jessica looked at him intently. Her eyes, which used to be clear green, had taken on a blue cast from melange usage over the years. Beyond that, he thought he saw a hint of affection for him there, more than usual.

She turned back to stare at the rock wall of the cistern. "Thank you for trusting me, Gurney. I appreciate that more than you can ever know."

Evil does not have a face, nor does it have a soul.

—ANONYMOUS

Though Rheinvar the Magnificent had kept a low profile for many years since the debacle at Balut's Theater of Shards, his Jongleur troupe still performed on backwater worlds and fringe outposts. The ubiquitous Wayku kept track of their movements as they slipped from system to system.

Bronso, traveling under a succession of assumed names and theatrical disguises, thought fondly of the troupe leader, one of the rare Master Jongleurs. Now, he needed Rheinvar and his Face Dancers to help him on his mission.

When the Guildship arrived at the secondary world of Izvinor, the Ixian used his ID scramblers to pose as a steerage-class passenger and travel down to the surface. There, he changed clothes, altered his identity again, and became a businessman looking for investment opportunities in keefa futures.

He had already sent word ahead to the Jongleur encampment, and as he made his way to the rendezvous hotel, he saw leaflets and placards advertising the upcoming performance. He smiled. Very little seemed to have changed.

"This suite is our finest," the bellman said, guiding a suspensor platform filled with Bronso's luggage into the parlor room. A smooth-faced man with a narrow black mustache and a bald head, the bellman was the sort of fellow whose age could have been anywhere between thirty-five and fifty-five.

After the door closed behind them, the man dutifully began to unload the bags. "Do you have fresh fruit?" Bronso asked.

"The mumberries are ready for picking." The bellman began to hang clothing in a closet.

"Too sweet for my tastes." With this exchange of code words, the other man's features shifted, rearranged, and then settled into an appearance that Bronso recalled warmly from his youth. "Ah, now you look like Sielto—but are you truly him?"

"Who is truly anyone? Every person is illusion to some degree. But . . . yes, I am the Sielto you remember. Rheinvar awaits you with great anticipation."

After a series of secretive movements through the city, doubling back, changing clothes, Bronso walked with the Face Dancer to the simple camp—very much the same as the tents he remembered from his boyhood, though they were a bit more battered and threadbare. Ten dancers practiced on dry grass, turning somersaults and vaulting over one another.

"These days, we no longer play the big palaces and theaters," said a familiar, rich voice. "But we get by."

Bronso felt years of anxiety and heavy responsibilities lift away as he turned to face the Jongleur leader. Rheinvar wore one of his trademark white suits, though his top hat was nowhere in sight; his dark brown hair still had only a little gray in it. "You haven't aged a day in twenty years!"

"Many things have changed . . . only appearances remain the same." The troupe leader gestured for Bronso to follow him into an administrative tent. "And you, young man—you've become quite infamous. I could lose my head just for speaking with you." Rheinvar gave a self-deprecating shrug. "Though some say that would be no great loss to the universe." He extended his hands, locked his fingers together, cracked his knuckles. "Your message said you need my help. Have you come to work as a roustabout again?"

"I'm not applying for a job, old friend. I am offering one for your Face Dancers in their . . . extracurricular capacity." He glanced over his shoulder at Sielto. "Years ago, before I fled Ix, I transferred my entire fortune from House Vernius to hidden accounts. I can pay you quite extravagantly."

"Very interesting. And the job?"

Without flinching, Bronso looked into the Jongleur leader's eyes. "I want you to help me assassinate someone."

"If you're willing to pay a vast fortune, the target must be an incredibly important person. Who could possibly warrant so much money?"

Bronso glanced through the partially open flap of the tent and lowered his voice. "The Emperor Paul-Muad'Dib."

Rheinvar took a step backward, then burst out laughing. "You've come to us too late. Haven't you heard? Muad'Dib is already dead."

"I don't mean physically. I mean his reputation, the myth and distortions around him. I have eyes inside the Citadel of Muad'Dib, and I watch what is happening there, and while I disagree with a great many political decisions, I have a very specific focus. I need to kill the idea that Paul was a messiah. The people, and the historians, must see that he was human—and deeply flawed. I need you to help me assassinate his character."

"I hear that Muad'Dib killed a Face Dancer, at the end," Sielto said with no emotion whatsoever. "An infiltrator and conspirator named Scytale. Maybe that's a good enough reason for us to help you against him."

Rheinvar continued to scowl. "It will be dangerous. Very dangerous."

Bronso paced the tent floor, talking quickly. "You only need to provide me with cover and help me distribute propaganda against him. The Wayku have assisted me for years, but I want to do something even larger in scale now, building on what I have already done. I trust your skills and your subtlety, Rheinvar. In fact, in coming here I am trusting you with my life. I hope you deserve that trust, and that my childhood memories aren't deceiving me."

The troupe leader looked over at Sielto, and a wordless understanding passed between them. The Master Jongleur sat down behind a cluttered table, folded his hands in front of him, and grinned. "Then allow me to demonstrate a bit of trust myself, to seal our cooperation. I'm surprised you haven't figured it out, a bright man like yourself."

In front of Bronso's eyes, the old man's features altered, flowed, and settled into a bland, emotionless countenance. Another Face Dancer! "Vermillion Hells! Now I see why you haven't changed in all these years."

"The first Rheinvar—the one you knew as a boy—was indeed human. But seventeen years ago, after an assassination job went awry, he was severely injured during our escape. He died aboard the Heighliner shortly after it left orbit. Fortunately, no one but us saw him perish. We decided not to throw away his fame and reputation, his *worth* as the troupe leader, and our perfect cover.

"And so I was the Face Dancer chosen to take his place. But without the real Rheinvar, we lost our inspiration, and our stature as performers declined. I can mimic some of his skills, but I am not truly a Master Jongleur. I do not have his amazing hypnotic and manipulative powers. I can only pretend to be who he was. Without him, we lost something indefinable."

"Something human, perhaps?" Bronso asked.

The two Face Dancers shrugged. "Do you still want our help?"

"More than ever, since now I've learned something about you that others do not know—something you might not even know yourselves."

The shape-shifter assumed Rheinvar's familiar appearance again. "Oh? And what is that, my friend?"

"That all Face Dancers are not the same inside."

We live our lives, dream our dreams, and scheme our schemes.
Shai-Hulud watches all.

—Fremen wisdom

Before Alia could become too involved in her wedding preparations, she went to Jessica, preoccupied with another matter. She wasn't distracted or disturbed, but engrossed. "I have something you and I should do together, Mother—something I'd like us to share. It will put us both on the same course." She seemed very excited by the prospect.

Curious, Jessica followed as Alia and Duncan led her down numerous corridors and stairwells beneath the keep into a large underground chamber, hewn by hand. Glowglobes bathed the grotto with light tuned to the white spectrum of Arrakis's sun, so that the sandplankton could survive. Jessica smelled powerful conflicting odors—dust, sand, water, and the rough flinty stench of a worm.

"My brother created this place in the second year of his reign." Alia inhaled deeply. "You know why, don't you?"

Jessica looked across the large, deep sandy area encircled by a wide trough of water. Staring with intense focus, she could see tiny vibrations, ripples of movement beneath the sand. "Paul consumed the spice essence to enhance and pursue his visions. He kept a stunted worm here for whenever he required the Water of Life."

"Yes. Sometimes he shared the converted spice essence with his circle of closest advisers. Other times he made the inner journey alone." She paused, as if hesitant to make her suggestion, then smiled at Jessica. "Would you travel that path with me now, Mother? We did it together when I was but a fetus in your womb—when you were changed into a Reverend Mother, and I was changed into . . . myself." She warmly took Duncan's hand, but kept her eyes focused on her mother. "This will be the last opportunity before our wedding. I would consider it a sacrament. Who knows what we might discover together?"

Though she was uneasy, Jessica could not turn down her daughter's request. The awakening effect of the awareness-spectrum drug intensified mental connections, creating a blurred form of shared consciousness. She and her daughter had already experienced a oneness, a unified pattern of thoughts that had gradually faded as Alia matured, and Jessica lived at a distance on Caladan. Now, Jessica did not want to expose all of her secrets to her daughter. All of *Paul's* secrets. There were some things Alia could not know, would not understand.

Fortunately, Jessica was much stronger than she had been on that first night long ago during the tau orgy in sietch. In addition to her own experiences, the damaged and changed Tessia Vernius had shown her many ways to protect herself back on Wallach IX. Jessica could build mental walls securely enough. She would be safe. "Yes, Alia. This is something we should do together."

Five amazon guards had followed them into the underground chamber, accompanied by a Fremen watermaster. Duncan signaled to the watermaster, who turned a heavy iron wheel on the stone wall. Gears shifted and machinery dropped, releasing a false floor beneath a narrow area of sand to create a trough, into which water flooded. The channel divided the enclosed dry space in half. A small worm erupted from beneath the sand, thrashing away from the flowing water as if it were acid.

It was a monster by any definition—a long serpentine form, a meter in girth and five meters long, the round mouth full of crystalline teeth, its eyeless head bobbing to and fro. By Arrakis standards, however, this was a stunted, immature specimen.

With a yell, Alia's amazons lifted their metal staffs and jumped down onto the sand. They encircled the worm and struck its rippled segments with sharp blows. The creature thrashed and attacked, but the women dodged out of the way. Jessica realized the guards had done this before, and perhaps often. She wondered how frequently her daughter consumed the spice essence. And how frequently Paul had done it.

The watermaster worked another metal wheel, which created a new trough across the sand, blocking the worm with a second line of water, forcing it into a smaller and smaller area. As though it were an exhilarating sport, the women threw themselves upon the creature, grappling with it, wrestling it down to the sand.

The Fremen watermaster flooded more of the sand, and the stunted worm writhed against the liquid touch, jerking with electric spasms of fury. But the women caught the creature, pushed it down, submerged it until its head was beneath the deep water, its mouth agape. With splash and spray turning the sand to a slurry of brown grains, they held the beast under until the poisonous water had filled its gullet.

In its last spasms, the amazons hauled the worm's dripping head out of the trough, while the watermaster ran forward with a large basin. Dying, the worm spewed out a cloudy liquid. The thick and potent bile was one of the deadliest known poisons, yet when catalyzed by a Sayyadina, it became a means of euphoria, a way to open the Inner Eye of awareness.

With a flushed face and bright gaze, the muddy watermaster stumbled up to them carrying the basin; its poisonous contents sloshing against the sides of the container. "Lady Alia, Lady Jessica—a bountiful harvest. Enough to make the tau drug for many of the faithful."

Alia removed a small copper dipper from the side of the basin, filled it, and extended the ladle toward her mother. "Shall we both do the honors?"

Jessica took a mouthful of the foul-tasting alkaloid fluid, and her daughter followed suit. Holding it in her mouth, Jessica altered the chemical signature of the substance, manipulating the elemental bonds with her Bene Gesserit abilities, turning it into a seed chain of molecules that, when she and Alia both spat it back into the basin, transformed the bile from the dying worm. In a chain reaction, the liquid became something else.

The amazon guards and the watermaster watched with awe and hints of greedy hunger. Alia took the ladle again and drank deeply of the converted substance, as did her mother.

Alia extended the ladle to Duncan, who stood guard behind them, but the ghola refused. "I must remain alert. I have seen what this does to you."

"You must see what it does to *you*. Take it, Duncan. Marry me in another way."

Like a good soldier, he did as he was commanded. *Duncan, always the same, always loyal to the Atreides. . . .*

Before the drug could take effect, Alia offered the basin to her guards. "This is a blessing from the sister and mother of Muad'Dib. Take it, share it. Perhaps others will find the truth they seek."

As the others hurried away, Jessica felt the drug thrum more and more loudly against her consciousness. Alia reached out to touch her, and Jessica responded, but she maintained her reserve, erecting a protective barrier inside her mind, letting her daughter see her and know her . . . but not everything.

Instead of answers, Jessica felt questions growing louder in her consciousness, the doubts, the turmoil that lay ahead, the empty and dangerous gulf of an uncontrolled future and the many paths that stretched out for humankind . . . possibilities upon possibilities upon possibilities. She knew this was the trap of prescience. *Seeing* futures did a person no good, unless one could determine the actual future that would occur.

Feeling the pull of the drug, Jessica heard and experienced changes in her body's chemistry. She began to drift across endless dunes in her mind, back through countless generations, a chain of female ancestors all standing there to advise her, to reminisce about their long-forgotten lives, to criticize or to praise. Jessica had always kept them at a secure distance; she had seen what could happen to a Reverend Mother who let those constant haranguing voices dominate an individual personality.

How had Alia protected herself against the inner clamor? Unprepared and unborn, she could have initially drowned in the onslaught of all those lives. How had she protected herself?

And now, at the end of that long succession of past lives, Jessica discovered a figure standing before her in a robe, the face covered by a hood that flapped in a silent wind. A male figure. *Paul?* Something compelled her to turn, and at the other end of eternity she found her son standing there as well, but he had no face or voice.

Finally, she heard his words in her head: "There are few who can protect me . . . but many who would destroy me. You could do both, Mother—as could Alia. Which will you choose?"

She tried to ask for more information, but could not find her own voice. In response to her silence, Paul said only, "Remember your promise to me . . . the one you made on Ix."

The sands whipped around her, bringing dust and haze that swirled faster and faster, scouring at her—until finally she was rubbing her eyes, looking around at the underground chamber, smelling the splashed water, the dead worm, and bitter bile.

Alia was already awake. Being more accustomed to the drug, her body had metabolized it faster. The girl's spice-addicted deep blue eyes were open wide, her lips parted in a smile of amazement. Next to her Duncan sat rigid and cross-legged, still apparently dreaming.

"I saw Paul," Alia said.

Jessica's heart pounded faster. "And what did he say to you?"

Alia's smile became mysterious. "That is something even a mother and a daughter cannot share." Jessica realized, belatedly, that Alia had walled *her* off, too. "And what did you experience?"

Jessica shook her head slightly. "It was . . . perplexing. I need to meditate upon it further."

When she rose, the stiff soreness in her limbs told her that she had been in a trance for quite some time. Her mouth was dry, with a sour residual taste from the liquid she'd consumed . . . and the strange vision she had experienced.

Jessica left Alia sitting beside Duncan. The young woman held the ghola's arm, watching him, and guarding him as he finished his own inner journey. But Jessica was gone before he woke up.

When the true motive is love, there are no other explanations.
Searching for them is like chasing grains of sand in the wind.

—Fremen proverb

A long with the wedding preparations, construction work continued at great speed to erect magnificent new temples to show the glory of St. Alia as well as Muad'Dib. Towering in a public square, a tall statue depicted the Janus figure, the duality of brother and sister, two visages facing opposite directions—the future and the past—Alia and Paul.

Newly minted coins bore the profile of Alia on one side, Madonnalike over two small babies, surrounded by the faint image of Paul-Muad'Dib, like a benevolent spirit watching over them; the flip side bore the Atreides hawk crest embellished with imperial styling and the words ALIA REGENT. Alia seemed to have learned the power of mythmaking from the example of her brother; even during Paul's reign, the girl had made herself into a powerful religious leader on Dune.

Despite the anticipated joy and excitement of the wedding, Alia quietly asserted that there was danger all around—and Jessica could not discount her fears. Such a spectacle would indeed be a tempting time for someone to commit violence. A team of amazon guards never left the Regent's side, and a Fremen troop led by Stilgar remained stationed outside the entrance to the conservatory where the twins were held.

All offworld ships were searched thoroughly, every passenger questioned, each cargo deep-scanned.

Alia's inner-circle priests carried the brunt of the expanded protective measures, with the Qizara Isbar proudly accepting a much more
important role than he had held before. Jessica had not liked the fawn-
ing man when he'd come to Caladan to deliver the news of Paul's death.
Now, the more Isbar insisted that he was helping Alia, the less Jessica
approved of him.

When she received a secret coded message revealing an assassination plot spearheaded by Isbar, even Jessica was surprised at the audacity of it. She studied the secret message again and again, listened to the
surreptitiously recorded conversations that revealed Isbar's plan in all
its detail. Then she summoned Gurney Halleck to her quarters.

" 'Beware the viper in your own nest.' " Gurney's scar flushed. "Didn't
Paul's man Korba attempt something similar?"

"Yes, and that's why he was executed. Korba wanted to make a martyr out of Paul so that the priesthood could use his memory for their
own ends. Now, these people mean to do the same with Alia. If they
remove her as Regent, they will have only the baby twins to worry
about."

"You might be on their target list yourself, my Lady. And Irulan.
'Ambitions grow like weeds, and are as difficult to eradicate.' " The big
man shook his head. "Are you sure of the information? Who provided
it? I don't like this anonymous source."

"The source is not anonymous to me. I believe it to be unimpeachable, but I cannot reveal the name."

Gurney lowered his head. "As you wish, my Lady." She knew she
was asking a great deal from him, but she expected his full acceptance.
Jessica had come to Dune to honor Paul, to strengthen the name of
their Great House, and to revere a fallen leader—her son. But she
could do no less for her daughter. Alia was as much an Atreides as
Paul.

Jessica tapped the scrap of spice paper and the words she had written there. "These are the three names. You know what to do. We can't
trust anyone, even those in Alia's inner circle, but I trust you, Gurney."

"I will take care of it." His fists were clenched, his muscles bunched.

As he departed, Jessica let out a long, slow sigh, fully aware of what she had set in motion.

THAT EVENING, AFTER Isbar completed his service in the Fane of the Oracle, celebrating St. Alia of the Knife, the priest bowed to the cheering congregants, raised his hands in benediction, and stepped back behind the altar. His skin gleamed with scented oils. Isbar's neck had begun to thicken with soft flesh, a plumpness that resulted from unlimited access to water for the first time in his life.

Parting the rust-orange curtains of spice-fiber fabric, he entered his private alcove and was surprised to find a man there waiting for him. "Gurney Halleck?" Recognizing him, Isbar did not call for the guards. "How may I help you?"

Gurney's hands moved in a blur, fingers clenched around a thin cord of krimskell fiber, which he flashed around the priest's neck and yanked tight. Isbar flailed and clawed at the garrote, but Gurney's grip remained firm. He twisted and pulled tighter, and the cord swiftly cut off the priest's breath, broke his hyoid bone, and silenced his larynx. As Gurney sawed deeper with the cord, Isbar's eyes bulged; his lips opened and closed like a beached, gasping fish. In a fleeting thought, Gurney wondered if the desert man had ever seen a fish.

He spoke quietly into the priest's ear. "Don't pretend to wonder why I am here. You know your guilt, what you intended to do. Any plot against Alia is a plot against all Atreides." He jerked the garrote tighter still. Isbar was beyond hearing, his throat nearly severed now. "And therefore it must be dealt with."

Outside, the worshippers continued to file out of the temple, some still praying. They hadn't even seen the hanging fabric panels stir.

When he was absolutely certain the traitor was dead, Gurney let him slide to the dusty floor. He peeled the krimskell fiber out of the deep indentation in the priest's neck. Coiling the strand once more into a neat loop, he left silently through the back entrance. He had two more men to visit this night.

WHEN SHE LEARNED of the murders of her three supposedly loyal priests, Alia was outraged. Without being summoned, Jessica came into the Regent's private office, ordered the amazon guards to wait outside, and sealed the door.

Seated at her writing table, Alia wanted to lash out at some target, any target. She had laid out a pattern of the new Dune Tarot cards, though the reading had not gone as well as she'd hoped. When her mother entered, Alia scattered the cards on the table, a panoply of ancient icons modified to have relevance to Dune—a Coriolis storm of sand, an Emperor resembling Paul, a goblet overflowing with spice, a sandworm instead of a dragon, and an eerie Blind Man, rather than Death.

Jessica withstood the brunt of her daughter's buffeting rage, then spoke calmly. "Those priests are dead for good reason. Gurney Halleck killed them."

That stopped Alia in midsentence. The willowy girl raised herself to her feet from behind the desk, the clutter of tarot cards before her. Her face turned pale, her eyes widening. "What did you just say to me, Mother?"

"Gurney only followed my orders. I saved your life."

While her daughter listened, astonished and scowling, Jessica revealed the full details of the plot that would have assassinated both Alia and Duncan at their wedding ceremony. She extended the recordings, letting her daughter listen to the schemes of Isbar and the other two priests. There could be no denying their guilt. "It seems your priests would rather speak as surrogates for dead prophets than for live rulers."

Alia sat down heavily, but after only a moment's pause, her mood shifted once more. "So you've set spies on me, Mother? You don't trust my security, so you have your own inside sources?" She jabbed a finger at the surreptitious recordings and her voice grew louder, more shrill. "How dare you secretly keep watch on me and my priests? Who among my—"

As Alia began to lose control of her temper, Jessica took a step closer and slapped her like a mother disciplining an unruly child. Calmly. Once, hard. "Stop this nonsense and think. I did it to *protect* you, not to weaken you. Not to spy on you. Sometimes it is beneficial to have an independent set of sources—as this proves."

Alia rocked backward, shocked that her mother had struck her. Her lips tightened until they turned pale; the red mark stood out on her cheek. With great effort, she composed herself. "There are always plots, Mother. My own people would have uncovered this one in time—and I would much rather have publicly executed the traitors, rather than killing them in secret. The wedding ceremony would have been an obvious opportunity for someone to move against me, and I've already taken security measures—measures that even your 'sources' don't know about."

"I am not your enemy, nor am I your rival," Jessica insisted. "Can you fault a mother for wanting to prevent harm to her daughter?"

Alia sighed and tossed her hair back behind her shoulders. "No, Mother, I cannot. By the same token, don't fault me for saying that I will feel less . . . unsettled, when you return to Caladan."

When yet another of Bronso's manifestos appeared only days before the wedding, Alia reacted swiftly and angrily, ordering the
destruction of all copies. She demanded that anyone who was found
distributing, or even carrying, the document be executed without further ado.

Deeply concerned and hoping to mitigate any damage, Jessica rushed
to meet with her daughter in private. "Such bloodshed will backfire on
you. In two days you and Duncan will be married—do you want the people to hate and fear you?"

After expressing her disgust at the situation, Alia relented. "All right,
Mother—if only to appease you. Amputating the perpetrators' hands
should be harsh enough to get the message across, I suppose." Her mother
departed, not entirely satisfied.

Alia spent the rest of the day in the throne room, then left through
a guarded doorway and pushed aside a Fremen wall hanging, just as
she had seen her brother do many times. It was difficult to believe he
was gone. She churned with a feeling of helplessness that only made
her angry. Why had he left *her* with such a messy state of affairs? Did
Paul expect *her* to act as the mother of his twin babies? Or perhaps

Harah could do it? Or Princess Irulan? Or Jessica? How could the most important man in the known universe simply turn his back and . . . leave?

She wished her brother could be here now.

A terrible sensation of sadness and longing threatened to make her cry, but Alia had not shed tears for him, and doubted she ever would, especially on Dune. Yet she had loved Paul in life . . . and might love him even more now in death.

His presence was like a supergiant star whose gravitational pull affected everything that came within his sphere of influence. Paul shone so brightly that he blinded all other individual stars and constellations. The Emperor Muad'Dib, the Fremen messiah Lisan al-Gaib. He had overthrown an Emperor, conquered a galaxy, and used a Jihad to sweep aside the clutter of ten thousand years of history.

But without his charismatic personality dominating the daily workings of government and the Atreides family, Alia was beginning to see her brother from a different perspective, actually getting a chance to know and respect him in new ways.

After Chani's water was mysteriously stolen—and no blackmail threats had ever emerged, thankfully—she had sealed off Paul's private quarters in the Citadel, and allowed no one into these rooms. Alia liked to come here alone, just to think, imagining that he might still be there.

Paul-Muad'Dib had left a remarkable legacy, and she was its custodian as Regent and as his *sister*. That was not a duty she took lightly. Given time and the proper circumstances, Alia might stand one day as the equal to Muad'Dib in the histories. She already had chroniclers compiling records of her achievements, just in case.

Standing on stone floor tiles just inside the room's entrance, she smelled the lingering odors of the former inhabitants, a bit of staleness in the air. Not so long ago, Paul and Chani had filled these rooms with their personalities, their dreams, their hopes, and secret words for each other. They had made love here and conceived the twins, Leto and Ghanima.

Oil murals painted on the walls depicted common Fremen scenes: a woman counting water rings for her hair, children out in the sand catching sandtrout, a robed Naib standing high on a promontory. Everything was exactly as the occupants had left it, Chani's shoes and clothing were laid about casually as if she had expected to come back, just like any other day . . . but Paul's clothes were neatly put away. Seeing this, Alia felt a chill, wondering if her brother had known he would not return.

Ultimately, Alia contemplated what to do with these private quarters. The hallowed place reached beyond her own feelings of devotion for her brother. She felt the sacredness in the still shadows of the sietchlike suite with its austere wall tapestries, the bed Paul and Chani had shared, the jasmium spice-coffee service that had once belonged to Jamis.

After long deliberation, Alia decided that she needed to share this place with others. But with whom? A place limited to herself and a few invited guests, only those who had been close to Paul, and to Chani? What about a museum that only Fremen could visit . . . or should it be something more accessible that drew pilgrims from all over the Imperium?

Valefor's voice called to her from the other side of the closed door. "Regent Alia, your mother requests entrance."

Alia pushed past the wall hanging, opened the door and saw her chief amazon guard standing next to Jessica. "Of course."

Her mother entered, the first time she'd ever been inside these rooms. She said nothing about the crackdown, or Bronso's writings, or any of their previous discussions as she walked around the chamber, sadly inspecting the extra stillsuits, the filmbooks that Paul or Chani had been reading, the holophotos. She wiped a finger across a tabletop, came away with a thin layer of dust; she took several deep, agitated breaths.

"This is not easy for you, is it, Mother?"

"No."

In the sleeping quarters, Jessica paused to look at a detached wooden headboard that featured carvings of a leaping fish and thick brown waves . . . a piece that had been salvaged from the original Arrakeen Residence. That headboard had once concealed a hunter-seeker used in a Harkonnen attempt to kill Paul. Later, after becoming Emperor, Paul had kept it as a reminder never to let down his guard.

Moving on, Jessica paused to examine the contents of a table by a filterglass window, a pottery jar set all by itself as if in a place of special reverence. Her gaze flickered over to her daughter, asking an unspoken question.

"It's the jar Chani sent me to fetch after Count Fenring stabbed Paul. It held the Water of Life that stopped his heartbeat long enough for us to control the bleeding."

Jessica stared at the pottery. "After what we observed in the bazaar the other day, it heartens me to see *authentic* objects here. I think I should collect a few keepsakes of my own."

Alia felt a rush of enthusiasm. "Yes, Mother. After our conversation, I instituted a close watch on the black marketeers with their phony relics. The memory of Muad'Dib should not be cheapened by counterfeits." She smiled, hoping her mother would approve. "I have decided that the only way to prevent the fraud is to create a seal of approval, an official mark that reassures buyers—the faithful—that a particular object has been authenticated as the original. All additional profits shall go into the government treasury."

Jessica's brow furrowed. "But the demand will be far higher than the amount of items available."

"Yes, and since copies will be made anyway, we will manufacture our own replicas and sell them as such, blessed by the Qizarate. Official facsimiles, rather than fakes. I'll be on a consulting board, and I'd like you to act in that capacity as well."

"Remember, I'm going back to Caladan soon. I've seen enough . . . scraps of Paul's life." She took another long look around and then slowly left. "Yes, I've seen enough."

Afterward, Alia lifted a seashell fragment from the table and held the broken piece up against the light from the window. It was an object from Mother Earth, if Whitmore Bludd's story about it was true. He'd given it to Paul as a token of allegiance from Archduke Armand Ecaz. But the seashell, like Bludd's promise, was broken.

She put the artifact back down in exactly the same position. Then on impulse, she spun the piece around so that it faced the other way. Making her own mark. These objects were not really sacred, though she would continue to act as if they were. They were just . . . things.

Is a ghola capable of love? This was one of my questions at first, but not any longer. Duncan Idaho and I have an understanding.

—ALIA ATREIDES, private notes

Only hours before Alia and Duncan's wedding would begin, three stern amazon guards escorted Lady Jessica out to a place of honor at the edge of the desert beyond the Citadel walls.

Stilgar was her companion as they moved through the festive crowds, both dressed in formal robes for the joyous occasion. She had intentionally kept her distance from the Fremen leader since returning from the secret ceremony to honor Chani. Keeping their silence, Jessica and the Naib took seats in the viewing stands overlooking the perfect expanse of desert. Hundreds of diligent workers had combed the dunes with fine rakes and used gentle blowers to erase footprints and remove any appearance of clutter—an extravagant and unnecessary waste of effort, Jessica thought, for the swift winds would erase any mark soon enough.

As the crowds gathered, Stilgar mused, "I was the one who first told Usul that your daughter should be wedded. It was a thing any man could see, at the time." He narrowed his eyes and gazed out at the dunes where the ceremony would take place.

Jessica was glad to share her thoughts. "In some cultures, my daughter would be considered too young for marriage, but Alia is unlike any other girl. In her memories, she can recall all the pleasures of the flesh, all the joys and obligations of marriage. Even so, it's always challenging for a mother to think of her daughter being married. It is a fundamental change in relationships, the crossing of a Rubicon."

Stilgar raised his eyebrows. "Rubicon? The term is unfamiliar to me."

"A river on ancient Terra. A famous military leader crossed it and forever changed the course of history."

The Fremen Naib turned away, muttering, "I know nothing of rivers."

Princess Irulan arrived with Harah and the two children, attended by another cluster of guards. Gurney moved along the stands, ever suspicious and alert. Jessica understood his reasons for concern. By removing Isbar and the traitorous priests, they had eliminated one plot against Alia . . . but that did not mean there weren't others waiting to be sprung. Alia had mentioned her implementation of other unusual "security measures," but Jessica did not know what her daughter had meant by that.

Grand spectacles seemed to invite tragedy: Rhombur's death during the Jongleur performance in the Theater of Shards, the slaughter during Duke Leto's wedding, the swarms of unleashed hunter-seekers during Muad'Dib's Great Surrender ceremony, even Bronso's recent disruption during Paul's funeral. From the stands, she glanced at the twins, aware that Leto and Ghanima would spend their entire lives fearing an assassin's blade, a conspirator's explosion, a poisoner's special ingredient, or some weapon no one had yet contemplated.

But a state wedding could not be held behind closed doors and drawn shutters. Duke Leto Atreides, and the Old Duke before him, had understood the power and necessity of diversions, of bravura. "Bread and circuses," the ancient Romans had called it.

Her heart went out to Alia, wishing the young woman well on her wedding day. "She is *my* daughter," she whispered fiercely to herself. Jessica prayed that this ceremony, unlike those others, would take place without disruption or disaster, and that Alia and Duncan could actually be happy together.

It was time for that in the Atreides family.

OUT OF VIEW, Alia stood naked on the balcony of a palace annex at the far edge of the city. The sun was setting on the horizon, throwing long shadows across the rock escarpments. On the sands below, young Fremen women whirled and chanted, their hair flying loose and free. The traditional marriage dances were under way.

Behind her, Duncan Idaho lay on the bed they had recently begun to share. She and Duncan had just made love, a passionate release of their anxious energies as they waited, and waited, for the time of the ceremony. He was her first physical lover, though she remembered plenty of others in her deep layers of memories.

All day long, crowds of onlookers had gathered at the edge of the city and spilled out onto the sands. Weaving their way through the throngs, vendors hawked memorabilia bearing the faces of the bride and groom, and Alia's government would receive its percentage of it all.

A number of viewing stands had been erected for the visiting dignitaries of various Houses, CHOAM, the Landsraad, the Spacing Guild, the Bene Gesserit, and the Qizarate. Each important personage would receive his own memorabilia, inscribed and authenticated.

As both the sister of Muad'Dib and Regent of the Imperium, Alia had designed her wedding to combine Fremen and Imperial elements in a hybrid ceremony. She and Duncan had gone over the details that would combine vows from both traditions. Far out on the dunes, the two of them would be wed under the double moonlight—at least, that was what the people would see, and hear. Their preparations would make the illusion perfect.

To the left of the bed stood a blackplaz cubicle with a sealed door— one of the new technologies that the Ixian Confederation had recently given her, hoping to buy their way back into her good graces. Because of the usual death threats that hovered around her, Alia was increasingly resorting to technological security measures.

Her mother and Gurney had thwarted Isbar's plot to kill them during the wedding. Alia knew of the deadly conspiracies that had sprung up around Paul. And Irulan had once told her stories about the countless plots, conspiracies, and assassination attempts Shaddam IV had faced on Kaitain. *What is it about human beings that they invariably develop hatred toward their leaders?*

Just yesterday, Qizara security had seized a lunatic in the streets shouting that the wedding was "an unholy alliance of Bene Gesserit Abomination and Tleilaxu ghola." Under interrogation, the man had implicated others, and provided credible evidence that there were deeper plots afoot against Alia and Duncan. But the man himself had been an inept fool, and had never posed much of a threat.

She worried more about the *quiet*, well-concealed plots, conspirators who were not so foolish as to shout out their anger in the streets of Arrakeen. She would have liked to blame all the threats on Bronso of Ix, but she had never been his target, though many others had resentments against her. For her purposes, however, Bronso provided a convenient focal point, and she could use his reputation to turn the tables and incite a backlash against critics of the regime. She had already taken steps to exploit the situation, secretly writing her own counterfeit "manifesto" that would be released immediately after the wedding, under Bronso's name.

Adaptation was a Bene Gesserit strength, one to which she had been born. Her brother had changed the human race forever, but Alia would take her place in history as well, since Paul had left her to pick up the pieces and arrange them as she saw fit.

If she could make the Imperium strong and enduring, historians might even elevate her above the stature of Muad'Dib. For her, it was a matter of diminishing Paul's memory in calculated ways, while brightening her own accomplishments. She would stand on his shoulders and benefit from his victories.

In honor of her wedding day, Alia had ordered the temporary cessation of all torturings and executions. In addition, one fortunate prisoner would be exonerated each day, based upon a public drawing to be held outside the main prison, and Duncan had been giving away valuable gifts to hundreds of lucky citizens selected at random, to demonstrate Imperial largesse.

Stepping away from the slanted dusk light on the balcony, Alia turned to see Duncan dressing in front of a mirror, putting on green uniform trousers and a black jacket that bore the red hawk crest of House Atreides. He was always precise, the result of the original Duncan's Swordmaster training and years of military service to House Atreides.

She closed the plaz doors behind her and activated the moisture seals, shutting off noises from the crowd outside. With a tingly feeling of anticipation, Alia put on a black velvasilk dress that had the cut of a Fremen robe, but with the materials, fittings, and resplendent jewels of a noble lady. She braided her hair with water rings and wore a white pearline necklace—the perfect combination of Fremen and Imperial elements. She also put on a satisfied smile.

When sunset faded into darkness, multicolored lights played across the sands and the windows of the palace annex. Duncan stood at a viewing scope on one wall, and Alia joined him so that they could observe the crowd. While the couple watched from behind the walls of Alia's high bedroom, her amazon guards marched out onto the sands and took their stations to guard the participants and guests. Enhancing the magnification, she spotted a black-robed Sayyadina, along with a Qizara priest in a yellow robe, standing in a pool of light at the crest of the dune. Everyone was waiting for her and Duncan to arrive.

She squeezed his hand and led him to the blackplaz cubicle at the back of the room. "Shall we make our appearance?"

The two of them stepped inside the booth. The cubicle door shut, and the golden lights of scanners and imagers bathed them. Abruptly, out in the desert, Alia seemed to be standing on the dunetop with Duncan, but they were merely solido holoprojections, unbeknownst to onlookers. Alia and her husband-to-be seemed to emerge out of nowhere, like a miracle . . . or a stage trick. No one in the audience would believe the two were not actually present. Even if an assassination attempt occurred now, neither of them was at risk.

Alia had studied the details of the ceremony so many times that she barely noticed as the Qizara spoke in Chakobsa, following traditions as old as the Zensunni wanderers who were the forebears of the Fremen, while the Sayyadina spoke afterward in flowery ancient Galach, using words that had once been uttered by Priests of Dur in royal wedding ceremonies, before their recent fall from grace.

The perfect projected images of Alia and Duncan uttered the responses they had memorized, received the blessings of the two officials, and kissed to a roar of approval from the population of Arrakeen. Then the two newlyweds glided off onto the sands. Miraculously leaving no footprints, they vanished into dune shadows, bound for their secret honeymoon destination.

When it was over and the two of them stepped out of the projection booth and found themselves back in the suite, Duncan produced actual wedding rings from a pocket of his jacket. Blushing almost shyly, they slid the bands on each other's fingers. Duncan was such a traditionalist.

Smiling at him, feeling the warmth of genuine though unfamiliar emotions, Alia said, "It all happened so fast. I turned my head and we were married."

"You turned my head some time ago," he said and folded her into his embrace.

Wellington Yueh, the Suk doctor of House Atreides, is the most no-torious traitor in the long and checkered history of the Imperium. Bronso of Ix, on the other hand, is more than a mere turncoat—he is a defiler of Muad'Dib's memory. He does not simply betray, but rather hopes to destroy everything Muad'Dib created.

If a million deaths were not enough to punish Yueh, as the refrain goes, how many deaths would be sufficient for Bronso?

—*The Legacy of Muad'Dib* by the PRINCESS IRULAN

In the continuing search for Bronso of Ix, Duncan Idaho's network of disguised Mentats patrolled the streets or worked menial spaceport jobs. They observed and processed millions of faces, then ignored them. They paid no attention to other criminals, fugitives from the Jihad, or rebels who had fought against Muad'Dib but were never caught. They sought only Bronso. *That* was Alia's priority.

Gurney tried unsuccessfully to trace the treatises to their origins, and reading some of the outrageous claims made his blood boil. The Ixian had once been Paul's friend, and now he had become a particularly malicious gadfly.

Still, Gurney had sworn to honor Jessica's request, no matter how odd he found it, no matter how infuriating the Ixian fugitive was. And so, to throw Duncan off the scent, he chose carefully where to focus his efforts. He "misplaced" a few particularly promising leads, while expend-ing manpower on dubious sightings. Through the weeks of hunting, Gur-ney surrounded himself with a flurry of activity, conducting dozens of interrogations personally. He dispatched spies and searchers and made a great show of his determination.

All the while, he did his best *not* to find Bronso.

Thus, when the fugitive was actually apprehended at the Arrakeen

Spaceport, Gurney could not have been more astonished. "Gods below, they caught him? They have him in custody?"

The high-spirited messenger who pushed his way into their headquarters office could barely contain himself as he delivered his fresh news.

Duncan didn't seem surprised at all. "It was only a matter of time, effort, and manpower. Bronso Vernius is a worthy adversary, but he could never match the resources we brought to bear against him. And now we've stopped him. We have done what honor demanded."

Honor.

"That's . . . good, Duncan," Gurney managed, but a weight remained on his shoulders. He had failed Lady Jessica. She had seemed so earnest, and he had done what he could. Despite Gurney's efforts to stall and divert attention, Duncan's men had caught Bronso.

After Bronso's earlier escape from a death cell, security was bound to be tighter than ever before. Gurney struggled to think of something he could do to honor his promise to Jessica. His stomach was in knots. Should he try to free the notorious prisoner? To what lengths did Jessica want him to go? If Gurney's efforts became obvious, then questions would be asked, and Jessica's involvement could be exposed. "Let me interrogate him in the prison. I'll learn what we need to know."

The breathless messenger shook his head, but the motion did not dislodge his smile. "No interrogations are necessary. Regent Alia has sent out a summons, and already the crowds are gathering. Bronso's guilt has been plain for years, and she will not risk another escape. We learned our lesson that first time. The Regent says there is no need for a drawn-out trial. He is to be executed swiftly, so that we can all move on to other pressing matters."

Gurney could not conceal a scowl. "No matter how apparent his guilt may be, the law is the law. You know as well as I that Duke Leto would never have allowed conviction and execution without due process. That's a Harkonnen way of dealing with problems . . . not the Atreides way."

"Ways change," the ghola said, his facial expression unreadable. "Those things take time, and Alia believes she has no time to spare. She's in a hurry to be done with the man."

The messenger seemed much too happy. "The people already know the justice of Muad'Dib, and they are eager to have it carried out."

CROWDS HAD ALREADY gathered in the central square near the sun-washed tower of Alia's Fane. Angry bodies pressed against one another with a roar of vengeful cheers and shouts, a mounting thunderstorm of humanity. The Qizarate did not have to work hard to whip up fervor against Bronso.

Dressed in an extraordinary black and gold outfit that made her look like a goddess, Alia sat on a shaded platform high above the masses. Beside her sat a stony-faced Jessica, whose mood Gurney could not decipher. When he and Duncan presented themselves on the high observation platform, Jessica showed no reaction, but Gurney felt sick inside. He had never failed her before. No excuses would matter now.

Alia looked at them with a bright smile. "Ah, Duncan and Gurney— thanks to your efforts, the vile Bronso has been snared, and he's confessed his crimes, even without coercion! He actually seems proud of what he's done." She steepled her fingers and looked out at the masses. "I see no reason to make this a prolonged affair. We know what the people want, and what the Imperium needs." Alia looked at her mother as if hoping for approval, then back at Gurney and Duncan. "In the execution after the Great Surrender ceremony, the crowds tore Whitmore Bludd limb from limb. I wish you all could have seen it." No one else seemed to share her enthusiasm.

She sat back in her elaborate chair. "But I've decided to be more Fremen about the execution today. Stilgar will use his crysknife. Do you see him down there?" Gurney could make out the Naib standing alone on a platform; he wore a full stillsuit and desert robes, without any badges of office.

Bronso's outrageous writings were so treasonous that any government would have seen the need to cauterize the wound and proceed with the healing. But since Jessica had told Gurney *not* to let Bronso be captured, something else must be at stake here.

Gurney searched her face for any signal, trying to guess what she wanted him to do. Should he suggest that Bronso might serve as a more effective tool of state if he repented and retracted his claims against Muad'Dib? He doubted Bronso would do that without protracted turmoil and torture, but at least it would cause a delay. . . .

The crowd's roar increased to vocal thunder as the captive was brought forward. Despite their distance from the platform, Gurney could tell by the man's manner, the exposed facial features, and the shock of copper hair that the prisoner truly was Bronso of Ix, the son of Rhombur Vernius.

Three Qizaras spoke in odd unison, bellowing through voice amplifiers in Galach, listing Bronso's crimes, condemning his acts, and sentencing him to death. Gurney felt swept along by it all. He could discern no expression on the captive's face, neither terror nor contrition; Bronso stood straight, firm in his convictions and facing his fate.

Stilgar did not draw out the suspense, adding only a traditional Fremen curse. "May your face be forever black." He raised the crysknife high, displayed its milky-white blade, and let the crowd cheer for a few moments.

Then he drove it home into Bronso's chest.

When the blade struck, the victim spasmed as if jolted by lightning, and then fell to his knees. Stilgar withdrew the dagger, satisfied that it was an efficient killing, and Bronso fell backward to lie still at the Naib's feet.

The crowd let out a collective gasp, after which a resounding silence fell, as if all their heartbeats had stopped, not just the prisoner's. Stilgar stood like a man encased in stiff body armor.

Suddenly he recoiled, as if from a serpent. Gasping members of the audience withdrew from around the dais. Someone screamed.

Alia shot to her feet, unable to believe her eyes.

Bronso's features blurred and then seemed to be erased, leaving a blank, expressionless visage, a smooth face with the requisite eyes, mouth, and nostrils . . . nothing else.

Jessica bolted upright from her shaded seat, astonished and vaguely pleased, as far as Gurney could tell. "It's a Face Dancer! Not Bronso at all—a Tleilaxu Face Dancer!"

To his knowledge, Gurney had never seen one of the shape-shifters before, and certainly not in its natural state. Even viewed from a distance, the thing had a bizarre inhumanness.

HIDDEN IN THE crowd, he was jostled by elbows and shoulders. The smell of packed human bodies and dry dust penetrated the scarf he'd wrapped around the lower half of his face. He pulled his hood farther forward to conceal his features.

With great sadness and unrelenting defiance, Bronso of Ix watched his duplicate die before a bloodthirsty mob. As the people withdrew in horror and disgust, cheated of their true victim, he had an excuse to turn away from the dead shape-shifter—the man, his friend—who had sacrificed himself.

Bronso had accepted many necessary and painful tasks, but he'd never before asked anyone to die for him. Sielto had seen the need, and had volunteered. Another "necessary" death. Bronso didn't think he could have made the request alone. . . .

Aboard the Guild Heighliner, where he had gathered with Sielto and other members of Rheinvar's troupe, the plan had been obvious and ingenious. "They are looking for you everywhere," said Sielto. "Therefore, it is best to let them find you." The Face Dancer had shifted his features to mirror Bronso's. "They will find me instead, and they will be fooled."

"But you'll be executed." He remembered with a shudder the time he had been held in the death cell. "And no one will help you escape."

"I am aware of that. All Face Dancers have agreed to wear your features—on cue. Immediately after my execution, 'Bronso of Ix' will seem to appear everywhere at once. There will be hundreds of sightings around the Imperium."

Bronso remained guarded. "But once Alia's men have been fooled, they will develop tests and find ways to expose the Face Dancer imposters."

Sielto shrugged. "Let them do so. After a hundred false arrests, even Alia will grow tired of chasing false trails, humiliated by being tricked time and again. You will be safe."

"I'll never be safe . . . but this may give me some breathing room." Bronso hung his head. "Sielto, I've known you for so many years. The time when Paul and I worked with you was so happy, until . . ." His expression fell. "I don't want you to do this for me."

Wearing Bronso's face, Sielto had remained undisturbed. "You make an error when you consider us to be individuals. I am just a Face Dancer and a Jongleur—malleable and adaptable to any circumstance, including my own execution. I was *designed* to play a role, my friend, and this will be my finest performance."

And it had been, indeed.

Swallowed up in the angry crowd, Bronso watched it all, hardly able to bear the gruesome sight. If anything, he had underestimated the magnitude of the audience's shocked reaction. This trick with the Face Dancer now made all these people consider Bronso to be even more the genius, even more the villain. He had fooled them again!

It wasn't what Bronso wanted, but it was what he *needed* in order to continue tearing down the myth. And that was what Paul needed. Beyond that, nothing else mattered.

Murder? The word, the very concept itself, is not in my lexicon—
at least not as it can be applied to my Imperial rule. If killings are
needed, I order them. It is not a matter of legality or morality; it is
one of the necessities of my position.

—ALIA ATREIDES, in the seventh month of her Regency

Dressed in an austere black robe so that no one would recognize her, Jessica hurried along a crowded, dusty boulevard in Arra-keen. In the early evening, yellow lights from narrow sealed windows and recessed doorways cast pools of illumination. When darkness fell, young people frequented this main thoroughfare, some doing the cir-cuit of taverns, others attending services at countless new temples and shrines that had sprung up after Paul's death. She made her way around the small crowds that blocked the entrances to their favorite places.

For the past hour, she had been inside the newly renamed Temple of Muad'Dib's Glory, and now she was on her way back to the Citadel. The temple was the grandest of several such structures that had not quite been completed before the wedding. Alia herself had chosen this par-ticular building to be refurbished, ordering her teams of workmen to la-bor around the clock. It was not yet open to the public, but she had insisted that her mother see it today. Jessica doubted Paul would have wanted such an ostentatious temple dedicated to his memory and leg-end.

The priest in charge had given her a private tour, and Jessica pre-tended to be impressed. At her daughter's behest, she had given the holy man an authentic artifact of Paul—a red braid from an Atreides uniform he'd worn as a boy. The grateful priest had stammered his thanks as he held the object in its clearplaz box. He promised to place it in a secure reliquary and henceforth exhibit it inside the temple. Before sending the braid to him, however, Alia had ordered it duplicated, so that facsimiles could be sold along with other artifacts.

On the edge of the thoroughfare ahead, Jessica saw a man running, brushing against the dry, tan buildings, while gunshots rang out. A small police 'thopter, flying low, roared around the corner of the street beyond the man, spraying projectile fire at him, thin needles that glinted in the dusk.

Screaming people scattered in the streets and into doorways; a number of them were struck by stray or ricocheting projectiles, since most townspeople did not wear body shields. Jessica dodged into a doorway and pressed her back against the moisture seal as a spray of gunfire tore up the place where she had been walking. The hunted man ran past her, panting like a laboring engine as he fled. For an instant, he gaped at her; his eyes were large with terror, and he dodged back out into the street toward a group of people outside a drinking establishment.

Moments later, she heard another burst of gunfire and more 'thopters. Men wearing the black-and-green uniforms of Alia's Imperial guard ran past, shouting; some of them grinned like hunting jackals. Peering out of her meager shelter, Jessica saw the hapless man lying motionless in a widening pool of blood. Moisture wasted, flowing away on the pavement.

Jessica moved quietly forward with a gathering crowd of onlookers. A woman knelt over the body, sobbing. "Ammas! Why have they killed my Ammas?" She stared at the appalled spectators as if they could give her answers. "My husband was just a shopkeeper. In the name of Muad'Dib, *why?*"

Alia's guards quickly hauled the woman away, pushing her into the back of a groundcar that sped off.

Jessica marched angrily up to an officer who was trying to disperse the crowd around the man's bleeding body. "I am the mother of Muad'Dib. You know me. Explain your actions."

The man recoiled as he recognized her. "My Lady! It is not safe for you to be out by yourself. There are dangerous elements in the streets, threats against the Regent, people spreading sedition."

"Yes, I can see how unsafe it is, particularly for that man. But you have not answered my question."

He seemed perplexed. "Any person who speaks out against the sacred memory of Muad'Dib is subject to arrest and prosecution. Any propagandist may be in league with Bronso of Ix. We do it to honor your noble son and daughter, and . . . and the entire Atreides family, including yourself."

"You do not commit murder to honor *me*. What was your evidence against this man?" She could still see the terrified expression on the poor victim's face, the hopelessness. "Where is his conviction order from an Arrakeen court?"

"We were trying to arrest him, and he fled. Please, my Lady, let me escort you back to the Citadel. The Imperial Regent Alia herself can answer your questions much better than I."

Though the smell of blood and violence clung to the guard, he was only a follower, a tool that had been used by Alia's hand. "Yes, I would very much like to see my daughter right now."

ALIA WORE A white dressing gown when she came to the door. Her dark hair was wet. *Wet*, letting the moisture simply evaporate into the dry air. Scrubbers on the walls and ceiling recaptured most of the humidity, but the lax water discipline still surprised Jessica, even here in the keep.

Standing in the open doorway, Jessica said, "I want to know why your guards shot and killed a man in the street tonight. A woman—apparently his wife—said he was just a shopkeeper, and she was taken away as well."

"You must be referring to Ammas Kain? Yes, I signed his arrest order and followed the proper forms. He is a seditionist, promoting hatred against me, destabilizing my regime."

Jessica crossed her arms, not softening her position. "And your evidence?"

Alia brushed a strand of wet hair away from her face. "A copy of an appalling new manifesto from Bronso was found in his smoke shop."

"Simply finding such a document is sufficient reason to call for his execution without further investigation?" Jessica remembered how she had seen the Wayku aboard the Heighliner discreetly depositing Bronso's tracts in public places. "In whose court of law?"

Alia stiffened. "Mine, of course, because I *am* the law. Have you read Bronso's most recent manifesto? Instead of limiting his venom to Paul, the new document calls me and my husband 'the Whore and the Ghola.' Bronso names you the 'Mother of all Evil' and claims you took so many secret lovers that no one can know whether Duke Leto was really Paul's father."

Jessica drew back in surprise and puzzlement. *Bronso* had written that? "All along, Bronso's stated purpose has been to correct the historical record about my son and his rule. Why would he stoop to insults against you and me?"

"Why does he need any further reason? He lives to spread hatred." Alia invited her inside the chambers, offering to share a pot of melange-laced tea. "I'm glad that you're here with me. This will be a particularly dangerous night. Many operations are under way."

Jessica heard alarms sounding outside. She crossed Alia's quarters, still smelling the bathing perfumes and moisture in the air, making her way to a high window. Through the plaz pane, she saw an unusual number of aircraft flying over the city, playing their spotlights across the night sky.

"Duncan is in charge of the details," Alia said. "I could have asked Gurney to join him, but my husband was sure he could handle it himself. He is so dedicated and loyal! Tonight, the streets of Arrakeen flow with the blood of those who hate us, and tomorrow, our city will be much cleaner."

Jessica's horror was tinged with amazement. As she looked at her daughter, the events seemed unreal. She realized with a further chill that Alia had sent *her* to the refurbished temple without warning her of the violence that was about to be unleashed. *Did she want me out there? In harm's way?*

Coldly, Jessica said, "Bronso wrote terrible things about your brother for years, but *Paul* never felt the need for such an extreme reaction. Why are you so sensitive?"

"Because Bronso has escalated his campaign against the Imperial government. Therefore I am escalating the response."

"By reacting so extremely, you give his words a legitimacy they do not deserve. Just ignore Bronso's criticisms."

"Then I would look weak, or a fool, or both. My response is entirely appropriate."

"I disagree." Jessica considered using an appropriate shifting of Voice, in an attempt to bring her daughter to her knees, but that could precipitate a confrontation between them. Alia was not without her own defenses. Still, she wanted to make Alia see what she was doing. "Your father was called Leto the Just. Are you your father's daughter, or are you something else? A changeling?"

With a sudden movement, Alia slapped Jessica on the face. It stung.

Jessica saw it coming, and chose not to evade the blow. Was this a petulant retribution for when she had struck Alia only weeks before? Marshalling all the calmness she could, Jessica said, "The mark of a true leader, a true human, is to find a reasonable solution to intractable problems. You have stopped bothering to try. The ripples spread wide from here, Alia. There are consequences for everything."

"You threaten me?"

"I *counsel* you, and you would be wise to listen. I am only here to help you—and I won't be here for long." Gathering her dignity, Jessica left the room.

The hearts of all men dwell in the same wilderness.

—TIBANA, one of the leading Socratic Christians

Standing in row after row, the men looked like a sequence of images in a hall of mirrors, one Bronso Vernius after the other, each indistinguishable from the next. Dressed in identical white tunics and brown trousers, with similarly unkempt hair, they stood side by side in morning mists on the distant world of IV Anbus.

Only one of the Bronsos was real; he looked surreptitiously at the others. The Face Dancers asserted they were all the same; some still claimed to be Sielto, despite the very public execution in the Arrakeen square. Bronso didn't think the shape-shifters even knew the difference among themselves, but that did not diminish the sick feeling he felt inside. He would never be able to wash away the nightmarish memory of Stilgar's crysknife flashing into a body that looked indistinguishable from his own.

That was meant to be me.

After the spectacle, Face Dancers had appeared all around the Imperium, dozens of them in Arrakeen itself, providing enough diversions and distractions that the real Bronso could escape from Dune. In countless star systems, the shape-shifters would continue to take his place, and sightings of Bronso would occur on planet after planet. After much wasted time and effort, after interrogations and blood tests, all the captives would be exposed as imposters. Already, he was making Alia look foolish in her pursuit of him.

At least five additional shape-shifters had been executed, but none had revealed anything during protracted interrogation sessions. Such great and noble acts were seemingly incongruous among Face Dancers.

As Bronso thought about it, he remembered that the original Rhein-var the Magnificent had selected only the finest shape-shifters for his troupe, those who would adhere to noble Jongleur traditions. And as perfect mimics, picking up on nuances of behavior, the Face Dancers must have imitated the Master Jongleur at some point and absorbed his sense of honor.

Now Bronso was in the midst of those he could trust, humans of a different cut. He and his doppelgangers were meeting on a planet whose once-powerful civilization had long ago faded into history. The group stood together on a wide, flat promontory above the confluence of two rivers whose waters churned and flowed far below in the deep canyons they had cut. A sparkle of closely orbiting moons rode in the sky, visible even in daylight.

Long ago, a monastery had stood on this site, where the first So-cratic Christians had gained and consolidated political power. IV An-bus was a spiritual place, a beacon for their souls, but in the distant past, unremembered enemies had killed every person on the planet and erased most evidence that their sect had ever existed; the victors had shattered the stones of the monastery buildings and tossed the fragments into the raging torrents below.

Only the evening before, Bronso and the Jongleur troupe had ven-tured down to the planet, which remained only sparsely inhabited after so many centuries. Bronso had made certain that several Wayku atten-dants and others on the ship realized who he was and where he was going. Boarding another Heighliner under an assumed identity afterward, altering his features and clothing with sophisticated Jongleur makeup and costuming, he would continue his journey, staying for a while and then moving on, as usual.

Striding to the front of the group, the Face Dancer replica of Rhein-var the Magnificent scrutinized the identical Bronsos. The Jongleur leader scratched his head and muttered to himself, unable to identify the real Ixian among the imitators. Finally he said in a booming voice,

"Even to a Face Dancer of my perceptive abilities, your voices, eyes, and mannerisms reveal nothing."

All of the Bronsos smiled, in unison.

DESPITE REGENT ALIA'S strict prohibitions against anyone possessing or even reading Bronso's inflammatory publications, the new manifesto was widely distributed and discussed. The extreme writing was more insulting and hateful than anything he had published before.

The problem was, Bronso hadn't written it.

When he read the provocative insults against Alia, Duncan, and even Lady Jessica, Bronso simply stared in disbelief. Even Ennzyn, who brought him a copy while the Heighliner was en route to its next destination, assumed that it was genuinely one of the Ixian's writings. Wanting to help, the Wayku had surreptitiously spread it to a wider audience, as usual.

But it was a forgery. Bronso found that extremely disturbing.

He wondered if the author could possibly be Irulan. The Corrino princess had spread plenty of her own falsehoods, but nothing in her writing—especially the recent insipid and glorified "revisions" to history—had contained this sort of maliciousness. Even his most critical analyses of Paul Atreides had never been so boorish and rude, had never contained such vehement and personal attacks.

Sealed in a small inner stateroom, he pored over the alarming counterfeit manifesto, searching for clues. The words sounded as if they'd been written by a madman. No wonder Regent Alia had ordered her guards to hunt him down at all costs and had increased the bounty on his head. No wonder the people were growing more unified against him in common disgust.

A chill went down his back as the answer dawned on him. *Alia herself* had the most to gain from such invective! If she had not written it with her own hand, one of her agents must have compiled it. And the Regent had the ability to distribute many, many copies.

Anger clenched his muscles. Of course, Alia did not know that *he* was the one who'd sent Lady Jessica the covert recordings of the priest Isbar's assassination plan. Bronso had many secret surveillance devices planted in strategic places in the temples and in the Citadel of Muad'Dib itself. He had saved Alia's life, even if she didn't realize that he was her benefactor.

And now she had done this to him!

The sole purpose of his writings was to provide the unvarnished truth about Paul-Muad'Dib, exaggerating his weaknesses to make up for the fictions that were being written about him by starry-eyed Irulan. The pendulum had to swing both directions. Trying to set the record straight, Bronso had already sacrificed his wealth and noble title, risking his life for years on the run.

And now Alia was publishing lies—*under his name.*

Writing feverishly, he began to compose another manifesto to refute the forged document and deny responsibility for it. He could not allow such lies to go unchallenged.

There comes a time when every relationship is tested, and the true
strength of the bond is determined.
  —from *The Wisdom of Muad'Dib* by the PRINCESS IRULAN

Weary after a long day, Irulan entered the northwest wing of the
great citadel, interested only in reaching her private quarters.
She carried a ridulian crystal recorder under one arm, which she had
used to collect information from people on the streets of Arrakeen.
How strange for the eldest daughter of Shaddam IV, the lawful wife of
Emperor Muad'Dib, to be employed as a gatherer of data, a survey taker.
Alia had given her the capricious, nonsensical instructions; Irulan didn't
understand what she really wanted.

Even while Paul still lived, Irulan's role had been unclear, her as-
signments beneath her abilities. The eldest daughter of Shaddam Corrino, relegated to a mere chronicler . . . but even that was preferable to
performing such menial work. Did Alia intend to demean her?

Pursuant to the Regent's instructions, Irulan and an entourage of
guards and functionaries had gone out into the city on a special assignment to interview common people. "I want honest opinions, candid
responses," Alia had said, obviously knowing she would get no such
thing. Considering the recent purges—not to mention the intimidating amazon guards at the Princess's side—no one would voice criticisms of the Regency. Over the course of the day, Irulan had collected
thousands of glowing responses. Exactly what Alia wanted. But why?

Irulan had never been averse to manipulating answers herself. No matter what Jessica had told her, she felt obligated to continue building the myth of Muad'Dib, developing and revising his history in order to cement his place as prophet, the Kwisatz Haderach, the Lisan al-Gaib. By extension, that strengthened the legitimacy of Alia's rule. There could be no doubt in the minds of the people, no questions. That was why Bronso posed such a threat.

Irulan feared what would happen when the twins grew older. What if Alia began to scheme against little Leto and Ghanima? As Paul's wife, albeit not the mother of his children, she would continue to watch over the babies, help Harah to raise them, and guard them if necessary.

All the while, her father remained in exile on Salusa Secundus with Count Hasimir Fenring. The fallen Emperor Shaddam had been strangely silent since the "accident" had killed his ambassador Rivato just after Paul's death, but she knew her father—and Fenring—very well: Sensing weakness, they would be like wolves sniffing at Muad'Dib's wounded Empire. She wondered what her father would do next.

Walking along hallways of polished stone, she passed priceless paintings, statuary, and sealed bookcases containing ancient illuminated manuscripts. After a lifetime of familiarity with ostentatious trappings, both on Kaitain and here, she barely noticed the finery anymore.

But inside her own inner rooms, she sensed that something was not right.

With the door to the hallway still open behind her, she paused, her senses heightened from her years of Bene Gesserit schooling. She detected peculiar odors, things a bit out of place, heavy tables moved slightly, a sheaf of documents in a different position, the jewelry case visible through the doorway to her sleeping chamber open just a crack.

It was ridiculous to think that a burglar had broken into her chambers deep inside the Citadel. A quick inspection revealed that nothing had been taken. But objects had been moved around. Why? Had the intruder been searching for something?

Suddenly, she understood why the Regent had sent her on an unusual, and pointless, assignment all day. *Alia wanted me away from my rooms.*

Irulan checked a cleverly concealed sliding wall compartment, confirmed that her private journals had not been disturbed. On impulse, she went back to her jewelry case and took out a strand of varnished reefpearls that she had received as a gift during a party game in the Arrakeen royal court.

She remembered that celebratory night, an intentional throwback to the early years of Paul's reign. Clinging to their former glory, despite the ongoing destruction of the Jihad, Landsraad members had been invited to an especially lavish celebration intended to resemble similar parties back on old Kaitain. Paul had been much too busy for such court games.

As the highlight of the evening, the participants opened random packages provided by the organizer, a bubbly woman who had once been a countess but had lost most of her fortune in a scandal that had nothing to do with the Jihad.

Casually, Irulan had selected an item from the assortment of gifts arrayed on tables around the room—just a light amusement for all—but when she opened her package, Irulan had immediately seen that her gift was unusual. The reefpearls appeared to be genuine, which she'd confirmed afterward through a wizened old jeweler. The jeweler had noticed something else on the necklace, which he showed to her under a magnifying lens: an unmistakable hawk crest etched into the golden clasp. "It appears to be an authentic Atreides heirloom, Highness."

Later, Irulan had walked into Paul's private study and interrupted a meeting with Stilgar, freshly returned from an offworld military mission. While the Fremen commander watched, looking at her sourly as he often did, Irulan had handed the reefpearls to Paul. "I believe this keepsake belongs to you, my Husband, not to me."

"I am Muad'Dib now. Atreides heirlooms are no longer important to me." With a casual motion Paul had tossed the reefpearls back to her. "Keep them yourself, or send them to my mother on Caladan, as you like." The Princess had gone away with the necklace, questions churning through her mind. . . .

Now, as she held the strand of pearls up to the light from an overhead glowglobe, Irulan looked through a handheld magnifier and found the minuscule hawk crest, as expected. But something wasn't right. Laying out the reefpearls, she looked at them under a focusing lens. Previously, the second pearl from the clasp had been distinguished by a barely perceptible scratch that the jeweler pointed out to her. Now she could not locate it. Her heart racing, Irulan looked again, increasing the magnification just to verify her suspicions.

Not there.

Carrying the pearls, she marched off to the grand ballroom where servants were setting up dinner. She still wore wrinkled and dusty clothing from her day on the streets of Arrakeen, but she did not care about decorum.

When Alia arrived with Duncan and took her customary place at the head of the table, Irulan laid the pearls on her own dinner plate. "I must commend you on an excellent job of copying, Lady Alia. However, your craftsmen failed to take into account a small scratch on one of the pearls."

Rather than being incensed, Alia responded with a wide smile. "You see, Duncan! Irulan is not as easily fooled as you expected. She noticed a flaw that even our experts disregarded."

Her new husband wore a slight frown. "I did suggest that we ask her openly for the original, instead of attempting secrecy."

Irulan waited for an explanation, and Alia said lightly, "We confiscated the original because it is a relic of House Atreides. It has nothing to do with you, Irulan."

"Paul himself told me I could keep it."

"You received many items from my brother."

"Legitimately. I was his wife."

"We both know the truth of that, Irulan. Because of their important religious significance, all of your original keepsakes have been replaced with copies. The true relics will be placed under the care and guard of the Qizarate, and select authorized replicas will be made available to certain devout and generous collectors."

Irulan felt anger, but used her Bene Gesserit training to remain calm. "Those were my possessions. Gifts from my *husband.*" She was edging into dangerous territory, but she set aside her fear and tried to keep her voice steady. "With all due respect, because of my dedication and loyalty, I have earned the right to keep my own things."

"Oh, enough melodrama, Irulan Corrino! They were never *your* things. I don't see how any of this can matter to you. You are not really an Atreides." Giving her a dismissive gesture, Alia called for the first course. By now, other diners had halted their conversations, and the usual dinner table murmurings had dwindled to a few tinklings of silverware, glasses, and plates.

Servants rushed about in a great flurry, serving extravagant salads, lush greens, and succulent raw vegetables grown in moisture-sealed greenhouses inside the Citadel. It was clear Alia wanted to speak no more of the matter.

In a voice as brittle as dried bone, Irulan asked, "Will the Lady Jessica be joining us for dinner?"

"My mother has chosen to meditate in her own rooms."

Irulan decided to pay a visit to Jessica later in the evening. It was obvious that the other woman had much more to tell her, but Irulan hadn't been ready to hear it. Irulan ate and then excused herself as quickly as possible.

WHEN JESSICA RESPONDED to a subdued knock at the door to her private apartments, she found the Princess standing there alone and troubled. In an instant, she read many things in the younger woman's expression. "Please come inside for a cup of spice tea."

After Jessica had closed the door behind them, Irulan used finger talk to silently explain what Alia had done; her coded words were tentative at first, but she gained energy as she allowed herself to become more upset. She felt a need for secrecy—perhaps irrationally, since Alia had just confirmed what she'd done in front of all the attendees at the banquet.

Absorbing the new information, Jessica let out a long sigh. Her fingers flashed in subtle communication, acknowledging the potential danger they faced. "My daughter grows increasingly unpredictable, and the challenge before you is great. You walk a dangerous, fine line—just as Paul did when he looked into the future and saw only a treacherous and uncertain path. Alia is the rightful Regent of the Imperium, and we must accept that. But even Alia doesn't see everything. You have an important role, as do I. As does Bronso of Ix."

Irulan was startled. "*Bronso* has an important role?"

"Paul understood it before I did, Irulan, and he asked us for help."

She gave a finger sign for added caution. Alia knew every Bene Gesserit code, and if there were hidden spy-eyes. . . .

Feigning casualness, Jessica sat back against her comfortable cushions, and reached over to pour them tea. Openly, as a diversion, she spoke of how much she missed Caladan and hoped to return there soon; all the while the fingers of one hand flashed subtly with the real message: "You will make your own decisions, Irulan. But in determining what to write, you must first *know* the truth, in all of its dimensions. Your special duty is to protect Paul's legacy."

Hunching over, hiding her hands in her lap, Jessica continued her quick finger signs. "You must hear the rest of the story about Bronso and Paul. Only then will you understand why Bronso writes what he does. We cannot speak here. I will arrange a safe time and place."

Alas, history can be rewritten according to political agendas, but in the end, facts remain facts.

—*Conversations with Muad'Dib* by the PRINCESS IRULAN

After establishing an acceptable pretext that she and Irulan wished to attend a Fremen ceremony at Sietch Tabr the following evening, Jessica specifically requested Gurney Halleck to pilot the ornithopter. Preoccupied with a new set of motions that had been delivered from the latest Landsraad meeting on Kaitain, Alia sent them off without any apparent concern.

Gurney made the 'thopter preparations with good cheer, meeting the two women in a vehicle bay that was normally used for Regency business and security operations. "The guards assigned us this craft, my Ladies. I have loaded aboard literjons of water, a Fremkit, and other emergency supplies. We are ready to go."

Jessica paused, then looked over her shoulder. "We'll take that one instead, Gurney. I like the look of it better. You can go over the checklist yourself quickly enough." Any 'thopter that Alia had assigned to them might contain hidden listening devices, and Jessica wanted no one to hear what she was about to reveal.

Though surprised by the unexpected change, Gurney called for assistance in preparing the second craft. Catching his eye, Jessica made a subtle half-hidden signal with her hand, using an old Atreides battle code to inform him that he was to ask no further questions. A troubled cloud came over the man's face, darkening the line of his inkvine scar, before he returned to his casual demeanor.

The mechanics and uniformed guards were thrown into confusion by the sudden change, but Gurney brushed them aside and quickly transferred over the supplies, checked the fuel level, and tested the 'thopter systems, while Irulan and Jessica waited in the vehicle bay. Both of the noble ladies looked out of place.

When he was satisfied, Gurney opened the door of the craft and extended a hand to help Irulan and Jessica aboard. After they had secured themselves inside, he powered up the engines, extended the stubby wings, and activated the jetpods.

The craft flew away from the Citadel of Muad'Dib, into the sparkling traffic patterns of the desert night. Both moons shone overhead, widely separated in the sky. Gurney fixed his gaze ahead through the cockpit plaz, guiding them through the thermal turbulence caused by temperatures falling after sunset. They flew up and over the rugged barrier of the Shield Wall.

Jessica drew a long, deep breath. "I wanted you to be my pilot, Gurney, because I trust you completely. Even if Duncan is the old Duncan, Alia has him too ensnared." She glanced over at Irulan, who looked willowy and beautiful, though not fragile. "And I'm not certain that I share Alia's goals in all things. For what I am about to reveal—to both of you—I require absolute privacy. Alia cannot be allowed to know what I tell you."

Though he concentrated on his flying, Gurney was troubled. "I am always loyal to you, my Lady, but for a mother to keep such secrets from her daughter, it's not to my liking."

Jessica sighed. "They are secrets about my son, and they concern you as well, Gurney. Back in Arrakeen, there are too many eyes and ears, as there will be in Sietch Tabr. We need time alone. Absolutely alone." She leaned forward, spoke into his ear over the thrumming of the articulated wings. "Find us a place to land—a rock outcropping somewhere not too obvious. Once I begin, I'll want your full attention, and this could take some time."

Flying over the open desert, Gurney passed several low ridges, black islands in the sand that he did not find satisfactory. At last he selected a reef of rock far enough outside their anticipated flight path. He circled, then fiddled with the control panel. "I can contrive a minor malfunction in one of the engines so that the 'thopter log shows we were required to land and make repairs."

"Good thinking, Gurney."

He set them down on the rugged surface, where they were entirely alone. "There, my Lady, I hope this place will serve. I know of no Fremen caches or formal sietches near here. It's too small to be worth anything." His glass-splinter eyes were bright, but she saw a dread within them: He did not relish the prospect of what she would have to say.

Jessica fitted her noseplugs, adjusted her face mask, checked other fittings on her stillsuit. "Come, we will go outside onto the rocks, away from the 'thopter." She couldn't be too careful. Saying little, she and her two companions went outside into the quiet desert night.

Jessica led them to a sheltered overhang of dark rock, where they could still see the 'thopter sitting like a large, ungainly insect where it had landed. Wind whispered around them as they found places to sit on the hard surfaces. "This will do fine," she said.

Irulan composed herself, waiting attentively in the shelter of rock. "I'm eager to hear you explain why you seem to keep defending, or at least shielding, Bronso."

Gurney perked up. "I would like to know that as well, my Lady, but I refrained from asking questions, as you requested."

"You'll know the hard truth I learned about Paul, and you'll know why—wrongly—I decided that I had to kill my own son."

Before her listeners could recover from what she had said, Jessica drew a long breath, marshaled her thoughts, and spoke openly. "After the death of Earl Rhombur in 10,188, House Vernius remained estranged from House Atreides for a long time. But twelve years later, during the worst excesses of the Jihad, while Paul was Emperor, events conspired to bring the two Great Houses together again. . . ."

PART IV

10,200 AG

The Reign of Emperor Paul-Muad'Dib

*It has been seven years since the fall of Shaddam IV,
who remains in exile on Salusa Secundus. Two years
have passed since Count Fenring's failed assassination
attempt on Paul Atreides.*

*Muad'Dib's Jihad rages across hundreds of worlds, but Lady
Jessica and Gurney Halleck have withdrawn to Caladan,
hoping to avoid the bloodshed and fanaticism.*

There are those who think that to revere Muad'Dib takes nothing more than the utterance of a prayer, the lighting of a candle, and the casting of a pinch of sand over one's shoulder. There are those who think that building shrines, waving banners, and collecting trinkets is sufficient. I have even heard of those who slice open their hands to spill blood on the ground because they think this honors Muad'Dib. Why does my son need more careless blood spilled in his name? He has enough of that. If you truly wish to honor Muad'Dib, then do it with your heart, your mind, and your soul. And never assume you know the complete Muad'Dib; there is much about him that can never be revealed.

—LADY JESSICA, address to pilgrims at the Cala City Spaceport

Following the fall of Shaddam IV, Paul's zealous followers had surged across the Imperium for seven years. The prospect of peace seemed as distant as sunshine during Caladan's months-long stormy season.

Unable to stomach the absurd distortions spread by the Qizarate and Muad'Dib's propaganda machine, Jessica had left Arrakis and returned to Caladan, where she kept her opinions private and ruled her people with the assistance of Gurney Halleck.

But because of the fervor that Muad'Dib inspired, pilgrims followed her—great numbers of them—and clamored for her blessings.

Before the end of the Corrino Imperium, Caladan had been only a secondary world ruled by a somewhat ordinary Landsraad family. Though the leaders of House Atreides were well liked in the Landsraad, they had never been as wealthy or powerful as House Harkonnen, House Ecaz, House Richese, or others at the front ranks.

Ruling the Imperium from his distant throne on Dune, Paul-Muad'Dib had not visited his home world in some time, yet pilgrims still came to Caladan, and they kept coming. The Cala City spaceport was not designed to accommodate the relentless traffic that swept down like a raging flood. Veterans of uncounted battles, desperate refugees, and pilgrims too infirm to fight—all went to touch the soil upon which Muad'Dib had spent his childhood, and to take a little of it home with them. . . .

Jessica glided down a staircase to the main level of Castle Caladan, knowing that a crowd waited inside the audience chamber, where Leto had once listened to the complaints, demands, and needs of his people. More than twenty generations of Atreides had done the same before him. Jessica could not break that tradition now.

Outside on the winding path that led up from the seaside village, she heard the clink of hammers as stonemasons repaired cobblestones and added gravel. Gardeners uprooted dying shrubs and planted new ones, knowing they would have to repeat the process in less than a month. Despite posted signs and guards patrolling the road, offworld pilgrims pocketed pebbles and plucked leaves from bushes as keepsakes of their visit to holy Caladan.

Offworlders came in a variety of clothing styles, carrying ribbons with the name of Muad'Dib, holding tiny sacks filled with sand that purportedly came from Arrakis, or collectibles said to have some connection with the Holy Emperor. Most of these items were cheaply made or fraudulent, or both.

Entering the chamber, Jessica strengthened her resolve when she saw the sheer number of people there. Gurney had arrived early to sort those who wished to present petitions from the larger number of visitors who simply wanted to glimpse the mother of Muad'Dib. Of those who asked to address her directly, Gurney gave precedence to the true Caladan natives, and relegated to the end of the line those who merely wanted to prostrate themselves before her.

When Jessica walked down the aisle to the front of the room, a hush rippled before her, followed by a curling aftershock of whispered awe. She kept her gaze forward, knowing that if she deigned to notice any particular supplicants, they would reach out their hands or raise up their children for blessings.

If Reverend Mother Mohiam could see her now! Jessica wondered if her old teacher would be impressed or disgusted. The Bene Gesserits despised and feared what Paul had become, though they themselves had worked for many generations to create a Kwisatz Haderach. Under

Muad'Dib's reign, the Sisterhood had fallen on excessively hard times, and Paul made no secret of how much he resented them. Even so, the women continued to make overtures to Jessica, pleading for her assistance and understanding. So far, she had ignored them. They had done enough damage, as far as she was concerned.

Beside her elevated chair at the front of the room, Gurney stood like a master at arms. Though he was an earl in his own right and an esteemed hero of many battles, he abdicated authority to Jessica whenever she took her duchy seat. "Very well, let's begin," she said. "You people must have more important things to do than stay here all day." The audience members seemed not to notice her wry humor.

Jessica recognized the first supplicant who stepped forward, a bearded old man clad in traditional fishing clothes, wearing a medallion on a blue ribbon around his neck. With a potbelly and stick-thin legs, Mayor Jeron Horvu had been the elected leader of Cala City for most of his life, groomed by the Old Duke himself.

The mayor was obviously distressed. His cheeks were gaunt, his eyes red and weary from lack of sleep. He gave Jessica a quick formal bow, which some in the audience regarded as an insufficient display of reverence. "My Lady, we are *besieged*. I implore you to help us. Save our world."

Many pilgrims looked from side to side with clenched fists, ready to fight anyone who dared to threaten Caladan . . . not realizing that the Mayor referred to *them*.

"Describe exactly what you mean, Jeron." She leaned forward to encourage him. "I've always known you to have the best interests of Caladan and its people at heart."

"All these offworlders!" Horvu gestured behind him at the crowds. "They say they come to honor Paul Atreides, the son of our noble Duke, yet they plunder our towns, trample the headlands, muddy the shores! I'm sure they mean well," he added quickly, trying to placate the angry buzzing that rose in the audience chamber, "but their intentions are irrelevant when everything we hold dear is stripped barren."

"Go on, man, be specific," Gurney prodded. "These others need to hear it."

The old man began to tick off items on his fingers. "Just last week, we had to replace three docks down in the harbor because the wood was so badly splintered and weakened from countless people taking slivers as mementos. Simply because Duke Leto Atreides used to dock his boat *Victor* there!" He rolled his eyes to show how absurd he considered the idea to be.

"Our inns have been ransacked. Our streets overflow with people who sleep in the gutters, steal things from merchants, and justify their thievery by claiming that 'Muad'Dib would be generous to all of his followers'! And let's not forget those charlatan souvenir vendors who sell counterfeit scraps of things they say Muad'Dib touched or blessed. It is well known that they simply gather any items they can find and sell them to gullible pilgrims, who pay sizeable sums, with or without proof."

Now that his passion had gained momentum, Horvu did not slow down. "The fishing waters are so crowded with tourist boats that our catches have drastically decreased, at a time when there are thousands more mouths to feed! Our very way of life is being trampled, Lady Jessica. Please help us." Horvu raised his hands. "Please, make them stop coming."

"You must not, Sayyadina!" someone cried from the audience. "This is the first home of Muad'Dib, a sacred place on the Hajj. The Messiah will strike down anyone who denies us, with a vengeful bolt from the heavens!" Shouts of support sounded.

Horvu quailed at the sheer venom in the audience's reaction, but Jessica rose to her feet. She'd had enough. "It is not for the Emperor Paul-Muad'Dib to strike *anyone* down from Heaven. That is the purview of God Himself. How dare you insult both God and my son by pretending he has such power!" The people were shocked into silence by her words. "Don't you want to be protected from those who would cheat you? Very well, this is my command. As a first step, I order that all vendors must prove their claims to *my* satisfaction before they are allowed to market any artifacts.

"Second, I hereby alter our law: Anyone caught stealing from the good people of Caladan will be considered to have stolen from Muad'Dib himself. Let a Qizarate court deal with them." That stunned them into silence, since all knew how harshly the priests would punish such a crime.

"And third: We will limit the number of pilgrims who come here, and those who are allowed to visit Caladan will henceforth be charged a substantial fee for their visa, with the funds used to replace things damaged or stolen by pilgrims." Satisfied with the pronouncement, she nodded to herself. "Gurney, please work with Mayor Horvu to develop and implement a suitable plan." She added a hard edge to her words, a ripple of Voice to take advantage of the reverence these followers held. "Thus, I have spoken, in the sacred name of Muad'Dib."

Jessica saw tears of gratitude brimming in the Mayor's rheumy old eyes, but she did not detect any similar reaction in the faces of the by-standers. They respected and feared her, but did not like the pronouncements she had made.

So be it, she thought. Elsewhere in the Imperium, Paul's fanatics could run loose and out of control. But not on Caladan.

Few forces can match the power of fanaticism. One that comes close is wounded pride.

—*Conversations with Muad'Dib* by the PRINCESS IRULAN

Over the past several years, Jessica had already heard enough news about the Jihad's atrocities, things that Paul allowed to be done in his name. But more stories found her, whether or not she wanted to hear—or believe—them.

Each time a Heighliner passed over Caladan, Mayor Horvu and the redoubtable village priest Abbo Sintra hurried to the Castle to report the travelers' tales. Meaning well, the two men showed Jessica official Qizarate releases as well as unofficial documents spread by horrified survivors of Jihad attacks. "We beseech you to review these stories, and please *do* something, my Lady!" Horvu pleaded. "He is your son!"

"Help him return to the just and honorable path," said the priest, who had long ago officiated at Duke Leto's disastrous wedding ceremony. "Paul will listen to his mother. Help him remember that he was an Atreides long before he became this fanatical desert leader."

After Jessica shooed the men away, she avoided looking at the reports for a long time. Finally, she retired to a private room, calling Gurney to join her. The two sat with disturbed expressions as they read the reports.

Three more planets had been completely sterilized, scalded clean of all life, their populations exterminated. Every living thing. And this was condoned by *Paul*, a man who espoused the ecological awakening and careful terraforming of Arrakis, a man who had just established and endowed a new School of Planetology in honor of Chani's father.

That makes four worlds gone now. And each atrocity seemed to be getting easier for him. Her voice was a chilling whisper. "What can he be thinking? It's murder!"

"Paul's first step down that slippery slope was when he punished Earl Thorvald and his rebels, wiping out the planet Ipyr, my Lady."

Jessica frowned. "In that instance, Thorvald was en route to Caladan, to annihilate us. All of Caladan was threatened, the Atreides homeworld. That was an attack aimed at Paul himself, something he could not ignore."

"Most of those who died on Ipyr—women, children, ordinary people—were undoubtedly innocent." Gurney could not tear his eyes away from the images he saw now.

Jessica's tone dropped off in sadness. "It was a dreadful price, but I can almost accept what he did in response. He had to send a message that would prevent further rebellious acts. But these other planets . . ." She shook her head and set her jaw firmly. "He must have had his reasons. I know my son—I raised him, and I cannot accept that he does this capriciously or vindictively." Making it more difficult on them, the Emperor had not explained himself, and his followers took it on faith that what Muad'Dib foresaw, and decreed, *must* be necessary.

Jessica could not brush aside her vivid memories of Paul as a precocious child, a talented youth who struggled against adversity and emerged victorious, stronger, and—so she'd always believed—with his core of Atreides honor intact. As his mother, she could not simply condemn him out of hand . . . nor could she ignore, excuse, or rationalize his recent actions.

"I would feel better if I understood his overall plan. I'm afraid Paul is slipping and sliding toward oblivion, making up new excuses as fast as he finds fresh targets, my Lady."

The pair reviewed images of smoking battlefields. A Qizarate spokesman, speaking into the imager, proudly identified the numerous bodies strewn across the fields as "those who refused the blessings of Muad'Dib." On each battleground, the slain numbered in the tens of thousands.

Jessica saw that the celebrants who ran across fields and plundered the bodies of the dead were Paul's jihadi fighters. In the foreground, vessels were clearly marked as medical ships carrying hospital troops and battlefield surgeons. But Jessica spotted something in the background of the high-resolution image that the Qizarate had either not noticed, or never intended to report upon. She enhanced the view, zeroed in on several large, unmarked ships that hovered at the edges of the bloody field.

There, small-statured men scurried out of transport vessels to comb over the slain, discarding many corpses, marking others. Handlers came afterward with suspensor-borne pallets and loaded bodies aboard, stacked them like split logs, then carried their grisly harvest back to the unmarked vessels.

"Gods below, those are Tleilaxu. Handlers of the dead retrieving corpses."

"But not all of the corpses," Jessica pointed out with a frown. "They're using some kind of selection process. If those were simply mortuary vessels, the Tleilaxu would gather every dead body. Why do they choose *particular* ones? And what are they doing with them?"

As soon as each cadaver craft was fully loaded, the cargo doors sealed shut and it lifted off, groaning with the weight of so many bodies aboard. As soon as one vessel departed, another unmarked ship dropped to the battlefield and began the same process.

Before either Jessica or Gurney could postulate any answers, a brisk knock at the door interrupted them. A young castle page spoke quietly, "A Guild Courier is here, my Lady, bearing a message from your son, the Holy Emperor."

The uniformed Guild employee who appeared moments later was female, though her short hair and loose singlesuit gave her an androgynous appearance. She handed over a message cylinder with a slight and efficient bow. "My Lady Jessica, Muad'Dib commissioned me to deliver this to you."

She accepted the cylinder and dismissed the woman. After the door closed, Jessica promptly unsealed the message, which was written in Atreides battle language. A personal letter from Paul. Jessica had no secrets from Gurney, and she allowed him to look over her shoulder:

"Dear Mother, I know you prefer to remain on Caladan away from Imperial politics, but I have an important favor to ask. It would mean a great deal to me. After my victory on Arrakis, I promised Shaddam in his exile that I would send terraformers to Salusa Secundus. Once I established my School of Planetology, I dispatched skilled workers to begin the task, and now the time has come for a thorough inspection of their work.

"I am sending both Chani and Irulan, who can speak and observe for me, but I would greatly appreciate your attendance. You see things from a different perspective, Mother. I'd like you to be my independent eyes and ears."

Jessica rolled up the message, deep in thought. "Of course I'll go. But first I have an important duty to perform tonight, for Caladan."

AS THE SUNSET colors deepened under a clear evening sky, Jessica led a small procession of villagers up into the coastal hills for the annual folk festival of the Empty Man. Each year, on the night of the autumn solstice, the people gathered to celebrate the legendary defeat of evil with a large bonfire and an effigy burning on the cliffs above the crashing surf. More so than in previous years, the procession had to be kept carefully private, the Caladan natives not wanting the offworld pilgrims to pollute their culture. Let the offworlders wonder what sort of ceremony was being held, and why they had not been invited.

Villagers streamed up a well-worn trail to the grassy headlands, leaving the harbor and town behind. They carried firebrands for torches to light after dark. Jessica walked regally at the head of the group with her chin held high.

The crowd reached their destination as the night's chill pulled a thin mist from the sea. A huge pile of twisted driftwood and kindling stood like an island at the edge of the cliff. Atop this, a stick framework held a sagging suit of clothes—the effigy of the Empty Man.

After the villagers took their places and sang a bright, powerful song to drive away evil, Mayor Horvu ignited a piece of kindling and applied the flames to the heart of the woodpile. Parents and children came forward to light their brands in the growing fire, and then stepped back.

When the people all fell silent, holding their flickering torches, she had everyone's attention.

Jessica would tell the tale, just as their fallen Duke Leto used to do.

"A long time ago in a quiet fishing village, there lived a man whose soul died within him after a terrible fever—but his body didn't follow in death. Even though everyone else thought he had recovered, the emptiness inside grew and grew . . . and no one could see the change, because his body *remembered* how to be human.

"The man discovered that the only way to stop the emptiness from growing was to fill it up with pain." She paused for dramatic effect, looked at the shining eyes of her listeners. "Children began to vanish from the beaches, and small fishing boats were found adrift and crewless. Bodies were discovered at low tide on the shore. Young men went out on errands and never returned.

"And as the emptiness inside the man grew hungrier, he became so bold in his need to find victims that finally he was caught." She whispered, leaning forward to three boys who stood close. "The towns-people pursued the man up into the headlands and cornered him at the edge of a cliff. But when they moved to take him into custody so that the Duke could dispense justice, the man hurled himself off the precipice, down to the wave-washed rocks."

Jessica turned to face the dark sea beyond the edge of the firelight. "The next morning, when they fished his body out of the water, they found only an empty skin, like a discarded suit with nothing else inside. An Empty Man."

Some of the listeners giggled, others muttered nervously. Jessica held up her small brand. "And now, let us all light our—"

A commotion came from behind the group. A party of five men marched up the trail in the darkness, dressed in the garments of Muad'Dib's priesthood, all yellow except the leader. Wearing an orange robe, he exhibited an air of self-importance, as if he were entitled to attend any private ceremony he chose. "I bear a proclamation in the name of Muad'Dib. These words are for the people of Caladan."

Jessica stepped forward. "Can this not wait? This is our festival."

"The words of Muad'Dib will not wait for a local matter," the priest said, as if the comment should have been self-evident. "This proclamation comes from Korba the Panegyrist, official spokesman for the priesthood and representative of the Holy Emperor Muad'Dib:

"'Because Caladan is sacred as the childhood home of Muad'Dib, its name must reflect its importance. People from ancient times named this planet Caladan, but such a name no longer has sufficient relevance. Just as Arrakis is now called Dune by the faithful, so Caladan has been renamed *Chisra Sala Muad'Dib*, which, in the language of the desert, means the Glorious Origin of Muad'Dib. Korba has hereby decreed that all future maps of the Imperium shall reflect this change. Henceforth, your people shall be honored to use the new name in all of your writings and conversations."

Jessica was amazed at the audacity of this man. She wondered if Paul even knew about this ridiculous idea; the supercilious Qizarate probably deemed the matter beneath Muad'Dib's notice. She cut the priest off immediately, addressing him with the full authority of her position as Duchess. "That is unacceptable. I will not allow you to strip these people of their heritage. You cannot—"

The priest interrupted her, much to her astonishment and annoyance. "This is about more than their heritage." He regarded each person who held a flickering torch to ward off evil. Now those lights seemed small and weak. The priest seemed to see nothing but his own importance. "We will provide copies of the proclamation so that they may be distributed among those who are not here. The word of Muad'Dib must be heard by everyone."

He placed a copy of the document into the trembling hands of Mayor Horvu. He also gave one to Gurney, who tossed it to the ground, where stray breezes snatched it and swept it over the edge of the cliff. The priest pretended not to notice.

The blazing bonfire grew brighter and hotter as the five priests wended their way back down the path, letting the crowd pick up the festival once more. But Jessica was no longer in any mood for celebrating.

The expectations of civilized society should afford all the protection
a person needs. But that armor is rendered as thin as tissue when
one is dealing with the uncivilized.

—Bene Gesserit archives

Entering the den of a lion . . . a Corrino lion.

Thanks to protocol machinations with the Guild, Jessica arrived at the same time as Chani and Irulan, and all converged at the new complex the exiled Corrinos had built. Shaddam's new city was a cluster of connected domes, each of which contained shielded buildings so that the inhabitants could, with some amount of imagination, pretend that they were still on Kaitain.

Ages ago, Salusa Secundus had been the lavish capital of the Imperium, but a disgraced noble family had unleashed enough atomics to devastate the world, wrecking the climate and deluging it with fallout and uncontrolled fires. Salusa had been a dead place for a long, long time, but by now the background radioactivity had dwindled to nominal levels, and persistent life emerged in a weak new spring. With the vigorous work of Paul's terraforming teams, Jessica expected Salusa to reawaken rather quickly.

The exiled court welcomed the representatives of Emperor Muad'Dib with great fanfare. Standing there as Chani and Irulan arrived in a suspensor-borne barge made for showy processions, Jessica wondered what other use Shaddam had for such a vessel here. She watched the fallen Emperor attempt to smile; after all his years of ruling on Kaitain,

Jessica thought he would have been better at it by now. His whole body seemed to cringe. She noted streaks of gray in the nobleman's reddish hair, and she could also see the unconcealed, simmering resentment on his thin face. Not surprising, since she represented *Paul-Muad'Dib*, the man who had defeated him.

Jessica observed Count and Lady Fenring, both of whom kept themselves surrounded by members of the large reception party. Shaddam's daughters clustered at the front of the group. Josifa and Chalice seemed eager to see their sister again, or at the very least pleased to participate in royal pomp and splendor again. Wensicia, though, wore a sour expression as she clung to her little boy's hand so tightly that he squirmed with discomfort.

The loud music played a dramatic sounding Kaitain march, then dropped off into sudden silence. Surrounded by yellow-robed priests and crisply uniformed Fedaykin guards, Irulan and Chani emerged from the ornate barge.

Chani slipped back her hood to reveal elfin features, dusky skin, dark red hair, and blue-within-blue eyes. She wore clothes fitted to desert environments, practical garments rather than showy. Next to the formally dressed Irulan, Chani seemed on edge, a Fremen fighter among known enemies. Jessica knew there was no love lost between the two women, but they had a common goal now.

Irulan regarded her family with an icy gaze and a stony expression. She did not seem overly pleased to visit them, and Jessica detected a similarly veiled animosity from the Corrinos. Such complex relationships here. . . .

The silence lasted an instant too long, as if no one knew who would speak first. Then, with a nudge, the unrealistically young-looking new chamberlain delivered the official greeting. "Shaddam Corrino IV welcomes the representatives of Emperor Muad'Dib."

The young man's voice was a bit too high, a bit too thin, and it quavered as if the volume of his own amplified words startled him. Jessica decided he must have been stuffed into a uniform and told what to say, without being given much training. Shaddam's last formal chamberlain, Beely Ridondo, had been executed in front of Alia six years ago, because he'd made too many demands about the ecological restoration of Salusa Secundus.

This one bowed awkwardly. "May you be inspired to accelerate the terraforming work being done here, in the name of God."

With a smooth step, Jessica reached out her hands to greet the two women. Clasping Chani's hand in her right and Irulan's in her left, the movement also neatly put herself in front of the fallen Emperor. "My son asked me to join both of you here to ensure a successful visit."

Chani bowed, and her expression showed genuine warmth. "Thank you, Sayyadina. It has been too long, and I'm glad you're here."

Irulan chose to address Shaddam, and she did not bow. "We welcome this visit to your home on Salusa Secundus, Father. In return, please accept the good wishes of my beloved husband, the true Emperor."

So many sharp barbs loaded in that one statement, directed at both Chani and the Corrinos, Jessica thought. And Irulan knew exactly what she had done.

THE WILLOWY LADY Margot Fenring escorted Jessica to her quarters inside the domed city, an obvious ploy to keep her, Chani, and Irulan separate. "I am pleased to have a little time with you, Lady Jessica. Our paths do continue to cross, don't they?"

Jessica controlled her voice. "Are you my ally or enemy this time, Lady Fenring? You have been both in the past." The Count's wife had left her a secret message in the Arrakeen Residency, warning Jessica of Harkonnen treachery . . . but she had later sent her monstrous little daughter Marie as a pawn to kill Paul.

"This time, I am just an associate of the Sisterhood," Margot said, showing her to her room. "We have chosen our own paths, for good or ill."

Left to freshen up inside the room before a planned evening banquet, Jessica regarded the gaudy trappings: the intricate carvings, gold filigree, interlocked stained-plaz windows. The decorations seemed rushed and showy, a desperate effort to demonstrate that House Corrino had not lost all of its glory. Sparse artwork hung on the walls. Jessica gleaned the impression that the exiled Corrinos didn't have enough possessions to furnish every room. Then she wondered if that, too, was a carefully calculated impression designed to make her believe that the deposed Emperor's circumstances were more difficult than they really were. Was that what they wanted her to report to Paul?

Later, Count and Lady Fenring smiled as Jessica entered the banquet room. At the opposite side of the long table, Shaddam Corrino IV sat with his surviving daughters: Chalice, Josifa, and Wensicia. Irulan and Chani had been seated next to each other—an attempt to promote friction, Jessica wondered.

As she faced Shaddam before taking her seat, she hesitated, realizing that she had not decided how to address this man. Shaddam still deserved a certain degree of respect, but not too much. She swept her gaze around everyone in attendance. "Thank you for the kind reception—all of you."

Irulan turned to the small boy who sat at the table next to Wensicia. Little more than a year old, his eyes were bright and intelligent. "This is your son, Wensicia? Where is his father?"

The temperature in the air seemed to drop. "Farad'n is now the heir to whatever is left of House Corrino."

Wearing a vinegary expression, Shaddam glanced to his immediate right, where Count Fenring sat. "His father unfortunately passed away in my service."

Jessica noted a fractional flash of annoyance on Count Fenring's face, instantly hidden. *Interesting.* What did Fenring have to do with the child's father?

Chani drank sparingly from a goblet of water in front of her. She did not touch the wine. "His Holiness the Emperor Muad'Dib has dispatched us here to ensure that terraforming operations are being conducted with all due speed, to make Salusa into the garden world he envisions, full of gentle things."

Jessica wanted to twist the knife. "Paul is always true to his word."

Shaddam did not try to conceal his scowl, and then called for the first course, apparently anxious to be done with this meal. Jessica made a swift assessment of Shaddam. The Corrino patriarch saw only what he had lost, not what he retained. For a man who could well have been executed as a threat to Muad'Dib, Shaddam still had plenty of comforts, and yet the man must grieve for his palace on Kaitain, which had long since been burned by Muad'Dib's fanatical hordes.

Count Fenring deftly raised a prickly subject. He looked from

Chani to Irulan, then finally rested his gaze on Jessica. "Aaah, tell me, now that we've had seven years of . . . *this*, do you truly believe the human race is better off under your son's leadership, hmmm?"

Shaddam put his elbows on the table. "Or would you say that more people prospered under Corrino rule? What do *you* say, Irulan? The answer is obvious enough to me."

"I am sure many planetary populations are asking themselves the same question," Lady Fenring added.

"And we know what their answer must be." Wensicia raised her voice, drawing attention to herself. Receiving a rebuking glance from her father, she fell silent again. To deflect her embarrassment, she scolded Farad'n for fidgeting.

Chani spoke up. "Here in exile, you must have endless evenings to debate the same topic, but the question is moot for all of you. Muad'Dib is Emperor now, and House Corrino no longer rules."

Shaddam drummed fingers on the table and let out a long, weary sigh that sounded rehearsed. "I should have seen it coming. I am ashamed to admit my failings as an Emperor." He had to drag the words out of his throat, because they would not come willingly. Jessica did not recall any previous instance in which the Padishah Emperor had admitted his own mistakes. She didn't believe for a moment, though, that he had been humbled. "Alas, I was not attentive enough to my people, and did not notice the growing weaknesses on the planets that served me. Storm clouds were gathering, and I did not see the signs."

When she noticed a tiny smile of approval on Fenring's face, Jessica realized who had coached the fallen Emperor for this conversation.

"My failings may have softened the Imperium and allowed the bureaucracy to swell, but what Muad'Dib has done is far more damaging to CHOAM, the Landsraad, the Spacing Guild, everyone. Any fool can see that."

Count Fenring quickly inserted himself into the conversation when he saw Chani ready to leap to her feet and reach for her crysknife. "Ahhh, my Ladies, forgive us, but my friend Shaddam and I have had many such discussions. And we cannot find a convincing answer as to what Muad'Dib really intends. He seems to be a force for chaos, driven by the blind energy of religious fanatics. How does this ultimately help the Imperium?"

Jessica looked at the first course that had been placed in front of her—sparkling imported fruits and thin slices of raw meat. She picked at it without eating. "I can't deny that the Jihad has caused a lot of damage, but Paul must fix many generations of neglect. That is, by necessity, a painful process."

"Corrino neglect, you mean?" Shaddam asked, with a glare.

"All Great Houses were to blame, not just yours."

Like a serpent about to strike, Fenring leaned forward, folded his hands together. "Ahhhh, hmmm, can you explain to us how these continuing massacres by jihadis benefit mankind, in either the short or long run? How many planets has your son sterilized now? Is it three or four? How many more does he intend to destroy?"

"Emperor Muad'Dib makes his difficult decisions according to the harsh necessities of his rule," Irulan interrupted, "as you well know, Father. We are not privy to all of his reasons."

Around the table, no one was eating. All were listening to the conversation, even young Farad'n Corrino.

Count Fenring shrugged his shoulders. "Even so, do you all remain convinced that Muad'Dib's work is necessary? Tell us, for we are eager to hear your answer. How is the sterilization of planets and the slaughter of populations *helpful* to humanity in any way? Explain this to us, please, hmmm?"

"Muad'Dib sees things that others cannot. His vision extends far into the future," Chani said.

The plates were taken away, hardly touched, and the next course arrived—small roasted squabs in a bitter citrus sauce, garnished with spears of fresh flowers. Pressed for a definite answer, Jessica used one of her common refrains, even though it had not sounded convincing to her for a long while.

"My son understands the pitfalls that await all of us. He once told me that the only way to lead humanity forward is to build bridges across those pitfalls. I believe in him. If he has determined that continuing violence is necessary, then I trust him implicitly."

Wensicia made a sarcastic noise. "She sounds like one of the fanatics herself. All three of them do." Her venomous glare was directed toward Irulan, who ignored her.

Shaddam gave a rude snort, then caught himself and wiped his mouth with his napkin, pretending that the sound had been no more than an unpleasant belch. "Paul Atreides implies he has good reasons, but won't reveal them? Know this, all of you—a man on the Imperial throne can *say* anything he likes and expect others to believe him. That is what followers do. They *believe*. I know—I took advantage of that fact myself, many times."

The day the flesh shapes and the flesh the day shapes.

—DUKE LETO ATREIDES

W hile the Duchess was away from Caladan, an old woman struggled up the steps of the Cala City town hall, refusing the assistance offered by two kindly onlookers. She muttered at them with
enough sourness that the two gave her a wide berth. The mood of the
gathered people was already stormy, which fit the weather outside. In the
past hour it had rained heavily, leaving the streets wet and the buildings
dripping.

She ascended the laid-stone stairs, step by painful step. A tall man
in a formal suit held the door open for her, and she moved past him
with a grunt of appreciation. To anyone watching, the climb had taken
its toll on her, and she needed a place to sit down, but she concealed
her strength. She had arrived early enough to secure an aisle seat in the
front row, where the most people would notice her.

So far, her performance was quite convincing. No one would suspect
that Gaius Helen Mohiam was a Reverend Mother of the Bene
Gesserit.

Her bird-bright eyes took in the surroundings. This was an old government structure, with frescoes painted on the walls depicting the ex-
ploits of famous Atreides dukes. In one of the newer paintings, she
recognized Paulus in his matador outfit, facing a huge Salusan bull.

Paul Atreides, the reckless, out-of-control Kwisatz Haderach, had become a Salusan bull in the political arena, rampaging and goring Imperial traditions. In only a handful of years, Muad'Dib had single-handedly stripped the Bene Gesserit of their power and influence, heaping scorn on them and sending them running back to Wallach IX . . . not in defeat, but to regroup. Mohiam knew with every fiber of her being that the Sisterhood had to remove Paul and hope that his successor could be more easily controlled.

He is my grandson, she thought bitterly. How she wished she'd never been a part of the Bene Gesserit breeding chain that led to such a monster. After what he had done, Mohiam found him to be even more loathsome than Baron Vladimir Harkonnen, who had gotten her pregnant in the first place. Now, she deeply regretted not killing her grandson when she'd had the chance. There had been numerous opportunities, including one shortly after his birth, when she killed the original Piter de Vries and saved the baby.

That was a mistake.

But a Bene Gesserit was capable of looking at the broader picture of history. Mistakes could be corrected. And she was intent on doing so now.

As she sat in the town hall, exaggerating her discomfort with sounds and sighs and restless shiftings, townspeople continued to stream into the hall. Mayor Horvu appeared on the stage, fiddled with something on the podium, then looked at the agenda with a preoccupied muttering. All around her, the noise level increased to a loud, buzzing murmur—a decidedly angry murmur, because of the Imperial edict that changed the name of their planet.

Patience. Mohiam concealed her smile.

She remembered another opportunity to kill Paul Atreides, and again she had failed to act. When he was but a teenager, wide-eyed and earnest, she had held the poisoned gom jabbar to his neck, testing him with the agony box. Just a little jab then, and none of the ensuing horrors would have happened, hundreds of billions dead in his name, four planets sterilized and no doubt more on the planning sheets, all of human civilization reeling from an onslaught of fanaticism. One little jab of a needle. . . .

Another mistake. A big one.

She vowed not to make another one, though Mohiam doubted if she would ever get close to Paul again, because of the political machinery of his empire and his religion all around her. Paul's stinging words that day after his victory against the Emperor lingered in her memory: *"I think it better punishment that you live out your years never able to touch me or bend me to a single thing your scheming desires."*

Instead, the Sisterhood would have to carry the battle into a different arena, one at which they were masters. They would use individual populations as weapons. And what better weapon to turn against the Atreides than the people of Caladan? Though explicitly forbidden from traveling to Arrakis, she had quietly made her way here.

Now, in disguise among the locals, she had all of the necessary identity documents, contact lenses to cover her spice-addicted blue-in-blue eyes, overlaid fingerprints, altered facial features—she would fool anyone. Mohiam had worried that Lady Jessica or Gurney Halleck might recognize her, but the Duchess of Caladan had departed on an errand for her son to Salusa Secundus, and Earl Halleck was at his rural estate. *All the better*. No one else on this planet would know her.

The Sisterhood's campaign to undermine Paul-Muad'Dib would begin here. She would stir up the anthill and watch what scurried out. Paul had already slighted the people of Caladan and lost their respect. He had turned his back on them, *offended* them with his proclamation to rename their world as "Chisra Sala Muad'Dib." A ridiculous mouthful. Mohiam couldn't have asked for a better opportunity.

The local mayor called the town hall meeting to order, coming forward on bird-thin legs that did not seem capable of supporting his pot-belly. He seemed avuncular, well-liked. "We all know why we're here today." His rheumy eyes scanned the crowd. "We cannot let some distant bureaucrat rename our world. The question is, what are we going to do about it?"

The audience roared their unfocused outrage, years of uneasiness and dissatisfaction with the pilgrim mobs, blundering offworlders, the intrusion of outside events that should have remained safely far away.

"Caladan is Caladan."

"This is our planet, our people."

Horvu shouted into the voice pickup at the podium. "So then, what if we propose 'Muad'Dib's Caladan' as a compromise?"

"What if we find a new mayor?" a woman called in response. The crowd laughed.

One man was particularly vehement. "Desert fanatics do not decide our daily lives. What do grubby, dirty people know about the sea and the tides, the fish harvest, the thunderclouds and storms? Hah, they've never even seen rain! What do they know of our needs? A Fremen wouldn't survive a week on the high seas."

"We have nothing to do with Muad'Dib's Empire," said another man. "I don't know this 'Muad'Dib'—I know only Paul Atreides, who should be our Duke."

"Let's build up our army and fight them!" a woman cried in a shrill voice.

Mohiam watched the interchange with great interest, but the last comment was so absurd that some of the shouts died down. The mayor shook his head, looking sad. "No, no, none of that. We cannot stand up to Muad'Dib's vast military—you all know that."

"Then don't fight them." Mohiam struggled to her feet and turned toward the audience. "We don't want war. We want to be left alone. As many of you have said, Caladan is not part of this endless, bloody Jihad, and we should declare our *independence*. Paul Atreides is our lawful Duke, not this man who calls himself by a foreign name. Caladan isn't part of this struggle. We never wanted a part of it. We never invited these crazed pilgrims who sweep like locusts into our towns. We just want things back the way they were."

Mohiam heard bits of conversation around her. "Independence . . . Independence! Wouldn't it be wonderful?"

Independence. The word was like a fresh sea breeze curling through the town hall. The people naively thought that this new idea would not require them to take up arms and go against screaming Fedaykin killers.

The mayor raised a bony hand in an attempt to silence the crowd. "We are not here to discuss rebellion. I will have no part in that."

"Then you are in the wrong place," Mohiam said, very pleased with the discussion. "I am old and I have seen much. I was once a house servant for Old Duke Paulus, back when Atreides honor and human dignity still meant something. After he died, I withdrew inland where I have led a quiet life. Many of you may have seen me over the years, but probably didn't notice me." A planted idea, and the listeners would ponder and decide that, yes, they might have seen her in the town from time to time.

"What happened to Atreides honor? We just want a measure of respect. Enough of this folly. Either stand up to those priests or become doormats for them. Do not lose your backbone! If Paul Atreides bears any love for Caladan—and I believe he must—then surely he will accept the will of the people. We mean him no harm, but we must retain our identity. For the people of Caladan!" Her eyes scanned the crowd one last time. "Or would you rather be forever known as the people of *Chisra Sala Muad'Dib*?" She practically spat the name.

It was time to make her exit. The audience muttered, then began to cheer Mohiam as she worked her way down the aisle and back to the outer doors, the stone steps, and the damp night outside. She had barely needed to use Voice at all. . . .

As she departed, she heard Mayor Horvu changing his tune, enthusiastically accepting her suggestions as a reasonable compromise. Oblivious to her manipulations, he would carry the torch from here, and in later days no one would be able to name her, nor would they find her. Horvu would now lead them in increasingly dangerous directions. By the time Jessica came home from Salusa Secundus, the groundswell would be uncontrollable.

Mayor Horvu and all these people were mere cannon fodder in this new political battle, and Reverend Mother Mohiam felt no guilt about it. The entire Imperium was a large game of chess, and she was privileged to move some of the key pieces, never forgetting the line between the player and her pawns.

With a brisk step she walked into the drizzle, no longer showing signs of extreme age. *Sometimes it is so challenging to be human*, she thought.

Certain actions are taken out of mercy, necessity, or guilt. The logic may be impeccable and irrefutable . . . but the heart knows nothing of logic.

—GURNEY HALLECK, *Unfinished Songs*

When the gaze hounds were on the scent, Gurney loved the flood of adrenaline. As he ran with the animals, he became so engrossed in the chase that he could almost forget the painful memories he had accumulated over a lifetime. With Jessica away on Salusa Secundus and the front lines of Muad'Dib's Jihad far from here, he considered it an excellent time for a hunt.

Until recently, his life had been so turbulent that he'd never considered owning pets, but he was an Earl of Caladan now, a nobleman. He was expected to have a private estate, a manor house, a retinue of servants—and of course, hunting dogs.

Gurney had never meant to become so attached to the creatures, nor even to give them individual names, but he needed to call them something other than "Blackie" or "White Spot." For no better reason than that he had no other ideas, he named the six dogs after planets on which he had fought during the Jihad—Galacia, Giedi, Jakar, Anbus, Haviri, and Ceel. Each dog had its own personality, and they all reveled in the attention he gave them by patting their heads and rubbing their chests, brushing their fur, feeding them treats.

The gaze hounds could run for hours across the moors until they scared up a marsh hare, which they chased with a wild baying chorus.

Today, though, the prey had gotten away despite a long and exhausting chase. But at least the dogs got their exercise, and so did he. His clothes were damp with sweat, and his lungs burned.

When he took the dogs back to their kennel and fed them an extra bowl of food, the hound he'd named Giedi growled and sulked as he ate. Uncharacteristically, the dog had lagged behind in the chase today. Concerned, Gurney stepped into the kennel and saw that the animal's eyes were watery and red. Giedi let out a small defensive growl when his master touched him.

"You look sick, boy. I'd better isolate you from the others." Tugging on Giedi's collar, he hauled the reluctant black-and-tan hound to a separate run. If the dog didn't improve by tomorrow, Gurney would have to go into Cala City and find a skilled veterinarian.

The following morning, the gaze hound looked decidedly worse, eyes scarlet from scleral hemorrhaging. Giedi barked and howled, then whined as if in deep pain. When Gurney approached the kennel, the unfortunate animal threw himself against the barrier, growling and snapping.

Three of the other hounds—Jakar, Anbus, and cream-colored Haviri—had red-rimmed eyes as well and sulked in the backs of their kennels. Gurney felt a heavy fear in his gut, and immediately summoned a veterinarian to his estate.

The man took one look at the animals and shook his head. "Bloodfire virus. The symptoms are unmistakable, and you know it's incurable, my Lord. Much as you love your dogs, they will only grow worse. They'll suffer, and will begin to attack one another, even you. You've got to put all four of the sick ones down before the last two get infected. I can do it, if you like."

"No! There must be something you can do."

The veterinarian looked at him with heavy-lidded eyes. "Bloodfire is a rare disease among animals on Caladan, but once contracted it is always fatal. Separate out the two healthy dogs immediately, or you'll lose them too. But the others—" The doctor shook his head. "End their suffering now. A mad dog must be put down. Everyone knows that."

Gurney practically shoved the man back to his groundcar, then returned to the kennels. From their individual cages, the two healthy dogs, Galacia and Ceel, looked at their sick companions, whining mournfully.

Gurney asked one of his men-at-arms to help him separate the other three moody and lethargic dogs into empty cages. Haviri lashed out and tried to bite him, but with his fighting reflexes Gurney twisted away just in time. Feeling a chill, he realized that if *he* were to contract the disease, his own fate would be a long and painful series of treatments—with no guarantee of success.

The dog named Giedi, sick but not lethargic, threw himself against the kennel barrier, barking and scratching until his muzzle was bloody and his claws shattered. Mucus streamed from the dog's eyes, and Gurney wept. The animal didn't know him now, didn't know anything except its pain and virus-driven fury.

Gurney had faced horrific tragedies in his life: from his youth when he was tormented and forced to work in the Harkonnen slave pits, and they had raped and murdered his sister, to his days in the service of House Atreides, when he tried to stop the horrific massacre at Duke Leto's wedding, and later when he served on the battlefields of Grumman, Dune, and countless places in Paul's Jihad. Gurney had been forged and tempered in a crucible of extreme pain.

And this was just a dog . . . *just a dog.*

Gurney quivered as he stood there, unable to see through the veil of tears in his eyes. His knees were weak; his heart pounded as if it would explode. He felt like a coward, unable to do what was necessary. He had killed a great many men with his own hand. But this, what he had to do to a loyal animal. . . .

Moving like an ancient automaton, he went to the hunting locker and returned with a flechette pistol. Time and again he had shot cornered prey and put them out of their misery, making it quick. But now the nerves in his fingers had gone dead. He aimed the pistol, but it wavered even as the dog snarled at him.

Somehow, he managed to fire a needle into Giedi's chest. The dog let out a final yelp and collapsed into merciful silence.

Gurney staggered to the other kennels, where the remaining sick dogs huddled uncertainly. But he could not bring himself to put them down. They hadn't reached that point yet. Letting the needle pistol drop to the ground, he staggered away.

Only two of his gaze hounds remained uninfected. He ordered them quarantined.

The next day, Ceel also showed reddened eyes, and Gurney dragged him out of the kennel with Galacia. Five of the six! He had been too afraid, had avoided the hard truth too long, and he steeled himself now.

He was forced to use the needle pistol four more times. It didn't get any easier. He stood there trembling, stunned, torn.

Afterward, only Galacia remained, the gentlest of the hounds, the one who most adored attention, the female who wanted to be treated like a princess.

When he was all alone in the silence of the kennels, smelling the blood, Gurney slipped into the cage with her and collapsed beside her. Galacia lay down, resting her head in his lap, her ears drooping. He stroked her tawny fur and felt sadness rage through his body. At least he had saved her. Only one . . .

If he had acted more swiftly, if he had taken the first dog into quarantine as soon as he'd suspected the illness, if he had gone to the veterinarian earlier, if . . . if . . . if he'd been brave enough to face the pain of losing a few dogs, he might have saved the others. He had hesitated, denied his duty, and the other gaze hounds had paid for it.

No matter how much he loved them, killing the dogs had been the only way to cut losses, to stop them from doing further damage, to minimize the inevitable greater pain. As soon as the virus began to spread, the rest of his options had disappeared.

Gurney heaved a great breath. He felt so weak, so devastated. Galacia whimpered, and he patted her head. She looked up at him, helplessly.

Her eyes had begun to turn red.

Why is it that harm can be done in an instant, while healing requires days, years, even centuries? We exhaust ourselves trying to repair damage faster than the next wound can occur.

—DR. WELLINGTON YUEH, Suk medical records

Since the former Emperor decided to accompany the inspection group out to the terraforming sites, a simple trip out to the barren lands became a matter of such complexity that it rivaled the preparations for a major battle. The Imperial aerial transport was stocked with food and refreshments and staffed with at least one servant for every high-ranking passenger.

The Qizaras accompanying Irulan and Chani saw no benefit in the former Emperor's presence; many of them could not understand why he remained alive, since any fallen Fremen leader would have long since been killed—but Irulan told them to keep their objections to themselves. "It is the way things are done."

Aboard the large floating transport, Jessica remained alert for frictions among the Fedaykin, priests, and Corrino household guards. A few Sardaukar troops formed a personal bodyguard around the fallen Emperor to protect him in case any of Muad'Dib's men secretly tried to assassinate him. Jessica knew, though, that if Paul ever decided to get rid of Shaddam IV, there would be nothing secret about it.

When Chani directed the Fedaykin and the priests to their places, Shaddam made little effort to hide his scorn from her, remaining aloof in the forward observation area of the floating transport. "A mere concubine should not be ordering men about." His voice was loud enough to be heard over the hubbub of settling people.

Chani's hand went to her crysknife, and the Fedaykin and the priests were perfectly ready to go to battle, then and there. The Sardaukar moved close to the former Emperor in a tight protective posture.

But Jessica placed fingers on Chani's forearm. She said, also loudly enough to be heard, "The former Emperor is merely incensed that his own role is even less than that of a concubine. I was once a concubine, and now I am a ruling Duchess."

Shaddam was startled by the insult, and when Count Fenring chuckled loudly, he turned red.

"Enough of this posturing," Irulan snapped. "Father, you would be well advised to remember that my husband could sterilize Salusa Secundus all over again. Everyone here would be most pleased to complete this inspection as soon as possible, so let us go about our work without delay."

As the aerial transport departed, Jessica selected her seat, placing herself between Chani and Irulan. Though they shared no affection, both lived in the Arrakeen citadel and had long ago learned to tolerate one another. Each wanted something from the other: Chani wanted to be called Paul's wife, and Irulan wanted Paul's love.

Jessica showed no favoritism to either, lowering her voice to keep the conversation private. "I need your insights, both of you. I've been isolated from my son for so long I'm not sure I know him any longer. I see his decisions only through a filter of distance and biased reports, and frankly much of what he does disturbs me. Tell me about Paul's daily life, his mood, his opinions. I want to *understand* him."

Most of all, she wanted to know why he so easily accepted slaughter in his name. Long ago, when Paul had slain Jamis in a knife duel, Jessica had squashed his feeling of triumph, forcing him to feel the consequences and obligations of that one action, that one death. "How does it feel to be a killer?" Her son had been stung, shamed.

And now he blithely allowed the deaths of billions. . . .

I am Paul's mother, Jessica thought. *Should I not love him and support him, anyway? And yet, if he continues on this course, the whole galaxy will see him as history's greatest tyrant.*

Irulan's words were stiff and formal, but she allowed a faint glimmer of pain to leak through. "Paul does not speak openly with me. Chani is his confidante."

Jessica didn't think Chani ever criticized or questioned Paul's actions. Chani shrugged. "Muad'Dib is guided by prescience and by God. He sees what we cannot. What is the purpose in asking for explanations to that which is inexplicable?"

TRUE TO HIS promise, Paul had assigned his best planetology teams to Salusa, and they remained out in the field, combing the landscape, setting up testing stations. The men rarely had any need to come to Shaddam's domed city.

Jessica gazed out the leisurely vessel's plaz observation window, seeing clumps of hardy shrubs, arroyos carved by abrupt flash floods, and bizarre twisted hoodoos of rock sculpted by the hammerwinds. Despite its unpleasant environment, the planet supported a reasonable population of hardy survivors and descendants of prisoners who had been deposited over the centuries. Here and there, sheltered domes and prefabricated structures were nestled in box canyons. Crops struggled to grow beneath retractable reflective tarps that provided shelter from the worst blasts of weather.

"Salusa does not look so harsh in comparison with Dune," Chani said, standing next to her. "It is obvious that people can survive here if they are careful and resourceful."

Irulan came up behind them. "But not comfortable by any means."

Chani shot back. "Is it Muad'Dib's task to make them comfortable? That is something people must do for themselves."

"They are trying," Jessica interjected. "*Humans* caused this damage long ago, and now humans are trying to fix it."

Shaddam announced from the viewing platform on the bridge, "Our destination is the northwest basin, the site of the most extensive restoration work." He pointed to a prominent line in the terrain. "The ground team's current camp is in the base of that dry gorge. You can see all you need to see from the air."

"We decide what we will need to see," Chani said. "Take us down there. I would speak with the planetologists face to face. They are doing work in the name of Liet, my father."

"No, we can see quite enough from up here," Shaddam replied, as if he had the final word.

But Chani would have none of it. "Irulan and I have instructions to observe." She glanced sidelong at the Princess. "Unless you are afraid to get your hands dirty?"

Incensed, Irulan turned to her father. "Take us down, now."

With a beleaguered sigh, the deposed Emperor passed instructions to the pilot. The aerial transport and its accompanying ships landed like an invasion, startling the planetology team at their labors. Wearing dusty, stained jumpsuits, the terraformers left their machinery and hurried forward to greet the visitors.

The two men in charge of the dry canyon worksite were Lars Siewesca from the stark planet of Culat, and a stocky man who introduced himself as Qhomba from Grand Hain. Neither of those worlds was a pleasant place, Jessica knew.

Siewesca's appearance unsettled Jessica, for the man was tall and lean, with sandy blond hair and a neatly trimmed beard. Was he intentionally mimicking the late, murdered Dr. Liet-Kynes? Though the visitors included Shaddam IV, his daughter Princess Irulan, and Lady Jessica, the two planetologists were most impressed to meet Chani.

"Daughter of Liet! We are honored that you have come," Siewesca said, bobbing his head. "My companions and I all completed our training at the School of Planetology in Arrakeen. Please, let us show you our work! It is our heartfelt goal to honor your father's teachings and his dreams." They bustled around her, ignoring Shaddam, much to his annoyance, even though he had no particular interest in the operations.

Chattering to Chani, the two team leaders expressed unbridled enthusiasm, rattling off the hectares reclaimed, temperature gradients, and relative humidity traces. While they droned on with obscure numbers, percentages, and technical details, Chani dropped to her knees in the loose sandy ground of the canyon floor. She dug her fingers into the soil, working them deep, pulling up pebbles, sand, and dust. "This world is more dead than Dune."

Irulan remained standing, pristine and beautiful, profiled against the wasteland. "But Salusa is more hospitable and getting better. According to the reports, new ecosystems are catching hold, and the worst storms have abated in only a year."

Chani stood and brushed her hands on her thighs. "I did not mean dead in that way. Salusa was ruined by atomics and used for centuries as a prison planet—this place is dead in its *soul*."

The planetology team hurried to finish their preparations for a large test. "Deep scanning shows a substantial aquifer sealed beneath caprock," said Siewesca. "We were about to break open the barrier and create a channel so the underground river can flow again. It'll change the face of the continent."

"Very well, get on with it," Shaddam said, as if they had been waiting for him to issue orders.

Over the next hour, the crew packed their equipment and machinery, withdrawing their transports to the rim of the canyon above. Qhomba and Siewesca asked to be invited aboard the observers' ship in order to provide commentary. With the canyon work site abandoned and explosives planted in deep shafts, the rest of Shaddam's ships withdrew to a safe distance.

Qhomba and Siewesca pressed up against the observation windows, and Jessica sensed the genuine dedication of these men. The wait seemed interminable. Shaddam uttered a complaint about the delay, only to be interrupted by explosions that rumbled deep beneath the ground, hurling debris and dust in a feathery pattern against the wide canyon walls.

From behind the plume of smoke and debris, a roiling, stampeding wall of water spurted like pumping blood into the confines of the canyon, dragging layers of sediment with it. The surge swirled centuries-old dirt into a brown torrent that churned along.

Qhomba let out a high-pitched cheer. Siewesca grinned, scratching his sandy beard. "Salusa will become a garden in half the time it'll take us to reclaim Dune! In only a few centuries, this place will be a fertile world again, capable of supporting many kinds of life." He looked as if he expected them all to applaud.

Shaddam merely made a sour comment. "A few centuries? That does me no good." He did not behave as if he planned to stay here that long.

Jessica studied the man closely, and from the furtive look in his eyes she sensed that he was hiding something. She wondered what Shaddam and Fenring might be up to. She did not believe for a moment that the Corrinos had meekly bowed to their circumstances, abandoning all further ambitions.

We avoid what we do not wish to see; we are deaf to what we do not wish to hear; we ignore what we do not wish to know. We are masters of self-deception, of manipulating our perceptions.

—Bene Gesserit summation, Wallach IX archives

After Salusa Secundus, Jessica was glad to return to the calm beauty of Castle Caladan, where she could smell the moist salty air and see the colorful fishing boats in the harbor. Chani and Irulan had returned to Arrakis with their reports, along with a separate report of Jessica's impressions.

She could again forget about the Jihad and what Paul was doing.

And yet, she couldn't.

For years, her son had been slipping away from her, becoming a stranger, caught up in his own legend. She had always feared how easily he had accepted the religious mantle in order to make the Fremen follow him. Perhaps she should have stayed on Dune after all, as an adviser; Paul needed her counsel and her moral compass.

She had always given him the benefit of the doubt, but like constant water drops eroding a hollow in sandstone, questions continued to work their way into her mind. He had explained very little to her. What he foresaw might not truly be the sole path of humanity's survival. What if he had already lost his way and simply made wild pronouncements, expecting his followers to accept them, as Shaddam had done? What if Paul actually *believed* what his adoring sycophants said about him?

Before she could enjoy being home in the ancient castle, Mayor Horvu and the village priest, Abbo Sintra, arrived in the audience chamber, begging for an unscheduled conference. *Again*. Not surprisingly, they claimed it was an emergency. These two men, who had never been off-planet in their lives, did not have an adequate measuring stick to gauge a *real* emergency.

Dressed in homespun robes, the priest looked uncomfortable in the room where he had presided over Leto's ill-fated wedding ceremony, now thirteen years past. For his own part, Horvu had donned the formal clothes that he wore only at special ceremonies, prominent festivals, and funerals of state.

She was instantly on her guard.

"My Lady Duchess," Horvu began, "we cannot let this happen. It strikes at the heart of our heritage."

She took a chair at a writing desk rather than using her formal throne. "Please be more specific, Mayor. Which problem are we talking about?"

The mayor gaped at Jessica. "How can you have forgotten the priests' proclamation already? Changing the name of Caladan to . . ." His brow furrowed and he looked at the village priest. "What was the name, again, Abbo?"

"*Chisra Sala Muad'Dib.*"

"And who can remember that?" Horvu continued with a snort. "This planet has always been *Caladan*."

Sintra spread out a spaceport manifest, a record of ships arriving and cargoes departing. Each entry listed the planet under its unwieldy and foreign-sounding new name. "Look at what they have done!"

Jessica hid her own troubled expression. "That means nothing. The men who issued that proclamation don't live here. Fremen refer to Arrakis as *Dune*—and this planet is *Caladan*. If I speak with my son, he will change his mind."

Horvu brightened. "We knew you would support us, my Lady. With you on our side, we have the strength we need. In your absence we already began to deal with the problem. As you yourself have withdrawn from the Jihad, so has the population of Caladan."

Jessica frowned. "What are you saying?"

The mayor seemed quite proud of himself. "We have declared our planet's independence from Muad'Dib's Imperium. Caladan will do just fine on its own."

Sintra nodded vigorously. "Because of the urgency, we could not wait for your ship to return. The people already signed a petition, and we sent the declaration to Arrakeen."

These men were like lumbering oxen in a field of porcelain-delicate politics. "You can't just withdraw from the Imperium! Your sworn oaths, the Landsraad Charter, the ancient laws of—"

The priest waved his hand, seemingly unperturbed. "Everything will work out in the end, my Lady. It is obvious that we are no threat to Muad'Dib. In fact, Caladan is of little use to him except as a gathering place for his pilgrims . . . who have now been mostly turned away."

Thoughts rushed through Jessica's mind. What would have been a minor problem might now become a watershed event. If the people of this planet had quietly chosen to ignore the name change, perhaps Paul would have turned a blind eye. But not if they openly defied Muad'Dib. These fools were putting her son in an impossible position, one from which he could not afford to back down.

"You do not understand the repercussions of what you suggest." Jessica contained her temper only through the use of her most effective Bene Gesserit techniques. "I am your Duchess, and you acted without consulting me? Some rulers would have you executed for that."

Sintra sniffed. "Come now, my Lady, no ruler of Caladan would punish us for doing what is right. That would be a Harkonnen thing to do."

"Perhaps you don't understand Harkonnens," Jessica said. They could never have imagined that her own father was the Baron himself.

"Oh, we are just one world, and a small one," Mayor Horvu said. "Paul will see reason."

Impatience flashed in Jessica's eyes. "What he will *see* is that one of his planets has defied him—his homeworld, no less. If he ignores that, how many other planets will take that as implicit permission to break away? He'll face one rebellion after another, because of you."

Horvu chuckled as if *Jessica* were the one who didn't understand. "I remember when you came here as a young Bene Gesserit, my Lady, but *we* have been with the Atreides Dukes for century upon century. We know their benevolence."

Jessica could not believe what she was hearing. These men had seen none of the Imperium, knew nothing of galactic politics. They assumed that all leaders were the same, that one action was not connected to another and another. They might remember the *young* Paul Atreides, but neither of these men could possibly grasp how much he had changed.

"Where is Earl Halleck? Is he aware of what you've done?"

The mayor and priest looked at each other. Horvu cleared his throat, and Jessica could tell that they had acted behind Gurney's back. "The Earl is on his estate and has not come to Cala City for . . . some days. We did not feel we needed to trouble him with this matter."

"It is simple, my Lady," Sintra said. "We aren't a part of the Jihad, and we never were. Outside politics and outside wars have nothing to do with us. We just want our planet back to the way it was for twenty-six generations under the Atreides Dukes."

"Paul isn't just an Atreides anymore. He's also Muad'Dib, the Fremen Messiah and Holy Emperor." She crossed her arms over her chest. "What will you do when he sends Fedaykin armies to seize control and execute anyone who speaks out against him?"

The mayor's chuckle showed no anxiety. "Come now, my Lady, you dramatize. He is the son of our beloved Duke Leto Atreides. Caladan is in his blood. He couldn't possibly mean us harm."

Jessica saw that these men were blind to the dangers of what they had unleashed. Her voice was low. "You misjudge him. Even I don't know what my son is capable of any longer."

IN THE DEEPENING darkness of her first night back, Jessica rose from the private writing desk inside her bedchamber, leaving her papers and recordings unfinished. She walked over to the stone wall and threw open the windows to let the cool night air flow in. It came with a hint of fog and the familiar smell of iodine and salt, seaweed and waves.

Curling waves slammed harder against the base of the cliff with each advance-and-retreat. She could see the silvery line of breakers lit by starlight and a waxing moon. The rumble and roar of booming surf and the clatter of rocks moving on the shore soothed her with their constancy, unlike the turmoil that washed across other worlds.

Throughout his youth, Paul had listened to those gentle whispers of

Caladan seas, and they had given him a sense of serenity, a sense of place and family history. Now, as Muad'Dib, he heard instead the crackling hiss of sandstorms—*Hulasikali Wala*, as the Fremen called it, "the wind that eats flesh." And the defiant shouts of fanatical armies. . . .

She couldn't convince herself that Paul's priests would have tried to rename Caladan without at least his implied approval. Had he finally become a leader so powerful that his advisers were afraid to speak honestly to him?

Or was he a man without real advisers at all? Paul had prescience; he was the Kwisatz Haderach, with a kind of perceptive wisdom that Jessica did not understand. But did such powers and talents necessarily make Paul *infallible*? She kept coming back to that question in her mind, and she wondered what psychological damage the Water of Life had done to him in the Fremen ritual that had changed him forever.

Some time ago, Reverend Mother Mohiam had warned her about the dangers of this child, the superhuman Kwisatz Haderach who had emerged before his time and slipped out of the Sisterhood's control. When the old woman had tested Paul at the age of fifteen, it had been more than a test. What if the Bene Gesserit accusations about him were correct? What if Jessica *had* committed a grave, disastrous error by bearing a son instead of a daughter? What if, after all, he was *not* a messiah, but instead a terrible mistake . . . an abomination of historic proportions?

As she watched the surf, a pale mass of luminescence drifted along, a cluster of plankton shining in the night. Hovering above it with flitting wings and distant cries, sea birds dove down to feed upon the fish that, in turn, fed upon the plankton. Another patch of luminescence drifted closer, caught on an eddy that drove the two clusters together, mixing them in a clash of shifting colors.

It reminded Jessica of the Jihad. . . .

She had reviewed eyewitness accounts of battlefield horrors. Jessica could not delude herself into thinking that the zealous followers were operating beyond her son's control, that Paul did not know the things they did in his name. He had been there, in person. He had *seen* the atrocities happen, and he had not spoken out against them. Rather, he had urged his fighters onward, had inspired them.

"Has your son forgotten who he really is?" Horvu had looked at her with tired, pleading eyes, expecting her to have a ready and truthful answer for him. But she didn't know.

Out on the nearby headlands, she spotted a bonfire, which brought to mind the recent aborted festival of the Empty Man. A shiver ran down her spine, as she wondered if her son had become the Empty Man of local legend.

Have I created a monster?

Jessica slept restlessly that night, her thoughts brimming with concerns and realizations about what Paul condoned and why he was doing it. A vivid nightmare started out convincingly as a memory of herself as a young mother slipping into Paul's bedchamber, looking down at the five-year-old boy. He slept soundly, looking so innocent, yet with a dark potential hidden within him.

If only she had known then that this boy would grow up to be a man who sterilized entire worlds, who had the blood of billions of innocent people on his hands, who led a Jihad that showed no signs of ending. . . .

In her dream, the young mother Jessica looked down at the sleeping child and picked up a pillow. She pressed it hard against his face, holding it there as the boy struggled and fought her. She pressed harder. . . .

Jessica bolted awake in a sweat. Her stomach churned with revulsion. Had her fears simply guided her dreams, or was that in itself a warning of what she needed to do—what Reverend Mother Mohiam had always wanted her to do?

I gave life to you, Paul—and I can take it away.

WHEN THE MESSAGE arrived from the Mother School, even the written words seemed to have the imperative power of Voice. The Sisterhood demanded that Jessica go to Wallach IX regarding a "most important matter," and the order was signed by Reverend Mother Mohiam herself.

Because of her lifetime of training and obligations, Jessica's immediate reaction was to rush there in response to the summons. But she forced herself to pause and throw off the programmed reaction; she was annoyed at the way the Sisters tried to manipulate her, how they had *always* tried to manipulate her. They wanted something. And if she did not go to them willingly, on her own terms, they would find some other means of getting her there, some less obvious way.

Jessica had returned from Salusa Secundus only the day before, had just learned of Mayor Horvu's foolish and naïve declaration, and now another obligation pulled her away. Once again, she would have to leave Gurney Halleck in charge on Caladan. But he needed to be forewarned.

When he came to see her, she was gathering necessary items for her travel wardrobe. "Gurney, I will be back as soon as I can, but the people of Caladan are in your hands for the time being." As she regarded him more closely, she saw a gaunt difference in his expression. He looked deeply shaken. "Gurney, what is it?"

The man focused his gaze on the wall rather than directly at her. "A personal matter, my Lady. Nothing that need concern you."

"Come now, my good friend. Maybe I can help, if you'll just let me."

He hesitated for a long moment, then said in a stony voice, "My gaze hounds . . . bloodfire virus. If I had acted sooner, maybe I could have saved some of them. But I waited too long."

"Oh, Gurney, I'm so sorry."

He took an awkward step backward, separating himself from her. "They were just dogs. I've been through far worse, my Lady, and I will endure this." Now she understood why he had been unaware of Mayor Horvu's ill-considered message to Arrakeen. But he was a man who preferred to deal with his emotions privately, and her sympathy would only make it more difficult for him. "It is past, and we both have our jobs to do. Go where you need to go, and I will rule in your absence."

She nodded, but he needed to know what she was leaving him with. "Some of the townspeople have gotten a dangerous and foolish idea into their heads. While you were at your estate, they unilaterally declared Caladan's independence from the Imperium."

Gurney stood straighter now. "Gods below, they can't do that!"

"They already have. They sent a formal petition to Muad'Dib. While I'm gone, please don't let this get out of hand."

"It sounds as if it already is out of hand, my Lady. But I will do my best to limit the damage."

The most effective family unit is quite large—a community in which children are raised and trained in a uniform fashion, not in a random, unpredictable way. There is also the matter of good genetics.

—RAQUELLA BERTO-ANIRUL, founder of
the ancient order of Bene Gesserit

After arriving on Wallach IX, Jessica saw bright reminders of her childhood everywhere around the Mother School. And that was intentional, to emphasize what she had been taught, again and again. *We exist to serve.* But Jessica was not that same person anymore. For years, she had been little more than a serving girl to Mohiam; now she was returning as the Duchess of Caladan and the Mother of Muad'Dib, the Emperor of the Known Universe. Much more than a meek acolyte.

As she entered the central plaza, she refused to let herself feel intimidated about the meeting to which she had been summoned. The Bene Gesserit Sisterhood no longer controlled her. Jessica controlled herself, her decisions, and her future.

She walked around the sprawling complex to gather her thoughts before facing the other Reverend Mothers. She paused by a fountain, where a refreshing spray of water misted her face. She dipped a hand in the cool water of the fountain, let the cupped moisture run onto the cobblestones. A waste . . . a luxury. Water was not a precious resource on Wallach IX. Others might see Jessica as a moonstruck girl dawdling at her chores, but she was in no hurry. Though they had commanded her, she had come of her own accord.

Despite the failings of the Bene Gesserit order, this place was a hub of human learning and triumphs, where the greatest thoughts were assembled and transmitted far and wide. Jessica had learned much here, but only later had she learned the most important truth of all—that even the Sisterhood was not always right.

But they were predictable. Neither Reverend Mother Mohiam nor any other Sister had deigned to notice her arrival, but Jessica saw right through that as a ploy to emphasize her lack of importance. How different her reception was from how Muad'Dib and the clamoring populace of Arrakeen would have received her.

Jessica already had deeply conflicting attitudes about Mohiam. The two women had an odd relationship that alternated from hostile to cool, with all too brief moments that approached tenderness. The old woman considered her a disappointment and would always look for ways to make Jessica pay for daring to have a son.

For now, at least, the highest ranking Bene Gesserits wanted to speak with Jessica. She was curious and concerned, but not afraid.

A black-robed woman emerged from the half-timbered stucco and wood administration building and stared at her. It was Mohiam herself, sending a signal of impatience with a rigid stance, a twitch of an elbow, a flicker of the wrist before she turned and went back inside.

Now that Jessica understood them, the Sisterhood's manipulative mind games were amusing. *Let them wait for me . . . for a change.* She remained at the fountain for another minute, focusing her thoughts, then made her way up the stairs and pushed open a heavy door. Like other structures in the Mother School complex, it had moss-streaked sienna roof tiles and special windows to concentrate the minimal light from Wallach IX's distant sun.

She joined other robed Sisters inside the chapter chamber. Their footsteps creaked on the floor planks of the octagonal room as they found spots on elaccawood perimeter benches.

Even the ancient Mother Superior Harishka took a seat like an ordinary acolyte. The Mother Superior remained alert, defying her age, though an attentive Medical Sister sat close to her. Harishka's dark, almond eyes peered out from beneath her black hood as she leaned forward to speak to a much younger Sister at her other side, whom Jessica recognized as Reverend Mother Genino. Despite her lack of years, Genino had risen quickly to become one of the Mother Superior's key personal advisers.

When Harishka squared her shoulders and shifted her body to gaze across the chamber at Jessica, the rustling of low conversations ceased. The imposing Mother Superior spoke into the sudden silence. "We're grateful you have come such a long way to see us, Jessica."

"You summoned me, Mother Superior." They thought she'd had no choice. "What is this important matter you must discuss with me?"

The Mother Superior bobbed her head like a crow. "We are concerned about Muad'Dib and his dangerous decisions. We fear those who may be counseling him."

Jessica frowned. Like any powerful leader, Paul had numerous people who could advise him, some good and others bad. The self-centered Qizarate sought to increase its power and influence, especially the man Korba, but Paul's other advisers were trustworthy and earnest. Stilgar, Chani, even Irulan. . . .

With a thin, wrinkled arm, Harishka gestured to the Medical Sister at her side, who spoke up. "I am Sister Aver Yohsa. I was one of those who tended Emperor Shaddam's first wife, the Kwisatz Mother Anirul, after the voices within began to overwhelm her."

"I'm very aware of Anirul's story. I was there. What is the relevance now?"

"It is a reminder of the danger of falling prey to the inner voices." Harishka's eyes narrowed further. "The temptation to listen to such ancient wisdom is often irresistible." Several Sisters shifted uneasily in their seats; Genino slipped off one of her sandals and leaned down to rub what appeared to be a sore spot on her foot. "For Reverend Mothers, our ancestors-within trace only through the maternal lines, but your son Paul does not have those limitations. He sees into both his feminine and masculine pasts."

"He is the Kwisatz Haderach, as the Sisterhood itself has admitted."

Speaking for the first time, Mohiam cleared her throat. "But he has none of the preparations and precautions that we intended to provide. He is dangerous. We suspect that he is already listening to advice that could destroy the human race. Corrupt ancestors from his pasts. What if Paul-Muad'Dib listens to the greatest dictators in human history?"

Harishka added, "You know all the obvious names. What if he has inner conversations with Genghis Khan, Keeltar the Ubertat, or Adolf Hitler? What if he takes private counsel from Agamemnon, known to be an Atreides ancestor? Or from . . . others?"

Jessica frowned. She smoothed her expression to remove any obvious surprise or concern. Were they subtly reminding her that his grandfather was the Baron Vladimir Harkonnen? "Paul would never do anything so foolish," she said with insufficient conviction. "Besides, Other Memories cannot be searched at will, like records from a filing cabinet. Every Bene Gesserit knows that. The voices must come of their own volition."

"Is that true even for the Kwisatz Haderach?" Mohiam asked.

Now Jessica was angry. "Are you suggesting that Paul is possessed by voices within?" She didn't want to consider that possibility, but the idea had struck home. Paul himself had suggested a similar flaw, lashing out at her just after the Battle of Arrakeen. *"How would you like to live billions upon billions of lives? How can you tell what's ruthless unless you've plumbed the depths of both cruelty and kindness?"*

The Mother Superior gave an aloof shrug. "We merely suggest that possession is a possibility. It might explain some of his extreme and unorthodox actions."

Jessica remained firm, just as she had when Shaddam and Fenring pressed her to explain Paul's behavior during the banquet on Salusa. "My son is strong enough to make his own decisions."

"But can any person survive the constant pressure of so many internal voices whose goals are entirely different from those of the living? He may be an abomination, just as Mohiam insists his sister is."

Jessica clenched her hands in her lap, and then surprised the other women by laughing. "And there you have it—the standard Bene Gesserit response to anything you find not to your liking. Abomination!" Now that she had identified their flaw, she found them amusing. "You're just being petulant because my son has made the Sisterhood irrelevant. With your Missionaria Protectiva and your Manipulator of Religions on Dune, *you* set in motion the circumstances that created him. You placed a tool in front of him, and now you complain that he used it? He grasped the reins of the myth—*your* myth—and rode it to power and glory. After the way the Bene Gesserit treated him, do you expect him to respect you at all?"

"Maybe you could make him do so," Harishka said. "If your role were expanded, you could convince him of our worth."

Reverend Mother Genino slipped her sandal back on and said abruptly, "We have a proposal for you, Jessica—a proposal for the good of the Sisterhood and all humankind."

Finally, they are getting to the point, Jessica thought.

"The Sisterhood has decided that we must bring the Emperor down, by any means necessary. And we want you to help us end his reign of terror."

The cold statement stunned her. "What do you mean, bring him down?"

Mohiam said, "Paul Atreides is a genetic mistake—*your* mistake, Jessica. He grows more dangerous and unpredictable with each passing moment. It is up to you to rectify your error."

"He must either be killed or controlled." Harishka shook her head sadly. "And we very much doubt if he can be controlled."

Jessica drew in a sharp breath through flared nostrils. "Paul is not a monster. I know him. He has clear reasons for everything he does. He is a good man."

Harishka slowly shook her head from side to side. "Maybe at one time he was, but how well do you know him now? Do not hide from what you feel in your heart. Tens of billions have died in the past seven years of his Jihad, and the war shows no sign of ending. An incalculable swath of pain and suffering across the galaxy. Look at it, child! You know full well what your son has done—and we can only imagine the additional horrors that lie in store."

Jessica no longer feared this old woman, was beyond being impressed by her supposed strength and wisdom. "What makes you think I would ever choose the Sisterhood over my son?"

Seeming to change the subject, Harishka rose from the hard elacca-wood bench. "I am old, and I have seen much of life, and of death." She seemed small and frail. She pressed a hand to her back, as if it pained her greatly. "Here is the Sisterhood's offer: If you do as we wish, I will step down immediately as Mother Superior and elevate *you* to the position. You, Jessica, will lead the Bene Gesserit order. With that power, perhaps you can find a way to influence your son and bring him back under the Sisterhood's control—for the good of humanity."

The idea startled her. "And why do you believe such an offer would be attractive to me?"

Harishka said, "Because you are a Bene Gesserit. We taught you everything that is important in life."

"But not of love. You know nothing of love."

Mohiam spoke in a hard voice. "If Paul-Muad'Dib cannot be tamed, then we have only one alternative."

Jessica shook her head. "I will not do it."

But . . . as Mother Superior, Jessica knew she could change the focus of the whole Sisterhood, take them back from the brink, restore an order that had existed for more than ten millennia. She could change their teachings and rectify the mistakes that they had perpetuated. The consequences, the *benefits*, were immeasurable.

But she would not do it at the cost of betraying her son.

Jessica forced a wave of cold calmness through her body, summoning prana-bindu techniques to slow her breathing. She needed to leave the Mother School, but now she worried about what the Sisters would do to her if she refused them outright.

Harishka swayed on her feet, and Medical Sister Yohsa steadied her. "We realize this is a difficult decision for you, but remember your training. Think about all we taught you, all the things that you *know*. Do not let your love as a mother blind you to the ruin your son is causing. Make the right choice, or all of our futures are forfeit." Her dark eyes glittered with intensity.

Jessica clung to her dignity as she left the chamber. "I will give you my answer in due course."

Exile is among the cruelest of acts, for it separates the heart from the body.

—SHADDAM CORRINO IV

T hough she would have preferred to be away from the insistent eyes of the Sisters, Mohiam wanted Jessica to stay long enough to attend the Night Vigil two evenings hence. And Jessica knew the Bene Gesserits would continue to pressure her.

She was determined to keep her faith in her son, but she would have been stronger in that resolve if she didn't have some of the same doubts that others had voiced. Jessica wished she understood him better. Her intellect could achieve superiority over her emotions, but only if she had reasons. She scorned people who exhibited glaze-eyed faith, but now she exhibited the same behavior as the fanatics who blinded themselves to reason and accepted the myth that Muad'Dib was infallible. If she refused to consider that he might be wrong, might be misled by his own delusions, how was her devotion to him any different?

Because he is Paul, she thought to herself. She realized how foolish she had been, how blind to reality. *Because he is Paul.*

Jessica kept to her own thoughts and avoided socializing with the other Sisters. The cold days on the Bene Gesserit home world carried a whisper of snow that blew but did not settle. Bundled in a thick coat, she followed a path through the lower gardens of rare orchids, star roses, and rugged but exotic vegetable flora from Grand Hain, all of which flourished in the cool climate. Despite the chill in the air, the blossoms unfolded in the weak morning sunlight.

Hearing sudden screeching sounds, she ducked as a flock of songbirds flew low to the ground, streaked past her, and dropped into a thicket of shrubbery. Before she could see what had disturbed them, a rush of powerful winds whipped her hair and clothing, seeming to come from all around her.

A number of tall, thin wind funnels twice her height whirled toward her from a shaded area, brightening as if they collected available sunlight and used it for energy. Jessica spotted more of the whirling objects coming toward her. Dust devils? Contained whirlwinds? Some kind of bizarre attack, treachery from the Sisters?

She threw herself prone in the path, wary but curious, and the whirling funnels circled her, their progress stalled. The small tornadoes were stunning to behold, with hypnotic rainbows of morphing color, like crystalline life-forms. Additional funnels circled and danced over a nearby conservatory building, the only shelter in sight, knocking loose some of the plaz panels.

Lurching to her feet and keeping her head low, Jessica ran toward the building, darting through the dark spaces between the funnels. As she went through, the winds clawed at her, trying to drag her one direction or another, but she struggled to the conservatory. Just as she ducked into the doorway, a loose plaz panel shot past her and shattered against the hard wall.

Inside the building, she looked up through gaps in the ceiling where roof panels were broken or missing. The predatory whirlwinds kept circling until a loud, percussive noise sounded, and the funnels abruptly disappeared. Blue sky appeared overhead, leaving the garden grounds strewn with broken plants and debris.

"Quite a show," said a female voice. "Residual psychic energy. It's been doing that around here recently."

Jessica saw a brown-haired woman with creased skin and sepia eyes, weary eyes . . . a familiar face from long ago. She caught her breath, so surprised that it took her a moment to recognize the woman. "Tessia? *Tessia!*"

Rhombur's wife had aged perceptibly, as if she had barely emerged alive from a personal crucible. She came forward to take Jessica's hands in her own. Tessia was shaking, either from fear or from exhaustion. "No need hide your surprise. I know what's happened to me."

"Are you all right? We sent so many inquiries, but no one would say what had happened to you. The Sisterhood turned down my requests for information. How long have you been . . . awake? And after what happened to poor Rhombur, Bronso broke off all contact with House Atreides for the past twelve years." She wondered if Tessia even knew how the cyborg prince had been killed in Balut's Theater of Shards.

And what did she mean by residual psychic energy? Had the Sisters been tampering and testing, developing new skills? A weapon? And would that weapon be used against Paul? Jessica didn't trust them.

Before she could ask, two Bene Gesserit proctors rushed along the walkway in the aftermath of the bizarre windstorm. Seeing them, Tessia drew Jessica farther into the dimly lit conservatory. "This is my velvet-lined prison. I have recovered, but not entirely in the way the Sisters expected. I'm the only person ever to emerge from the hell of a guilt-casting." She glanced around uneasily.

Only a few rumors had leaked out about the Bene Gesserit guilt-casters, and most people did not believe in their existence. "We thought the Ixian technocrats had used some sort of weapon on your mind." Now Jessica understood what had happened to Rhombur's wife on that night in the Grand Palais. If not for the consequences of the guilt-casting, Bronso would never have had a falling out with his father, would never have fled with Paul, and on and on, ripples upon ripples. Hard resentment seeped into Jessica's words. "Rhombur sent you here in hopes you could be saved."

Tessia shook her head. "It was Reverend Mother Stokiah—a weapon from their psychic arsenal. My own Sisterhood crushed me and took me from my husband . . . and now he is dead." Her voice hitched, and Jessica heard the wind suddenly pick up outside.

"What did they want that was so important? What was worth such a tremendous cost?"

"A little thing, actually. They wanted me to be a breeding mother, but I defied their commands, and so they punished me. It did me no good to resist. They needed only my body, only my womb. Not my mind. Even while I was unconscious, they impregnated me. My body gave them the children they wanted." Her voice held heavy bitterness. "'I am Bene

Gesserit: I exist only to serve.' At least Rhombur didn't live long enough to find out about it. He never knew. Oh, how I miss him."

Jessica could not conceal her revulsion. What the Sisterhood had done to this woman, her friend! And now those same women were trying to convince Jessica to destroy Paul? These same women wanted to make her their Mother Superior? If she accepted their offer, she could put an end to breeding abuses . . . but to accept their terms would make Jessica a monster.

Tessia continued in a dreamy voice, as if her mind were far away. "It took years. I saved myself . . . I found my own way out of the darkness where their guilt-caster threw me."

Jessica's stomach knotted. "Does Bronso know where you are now? Can he help?"

"I've managed to smuggle out several messages. He knows what has happened to me, but what can he do? He is barely a figurehead on Ix these days. He has no real power and could never stand against the Sisterhood. He is as trapped as I am." She shook her head. "It's the fall of House Vernius."

Jessica hugged the other woman, held her close for a long time. "I wish I could get you out of here, but that is not in my power."

However, if she were Mother Superior, she could do so. . . .

Tessia smiled mysteriously. "Someday, I will find a way. I have already escaped from the mental prison they imposed on me, and oh, they would love to know how I did it. Now they test their techniques on me, alternately showing me compassion and then pummeling me with guilt. Even their guilt-casters don't understand."

"They continue to experiment on you?"

"Medical Sister Yohsa constantly tries to deconstruct my mind and build it back up the way the Sisterhood wants it, not the way I want it. But I know ways to deflect their attempts. Those mental defenses are mine, and I won't surrender them—not after what they did to me."

Tessia looked from side to side. By the whisper-rush of wind in the courtyard, Jessica heard what must have been another small, strange tornado, and the sharp cries of Bene Gesserits scattering in alarm. Apparently, the residual psychic energy was not completely under control.

Leaning close, Tessia whispered. "What do they want from *you*, Jessica? And will you give it to them? If not, you could be a target yourself. Have you defied them? You will—I know you. Then the guilt-casters will come for you." Tessia's voice came out in a desperate flood as she clutched Jessica's shoulders. "Listen to me! You must block your thoughts and prepare yourself ahead of time. Build up a bastion of powerful memories, a shield of good things. Have it *ready* at the forefront of your mind. Use it to guard yourself. They will not suspect you can stand against them, even for a moment. Guilt-casting is a psychic storm, but it can be weathered."

Jessica knew she might need the information. "Teach me how—please."

Tessia touched her own forehead, closed her eyes, and released a long sigh. "Let me show you what you need to know."

The very act of breathing is a miracle.

—teaching of the Suk School

An unusually warm wind blew in from the sea. Gurney had been hoping for heavy rain to discourage the crowds arriving for the scheduled rally, but as he looked up at the patches of blue sky, the clouds seemed to be scattering.

Jessica had been right to warn him about what the people might do. Mayor Horvu and his enthusiastic followers did not begin to comprehend the poisonous snake with which they were playing. In the name of Duke Leto, though, Gurney would try to use a compassionate, paternal touch. If it would only work. . . .

Wearing his best noble outfit for the occasion, Gurney stood scowling with a small group of local officials on a raised suspensor platform at the edge of Cala City's largest park. Over the past hour, an enthusiastic and boisterous crowd had gathered on the expanse of grass and starry flowers.

He wished he'd learned exactly what the clumsy rebels had in mind. With his disarming, often oblivious, smile, Mayor Horvu promised that this would be a peaceful demonstration, and Gurney wasn't sure what to do about it. He had called in soldiers to keep order, should some of the crowd become unruly.

After Jessica's complaints of damage done by pilgrims in previous months, Paul had stationed Imperial security forces on Caladan. Though Gurney didn't know the men well, they had been efficient and dedicated, as far as he could determine, but they were still offworlders. Today, especially, perhaps a more objective security force was best. . . .

Consumed with self-importance, Horvu had issued himself and his followers an unrestricted permit, according to the rules of the town charter. This seemed like a conflict of interest to Gurney, but the Mayor happily clung to outdated images of the way local politics worked in relation to the Imperial government.

"The people of Caladan know what they are doing, Earl Halleck," · the priest Sintra had said. Though pleased to see how many people had come to the rally, he was bothered that Gurney had chosen to bring armed guards rather than join them in their cause. "You have served House Atreides for a long time, my Lord, but you were not born here. You cannot possibly understand true Caladan issues."

Gurney was surprised at how efficiently this demonstration was organized, since Horvu and his followers were not known to have these skills. It was almost as if they had outside help. As the size of the crowd in the park increased, Gurney grew increasingly anxious. His soldier guards might not be able to impose order if the throng got out of hand.

Gurney looked around for Horvu. He doubted the old Mayor would be much of a firebrand, but that didn't make him any less problematic. Gurney didn't want Paul's homeworld to become another battlefield. Large groups of people, especially those with an agenda, were too malleable, their moods too easily swayed, their emotions too quick to turn. He'd seen the armies of Muad'Dib driven to frenzy because their passionate sense of rightness made them deaf to any concerns except the ones being pumped into them. If the local crowd got out of hand, that could in turn trigger his Imperial soldiers into uncontrollable, violent retaliation on behalf of Muad'Dib.

His soldier guards were veterans, but they did not know the character of these families who had been here for generations, the good-hearted people of Caladan who were now being misled by a Mayor who had no common sense.

As he looked out at the restless crowd who believed they had found an easy solution that their beloved Paul Atreides would honor, Gurney tried to recall the way he used to be: strong, valiant, and assertive in causes that mattered, writing heroic ballads for the baliset, going off to fight for House Atreides wherever duty sent him. His missed those days, but knew he could never go back to them. Sometimes now, he liked to spend time with his music as an escape, a refuge that made him forget the horrible realities from his past.

Several weeks ago, while sharing a pint of kelp beer with the patrons of a public house, he had picked up his instrument and begun to strum. The bartender had called across the heads of the crowd in the pub, "It's time for you to sing us a new song, Gurney Halleck. How about 'The Ballad of Muad'Dib'?"

People had chuckled, urging him on, but Gurney resisted. "That story is not yet finished. You'll just have to wait, men."

In reality, it wasn't a song he had any interest in writing. Though Gurney would never utter his opinion to anyone, he felt that "Muad'Dib" had fallen too far from glory to be worthy of such heroic words. It left him with a feeling of loss, on a personal level.

Paul may be the Emperor Muad'Dib, Gurney thought. *But he is not Duke Leto.*

Now part of the crowd made an opening on the grassy expanse, and Gurney saw the mayor making his way through, waving at people as he approached the suspensor platform. When Horvu stepped onto the lowered platform, he scolded Gurney, as if he were a child, "Earl Halleck, you will have to remove your soldiers. What kind of message does this send?" He scowled at the armed men stationed prominently around the park. "We've already sent our proclamation to the Emperor on Arrakis. This is just a celebration, a reinforcement of our resolve."

"If it's just a celebration, then go to the pubs and eating establishments," Gurney suggested. "If you disperse now, I'll even buy the first round for everyone." He didn't think the offer would work.

Sintra shook his head. "The people are quite pleased with how they have stood up to fanaticism and bureaucracy. Give them their moment of triumph here."

"It's not a triumph until Muad'Dib accepts your declaration." Gurney knew that wasn't likely to happen.

Wary but watchful, he stepped off the platform and motioned for his soldiers to accompany him to a cordoned-off clearing. As they moved away, the suspensor platform rose into the air and floated over the heads of the crowd, with Mayor Horvu waving down at them.

The commander of the offworld troops, a bator named Nissal, removed his cap and wiped perspiration from his brow. "The mayor claims he's just going to give a speech, sir."

"Wars can be started with a speech, Bator. Keep everyone on alert."

Shouting into a voice pickup, the priest called for the people to follow the platform as it glided through a wide opening in the park's trees. The audience moved with it from below, some running, some laughing, as if it were all a game.

Caught unprepared by the movement, Gurney called into his comm, "Bring in spotter aircraft. Have our people flank them and watch them, but don't let them do anything foolish. Remember the old phrase, 'Fools can cause more damage through reckless ignorance than an army can achieve with a coordinated assault.'"

Shouting encouragement, Mayor Horvu guided the crowd out of the park and down to the old fishing village, where the people gathered on the docks and on the rocky beaches at low tide. He hovered his platform over the water; many boats came in close, for the speech.

"We have members of every class, every profession here!" The public address system amplified Horvu's voice. "I have been your Mayor for decades, and I have earned your trust. Now I wish to earn your support. While we wait to hear from Emperor Paul Atreides, we must display our conviction and our strength. We'll show outsiders what the people of Caladan can do."

As Gurney listened with growing dismay, Horvu and the priest alternated their rallying cry. First, they urged fishermen to show their solidarity by not launching their boats, not bringing in the catch. They referred to petitions in support of Caladan's independence that were at that moment being circulated widely across the town, and the fact that merchants would refuse to sell goods to any person who had not affixed a signature.

This was very disturbing to Gurney, and it got worse. The Mayor declared that Jihad pilgrims were to be turned back from Caladan henceforth, no longer welcome unless Paul gave the planet an acceptable form of autonomy.

One of the soldiers spoke into the comm, startling the already edgy Gurney. "My Lord, they've shut down the main spaceport. Their people have scrambled the landing codes and are turning back any ship that uses the name of Chisra Sala Muad'Dib. Any inbound pilots have to agree to a binding document that reaffirms the name of this world as Caladan, and as nothing else."

Gurney was astonished by how swiftly the agitators had moved, how well orchestrated all the pieces of this . . . this *revolution* had come together. Now, with interplanetary commerce thwarted, Guild couriers and CHOAM officials would file stern complaints, demanding immediate action and spreading the embarrassing news throughout Muad'Dib's realm.

In all the years of the Jihad, Gurney had seen the appalling things that Muad'Dib's ruthless forces did when they decided to crack down. Caladan would not be immune.

He issued immediate orders. "Put House Atreides military aircraft in the airspace over the Cala City Spaceport. Prevent any ships from taking off or landing, and we'll shut down the facility our way—not the way the rebels want it. Block any ships disembarking from Heighliners and send them back up, without explanation. I don't want word getting out until we have this mess under control."

Using small military 'thopters—previously designated as search-and-rescue craft for fishermen on stormy seas—Gurney ordered his men to disperse the demonstration with a show of force. He boarded one of the vessels himself and led a fleet of the buzzing craft as they swooped low over the harbor village, firing bursts of compressed air that bowled the people over while doing little harm.

Gurney personally aimed the air cannon that knocked the confused-looking Mayor and the village priest off their suspensor platform and into the water. Imperial soldiers then rushed in with restraints to arrest the most outspoken demonstrators.

As Gurney's 'thopters flew over the city and his troops took control of every neighborhood, he received a flow of reports. Many of the off-world Imperial guards were failing to exercise the restraint he had specified. Gurney had used air cannons to confuse and deflate the situation, but as the soldier guards grew more zealous in their duties, many once-peaceful demonstrators were severely injured or killed, with their bones broken and skulls split open.

At the spaceport, Bator Nissal launched an impulsive and decisive operation of his own, storming the main terminal to rout out the demonstrators who had laid a primitive siege there. The panicked townspeople fought back, and eleven of the Imperial guards were killed, along with nearly a hundred agitators. The spaceport was reopened, and Gurney lifted his embargo, but felt no joy about it.

He had seen slaughters on the battlefields of the Jihad, but these were people of *Caladan*, not warriors, not blood commandos who had thrown themselves into a holy war. They were simply naïve citizens of Paul's home world.

Sickened, he walked among the bodies that were laid out on an old-town street, covered with blankets. Feeling an ache of grief and anger, he cursed, then stormed off to the village prison.

Gurney pushed his way into the prison cell that held a disheveled and astounded Mayor Horvu. The old man had a healing patch over one cheek, and he spoke with obvious disbelief, mixed with the acid of accusation. "I am disappointed in you, Gurney Halleck. I thought you loved Caladan."

"Be disappointed in yourself, not in me. I warned you not to hold your 'demonstration.' I *pleaded* with you, but you wouldn't listen. Now Muad'Dib's response is going to be a thousand times worse because of the disruption you've caused, which he cannot permit to occur on any Imperial world. I will call upon every scrap of friendship he still holds toward me, and I pray I can convince him to show mercy. But I guarantee nothing." Gurney shook his head. "How am I going to explain this to Lady Jessica when she returns?"

"Shame on you, Gurney Halleck! You were once a loyal retainer of Duke Leto, but you have forgotten Atreides principles." The Mayor glowered at him through the bars. The skin around his eyes was dark and bruised. "I have served the people of Caladan my entire life, and I never thought it would come to this. Our defiance will continue. One day we would be happy to welcome Paul back like a prodigal son, but only if he remembers who he is . . . and who we are."

Gurney sighed. "Others would call that blasphemy against Muad'Dib.

You fool, give me a way to order your release, not a reason to order your execution!"

The Mayor glared at him, but said nothing more.

TWO DAYS LATER, a response arrived from Arrakis, a dry letter congratulating Gurney for a job well done in defending the honor of the Emperor. The signature appeared to be Paul's, though the words likely came from some functionary. The filmpaper stationery bore a seal from the "Office of Jihad Administration." He wondered if Paul had even reviewed his report.

With a sigh of resignation, Gurney dispatched an immediate order to free all the demonstrators who had been arrested, including the leaders, without explanation.

On her last evening on Wallach IX, Jessica agreed to attend the Night Vigil. By tradition, she and the rest of the Sisters at the Mother School had spent the day in solitude, contemplating the life and travails of Raquella Berto-Anirul, who had founded their order from the rubble of humanity left by the Butlerian Jihad, thousands and thousands of years ago.

Jessica was eager to be away from the silent coercion of the Bene Gesserit. They had tried to bribe her with the position of Mother Superior—what Bene Gesserit didn't aspire to such a goal? She had avoided giving an answer, which in itself made the Sisters greatly suspicious. And knowing what they had done to Tessia because of her refusal, Jessica felt herself in significant danger.

As night fell, still reluctant to engage in conversation, Jessica joined a long line of black-robed women bearing candles as they proceeded up the long slope of Campo de Raquella, a prominent hill near the Mother School complex. In the ascent along a rocky trail, the serpentine procession of candles looked like bright eyes in the starry darkness. Another set of flickering flames descended the hill along a parallel trail.

The Sisters climbed to the broad rounded top with its cairn of stones that remained in the sacred place where Raquella had stood so long ago, where her life had almost ended prematurely. A cool breeze whipped up as Jessica reached the summit. She looked out at the diamondlike lights of the extensive school complex and pondered the Sisterhood's history, the millennia of power and choices they had made.

Unlike most of the indoctrinated acolytes, though, Jessica knew that some of those choices had been wrong. Very wrong.

Twenty women stood near her at the edge of a precipice on the sheer face of the hill, a marker on the drop-off where Raquella had once intended to jump. She had been despondent in those days, unable to keep the differing factions of her organization together, unable to see how to lead them on a common path into humanity's future. She had hoped that her personal sacrifice would force them to work together.

But it was on this spot that the internal voices of Raquella's female ancestry had first spoken to her. She'd consumed a great deal of the Rossak drug on that day, but the mysterious internal voices were no chemical-induced hallucination; the chain of voices emerging from her distant ancestors had urged her to live and to inspire others.

Holding her candle now, Jessica inhaled deeply of the night air to fully experience the moment. The ceremony was meant to be a time of reflection and contemplation, a chance to see the vast, unfurling tapestry of Bene Gesserit influence.

She faced outward at the top of the cliff as Raquella had done, standing closer to the edge than the other acolytes or Reverend Mothers with her. For the moment, she felt strongly connected to the core of the Sisterhood, the original purpose that had brought so many powerful women together, not like the corrupt self-interests that subsequently led the order so far astray.

A new Mother Superior could change all that. . . . This could be what Harishka wanted her to feel, an additional temptation of the glory of the Bene Gesserit and their shepherding of history. Despite the stirring she felt within her Bene Gesserit structured *emotions*, Jessica would not change her mind.

Finishing their meditations, one group of Sisters moved off to be replaced by others. Those with doubts or other concerns needed more time; others received their reaffirmation quickly, and surrendered their places.

A shadow moved up beside her, another black-robed Reverend Mother. *Mohiam.* "I am glad you stayed for the Vigil, Jessica. I'm sure you feel it." The voice was brittle, like a dry wind on Arrakis. "Every Sister needs to participate in this, to clarify her thoughts and her heart."

"It does make me think of the once-worthy goals of the Sisterhood . . . as opposed to its subsequent tactics . . . to what is going on now."

Mohiam scowled in the low light of her candle. "Mother Superior Harishka has made you a generous offer. I know you've had your complaints and criticisms of our Sisterhood, but now you can fix them all, and we ask little in return." The old woman stared across the dark-muddied landscape. "From this place, your view of the future reaches far . . . and your decision should be clear."

"Clear? You are asking me to kill my son." Jessica was beginning to lose patience. The edge of the cliff seemed symbolic of the choice they wanted her to make. Accept or leap. But was there another choice?

"A son you never should have had."

Jessica turned away and walked down the rough trail, picking her way back down the hill. She did not slow as the old woman hurried to follow her. "We will bring down Muad'Dib, one way or another. We will use his own violence against him." As the surprisingly agile woman caught up, her dark eyes sparkled in the candlelight. "You need to know these things if you are to become our new Mother Superior. You need to know that we will succeed. Cast your lot with us."

At her side, the old woman lowered her voice, but her words carried an undertone of excitement. "Already Bene Gesserit operatives have made preparations to launch scattered revolts around the Imperium. Caladan will be the first spark. There's nothing you can do about it. When that flame takes hold there, more than a hundred other planets will rise up simultaneously and declare their independence.

"The Emperor will have to withdraw his armies from other battles to deal with these unexpected problems and—if his fanatics perform as they always have—the sheer excesses of those crackdowns will ignite a cascade of other revolts, real ones that do not need our encouragement.

"Landsraad representatives will demand immediate reparations and unanimously push through legislation that imposes restraint. If Muad'Dib ignores or vetoes it, then he will lose the support of all the nobles who have sided with him. His government will not be able to contain them all. You see, Jessica? We will succeed with or without you."

Suddenly, Mayor Horvu's surprising and naïve idea of declaring Caladan's independence made sense. He had been led to it by a manipulative Bene Gesserit operative. Jessica fired words at Mohiam like projectiles: "How dare you try to start a revolt on Caladan. My Caladan!"

"Your Sisterhood should matter more to you than a mere planet. We want you to take power away from a tyrant who has already killed more people than any other leader in recorded history. What is one mother's love in comparison to that?" Mohiam sniffed, as if offended that she even had to convince Jessica. "Whatever decision you make, we will still bring him down."

Jessica tried to shake her away, but Mohiam kept up. The Sisters saw Paul only as a dangerous and destructive force . . . but she knew her son as kind, caring, intelligent, and clever, full of curiosity and love. That was the real Paul, not any adverse perceptions of him that had sprung up in the backwash of the Jihad!

The two women paused together, allowing other Sisters to pass in their progression downhill. Jessica stared into her burning candle, smelled the smoke, and struggled to control her emotions.

Grabbing her by the arm with surprising strength, Mohiam rasped, "You *owe* the Sisterhood. Your very life belongs to us! Remember that we saved you from drowning in your childhood. A woman died for you. How can you forget that? *Remember*."

As if the Reverend Mother's voice triggered a long-suppressed memory, Jessica suddenly recalled struggling for her life, going underwater in a fast-flowing river, the raging torrent all around her, in her mouth, in her lungs . . . and so cold. She couldn't swim against the swift current, remembered being swept against a large rock and bumping her head. She couldn't recall how she had fallen into the river, but she was just a child, no more than five or six years old.

Two brave Sisters had jumped into the raging river to rescue her. Jessica remembered being dragged to the shore and resuscitated. She'd learned later that one of the Sisters had lost her life in the attempt. Mohiam was right; she would have died that day if those women hadn't helped her.

Oddly, however, Jessica could not recall the name of the Sister who had perished, and couldn't remember the location of the river. Suddenly, as she slowed her thoughts and crystallized her memories of the event, she clearly remembered *two* Sisters dragging her onto the bank, both of them taking turns to clear water from her lungs, breathing into her mouth.

Two Sisters? How then, had one of them died in the rescue?

And why were other details faint? The Sisterhood left nothing to chance. Somehow her memory had been altered.

"Maybe I do owe the Bene Gesserit my life, or maybe you long ago planted that story in my mind to be used exactly in circumstances like this."

From the flicker of shadowy expression on the old woman's face, Jessica thought she had her confirmation. The near drowning had never occurred! What schemes did this old woman and her cohorts have in place, and what falsehoods did they hide?

Peering down her nose at Mohiam, Jessica said, "Thank you for helping me make up my mind. This night I have indeed achieved clarity. I owe the Sisterhood nothing!"

Mohiam grabbed Jessica's sleeve. "You will *listen*. You will make the correct choice." Jessica heard the commanding Voice, the importunate tone that she should not have been able to resist. Because she knew Mohiam so well, she identified the fringes of it, the dangerous undertones, and knew how to prepare herself mentally for the onslaught.

Another Reverend Mother stepped out of the tree-latticed shadows, a looming form whose wrinkled face became recognizable in the candlelight. *Stokiah*, a woman she had seen long ago on Ix . . . the woman Tessia had warned her about. Her heart stuttered with instinctive fear. *I must not fear. . . .*

Stokiah's voice was like a rough bone saw. "You disappoint us further by refusing to rectify your mistakes, Jessica. How can you bear such guilt?" The words were drawn out like a long, strained note on a tortured violin.

Powerful waves of psychic energy struck Jessica, infusing her with an awful, dragging despair that sapped her strength and hammered her with shame. Several Sisters had stepped off the trail nearby and drew in around her and Mohiam, joining in the attack. Stokiah pressed closer.

Jessica felt intense pain in her head, the demanding sensation that she *must* do what Mother Superior Harishka wanted and turn against her own son.

But Tessia had prepared her, showing her survival skills to use against such an attack. Rhombur's wife had been pummeled and damaged, but not defeated; she had found her own thread of strength, had resisted even as the Sisters tried to break her. And Jessica now shared that knowledge.

Rallying her strength and fury against what Stokiah, Mohiam, and these other women were trying to do to her—and to Paul!—Jessica steeled her mind and followed the mental channels she had prepared with Tessia's help, shoring up her defenses and drawing upon her own strength.

She fought the guilt, using the strongest aspect of her core, the foundation of her life. She did it with her abiding love for Duke Leto Atreides and for their son—and drew strength from them. In memory, she saw Leto's ruggedly handsome face, with his woodsmoke gray eyes looking at her so tenderly, so protectively—and she focused on that for a moment. With Leto's memory beside her, with his nobility and strength saturating every cell in her body, she had an armor that the Sisters could not penetrate.

With great effort, Jessica shouted, "Save . . . your guilt . . . *for yourselves!*"

Making a concerted surge, she threw off the attack, and as she focused harder and harder, Jessica felt the psychic pummeling recede, and heard screams of pain as she inflicted echoes of guilt on her attackers. As moments passed and she gained the upper hand, she stalked off down the trail, leaving the Sisters reeling and moaning.

INTERLUDE

10, 207 AG

Halfway to Sietch Tabr, the grounded 'thopter perched on its outcropping in the middle of the desert. The wind picked up, making the hull plates creak and rattle, which Jessica could hear from their sheltered place a short distance away. A hiss of sand scattered across the rocks, but the sound only deepened the sad silence as Jessica paused in her story.

Upon hearing the startling revelations, Gurney showed more overt emotion than Irulan did. " 'A memory can be sharper than a dagger and can cut more deeply.' Those were sad times, my Lady, and difficult for both of us, but I was not aware of the vile things the witches asked of you. It doesn't surprise me that you've distanced yourself from the Sisterhood."

"Oh, I've more than distanced myself, Gurney. I have turned my back on the Bene Gesserit entirely."

Irulan shifted uncomfortably on the rock. "The Sisters ask many things, without regard to the damage they may do. They're concerned only with their own goals." She drew a long breath through her filter. "But I still don't see how any of this changes or excuses Bronso's crimes. And I don't understand why you insist that you must keep this information from Alia. The Regent certainly has no love for the Bene Gesserit, nor did Paul. In fact, I think she'd be pleased to hear how you thwarted them."

Gurney said in a rumbling voice, "I am happy enough that you refused to do what the witches demanded, my Lady. Compelling a mother to kill her own son is appalling and inhuman."

"It's worse than that, Gurney." Jessica leaned back against the hard, rough rock and forced herself to say the words aloud. "Not long afterward, I decided they were right, and I did make up my mind to kill him. And because of that, I did even more terrible things."

Reverend Mothers are not mothers in the human sense. A real mother loves, understands, and forgives her child for almost anything.

But not everything.

—LADY JESSICA, private journal note

Even though Jessica had turned against them, the words of the militant Sisters had still penetrated, stirring her thoughts until they reinforced her own doubts.

As the Heighliner carried her away from Wallach IX, she isolated herself, in no mood for visitors or conversation. She had always clung to the certainty—perhaps delusion?—that Paul was right, that he did indeed know what he was doing, even if she didn't understand it fully.

In the quiet of her private stateroom, she meditated to calm her fears, while trying to reach a resolution in her mind. If love and misplaced kindness prevented her from doing a terrible but necessary thing, then how much more death and destruction would occur? How many more lives would be lost?

How could she even understand what Paul was trying to do?

Her son could be extremely persuasive, with charismatic and oratory skills he had learned from Duke Leto, from the Bene Gesserit instruction she had given him, and from his time among the skilled Jongleurs. Paul could make his followers believe in him and react in whatever ways he deemed necessary—mass persuasion.

But did he make the correct choices, or was he deluding himself? For years Jessica had been bombarded by adverse reports from a variety of sources. What if he was *wrong*? What if he had lost his way? Her son was *not* who she had once thought he was, not the man she'd hoped he would be. That was why she and Gurney had left Arrakis, left the Jihad.

What if the Bene Gesserit were correct?

She knew full well that the Sisters had their own agenda. Their arguments were not objective, no matter how persuasive they sounded or how vehemently the women argued their points. On this particular subject, the Bene Gesserit had shown their true colors by trying to destroy her psyche through guilt-casting. But that in itself did not mean they were *wrong*.

When the mocking silence of the stateroom grew too much for her, she disembarked onto the public decks. She did not want conversation or company, just the presence of other people; she hoped the background drone of their lives would fill the empty spaces in her mind.

While she was there, she did not intend to seek out news of the Jihad, but the stories were so horrific that she could not avoid them. The Heighliner had stopped at several waypoints, picking up new passengers, new rumors, and even eyewitness accounts. The buzz of shock and disbelief overwhelmed the unsettled crowds.

Her heart pounded with renewed urgency. What had Paul done now?

Fresh reports had come aboard with passengers embarking at the current planetfall, and the news hadn't yet had a chance to grow in the telling. Paul's propaganda scouts had not been able to sanitize or contradict the witnesses' statements. This was the true, raw reporting.

A pogrom had taken place on the planet Lankiveil, a former stronghold of House Harkonnen. In the snowy mountain fastnesses, Buddislamic monks lived in ancient cliffside monasteries surrounded by glaciers. The monks had been persecuted for years by Count Glossu Rabban, but not out of any particular religious hatred; Rabban merely liked to flaunt his power.

This time it was much, much different.

The Buddislamics had always been a quiet, peaceful sect who spent their days writing sutras, chanting prayers, and meditating on unanswerable questions. Members of Paul's Fremen Qizarate had swept down upon Lankiveil's religious retreats and demanded that the quiet monks erect a giant statue of Paul Atreides, as well as change their teachings and beliefs to reflect the fact that Muad'Dib was the greatest of all holy prophets, second only to God himself.

Although they had never spoken against Muad'Dib or the Jihad, and they had no political leanings whatsoever, the monks still had firm convictions. Meaning no disrespect, yet remaining adamant, they declined to follow the priests' orders. They refused to accept that Muad'Dib possessed the sacred aspects attributed to him by the Qizarate.

As a punishment, the monks were slaughtered to the last man. The ancient monasteries were blasted from the cliffsides, and avalanches were sent down to bury the rubble. In the aftermath, the Qizarate dispatched hunters across the Imperium to discover and eradicate any other enclaves of the "heretical Buddislamic sect."

Jessica sat down unsteadily in a hard, worn waiting chair, unable to deny how appalling the act was. Muad'Dib's religion was like a cancer, metastasizing across the universe. But the reports were conflicting, and she could not be sure whether this heinous act had been committed by out-of-control priests and warriors, or if Paul had given the direct orders.

Then she learned more.

After the initial outcry and uproar, Muad'Dib released a widely distributed video statement, which was played and replayed onboard the Heighliner. These words were not some bureaucratic proclamation issued by a sanctimonious official. *Paul* spoke them himself.

"Regarding the recent tragedy on Lankiveil, I am saddened by the foolish loss of life. Those poor Buddislamic monks did not need to die. I feel their pain and suffering.

"But while we grieve because they were human beings, we must not forget that those people had the power to save themselves. The responsibility for their deaths lies with them alone. My Qizarate explained how they could save themselves, and they ignored the warning." He paused, and his spice-saturated eyes blazed with fervor for his audience; he was like a master showman in his element. "And they paid the necessary price."

His Harkonnen side is showing, she thought. *That might as well have been his grandfather the Baron talking.*

In the projected image, the Arrakeen crowds roared their approval as Paul gazed calmly out upon them. The chant grew louder, like an accelerating wave that never seemed to crest. "Muad'Dib! Muad'Dib!"

Jessica felt anger building up inside. Instead of condemning the unnecessary brutality of his own fanatics, instead of ordering restraint, Paul had pinned the blame for the massacre squarely on the poor, innocent monks. He didn't even look troubled by what had happened.

When had Atreides honor died? She shuddered to imagine what Duke Leto would have thought if he'd seen his son's behavior.

On the scale of things, after the years of bloodshed in the Jihad, the Lankiveil massacre was a comparatively small event, but it spoke volumes about Paul, about his followers, and about the lengths to which they would go. It was a singular demonstration of how much he had changed, how passionately he had embraced the artificial persona he had created for himself.

In the recording, though, Paul had more to say. Raising his arms high in the air to quell the noise, he said, "I do not speak idle words. My voice carries power across the stars. You who are foolish enough to think that I know not of your heresies shall find no place to hide. You cannot avoid the hammer of fate you have brought on yourselves. I say this to those who continue to defy me: Soon, at a time of my choosing, Guild Heighliners will appear over eleven worlds. There, they will disgorge my warships to sterilize every planet that has displeased me. Eleven worlds . . . and I pray that will be enough."

The crowd grew strangely quiet, and as the recorder scanned over their faces, Jessica saw shock and surprise even among the Emperor's most avid supporters. Then, gradually, the expressions began to change, and the stunned people roared their approval. "Eleven more worlds!"

"This is the punishment I have prescribed. Let it be done, and let it be recorded in the annals of the Holy Jihad." With that, Paul turned and walked away, while the throng cheered wildly.

Jessica sat speechless. He had already sterilized four planets, in addition to the countless horrific battles that had been engaged in seven years of the Jihad. Now even more worlds were going to be erased . . . and she had no reason to believe the unspeakable violence would end there.

A sharp chill ran down the back of her neck. Emperor Muad'Dib no longer resembled the son she had loved and raised. In the past, Jessica had been able to see an echo of his father whenever she looked at Paul, but after hearing this speech, she could discern nothing of Duke Leto the Just. She'd heard enough, seen enough.

Paul had become the Empty Man, thirsting for the deaths of billions, a husk of a human being without a soul.

With a red haze around her vision, she hurried back to her stateroom and sealed herself inside. This was a turning point for her, the crack in the levee that allowed the long-denied truth to flood into her.

She had played a part in the creation of a monster. For so long, Jessica had believed that she would eventually understand Paul's rationale, if only he would explain himself. At one time she and her son had been a fine team, had relied upon each other through a series of challenges and crises. She had trusted him with her life. But her love for him had caused her to delay too long, just like Gurney and his gaze hounds infected with the bloodfire virus. Now eleven more planetary populations would be annihilated!

The conclusion was as inescapable as death: *Paul* was crippling the human race, and she could not pretend that events had simply slipped out of his control. He approved, even encouraged, the crimes committed in his name.

The Reverend Mothers had complained about Alia being an Abomination, but Paul was the real threat. Yes, Jessica's daughter was strange by any measure, but the girl could not help the accident of her birth, the voices in her mind. Paul, on the other hand, made his own decisions, had chosen his own path. As a leader, he allowed his soldiers to run like wolfpacks amongst otherwise peaceable populations.

How much more slaughter would Muad'Dib order? How many more planets would he destroy? If Jessica did not do something to stop him, was not she just as responsible? Sitting alone in her dimly lit stateroom, surrounded by the clamor of her thoughts, Jessica came to the inescapable conclusion.

She had to stop Paul . . . kill him. The Bene Gesserit were right.

He had surrounded himself with thorough protective measures, and his personal fighting skills were incomparable. But, as his mother, Jessica could get close to him. She was a force to be reckoned with in her own right, and she believed she had a chance against Paul, against Muad'Dib . . . against *her son,* because she knew his weaknesses. Just a moment's hesitation on his part—that was all she needed.

Lady Jessica knew Paul loved her. But the Bene Gesserit had taught her that she must not allow herself to feel love. Sadly, she realized, Mohiam may have been right about that after all. Muad'Dib was not merely Jessica's son: He was the product of a long, long breeding plan that had gone wrong. He was a product of the Bene Gesserit.

And he had to die.

At the Heighliner's next port of call, IV Delta Kaising, the immense ship disgorged small vessels from its belly—shuttles, cargo ships, military craft. A routine stop, Guild business as usual.

Jessica thought she might go mad from the delay in getting back to Caladan. She emerged from her stateroom again and stared out the observation window of a common area at the planet below. As she often did, she brooded over the terrible losses in the Jihad, which seemed endless. Her mind was angered and saddened by the news of continuing atrocities . . . and her heart was leaden from the horrendous decision she had made. But there could be no denying what she must do.

IV Delta Kaising was the planet where the vines for razor-sharp, metallic shigawire grew, a major cash crop that was exported to various worlds. Shigawire was used as a recording-base material, and had the interesting property of contracting when stressed, making it ideal for bonds to secure struggling prisoners—cruel, and often deadly bonds. Because of the ongoing Jihad, the market for the vines had boomed.

Such a long war. To Jessica, it seemed like centuries since young Paul had run off with Bronso Vernius, eager to visit the worlds of the Imperium, to travel to exotic places and cultures. He had been excited in those days, filled with wonder and curiosity. . . .

Jessica did not notice the approach of a Wayku attendant until the slender, dark-goateed man stepped up to her, solicitous but reserved. He held one hand behind his back. "You are the Lady Jessica, from Caladan." She did not hear a question at the end of his statement. Uncharacteristically, the steward's dark glasses were tilted back on his head so that he could peer at her with intense, pale blue eyes. "I checked the passenger manifest."

Wayku stewards rarely initiated contact with passengers, and Jessica was immediately wary. She hesitated. Then: "I am returning home."

From behind his back, the man produced a sealed cylinder and handed it to her. "Bronso Vernius of Ix asked me to deliver this important message to you."

She could not have been more astonished. She'd just seen Tessia at the Mother School, but she had not heard from young Bronso in years. Though he was the ostensible leader of Ix, he had broken all contact with House Atreides after Rhombur's death.

"Who are you? What is your connection to Ix?"

The Wayku was already trying to depart. "I have no connection to Ix, my Lady. Only to Bronso. I am Ennzyn, and I knew both him and your son when they were much younger. In fact, I helped your men locate Bronso and Paul when the boys were . . . missing. I have never forgotten them, and Bronso has not forgotten me."

He slipped away before she could ask more questions. Looking down at the mysterious message, Jessica cut the seal with a fingernail and unrolled a sheet of instroy paper bearing the purple and copper helix of the Vernius family.

My Dearest Lady Jessica—

    Though I turned my back on House Atreides for reasons that are painful to both of us, I now call upon the close relationship that our Great Houses once had. I know you have just visited Wallach IX, and I eagerly await word—the truth!—about my mother. I would be greatly in your debt if you would stop over at Ix and visit me, on your way back to Caladan.

    I still live in the Grand Palais, though I have been deprived of virtually all power. The Technocrat Council has stripped me of any real influence, and they dominate our society. It is also most urgent that I speak with you about Paul.

With all respect and admiration,
Bronso Vernius

Rolling the message tightly and returning it to the cylinder, Jessica marched off down the corridor to arrange for her departure at Ix. The planet was three stops away.

WHEN SHE REACHED the subterranean city of Vernii, Jessica noticed many changes over the past dozen years since she'd last visited— signs of great wealth, including many new buildings, expanded industry, throngs of people of various races bustling about in expensive clothing. The inverted skyline of stalactite buildings had grown more complex; the numerous new administrative buildings looked designed for utilitarian purposes rather than beauty.

Inside the Grand Palais, Jessica was greeted by a copper-haired man, whom she recognized immediately. Bronso looked careworn and tired with shadows under his eyes and fatigue etched into his features. His shoulders drooped. All happiness seemed to have been sucked out of his demeanor. "Lady Jessica, I can't tell you how much I appreciate this. It was imperative that you come." When he extended his hand to her, she noticed the fire jewel ring of House Vernius on his right hand, Rhombur had worn one just like it.

"Oh, Bronso! It has been so long." Words flowed from her like a flood. "I just saw your mother. She is alive and awake on Wallach IX, out of her coma."

The young man brightened. "That much I know, because she has smuggled out brief messages to me over the years, and I to her. If I had military strength or political influence, I would demand her release." His bony shoulders bounced up and down in a quick shrug. "But what could I do for her here? Are the Sisters taking good care of her?" He gestured for Jessica to follow him. "Tell me about her. How does she seem?"

Jessica talked quickly as he led her along a corridor, where the surfaces of tables and statues looked dusty. The furnishings were still of tremendous value, but did not look cared for. He stopped at the doorway of an inner room with no windows. As she finished her story about Tessia, she realized that he had been trying to distract her, and now she was puzzled that he would choose to bring her to a secure area rather than one of the more spectacular balcony chambers.

Bronso opened the door, and he was plainly nervous. "We can talk more inside." Jessica hesitated before entering, sensing something unusual, but unable to determine what. The room looked bright and sterile.

He sealed the door behind them, activated a series of security systems, and then visibly relaxed. Gesturing for her to take a seat near the faux fireplace inset in the wall, Bronso said, "House Vernius is not what it once was. Our factories hum, and customers pour in from every corner of the galaxy. All around me, Ix is an efficient machine of activity, generating vast profits. Yet, here I am in the midst of it, a lonely, forgotten man. Bolig Avati and the Technocrat Council do not see any need for a royal family on Ix. Instead, they have proposed an independent confederacy."

"I'm very sorry to hear that." She wasn't sure what he wanted from her, or what she could do to help him. "I wish I could do something to improve your circumstances. But your message said you needed to talk . . . about Paul?"

She could not reveal the crushing decision she had made.

"The summons did not come from me, my Lady."

A door opened on her right, and Paul strode into the room, wearing a black formal uniform of House Atreides with a red hawk crest rather than the Fremen desert garb he often wore, even away from Dune. He carried himself with an icy demeanor that reminded her of Duke Leto.

"I'm the one who asked you to come here, Mother."

If making a difficult decision is considered a strength, then does changing one's mind indicate weakness?

—*The Book of Mentat*

Jessica froze as Paul emerged to stand beside Bronso Vernius, the man who had supposedly broken all ties with House Atreides. *Paul!*

Time funneled down into a pinprick of an instant, and all of her Bene Gesserit schooling came to bear. If she truly meant to commit the unthinkable act, this was her chance. Paul suspected nothing.

Something had annealed inside her when she made up her mind to stop him. Her son had vowed to sterilize eleven more worlds. She *had* to remove him from power, end his reckless path of destruction.

She stepped closer, cautiously hoping for an embrace. She could deliver a single mortal blow—fast, irreversible . . . and necessary.

Seeing his strong-boned face and remembering the dear boy who had been such a dedicated student and eager learner, the pride of her beloved Duke Leto, Jessica almost lost her resolve. But this was what she *had* to do—not because the Bene Gesserit had suggested it, but because her own conclusions required it.

Paul said, "Mother, don't do what you're thinking." With surprising power and authority, his words stopped her in her tracks, just as she was about to strike out. Her arm flickered, hesitated. He added in a softer tone, "I desperately need your help."

Though he had seen the potential violence in her, he did not step back to put even a small buffer of safety between them. Paul remained exactly where he was. "No one else knows I'm here, and it has to remain that way."

The Ixian chamber was intensely quiet until Bronso said. "This is a very important matter. No one can know what we plan here. These walls are shielded, so we can speak plainly."

Paul nodded. "The excesses of the Jihad are too extreme. My own myth has grown too powerful, and Bronso is about to change all of that."

The Ixian's expression was hard, his skin pale from a life spent underground in the cavern city. "Paul has asked me to be his secret foil to counter the destructive myth of the messiah, to make people see that he is not the demigod that he's been portrayed as. And I have agreed to this." A cold smile crossed his lips. "Wholeheartedly."

Jessica jerked back her head in surprise. Her heart hammered in her chest.

Paul continued, "Bronso has made no secret of his animosity toward me since the night his father died—so no one will suspect that I put him up to anything. He's going to take me down a few notches, refute what the Qizarate and Princess Irulan say, ridicule those who blindly revere me. After so much bloodshed in the Jihad, it is time."

The words gave Jessica great pause. She felt stiff, heard no emotion in her own voice. "This is . . . not what I expected at all."

"I know the violence I have condoned, and I know that must seem inexplicable to you, unforgivable."

"At first I thought I was going to take pleasure in this," Bronso said, "but the more I consider the overwhelming task—and the perils involved—the more I doubt I'll get out of this with my skin intact."

Paul gave him a sincere smile. "Yet even with all that, my rediscovered friend has agreed to do as I wish, at considerable danger to himself. He will write the words that no one else has the courage to say, and people will talk about them. More and more, they will talk, and they will *think*."

"And, oh, how his fanatics will howl for my blood," Bronso said.

Paul's expression showed the determination that had overthrown an empire and launched fanatical troops across hundreds of worlds.

"Through destiny or fate, Mother—call it what you will—I found myself unable to prevent the Jihad. Through prescience, I saw horrific aspects of my future, yet I could not prevent it. Similarly, my father found himself caught in his own destiny, knowing that Arrakis was a trap set by his enemies, but knowing that he had to play it out and see if he could emerge victorious. I, too, know my own destiny— and it is not a glorious one. Perhaps it is the culmination of the Atreides curse." His words trailed away, and he stared at Jessica with his deep blue eyes. "Isn't there a Bene Gesserit saying—'Prophets have a way of dying by violence'?"

"Don't say that!" she said, then realized the irony, since she had been prepared to kill him herself only moments earlier.

"I am no longer just a nobleman making parochial decisions for Caladan and House Atreides. I have become something else entirely, a monstrous leader the likes of which this universe has never seen. When my warriors rush into battle, they shout my name as if it will protect them and strike their opponents dead with fear."

"I know, I know." She looked away, sadly.

Paul's words came faster. "The moment I became Muad'Dib, I reached the point of no return. As the Kwisatz Haderach, I saw portions of my future and of mankind's future, and I knew that I *needed* to lead my legions across planet after planet, carrying banners dipped in blood. And for what purpose, Mother? Just to kill, just to gain power, just to overthrow the old ways? Of course not!"

Glancing at Bronso, she saw the other man nodding as he listened.

"It was my fate to seize my role as the Lisan al-Gaib and the Kwisatz Haderach, in order to guide people through the whirlwinds of history, so that we could reach this point. The turning point."

Jessica narrowed her eyes, glanced sidelong at Bronso, then back at her son, without saying anything.

"Because of me, Mother, our noble House will be spoken of with hatred for years, maybe even centuries . . . no matter the noble deeds of our ancestors, no matter the good deeds I committed before the full violence of the Jihad became apparent."

She felt empty. "Then why are you ordering the sterilization of eleven more planets? How is that necessary to counter your myth?"

"Because I have seen that it must be done. In a way, it is the act that tips the balance and turns people against me, with a bit of persuasion from Bronso. It gives him a legitimate reason. If not for that, the situation would grow worse, much worse, and if he doesn't start now, it will be too late."

"But *eleven planets*? All those people, just to make a point?" Then, thinking of what Mayor Horvu and his followers had done with their foolish cry for independence, she added, "Is one of those worlds Caladan?"

He recoiled. "Caladan is my home planet. I would never harm it."

"Each of those worlds is somebody's home planet." She wondered if she had made a mistake in not killing him when she'd had her chance.

As if he could read her thoughts, he said, "I understand what you thought you needed to do to me, Mother. You hoped to save as many lives as possible, and that is my hope, as well. There are small deeds you aren't aware of. The recent massacre at the Lankiveil monastery involved fewer than one hundred and fifty deaths. Secretly, I arranged for forty-seven women and children to escape before the priests came in. Word has also been leaked to the rulers of the eleven target planets, and Guildships are taking away great numbers of people in an unofficial evacuation, though of course I would deny it vehemently."

Jessica caught her breath, almost sobbed as she asked, "But *why*, why do you want to be hated for all of eternity, and why must you take House Atreides down with you? Why must so many people die in the name of Muad'Dib? How can that be your destiny, or theirs?"

"I have had many visions that guide my course, some after great consumption of melange, others through dreams. I took my name from the desert mouse, the muad'dib, the shape of the shadow on the second moon—and in many visions I have seen the moon, and shadows, growing dark . . . maybe eclipsed." His voice trailed off, then he shook his head. "But that does not mean that all light is lost from that moon, or that my life has no purpose. Though caught inextricably in my own destiny, I will teach a lesson for all time, showing by example the danger of falling into the myth of the charismatic leader, the mistaken belief that following a heroic figure will always lead humankind to utopia. Such a myth is mass insanity, and must be destroyed. The legacy I leave is that my personal, very *human*, flaws are amplified by the number of people who carry my banner into battle."

Jessica began to comprehend the immensity of what Paul had in mind. His words were like an unexpected splash of cold water to open her eyes. He had done so many reprehensible things that she'd begun to believe that he had tumbled headlong down a slippery slope of his own justifications. She had begun to believe the worst of him, and using that chink in her armor, both Mother Superior Harishka and Reverend Mother Mohiam had tried to manipulate Jessica into murdering her own son.

With great sorrow, Paul said, "The things I have to do are my terrible purpose, revealed to me in my visions—the nightmarish path I must follow through darkness that seems never-ending, but which must ultimately emerge into light." His face was a grim mask that she would never forget. He looked so much older than his twenty-four years.

She felt a strange sense of calm. Paul had opened her eyes with his confessions, his immense personal sacrifice. Despite her fears, she realized that he really did know what he was doing after all, that his plans encompassed a much vaster canvas than any single tragedy, that he was not an abomination who needed to be slain just to stop a current crisis. Great numbers of people were being evacuated from targeted planets, but his part in saving their lives had to remain a secret. He was sacrificing himself, and the lives that were lost were the smallest price he could find.

She was appalled by how close she had come to killing him. How little she had understood!

Bronso broke the silence. "For a long time I considered myself Paul's enemy, and it took me a long time to find room for forgiveness. But I realized, eventually, that my father's death was not Paul's fault. The greatest blow was when my father's last words were about Paul . . . and only Paul." The Ixian nobleman drew a deep breath. "But then I realized something else. My father had made me swear to watch out for Paul, to protect him from dangers. By asking with his dying breath whether Paul was safe, he was asking *me* whether I had fulfilled my responsibility."

The young man raised his chin, and his eyes sparkled with a proud nobility. "Now I understand much more. And this gives me my own strong purpose—a purpose I have avoided for my entire adult life."

Bronso gestured to the shielded wall of the chamber. "The Technocrat Council runs Ix. Although I'm a Landsraad representative and still the titular ruler of the planet, my authority here is empty. The technocrats already regard me as irrelevant, and soon they'll conclude that I am an annoyance. Vermillion Hells, with all the dangers here, it may be safer if I hide out in the space lanes and spread dangerous tracts about Muad'Dib!" He smiled gamely at Paul, then at Jessica. "I'm ready for this task."

"It is my destiny to love you, Paul, no matter what," Jessica said. Paul turned to her with a plea on his face, and Jessica saw *her son* again, the bright, sensitive person she thought she had lost. She had conceived him in love and had given birth to him, and now she could do nothing to remove herself from the powerful historical current that carried House Atreides into the future.

Jessica could only nod when he said, "I want you to help Bronso, in secret, however you can. Help him to destroy me."

Each life is filled with secrets.

—AMAN WUTIN, adviser to Korba the Panegyrist

Everything in her life had changed—and changed again—but when Jessica returned home, Caladan was as beautiful as always . . . pristine, serene, and safe. When she stepped onto the Cala City landing field, she smelled the ozone-freshness of an ocean breeze. She drank in the vibrant late afternoon colors, the marshy pundi-rice fields, the tall coastal pine forests, the broad seas, the soaring inland mountains. *Home. Peace.*

Since the meeting on Ix, her impression of Paul had fundamentally changed. Jessica knew that he did have the clarity of vision he claimed, and that he was fully aware of the dangers of his own legend and the religion that had sprung up around him. Only she and Paul would ever know what Bronso Vernius was truly doing, and why. She couldn't even tell Gurney Halleck the truth.

Jessica knew as well that her own destiny was aligned with her son's, and that she could not extricate herself from it any more than he could. . . .

A contingent of guards met her at the edge of the spaceport grounds. For years, with the predictability of the daily sunrise, Gurney's expression had lit up whenever he saw her. But not now.

"You are returning home to a dire crisis, my Lady, and I fear it is only the beginning." He refused to say more until the two of them had climbed into the sealed groundcar. The offworld soldier guards took adjacent vehicles, making Jessica feel very uncomfortable. She had never seen so much security on Caladan.

During the ride to the Castle, Gurney described the surprisingly violent demonstrations, the increasing fervor for independence, the anger of Caladanians in response to how they perceived Muad'Dib had treated them.

"My solution may have made things worse." The rough-looking man shook his head. "We cracked down and stopped most of the demonstrators, and reopened the spaceport. But this morning, a few overly ambitious locals took four Qizara Tafwids hostage and are holding them until the Imperial government rescinds the change of Caladan's name." His hands knotted into fists. "I had hoped we could hold off any retaliation from Muad'Dib's government by claiming the problem was solved . . . but now what can we say to them? I am shamed to have failed you so, my Lady."

After what Mohiam had revealed to her on Wallach IX, Jessica understood that Bene Gesserit operatives had been manipulating the crowds all along, pushing them toward rebellion in hopes of triggering a cascade of planetary revolts.

"It's not entirely their fault, Gurney. The Sisterhood is trying to force Paul to overreact. They intend for Caladan's mostly innocent resistance to be the flashpoint for a chain of uprisings. The Bene Gesserits are playing a game of provocation, with the people here as their pawns."

"Unless I cut out the roots of this rebellion before it can blossom further," Gurney said.

"We, Gurney. *We* must cut out the roots of this rebellion."

His wide mouth formed a wolfish, almost involuntary, grin. "At your service, my Lady. . . ."

On Ix, after hearing Paul's shocking revelation, she had taken time to tell him of Mayor Horvu's plan to declare Caladan's independence. His demeanor had darkened. "Even if the Bene Gesserits are the instigators here, doesn't Horvu know what he'll force me to do? Such an act of defiance will incite a terrible retaliation that I won't be able to control! My followers are already incensed that you have turned away so many pilgrims. After hearing this, they will feel obligated to purify my original homeworld."

She had felt her own resolve harden as her breathing quickened. "Then before you act, Paul, give me a chance to mitigate the situation. If there's a price to be paid, I'll find a way to pay it, the smallest price possible—for Caladan. Let me do my job to protect the people."

Reluctantly, he had assented, but Jessica knew she would have only one chance, that Paul would not be able to maintain his role and stall his fanatics in the face of repeated provocation. Now the future of Caladan was in her hands, so many lives depending on her—if she could only make the difficult but necessary decisions. She needed to find the smallest possible price to pay. . . .

Now, beside her in the vehicle, Gurney carried a great weight on his shoulders. "I wasn't entirely sure how to respond, my Lady. I could not imagine that Duke Leto would imprison anyone who chose to speak out—especially since I myself am offended by the Qizarate's decree. Changing the name of Caladan?" He shook his head. "Ever since I released the dissidents from their holding cells, they have professed to be peaceful. You will see a crowd at your Castle . . . not much yet, but it increases in size every day. I fear it will get out of hand again, and soon."

"If it does, Muad'Dib's troops will come." Jessica's lips formed a grim line. "Leto was only the Duke of a single planet, and therefore could focus on the problems of his people. Paul is caught in an entirely different sort of whirlwind encompassing thousands of planets. It is the difference between a dust devil and a Coriolis storm."

When they reached Castle Caladan, Jessica saw the throngs, more numerous than even the hordes of zealous pilgrims during their unchecked days here. Gurney said, "Perhaps there's one last chance for sanity. They do revere you as their Duchess, my Lady. They expect you to stand with them and solve their problems."

Jessica looked out the windows of the groundcar. "I know. They must accept *some* responsibility for problems they created, however. We can't entirely blame the Bene Gesserit." The offworld security troops cleared a way for them to move ahead, and the crowd's shouting grew louder. "And they have to realize that theirs are not the only problems to solve."

"It will only grow worse, my Lady. The moment I lifted the restrictions on him and reopened the spaceport, Mayor Horvu drained half of the town's treasury to dispatch couriers to dozens of major planets to declare our independence. I stopped some of the couriers, and I have blocked dissidents from sending more messages offworld, but I'm afraid it's too late. Now, everyone will wait to see how Muad'Dib reacts to the situation."

"We can't wait, Gurney." Her voice was sharp. "Ultimately the solution to this crisis should lie in how *I* react to it, because *I* rule Caladan. I do not say that to diminish you in any way, because I *do* need your help, but there are certain responsibilities a ruler must bear alone."

As the vehicle passed through the crowd, she saw a large black balloon flying over the throng. White words printed on the surface read, PAUL-MUAD'DIB IS NO LONGER AN ATREIDES.

Seeing this, Jessica raised her voice to the driver. "Stop the vehicle. Here. Now."

"Here, my Lady? But it is unsafe."

After taking one look at Jessica, Gurney snapped, "Do as the Duchess says."

The crowd fell into a startled silence when she stepped out and faced them. She raised her voice as they began to cheer happily. The people were glad to see her, sure that she was the savior they needed.

"I have just now returned from my travels, and I am disappointed to see this unruliness! Is this how we solve our difficulties on Caladan? No! Hear me now—I want the hostage priests released unharmed. *Immediately*. Only after you have done so, can we discuss your complaints. Provided you do as I ask, this evening I shall invite the ten people you consider most important in this—" She searched for the right word. "—this *crusade* to meet with me in private. I only wish to see those who are truly *involved* in this matter, so that I may offer them my solution to your grievances. Until then, all of you please disperse, and let me deal with your concerns in a proper fashion."

The people hesitated for a moment, as if they had all drawn a deep breath at the same time. Then they cheered.

Jessica climbed back into the groundcar and told the driver to take them to the Castle. She leaned back in her seat, closed her eyes. "Gurney, I have to resolve this before Paul does."

He looked at her quizzically, then nodded. "Just give me my orders, my Lady."

EXPECTING JESSICA TO speak on their behalf, the people were eager to cooperate now, to show their faith in her. The four hostage priests were released within two hours. Gurney had put them in a safe building near the Castle and posted several of his offworld guards to watch over them. Satisfied with that at least, Jessica prepared for the evening. It would be her one chance to end this.

Gurney pressed her for what she planned to do, but Jessica refused to answer him. This was her decision, though she didn't like keeping such secrets from her trusted friend. *Paul has found the smallest price to pay, and I shall do the same.*

She had to prevent the oncoming disaster and hamstring the Sisterhood's plans to spark revolts across the Imperium, using the people of Caladan as cannon fodder. She had to stop it *here*.

When the ten specially chosen guests arrived, servants escorted them into the main banquet hall. These were the ringleaders, as selected by the dissidents themselves. Mayor Horvu looked relieved to see her. The priest Sintra, as well as the prominent leaders from Cala City and other coastal towns, all seemed delighted and victorious. Jessica had agreed to hear their grievances and present her solution.

Six men and two women accompanied the priest and the mayor, finding their places at the long table with an almost comical lack of efficiency. Most had never been inside the Castle before, and certainly not for such an important dinner. Food had already been delivered to the table, the portions served on fine plates next to goblets of clear spring water—a reminder of Caladan's bounty as compared to Arrakis.

After the servants departed, Jessica spoke in a clear voice. "Gurney, would you please excuse us?"

Gurney was surprised to be dismissed. "My Lady? Are you certain I can't be of assistance?"

She did not want him here. "For the moment, I must serve as the Duchess of Caladan, and this discussion is a private matter between these people and myself. Please close the doors behind you."

Though he looked concerned, Gurney departed straightaway, as instructed. The ten guests were flushed and excited; several looked smug. Sintra seemed to take special pleasure in seeing Gurney dismissed, apparently believing that Jessica disapproved of how he had handled matters in her absence.

She took her place at the head of the table. The Mayor and his cohorts had a festive air about them, expressing their concerns politely, at first. After a few minutes, however, the discussion grew heated and boisterous. As promised, Jessica listened. Mayor Horvu boasted that, with Jessica as their direct spokesperson, Paul-Muad'Dib would have no choice but to leave Caladan alone.

Jessica drew a deep breath and said cautiously, "I believe that my son still trusts my judgment. Now, eat. Drink. We have a hard night ahead of us, and I do not intend to leave this room until our problem is solved." She raised her goblet and drank, tasting the spring water.

Abbo Sintra raised his glass in a toast. "To solving problems." They all drank.

Horvu, his face seamed with worry, said, "My Lady, we don't want you to consider us troublemakers. But you must admit that your son's troops have taken aggressive actions across the galaxy. As an Atreides you cannot possibly condone such reprehensible acts? We only want Paul to remember his roots, and his Atreides honor, as well. That is all."

The guests ate their nut-and-cheese salads, then turned to the steaming bowls of traditional fish chowder.

The priest said in a bright voice, "When the other planetary representatives come here, we have decided that you may speak for Caladan. Assure everyone that all our people remain free of the stain of the Emperor's Jihad, commoners and nobility, united. Let history record that we rose up against tyranny and said *No* in a loud and unanimous voice." He ended with a grandiose flourish, looking very pleased with himself.

"On the contrary," Jessica said with a heavy heart, watching them all eat, "this is where *I* say no. This is where I save the people of Caladan from grave danger."

The men and women around the table appeared confused. Horvu said, "But *we* have already saved Caladan, my Lady." He seemed surprised that his voice was inexplicably slurred.

Jessica shook her head. "It is unfortunate, because I do sympathize with your outrage. The Jihad massacres are indeed tragic. But in the course of such sweeping, ambitious changes across an entire empire, there are bound to be excessive deaths. This saddens me, but Paul is my son, and I had a hand in his training. He knows what is necessary."

"But . . . you *must* help us, Lady Jessica," one of the two women at the table said. She seemed to be having trouble breathing and took a long drink of her water, but it didn't help.

Jessica recognized the woman as the daughter of one of the village fishermen. They'd met once, a rainy day on the docks where the woman had helped her father prepare his weather-beaten old boat. Jessica had overheard her cursing like one of the men, before she had abruptly changed her tone upon noticing the Duchess.

"In a way," Jessica said, forcing herself to calmness, "it is all of *you* who are helping me and helping Caladan. I'm sorry, but this is my solution—the only way I could see to avert a far greater crisis. I decided to save millions of lives."

Sintra began coughing. Several of the others looked dizzy, sleepy, sick. Their eyes rolled.

"The sacrifice you make here will preserve Caladan, as I know you meant to do. As Duchess, I make choices that affect the entirety of this world . . . just as Muad'Dib makes choices for all of the Imperium. Your deaths will demonstrate to the Emperor that I have taken care of the problem—that there is no need for him to send his armies here."

True to the Bene Gesserit records she had consulted, the poison she'd chosen had no taste, and it acted quickly . . . supposedly painlessly. For herself, she had consumed the same poison, but had easily transmuted the substance in her body, rendering it inert.

"It wasn't entirely your fault, which saddens me even more. You were all manipulated by skilled Bene Gesserits, and you did not understand where you were being led. I will issue a statement that you ten conspirators were tricked by Sisterhood agents, as part of a plot to overthrow the Emperor Muad'Dib. They will bear the brunt of the blame."

This addresses two problems at once, Jessica thought. *It deals with the uprising, and it serves as an act of defiance against the Bene Gesserit, along with my total rejection of their offer.*

349

"Every other Caladanian who participated in this rebellion will be pardoned," Jessica said. "Take comfort in that. But the ten of you . . . you are the price that must be paid."

Resigned, she sat straight-backed in her chair and watched the guests struggling, gasping, slumping over their plates or falling to the floor. As she watched, the Mayor slid off his chair with a heavy thud. His eyes went lifeless, while hers filled with tears.

Jessica fought back the emotion and said aloud to the room of death. "This thing needed doing, and I did it. Now, I've acted like both a Harkonnen and an Atreides."

Though I do not regret my years of service to House Atreides, there are no words to express some of the things I have witnessed, and done, and endured. I will not even try—I'd rather they were forgotten.

—GURNEY HALLECK, *Unfinished Songs*

Seeing the bodies slumped around the banquet table, Gurney was both furious and sickened. He stared for a long moment at the surprise and disbelief frozen on the faces of Mayor Horvu, the village priest, and the other instigators.

After letting Gurney back inside the room, Jessica made sure the chamber door remained securely locked, knowing this would test the depths of the man's loyalty. "You didn't do this, Gurney. *I* did. It was a terrible price to pay—but it was the smallest price I could find."

Gurney looked at her, his eyes red. "But you *knew* these people, my Lady! They were foolish, but they had good hearts. They were like children playing on a galactic stage." He gestured toward the sprawled figures. "They were *innocents*."

Jessica steeled her voice. She needed him with her now. "They were *not* innocents. Did we not both counsel them against rebellion? I myself warned them that there would be significant consequences if they proceeded. And do you believe it was an accident that they sent out those couriers behind your back, and while I was gone? And when did mere innocents start to take hostages? They let the situation get out of hand, and Paul would never have forgiven their revolt or swept it aside. If he showed any weakness or hesitation here, then other planets would have broken from the Imperium. The Emperor would have had to crack down on planet after planet, undoubtedly sterilizing even more worlds." She looked at the silent victims around the banquet table. "This . . . this was only ten lives. Not such a high price."

Gurney frowned, struggling to fit the tragedy into his concept of honor and decency, as well as loyalty to her and to House Atreides. With an effort, Jessica kept her voice from breaking; she sounded strong and firm, thanks to her Bene Gesserit training—and she hated herself for it.

"Without these instigators, the revolt on Caladan falls apart. Therefore, Paul doesn't have to respond at all. It remains a local matter, which *I* have dealt with, as Duchess. No need for the Fedaykin to get involved. Without these ten people, there will be no additional violence, or bloodshed, or repercussions on a hundred other worlds." She swallowed hard and added, "You know it yourself, Gurney. A mad dog must be put down before it can cause greater harm. These people were mad dogs. It was the only way. If I had hesitated . . ."

Finally, tears fell from her eyes, and she wiped them away with a quick gesture. Gurney turned his eyes away, pretending not to notice. All her life, the Sisterhood had forced her to build up impenetrable walls around her emotions, forced her not to *feel*, but in such an extreme case, after the terrible decision she had made, Jessica could not help herself.

The lumpy man nodded, very slowly. When she saw his mood change, Jessica realized she'd never had any doubt that Gurney Halleck would remain loyal to her.

He said, "So these ten are no different from the cannon-fodder shock troops in a war zone. They died in a battle that they helped create, and unfortunately they chose the wrong side." His voice sounded bleak. "I understand it better now, my Lady, but I still don't like it. I don't like what this changes in me. I've killed plenty of people in my service to House Atreides, but never before have I felt as if I participated in . . . murder."

Jessica took his hands in hers and said sadly, "Time and war change everything from bright and new to old, worn, and dirty. It is not murder. That's not the right word for it when a ruler performs necessary *executions*. As the Duchess of Caladan, that is one of my hardest duties."

She could no longer maintain any semblance of her composure. She rushed from the banquet hall, saying nothing else, giving no further orders. When she returned later, she knew that all the bodies would be gone, and everything would appear normal once more.

Inside her chambers, Jessica closed the door and threw the bolt home. She hoped the wooden barrier would be thick enough that no one could hear her. Fortunately, on Caladan there was no stricture against giving water to the dead.

HOURS LATER, AFTER she had drained away her grief, Jessica sat at her writing desk to compose a coldly worded message. The glow-globe cast a pool of light around her. Years ago, when she had asked the Bene Gesserit for help in finding the boys Paul and Bronso, she had received only a curt refusal. Now it was her turn to send a response that minced no words. She addressed the letter specifically to Reverend Mother Mohiam, her stern teacher, her secret mother.

"Your plan has failed. I know how you tried to manipulate me and others, but I am no longer a cog in your machine, and I will never be a part of your inner circle. So be it. I never asked to be Mother Superior.

"I know who you are, Gaius Helen Mohiam. I know your soul is filled with acid. Heed this warning—to you, personally, and to the entire Sisterhood: If the Bene Gesserits make another attempt to disgrace or destroy Paul, I will convince my son to send the full weight of his Jihad against the Mother School. I will ask him to sterilize Wallach IX, as he has sterilized other worlds. Believe me, I can persuade him to do it, so do not doubt my sincerity. He has wiped out other groups—religious and secular—that offended him. Do not add yourselves to that list."

She paused in her writing, but anger pounded in her temples. Mohiam had made her come so close to believing their lies, so close to killing her own son.

Jessica added a postscript: "Do not send me messages or dispatch your envoys to Caladan. I have no desire to hear from you again. You berated me for allowing myself to feel love. I assure you, I am also capable of feeling *hatred.*"

Those who worship Muad'Dib, read this.

Those who believe the lies of the Qizarate and the exaggerations of
Princess Irulan, read this.

Those who respect truth, read this.

—BRONSO OF IX, introduction to his first pamphlet (untitled)

Jessica prepared herself for any backlash from angry townspeople who had lost friends, family, or well-respected members of the community. However, the initial reaction to the execution of a handful of dissidents on Caladan could have been much worse. At least for now, many of the disgruntled and dissatisfied locals accepted the Duchess's pronouncement that placed the guilt directly on the shoulders of Mayor Horvu, the priest Sintra, and the other leaders of the revolt. After she explained how the good people of Caladan had been manipulated by the Bene Gesserits, the citizens reacted with shame and directed their anger toward the Sisterhood instead of her. When had the people of Caladan ever openly defied their rightful Duke or Duchess?

After being released, the hostage Qizaras applauded Jessica for her swift and sure justice, and they promised to speak on Caladan's behalf so that Muad'Dib's wrath would not fall upon this world or its people. They returned to Arrakis, ruffled but satisfied.

Then Bronso of Ix released his first shocking manifesto. It was late in the year 10,200, when the pundi-rice farmers of Caladan were preparing their paddies for the following season . . . when Muad'Dib had just sent a terrible force of ships to sterilize eleven more planets . . . when the Jihad seemed as if it would never end.

Distributed widely, copied, and passed from hand to hand, the treatise both horrified and titillated people with its bold and appalling claims. In a resounding reaction, the faithful rallied to protect the reputation and sanctity of Emperor Paul-Muad'Dib. On Caladan, those who might have complained about the executions of Horvu and his fellow conspirators suddenly found themselves infuriated by Bronso's damning passages—so infuriated, in fact, that they had to tell everyone else about the outrageous, insulting claims.

Paul's generals and priests issued an immediate order for the arrest and interrogation of the upstart Ixian, but Bronso Vernius was nowhere to be found. After transferring away most of his wealth, secretly draining House Vernius funds, Bronso had left the Grand Palais and vanished into space, leaving no trace of his whereabouts.

Jihad troops bearing the banners of orthodoxy encircled Ix, swarmed into the underground city of Vernii, and questioned all members of the Technocrat Council, demanding to know how they had aided the traitor in spreading his sedition. Fearing for their lives, the Ixian Council disavowed all knowledge of Bronso's actions and vehemently condemned him. Unfortunately for them, the military arm of the Qizarate did not find their denials convincing. Along with many others, Bolig Avati did not survive his interrogation. . . .

GURNEY BROUGHT ONE of the pamphlets to Jessica as she tended her new gardens in the courtyard of Castle Caladan. "Have you read what Bronso is saying, my Lady?"

She tamped down dirt around a new, fragrant-smelling rosemary bush. "No, I've chosen not to think about it."

He seemed barely able to contain his annoyance. "I snatched this from a bonfire down at the docks. The villagers confiscated copies from a man who found them in his baggage. They're so incensed at the insult to Paul that they wanted to throw the man in the flames as well. He insisted he didn't know how the documents had come into his possession, and I sent him back up to the Heighliner to save his life." He lowered his voice. "Like you, I didn't want to read drivel against Paul . . . but if I had read this beforehand, maybe I would have let them have their way with the man."

Gurney extended the pamphlet to her, but Jessica still made no move to take it. She brushed dirt from her palms. "And what exactly upsets you so much? Have you been reading Irulan's syrupy reports for so long you've forgotten that Paul doesn't actually walk on water?"

Gurney frowned and took a seat beside her on a stone bench in the garden. "Actually, Irulan claims that he walks on sand but leaves no footprints." He opened the pamphlet again, skimmed it, then threw it down on the ground in disgust to emphasize his point. Jessica did not pick it up.

"To be honest, my Lady, I can't claim that his facts are absolutely wrong. But ever since Earl Rhombur was killed and Bronso turned his back on House Atreides, I knew he'd be trouble. That boy has let his hatred fester, and now . . . *this*." In frustration, Gurney leaned closer to her. "Why aren't you more upset?"

Jessica gave him an enigmatic, pained smile, snipping an aromatic frond of the herb, inhaling deeply. "Oh Gurney, my son's government is strong enough to weather a little criticism—and maybe even benefit from it. The priests, of course, will cover their eyes and ears, but Paul might listen, and Alia too."

"I suppose you're right, my Lady. Duke Leto would never have been afraid of a few complaints." Gurney had a wistful look on his face. "I'm guilty of a similar thing myself. When I was much younger, I sang a few songs about the Baron Harkonnen." He hummed, then burst into a refrain:

"We work in the fields, we work in the towns,
and this is our lot in life.
For the rivers are wide, and the valleys are low,
and the Baron—he is fat."

He shook his head to drive away the bad memories. "When the Harkonnen troops heard me sing that, they smashed my baliset, beat me to within an inch of my life, and threw me into a slave pit."

Jessica covered his hand with hers, silently acknowledging everything he had gone through. "So you see, Gurney, we should ignore Bronso. He'll probably just go away."

But she knew that Bronso of Ix was just getting started.

PART V

10,207 AG

Two months after the end of Muad'Dib's reign

Knowledge is an impotent thing if a person refuses to believe.

—Bene Gesserit axiom

By the time Jessica finished her story and glanced back at the moonlit silhouette of the landed 'thopter, both Irulan and Gurney were deeply shaken. For the past seven years, that hidden knowledge had weighed like cold lead inside of Jessica.

She had paid a terrible price. Even after so much time had passed, the pain still burned deeply. To this day, Bronso of Ix continued to pay his share of the price, doing what Paul had asked him to do, even while the hounds of Alia pursued him . . . even while the populace reviled him for the truths he exposed.

"'A secret shared is a burden shared, but the weight can still be crushing.'" Gurney hung his head. "Ahh, my Lady, all these years! I feel like a fool for not having guessed, for some of the things I said to you, which made your pain even heavier, and more lonely." His scar looked like a dark line of blood in the light of the two moons. "I understand war, and I thought I knew the logical reasons for what you did to those ten ringleaders . . . but even so, I didn't understand it all. I was bound by my oath to House Atreides, and to you. Now at last I comprehend all of what you were doing, and why . . . but it isn't easy knowledge to have."

"I sacrificed a great deal for Paul—something of my humanity, perhaps, but the options before me were difficult." Jessica led them back toward the 'thopter, knowing it was time to go. They could only cover up their secret meeting for a short while before Alia would grow suspicious.

She paused before they reached the ornithopter, still wary that there might be listening devices hidden inside, despite the precautions they had taken. "Now you understand why I had to speak of these things away from the Citadel. The Qizara Tafwid would call it blasphemy and execute me before I could tell anyone else. And they would kill you for what you know. I'm not sure Alia would try to stop them. She doesn't recognize what she owes me—or Bronso."

"What could Alia possibly owe Bronso?" Irulan asked.

Jessica smiled. "He is the one who revealed to me the plot of Alia's priests, Isbar's intention of assassinating her and Duncan during their wedding. She doesn't know she owes him her life."

Gurney's eyes grew large. "*Bronso* was your secret source? Your spy in the Citadel?"

"He wasn't actually there, but Ixians have their ways of collecting information. Rest assured, he doesn't have any personal vendetta against Alia. He only wants to spread the real story about Paul."

Gurney's features looked sallow in the starlight. "Oh, I wish I had brought my baliset along, since now is the time for a long, sad song."

Jessica drew a deep breath. "Even though some of his harshest criticisms are as wildly untrue as the glorifications Alia wants written, Bronso still serves a vital purpose, and must be allowed to continue. It's a purpose that Paul himself asked him to take on, to counterbalance the things done in his name, a necessary weakening of the too-powerful bureaucracy and the priesthood that he could not defeat any other way. Paul saw only danger ahead if his myth grew even more out of control." Her voice hitched. "Bronso of Ix is the only hope I have of keeping my son *human* instead of letting him be reduced to a legend."

Over the years, Princess Irulan had taken a great deal of offense at Bronso's writings because they directly clashed with her version of history, but now she wrestled with the reality, obviously finding it difficult to accept the hard truth. "If I believe you that Paul requested this himself, Lady Jessica, then you're placing me in an impossible situation.

Paul's wishes are utterly incompatible with what Alia wants me to write about him."

"And where does your true loyalty lie?" After opening herself, Jessica felt empty and naked before her fellow Bene Gesserit Sister, her daughter-in-law. "Won't you protect Paul and what *he* wanted for his legacy?"

In the low light, Irulan's face was distraught. "Would Alia let me? That is not a simple question! There are already too many people who think that the daughter of Shaddam Corrino is more threat than benefit to the Regency. Alia could have me executed for not cooperating. Or she might send me away to Salusa Secundus and never let me see Paul's children again."

Jessica was a bit surprised by this last statement. "They are not your children."

"They are Paul's, and I loved him."

Finally reaching the 'thopter, they climbed in silently, each of them deep in thought. The interior of the cabin glowed with greenish light from the craft's standby control panel. Looking out glumly, Jessica saw that First Moon was just setting into the rugged horizon.

Beside her, Gurney reactivated the systems, prepared to take off. One of the panels on the console sent a signal, and he reacted quickly, gazing out through the curved cockpit window, scanning the starry skies. "Searchers are out there, trying to find us. They've locked on to our locator beacon."

"Already?" Irulan said. "Sietch Tabr could not have reported us overdue or missing yet."

"Even though we switched 'thopters, Alia's men could have been tracking us ever since we left Arrakeen," Jessica said. "When we dropped off their screens, searchers would have been dispatched immediately." She pointed to approaching lights in the distance.

Gurney worked the controls, pushing his emotions aside and focusing his mind on the ornithopter, running through a checklist. All business. "Time to fix our little mechanical problem, then." He activated the comm, took up the microphone, and spoke brusquely into it. "This is Gurney Halleck, pilot of Imperial flight six six five alpha. Sorry if we caused you concern. We needed to set down to adjust an unbalanced rotor and fix a stabilizing linkage."

A voice crackled back, "Do you require assistance?"

"No, no, it's just a minor inconvenience. Nothing a good field mechanic couldn't handle. Both passengers are fine." He powered up the engines, set the wings in motion. "We're on our way."

"We warned you against taking one of the 'thopters that had not been approved for your use," the voice said.

Gurney looked meaningfully at Jessica, then picked up the transmitter. "I'll remember that next time. No harm done."

Jessica and Irulan sat in silence as the 'thopter lifted off from the rock outcropping into the empty, moonlit sky. In a matter of moments, the focused lights of search 'thopters swirled around them like the luminous night insects in a Caladan marsh.

"We will escort you safely to Sietch Tabr," transmitted one of the 'thopter pilots. Gurney thanked them as they flew together over the harsh desert.

I have long disagreed with the fundamental Bene Gesserit admonition against falling in love. Love itself is not the danger. People who do not understand the sentiment, or who care nothing for it, are far more dangerous.

—LADY JESSICA in a letter to Mother Superior Harishka
on Wallach IX

The next day, returning from Sietch Tabr after an uneventful visit with the Fremen, Jessica went to her private chambers in the great Citadel of Muad'Dib. She felt exhausted, and was experiencing second thoughts about having shared her heavy secrets. The knowledge of Bronso's mission would only make circumstances more difficult for Gurney, and especially for Irulan. She had placed the Princess in an untenable situation, and Jessica wasn't entirely sure that Irulan wanted to believe what she had heard.

But they were truths, painful and necessary truths.

Forcing calm upon herself, Jessica prepared to meditate and practice subtle exercises of precise muscular control, to relax her body and clear her mind. Soon she would return to her Atreides homeworld. Caladan, oh Caladan! She missed the sound of the rushing sea and the fresh smells, in stark contrast with the sensory-deadening rasp of blowing sand from the constant winds of Dune. Even so, she didn't think she could ever leave the desert planet behind entirely.

When she entered her main chamber, however, she discovered that Alia had left her a grim gift.

Two battered literjons of water rested on the writing table. The containers looked old and scuffed, as if they had been carelessly tossed out of a spice factory to be weathered on the sands. She didn't understand the significance. Intriguingly, the literjons bore the worn mark of the Regency.

Considering her growing disagreements with Alia and the tensions brewing in the government, Jessica wondered what her daughter could mean by this gift. No person on Dune would refuse a gift of water, especially such a substantial amount. Was it a peace offering? Alia was certainly aware that her mother disapproved of the purges, the growing repression, the willful exaggerations of Paul's myth. Still, Jessica did not want to be at odds with her daughter, and she sensed that Alia longed for acceptance as well.

A spice-paper note written in Alia's hand sat beside one of the literjons. "This water belongs to one who was close to both of us, Mother. Dispose of it as you will."

Looking more closely at the containers, Jessica saw code letters in Atreides battle language. Even the amazon guards who had delivered the literjons would not have been able to read the message:

Reverend Mother Gaius Helen Mohiam.

Jessica froze. This was the reclaimed water of the scheming old woman who had called Alia an Abomination, who had worked repeatedly to destroy Paul and bring down his rule. The water of Jessica's own birth mother, whom Stilgar had executed.

The water of her mother . . . Did Alia mean this as some kind of threat, warning Jessica that she too could be removed and distilled? No, that didn't seem correct.

Despite her noble birth, Alia considered herself a Fremen, and the people of the desert revered the water of the dead, considering it a gift to the tribe. The distilled water of one's mother was also considered sacred, yet Jessica knew what this hateful old woman had done. And she knew how close Mohiam had come to succeeding, not only in her conspiracy to start revolts on numerous worlds, but in duping Jessica. If not for a moment's hesitation, Jessica might have killed Paul. . . .

Alia was letting *her* decide what to do with the old witch's water.

Jessica glowered long and hard at the literjons, and said, as if Mohiam could still hear her, "My son always meant more to me than you could imagine—far more than my mother ever did." Having just relived all those emotions from telling the story to Gurney and Irulan, she could not contain her bitterness. "You tried to make me murder him."

Fremen also said that water tainted by an evil spirit must be spilled upon the ground.

Not caring if Alia watched through a hidden spy hole, Jessica twisted off the sealed caps of the literjons. Without hesitation or regret, she poured the water of the loathsome old witch onto the dry stone floor.

*Shai-Hulud manifests himself in different ways. Sometimes he is
gentle, and sometimes not.*

—*The Stilgar Commentaries*

A rogue sandworm broke through the moisture barrier that blocked
the gap in the Shield Wall, and now the rampaging monster found
its way through the narrow passage. It plunged into the squalid settlements that spread outward from Arrakeen like dust seeping through a
ragged door seal, and plowed a track of destruction, swallowing entire
buildings in monstrous gulps.

Receiving emergency reports, Stilgar grabbed two reliable Fedaykin
soldiers and raced for the nearest launchpad. He was not a man to ponder overmuch during a crisis, but the very idea puzzled him. "This
makes no sense. The qanat should have made an impenetrable water
barrier."

"Maybe sandtrout got into the canal and broke it open, Stil," said
the Fedaykin pilot, throwing himself into the craft and activating the
prestart sequence on the rotors. "Millions of them could have breached
the liner seal and stolen the water."

Stilgar shook his head as he made sure the 'thopter was desert-rigged,
complete with Fremkit, ropes, and survival tools. "How could the inspection teams not have noticed the water line drying out?" He already
suspected a far more sinister answer.

The city of Arrakeen had considered itself safe. No sandworm had managed to pass through the gap in all the years since Muad'Dib had blasted open the Shield Wall during his final battle with Shaddam IV.

But something had allowed this monster worm through. It could not have been an accident.

Scrambling into the cockpit, he settled in beside the pilot, who set the articulated wings in motion, just as the third man jumped into the back. Within moments, the craft lifted off like a predatory bird startled from a fresh kill.

They soared out over the patchwork mosaic of Arrakeen, above the helter-skelter shacks of people who had given up everything to make a pilgrimage to Dune. Stilgar touched the comm in his ear, listening to frantic descriptions. He guided the pilot, although the area of tumult was clear even from a distance.

In a rush, the craft came upon the large segmented worm rolling through and crushing habitation complexes, with no apparent goal. The Fremen pilot stared in such open amazement that he reacted sluggishly to a sudden downdraft, and the 'thopter gave a sickening shudder before he regained control and brought them level again. The second Fedaykin uttered an automatic prayer before adding, "It is the spirit of Muad'Dib! He has taken the form of Shai-Hulud and returned to avenge himself upon us."

Remembering his earlier encounter with a worm in the desert, when it seemed that Paul *might* have been inside the beast, Stilgar felt a thrill of superstitious fear himself. Nevertheless, he infused his retort with scorn. "Why would Muad'Dib be angry with *us*? We are his people, and followed his orders."

That other worm had not tried to harm him.

Even so, he knew the awestruck people down there would make up their own stories. Stilgar could imagine the chants that the doomed victims would shout as the behemoth approached, "The spirit of Muad'Dib! The spirit of Muad'Dib!" Those devoured by the rogue worm would be celebrated as martyrs by the Qizarate.

Though he did not understand what drove this sandworm, he did know how he could stop it. Stilgar reached behind him. "Hand me the Fremkit." Opening it, he set aside the first-aid supplies, paracompass, thumper, and stilltent. He needed only the hooks, goad, spreaders, and rope.

He raised his voice to the pilot over the louder-than-normal throb of the wings; something must be wrong with the soundproofing and moisture seals in the cabin. "Take me down as close as possible. I need to jump onto its back."

The pilot was astonished, but he was Fremen and Fedaykin. "The vibration of our engines will surely disturb the creature, Stil. There is a risk."

"We are in the hands of Shai-Hulud."

This would be entirely different from summoning a worm in the open desert, which Stilgar had done countless times before. A man alone on the dunes could make preparations; he could plant a thumper in the proper spot; he could watch the worm's approach by the ripple in the sand; he knew where it would emerge and could make his move at the precise moment.

But this worm was already aboveground, and highly agitated. The slightest misstep and he would fall into that maw.

Stilgar opened the 'thopter's hatch to a sudden roar of engine noise. Angry winds rushed by, bringing with them the distant racket of panic and destruction. Stilgar secured his tools tightly to his body where they would be readily accessible. He held a climbing hook in each hand and extended the long telescoping rods to their full length. He would have to secure himself to the worm before he could take out his spreaders, before he could anchor his rope.

"I am ready."

The pilot lowered the 'thopter, and Stilgar prepared to leap out of the hatch. He knew that when he landed on the behemoth's back, the curved ring segments would give him little purchase.

At the last moment before he could jump, the sandworm thrashed about, reacting to the vibration and noise of ornithopter wings. It turned its sinuous neck upward and lunged up at them.

With a squawk, the pilot aborted and used the jetpods to lift the 'thopter higher in the air. Stilgar clung to the open hatchway to keep himself from being thrown out. The worm continued to stretch itself upward in response to the annoying pulse and noise, and reached its apex only meters below the fleeing aircraft. The stench of spice exhalations boiled out of its tunnel-like maw as the monster paused for a quivering motionless instant, then began to withdraw.

Stilgar saw his chance—and leaped. He fell, dropping and drop-ping, as the worm retracted below him. The additional few seconds gave him time to spread his arms and point his hooks. He smashed hard against the worm's back and began to slide down the pebbly surface, bouncing from one ring segment to the next, whipping his long, flexi-ble hooks as he struggled for purchase. Finally, the sharp end of a hook snagged in a gap, and he anchored himself there, hanging on by one hand. He swung his other arm up and set the second hook between the rings.

Not pausing, he roped himself in place and then planted the spreader, ratcheting it open to expose raw, tender flesh. Normally in such a pro-cess, other Fremen would help him plant additional spreaders and set more hooks, but Stilgar had to do this alone.

Above, the 'thopter hovered out of reach.

Leaving the spreader where it was, Stilgar climbed up to the next ring. Fortunately he had landed near the worm's head, so he didn't have far to go. Meanwhile, the creature continued its rampage, and only the rope prevented Stilgar from falling to his death.

When he was in place on top of the head, he cranked the next spreader open wider and took up his goad. He jabbed the worm, yelled in an attempt to turn it. "Haiiiii-yoh!" He had no reason to believe this beast had ever been ridden before, had ever heard a steersman's call. The sandworm fought back like a nightmare bull, intent on *him* rather than on the cacophony of tempting noises at the outskirts of the city.

The beast balked and thrashed, but Stilgar persisted, inflicting pain until at last it turned its bulk and began to retreat. The cracked Shield Wall towered ahead, where only a narrow slot allowed access to the safe desert beyond. He drove the creature to greater speed, and it plunged forward along its swath of destruction as if it sensed the arid dunes be-yond. Reddish-brown cliffs towered on either side of him, and Stilgar held on. If the worm thrashed at the wrong instant, the rider would be thrown off or smashed against the rock.

The creature shot through the broken qanat barrier, flinching as it squirmed over the line of moist sand. Looking down, Stilgar saw that the qanat had been smashed, and the water it contained had seeped out into the desert. From this height, he could not tell if this particular worm, or something else, had initially destroyed the canal barriers.

Exhausted after the destruction it had caused, the worm plunged toward the arid basin. Stilgar prepared for a dangerous dismount. Thank Shai-Hulud, he had done it many times before—and down he slid, skillfully landing on his feet on the sand before tucking his knees, and rolling.

After the worm had charged off into the distance, fleeing the inhabited zone, Stilgar got to his feet again and brushed sand from his stillsuit. Trudging back toward the city, he realized that his ordeal had been exhilarating in another way: Of all the teeming millions in Arrakeen, only a handful knew how to ride a wild worm.

After too long, Stilgar again experienced the thrill of being a true Fremen.

*We are taught that patience is a virtue, but I have come to realize
that it is also a weakness. More often than not, a thing must be
done now.*

—BRONSO OF IX

The small ship arrived on Wallach IX carrying workers, visitors,
and four Sisters wearing traditional black robes and uniforms,
designating low to mid rank. These four had no particular importance;
their travel documents were in order, and they attracted no attention.
But they were not what they appeared to be.

Also among the passengers, segregated from the Sisters, were three
men who had been assigned to the Mother School as temporary gardeners. Bene Gesserit acolytes usually tended the courtyards and gardens, but outsiders were brought in for specialized activities.

After exiting, the four Sisters casually wandered among the crowd
at the spaceport near the school complex. The trio of quiet gardeners
waited their turn, leaving the ship last, moving to the cargo-claim area
where they picked up their tools. Giving no sign that they recognized
each other, they joined up with the four women.

Bronso had waited a great many years for this, and now he would
wait no longer. The pieces had finally fallen into place.

Shortly after the death of his father, Bronso had petitioned for the
return of his comatose mother from the Sisterhood's medical advisers,
and was flatly turned down. Later, when Tessia Vernius emerged from
her years of unconsciousness and managed to smuggle a message to him,

he had learned the truth. As Earl Vernius of Ix, Bronso again asked for her release . . . and was ignored. He then filed a complaint with the Landsraad, but the nobles would take no direct action to free Tessia, claiming that she was a grown woman and a Sister of the order herself. Bronso hadn't had the wealth, influence, or military might to take any action. When Jessica gave him her report seven years ago, she had told him little that he hadn't already known.

All the while he had never stopped thinking of his trapped mother, never stopped searching for a way to get her out of the clutches of the Bene Gesserit.

Now, after being on the run for years, he had managed to slip a few Face Dancer infiltrators onto Wallach IX, if only briefly, and his spies had discovered the information he needed to know, where his mother was, and the security arrangements surrounding her.

All that remained was to implement a plan. The four Sisters and the other two men with him were Face Dancers. *His* Face Dancers.

As the visitors walked to the garden area near the outbuilding where Bronso knew Tessia was being held, one of the "Sisters" signaled the three gardeners. "Bring your tools and prepare for a hard day's work. You have only a little time to complete your job."

Bronso and the other two men followed meekly, behaving exactly the way the Bene Gesserits expected them to.

The Mother School gardens were a parade of spectacular colors, with geometrically laid out shrubberies at odds with wild and unruly botanical displays. Mother Superior Harishka, so it was said, had a penchant for exotic flora harvested from other planets. Such unique plants required a great deal of maintenance and specialized care, which could be provided only by offworld experts.

Bronso and his incognito crew had come ostensibly to replant a failed botanical area where the rugged native plants from Grand Hain had all died and needed to be replaced with something else. Dump boxes had been dropped from orbit ahead of time, filled with carefully harvested mosses, mulch, and chemically precise fertilizers for a new species line. Another armored dump box, ready to be resealed for retrieval, waited outside the dead area, filled with the leftover and obsolete Grand Hain fertilizers and mulch, which would be shipped away.

The men worked for hours under the supervision of their companion

Sisters, who acted appropriately aloof around mere laborers. Not once did the Face Dancers let their disguises slip; they were all true professionals, true performers—and perfectly content to carry out a tense and complicated assignment that did not require assassination. Bronso and the two workers moved in perfect harmony—excavating dead plants, digging trenches, turning over the soil and adding the chemical fertilizers as if it were merely another dance for them, even if no one watched their show.

During those agonizing hours, Bronso cast surreptitious glances toward the outbuildings, saw whirlwinds whipping up, great gusting breezes that rattled the tall skeletal trees, winds strong enough to scatter pebbles. A cluster of transient tornadoes circled one particular building, eerie dust devils and pale, swirling winds that appeared and disappeared. His Face Dancer spies had reported strange weather disturbances in the vicinity of Tessia's conservatory, but they could provide no explanation.

A few capricious winds were not going to bother him. He had waited years for this; finally, the time was nearing.

As the day progressed, the work brought them closer to Tessia's building, where Medical Sisters prodded her, tested her, tried to understand how she had independently recovered from the guilt-casting. The Face Dancer "Sisters" spread out and busied themselves with supposedly important activities. Nobody had paid attention to their group all day. Bronso had seen to it that the proper papers were filed in the proper places.

The teams moved the large dump box that contained obsolete mulch material. In the gloaming, at the daylight's most uncertain point, two male workers opened the dump box and removed some of the mulch to create a makeshift nest. From their supply canisters, they swiftly removed thermal insulation, a breather pack, airtight clothes, sealants.

Bronso's heart pounded; he could feel cold sweat beading on his forehead and dripping down his back as he approached the conservatory building, supposedly to inspect the shrubberies. The strong, random winds gusted again, and shingles on the building fluttered and rattled. A spray of dust and minor debris hissed against the outside walls.

Then the door opened and Tessia stood there in front of him. She looked older; her face was gaunt but her eyes were bright, her lips drawn back in a smile. "I got your message in the family code, Bronso. Very clever. I'm ready to go."

He had so much to say to her—but that would come in time, if they succeeded in escaping. There were lost years to recapture in words and memories—too many experiences to describe in fragments. They would start anew. "There is danger getting you out of here, Mother. Are you sure?"

"If I escape or if I die, either way I won't spend another moment under their control. Humans can endure many things, Bronso—as you know by now—but I am through enduring their abuses."

The blurred funnel of one of the transparent tornadoes appeared behind her, and a second gained strength, but Tessia seemed unconcerned. The whirlwinds circled and dissipated as she hurried over to the waiting dump box. The Face Dancers clustered close to shield her from view.

"It will be uncomfortable, Mother, but it's the only way."

"I'm no stranger to discomfort." Tessia applied the breather to her face, wrapped herself in the thermal shielding, and climbed into the mulch. The Face Dancer workers connected the life-support systems and gave Tessia instructions.

Her voice was muffled through the face mask, but her eyes never left Bronso's. "I will put myself into a trance and wait as long as is necessary."

As the conspirators worked, the tornadoes appeared and reappeared, seeming to gain strength until the group began to attract the attention of other Bene Gesserits, but the Face Dancer women moved in to intercept them.

As soon as the dump box was sealed and Tessia secured, the tornadoes vanished. The air fell still.

They moved the dump box and all their materials and equipment with as much furtive haste as possible. Bronso's heart did not stop racing until they were safely away from Wallach IX.

No man can be asked to do more than his best, even if he falls short.

—DUKE PAULUS ATREIDES

Now that Jessica had revealed the truth, Gurney understood why Bronso must not be captured. Duncan, though, unaware of any subterfuge, continued to throw himself into the task with all his energy.

While the ghola gathered details, Gurney labored to deflect the search subtly, trying not to get too close to the target. Thankfully, Bronso and his mysterious allies were masters of deception, planting false leads to establish dead-end trails that Gurney methodically followed, knowing they would lead nowhere. He didn't like to deceive his friend, but his greater loyalty lay with Lady Jessica, and to House Atreides. He understood what Paul wanted, and why—while Duncan did not.

However, the ghola was not only a Swordmaster, but also a Mentat, and not easily fooled. Gurney's many intentional failures were beginning to make him seem gullible or inept; before long Duncan would undoubtedly stop taking his advice or, worse, grow overtly suspicious.

Gurney paced their headquarters chamber in the Arrakeen citadel. "Face Dancers are Tleilaxu creations, so Bronso must have some sort of business arrangement with the Bene Tleilax. Maybe we should go to Thalim and interrogate some Tleilaxu Masters."

Duncan shook his head. "The Bene Tleilax hate House Vernius for ousting them from Ix, and the feeling is reciprocated. That is bound to be another dead end."

Since the ghola also had his own unsettling connections with the Tleilaxu, Gurney wondered if he could be reluctant to return to their worlds. "At least it's a new approach. At this point, I'm willing to try anything."

"I have another approach," Duncan said. "We can search among the Wayku aboard Guild Heighliners. We know the one named Ennzyn has a previous connection with Bronso Vernius. Find that one, and we might get some answers."

Gurney concealed his alarm as best he could. "It's been, what— nineteen years since the boys ran away? How do we even know Ennzyn is still working for the Guild?"

"Because the Wayku are forbidden to disembark on any planetary surface. He cannot have gone anywhere. And we know the Wayku are involved with Bronso because you and Lady Jessica observed them distributing the seditious literature during your passage to Arrakis."

"Ah, so we did." At the time, though, Gurney had not been aware of what he knew now.

BOARDING THE NEXT Guildship that arrived at Arrakis, Duncan and Gurney marched to the restricted decks bearing authorization documents signed by the Regent Alia herself. The cowed Guild security officials led them to a suite of windowless office cabins where sallow-skinned administrators sat at a row of desks. Though the administrators showed no enthusiasm for the task, the Guild knew the source of their spice and knew not to interfere.

One administrator gave a brief bow, not rising from behind his desk. "We will provide complete access to our personnel data, but we have very little information about individual Wayku employees. They have lived aboard Guildships for many, many centuries. They are . . . company assets, like equipment."

Gurney scowled. "Gods below, man! Even your equipment has serial numbers."

The Guildsman pondered for a moment, then left the chamber. He returned a short time later with printed records, shigawire reels, and crystal-etched documents. "Perhaps the information you seek is here."

To Gurney the task seemed hopeless—and thankfully so—but Duncan dove into the records with dogged determination, dropping into Mentat focus to scan the considerable amount of data.

An hour went by, then two, then three, while Gurney waited patiently. Finally, Duncan rose behind the pile of documents on the table. His ghola face held a satisfied smile, though his metal eyes were unreadable. "I've found him, Gurney. I know which ship carries Ennzyn. We will command the Navigator to divert this vessel so that we may intercept it."

Gurney's heart was heavy, but he pretended to be pleased.

INSIDE A CHAMBER hidden in the deep desert, Bronso Vernius examined the tiny silver capsule that he had just removed from the back of his mother's neck. Hours before, at the Carthag Spaceport, he had discovered it with a scanner and had disabled it electronically.

An Ixian locator beacon. The very fact of its existence angered him. "Part of their testing, Mother. While you were comatose, maybe even when you were pregnant with your unwanted babies, the witches implanted a tracker."

Tessia pressed a healing pad over the wound on her neck. "I always wondered why that spot itched." She gave him a gentle smile. "You sound surprised. Do not underestimate the Bene Gesserit. Many of their monitoring devices were merely to study me. I was their experimental animal."

"And their brood mare."

"No matter how many other offspring they forced me to bear, you are my only true son, Bronso." She patted his arm. "And you have freed me. I'm safe now, with you."

He frowned. "You are never truly safe with me, Mother. There's been a price on my head for years. But we're here on Dune now, so there's a chance. We have important allies." Bronso placed the capsule on the hard plazcrete floor, and smashed it with the heel of his boot.

THE HEIGHLINER CARRYING Ennzyn was forcibly delayed in orbit above Balut, its next stop, and the Guild offered no explanations to the numerous passengers aboard. As soon as the second Guildship arrived, Duncan and Gurney shuttled across, aided by Guild security.

Following his companion, Gurney's mind spun. After so many years, he couldn't believe that Ennzyn truly had any continuing contact with Bronso, yet the Ixian obviously had supporters amongst the Wayku. What better place to start than with Ennzyn? It made perfect sense, and he saw no way he could divert Duncan's attention.

As soon as the two men came aboard, the Heighliner's security launched a thorough search of the lower crew decks. Duncan and Gurney hurried without additional escort directly to Ennzyn's private cabin.

Gurney tried to convince his companion to show restraint. "Bear in mind, Duncan, that this man showed us how to find Paul and Bronso when they were with the Jongleur troupe. He helped us save them."

Duncan paused. "I remember that full well. Is that another test of my memories?"

"No, a reminder of our obligations."

"If he is involved with spreading sedition against the Imperium, then we have no obligations to this man." Using an electronic master lock tool, Duncan unsealed the cabin door and forced it open.

Gurney hoped the Wayku steward wasn't there, but this hope faded quickly. As soon as the corridor light flooded the chamber, the Wayku man lurched to his feet, where he stood surrounded by piles of instroy paper documents, stacks of reproduced manifestoes.

Sighting his quarry, Duncan lurched inside with a speed that Gurney had seen him use only in battle. As the Wayku reached for a small device under the metal table, trying to activate a switch—an incendiary?—Duncan pushed Ennzyn aside, and Gurney caught him, holding his arms behind his back.

The steward seemed unruffled by the unexpected vehemence of their reaction. His dark glasses and headphone had been knocked askew and fell to the cluttered deck; data streams poured onto the backs of the lenses, and faint voices emanated from his headphones. As soon as the units fell off, wisps of smoke emerged from the electronics.

With an attitude of forced calm, Ennzyn studied the two men, recognized them. "Why, it is Duncan Idaho and Gurney Halleck from House Atreides. Do you need my help once more?"

"We need to find Bronso again," Gurney said. "You helped us track him down before."

"Oh, but the circumstances are entirely different now. That other time, it was in the young man's best interests to have him return home to his father. This time, I don't trust that you two gentlemen are quite so altruistic. It would be no kindness to Bronso if I were to help you find him."

Duncan showed no sympathy or patience. "We are under orders from Regent Alia to find him." He gestured to the incriminating documents. "You are obviously in communication with Bronso of Ix."

Ennzyn didn't seem the least bit afraid. "I receive information only via complicated channels, and I am not in contact with him at this time. I believe he is involved in another important mission unrelated to his literary and historical endeavors." He smiled faintly. "Bronso knows how to hide, and the Wayku know how to keep secrets."

"That is unfortunate for you. Gurney, we will take him back to Arrakeen to stand before Alia."

Oddly enough, this caused Ennzyn great distress. "Wayku are not allowed to set foot on any planet. It is forbidden."

"Then I am dubious about your chances for survival." Duncan turned to his companion. "Did you find anything unusual among these?"

Gurney stopped his casual sifting through the stacked documents. "No. Just multiple copies of the same thing." He looked heavily at the Wayku captive, knowing what would happen to Ennzyn as soon as he was brought before Alia's interrogators. "Duncan, this man was Paul's friend, as well. Ennzyn came to us, revealed the boys' location, and by doing so he probably saved Paul's life. Duke Leto would have considered that a debt."

"Duke Leto is dead."

"But is honor dead, as well?"

The ghola looked troubled by the conundrum. "What do you propose we do with this man? He has obviously committed crimes."

With a loud clamor, five Guild security men rushed down the corridor and met them at the open doorway to Ennzyn's cabin. "We found other stockpiles of documents, sirs. We don't yet know which of the Wayku are involved."

"Ennzyn is involved," Duncan said.

Gurney looked at the captive, tried to understand what had driven this man—and so many of his vagabond people—to assist an outlaw like Bronso. Seeing no easy way out of the problem, but certain of what Alia would do to Ennzyn, he said, "Let these Guildsmen take care of the matter. The Wayku are their responsibility."

The lead guard snapped to attention. "We will bring this man and his allies before the highest levels of Guild administration. We will prove our loyalty to Regent Alia."

Duncan hesitated a long moment, choosing among orders, obligations, and humanity. Ennzyn looked at him as though he didn't care one way or the other, but Gurney could detect a gray pallor and a faint sheen of perspiration on his skin.

"Very well, but on one further condition. Dispatch a message throughout the Guild. All Wayku are to be questioned, all their decks to be searched, all copies of Bronso's documents to be confiscated. We will eliminate this distribution method for the traitor, here and now." Duncan appeared satisfied. "We have shut down Bronso's ability to spread his lies. That is a sufficient triumph."

Gurney's shoulders sagged, and he wondered if his suggestion had caused even greater damage. Now Bronso would be painted into a corner, and more desperate. Even so, he wasn't likely to give up.

In the court of public opinion, suspicion alone is often enough to convey guilt. Mentats do not think that way. We ask questions.

—*The Mentat's Handbook*

B ecause so many people in the demolished shantytown of Arrakeen were unofficial immigrants—without citizenship papers, jobs, or families—the total number killed in the sandworm attack was impossible to determine.

Workers, former soldiers, pilgrims, and beggars threw themselves into the recovery effort, working tirelessly because Alia called upon them to, in Muad'Dib's name. For his own part, Stilgar thought the Regent's request had an impatient edge. Though it was an unkind thought, he believed she summoned so many workers not because she wanted to help suffering people, but because she wanted to clean up the mess as quickly as possible.

Meanwhile, the Qizarate issued a joyful pronouncement that all those devoured by the rogue worm had been transported immediately to Heaven and incorporated into Shai-Hulud. Stilgar was not surprised to hear it.

Despite the destruction, he was glad for the fact that even greater mayhem had not been done. The wild worm might well have torn a path all the way to the Citadel of Muad'Dib, but Stilgar had diverted it in time. Sooner or later, Alia would probably present him with a medal for what he had done, but he had no time for trinkets or celebrations.

Instead, he was determined to find out who had caused the disaster. He had spent his life understanding the desert and the magnificent worms. He knew in his heart that it was no accident.

Stilgar gathered a handpicked team of sandwalkers and wormriders, desert men who could interpret the whispered secrets of the dunes, to read signs even though the winds tried to erase them. His grim assemblage went to the gap in the Shield Wall and combed over the scene.

Stilgar stood by the wrecked qanat, briefly removing his noseplugs so he could absorb the atmosphere around him, staring and sensing as he tried to pick up hints of what had occurred here. He stationed eight spotters out in the open desert to watch for other worms. He turned, looked around, felt the sting of grains against his exposed cheeks with the skirling gusts near the Shield Wall. *Cueshma*, he thought, the Fremen name for a twenty-klick wind, strong enough to stir the desert but not enough to be considered a storm.

Other than the wind, though, the desert was silent and secretive. He couldn't understand what had drawn the beast here in the first place, why it had crossed the moisture line and attacked Arrakeen with such a single-minded purpose. What could have driven it to such erratic, unnatural behavior?

His men dug through the sand, pulling out chunks of the plazcrete canal wall. The worm had destroyed much of the evidence, but that did not stop the Fremen from searching. Several men poled the sand in widely separated locations, pushing probes down far enough to measure any detectable moisture.

Finally the lead man reported, "It's dry, Stil."

"If that qanat was full when the worm smashed it, there would still be water down deep. The bulk of the flow was diverted beforehand, the water drained. Sandtrout would have gotten the rest," Stilgar said. *No accident. Someone wanted the worm to have access into the basin.*

Turning around, he passed his gaze along the impressive mountainous barrier that blocked all encroaching worms. During the Battle of Arrakeen years ago, the Padishah Emperor had stationed his forces inside the basin, assuming the area safe, not expecting Muad'Dib to use atomics to blast through the cliff, which enabled his Fedaykin to ride worms into the battle. It had been the turning point in modern history.

But those creatures had been *deliberately* guided through the gap by seasoned wormriders. How had a lone worm threaded the needle and entered the sheltered area? Even if the barrier qanat had dried, how had the sightless creature *found* such a relatively small opening?

Stilgar was not surprised when his men discovered the remains of a thumper. This suggested that several more might have been strung along like bread crumbs to lead the creature onward. The inexorable throbbing beat would have drawn the blind worm like a magnet, luring it through the passage.

"Treachery," one of the Fedaykin murmured. "Shai-Hulud was summoned intentionally."

Stilgar had suspected as much. But by whom?

One of the men held up a lump of twisted metal. "See this thumper's unusual design. Looks like Ixian technology to me. Bronso of Ix!"

The Naib scowled. "A thumper is no proof of that." With their clockwork mechanisms and syncopated tampers, the devices were quite simple. "No Ixian expertise is required to make one."

Under the bright sun and the briskly blowing grains, Stilgar's searchers kept sifting through the sands. Toward dusk they uncovered the fused circuitry of a shield generator, and another one farther along. Again some of the discoveries suggested Ixian technology, perhaps evidence against Bronso . . . though shield generators could be purchased anywhere.

Shields would drive a worm into a frenzy. Always. After thumpers attracted it to the remains of the qanat, the hidden shield generators would goad the creature into the Arrakeen basin. Someone had meant to create havoc here.

He knew why the men were so quick to conclude that Bronso was to blame. Alia had already announced her suspicions, and the Ixian's guilt would be proven to *her* satisfaction, one way or another.

I see darkness everywhere, but also the tiniest pinpoint of light marking the hopes of mankind.

—*Conversations with Muad'Dib* by the PRINCESS IRULAN

Inside the Citadel's vaulted exhibition arena, Lady Jessica sat on a hard stonewood bench between Alia and Irulan, watching a private performance of barefoot Jervish Updancers. They moved in a lissome blur, dressed in the blue and gold costumes of their remote planet.

On the other side of Irulan, Harah dutifully kept an eye on the twin babies, who were propped up in traditional Fremen baskets. Though only three months old, little Leto and Ghanima watched the dancers with obvious delight. Irulan also watched over Paul's children, still in the process of redefining her own role. Duncan and Gurney were both offworld, chasing a lead in the endless hunt for Bronso of Ix. . . .

For the past several days, Jessica had watched Irulan wrestle with her conflicting obligations to balance the difficult thing that Paul wanted with the equally impossible task that Alia demanded.

Following the sandworm attack, Alia had sponsored the day's private show in the Citadel to prove that all was right with the Imperium. "The people are done with mourning, and it is time to find things to celebrate. The Regency is strong, Muad'Dib is remembered, and all worlds will prosper."

The performance floor was made of rough paver bricks, like broken rubble, but the Updancers handled themselves with no missteps in a remarkable series of airborne flips and inverted moves, using their hands and feet interchangeably.

"Once when I was a girl, a similar troupe came to perform at my father's Palace," Irulan said, brushing a bit of grit off the lap of her elegant white dress. "My father placed hot coals across the dancing arena."

Jessica found it difficult to concentrate on the dance. A fly buzzed near her, and she swatted it away; somehow it had gotten inside the huge conservatory arena.

Paul had pondered deeply about his dangerous legacy, about the risks of letting himself be deified . . . but what had it done to the Atreides name and to those in the family he had left behind? His sister Alia was not ready to be thrust into the middle of such a windstorm of history, though she was struggling mightily to prove to all of her followers, and to herself, that she could be the equal of her brother.

And, Jessica knew, there were the twin babies—her grandchildren— to consider. In attempting to destroy the false holy aura that surrounded Paul's actions, what if Bronso was creating even more danger for the twins? She hadn't considered that before.

Ignoring the Updancers, Jessica watched how Irulan behaved next to the children. Jessica wondered how much Irulan could possibly have learned about being a mother from all her Bene Gesserit training and her experiences growing up in the Imperial court on Kaitain. Still, she definitely seemed devoted to the babies now.

The twins and their potential raised so many questions in Jessica's mind. If Paul was the Kwisatz Haderach, what powers might he have passed on to his children? How soon would anyone know if the two babies had access to Other Memory—and if so, would it become a challenge for them, as it was for Alia? Already, Leto and Ghanima demonstrated advanced behavior, oddities of personality. They were the orphaned children of a messianic Emperor who had been surrounded by fanatics: Of course these two would not be normal children.

During a lull in the performance, Jessica leaned closer to Alia and finally raised the point that had weighed on her for some time. "As your mother, I remember how difficult it was for you to be different at a young age, an unusual child treated as an outsider, an . . . abomination."

Alia responded sharply. "My differences made me strong, and I had my older brother's help."

"Mine, as well. And now I am concerned for my grandchildren. They need special study, special training."

"Leto and Ghanima will have my care and assistance. As the children of Muad'Dib, they will grow up to be strong." She gazed wistfully at the babies in their baskets. "I'll make sure of it. Don't worry about them, Mother."

Walking on their hands, the Updancers circled in front of the small audience, kicking their bare feet and calling out boisterously in their own language. The distracting fly came back to buzz around Jessica's head again.

"Of course I worry about them. The court of Muad'Dib is not the safest place in the Imperium. They would be perfectly protected with me on Caladan. I could raise the twins in the ancestral home of House Atreides, away from conspiracies and schemes here. You know how many threats you have already faced. Let them come back with me."

Alia reacted with surprising vehemence. "No, they will stay here! As Muad'Dib's children, they must be raised on Dune, and be part of Dune."

Jessica maintained a hard calmness. "I am their grandmother, and I have more time to spend on their welfare than you do. You're the Regent of the Imperium. Caladan is a place where Leto and Ghanima can study careful meditation, learn to control any voices that might be inside of them."

"The Atreides homeworld would only make them soft, water fat, and complacent. How many times did Paul speak of that? Paradise and ease make men lose their edge." She half rose out of her seat. "No, the twins are children of this planet, and they belong in the desert. I will not allow them to leave."

Irulan interceded. "I have already sworn to watch over his children and care for them as if they were my own." The Princess looked from Alia to Jessica and back again, torn between the choices. "But the Lady Jessica also has a point, Alia. Perhaps Leto and Ghanima could live alternately on Caladan and on Dune? It would give the children balance and a sense of their own history."

"They are also Atreides—" Jessica said.

"No!" Alia seemed on the verge of violence, and Irulan flinched despite her best efforts at control. "No one can understand those children better than I do. I will be the first to note the danger signs of possession. I will hear no more of this—from either of you."

Irulan fell immediately silent. Jessica realized that, even after she returned to Caladan, the Princess would remain here, at the mercy of Alia's whims, forced to keep herself useful and prove her loyalty to the Regency.

Barely noticed by their auspicious audience, the Updancers finished their performance and stood in a line on their hands. One by one, they flipped right-side up, bowed, and scampered out of the building.

With the show over, and the discussion about the children still stinging in her mind, Jessica rose from the stonewood bench. "Please pass along my personal appreciation for the fine show. I will retire to my chambers to meditate." She walked away swiftly.

As Jessica reached a sunlit stone garden, the persistent fly buzzed near her again, swirling around her face and darting close to her ear. Jessica wondered which sloppy door seals in the enclosed citadel had allowed the annoying desert insect inside. She tried to swat at it, but the fly maneuvered itself close to her face.

She was shocked to hear it emit a tiny voice. "Lady Jessica, this is Bronso Vernius. I have placed my recording in this disguised device. I need your help—for my mother's sake. Please meet me in secret. Listen carefully." The Ixian insect device recited a location, and a time two days hence.

Knowing that she might be observed, even here, Jessica continued to walk away. She showed no surprise at the clever way that Bronso had found to contact her. Putting a hand over her mouth as if to cover a cough, she said, "I understand, and I'll be there."

The fly darted off.

The new soldiers were already dead to start with, but not so mangled that they couldn't be repaired. They would fight again. And Shaddam recognized that ghola soldiers had certain special advantages.

Under the blistering orange sky of Salusa Secundus, far from any of the terraforming activities, Count Hasimir Fenring and Bashar Zum Garon accompanied the former Emperor out to an isolated dry canyon. The next corpse ship would arrive soon.

Muad'Dib's inspectors constantly monitored cargo transports to and from Salusa, but the Tleilaxu handlers of the dead moved freely. In the normal course of events, so many struggling exiles died that a ship to carry off bodies was no particular oddity; no one, however, would suspect that the arriving Tleilaxu vessel was already full—with bodies that had been reanimated by axlotl tanks.

Years earlier, Shaddam had concocted the scheme, and it both pleased and startled Count Fenring that his friend had actually come up with a good idea. The fallen Emperor's loyal Sardaukar commander, Zum Garon, had negotiated secret terms with the Tleilaxu, and Shaddam had paid for many shiploads of gholas . . . soldiers that were already counted as dead and not marked on any rolls. Legion after legion of

completely untraceable fighters to be trained as fierce Sardaukar warriors.

For years now, in exchange for a ridiculous portion of the remaining
Corrino fortune, the Tleilaxu had harvested the corpses of dead soldiers
from Jihad battlefields and placed them in axlotl tanks to repair their
wounds. They restored the fighters to a semblance of life, their memories
washed away, their personalities clean slates. Regardless of the various
flags under which these men had originally fought, the laboratory-made
gholas retained no feelings of loyalty or patriotism. But their muscles remembered how to wield a weapon, and they obeyed orders. Fenring himself had watched the test subjects during a series of mock battles near the
Tleilaxu city of Thalidei when dear, sweet Marie was still alive.

Shaddam paced the dirt restlessly. "I am sick of this place, Hasimir,
and I want to leave. How many will be enough? The Tleilaxu charge
an outrageous amount for each shipment of soldiers. My resources are
not boundless!"

"But your ambitions are, Sire, and you must have the army to
match them. There is, aahhh, something to be said for soldiers who do
not fear death."

A flash of indignation crossed Bashar Garon's face. "Sardaukar do not
fear death." The military commander waited next to his Emperor, sweating in his full uniform as the big Tleilaxu ship finally came into view and
lumbered toward the ground.

Fenring gave a deferential bow. "As you say, Bashar. I meant no disrespect." He did the mental arithmetic. "Now that the usurper is dead,
ahh, yes, it is time for us to make our move. The Regent is weak and
frightened—her own actions demonstrate that."

Shaddam scowled. "She killed my envoy Rivato after he suggested
a perfectly reasonable compromise. Don't forget that she killed my
Chamberlain Ridondo, too, back when she was much younger. A devil
of a child."

"Ahh, hmm, and that shows her impulsiveness. What did she have
to gain by slaying Rivato? She must have been afraid of him. And of
you, Sire."

Shaddam kicked a dry clod of dirt as they waited for the Tleilaxu
transport to settle onto the landing area. "We have been building—and
feeding, and caring for—our ghola army for years now. We need to take

advantage of the Imperial power vacuum, and *now*. That girl cannot possibly hold her brother's government together."

"Hmmm, Sire, you yourself saw what that 'girl' was capable of when she murdered Baron Harkonnen before your eyes. And she was just a toddler then! Later, she killed my dear Marie, who was herself a trained assassin. As Regent, now, Alia is even worse." The Count cleared his throat. "Even so, she is incapable of being the leader that Muad'Dib was. She has no finesse, and her tendency to overreact will build resentment among the populace. Fanaticism can go only so far." He grinned at Shaddam. "Ahhh, yes, I am convinced that our ghola army is nearly ready. A few more shipments, a few more training exercises."

Bashar Garon had already spent years with the ghola soldiers, testing them with brutally efficient Sardaukar methods, fighting techniques that had made the Imperial terror troops unstoppable for centuries. Both Fenring and Shaddam had seen these huge new legions perform military maneuvers with cold precision that brought a thrill of awe and a shudder of intimidation. The Emperor longed for the restoration of his former glory, and Garon wanted the same thing—to bring back the proud Sardaukar name from the ash heap of history.

But Shaddam's secret army needed to attack at a precise time and place, a carefully calculated strike that would send shockwaves throughout the fragile structure of Muad'Dib's Imperium. Regent Alia could never withstand it.

Though the Jihad had officially been over for years, battles still raged on scattered planets, while new signs of strain appeared on the dominated worlds. The writings of Bronso of Ix continued to prod sore spots, raising doubts and emboldening many people to question the supposed "Messiah." Fenring could not have planned it better himself. As Regent, Alia Atreides must already be feeling her brother's power slip through her fingertips, after only a few months.

Bashar Garon remained cool. "I am eager to begin an open battle to restore you to the Lion Throne, Majesty. The rogue sandworm in Arrakeen was a good preliminary strike, an opening gambit."

The fallen Emperor frowned. "I had hoped for dozens of rogue worms to make it through the breach in the Shield Wall. Does that mean the plan was a failure, Hasimir?" His voice had a sharp accusatory tone.

"Even one rampaging sandworm caused a great deal of destruction, Sire, leaving Arrakeen in an uproar. Alia's Regency already has enough troubles to deal with, and we just added another significant disruption. Some of the locals are claiming it was Muad'Dib's angry spirit, returning for revenge."

"What superstitious fools they are!" Shaddam laughed, then paused. "Or did we start the rumors ourselves?"

"We did not need to, Sire." Fenring consulted his crystalpad, where an intricately coded message described the event on Arrakis. Two of their spies had been killed in the worm's onslaught, innocent bystanders in the Arrakeen slums, but one surviving operative had sent a detailed eyewitness account. "As the locals scramble to repair the damage, they're frightened, and some see it as a sign of God's displeasure in Alia's rule. *That* rumor is one of ours. . . ."

The rugged red-walled canyon opened into a sheltered valley, far from prison settlements or Shaddam's domed city. On schedule, the Tleilaxu corpse ship settled onto the hard-packed ground, stirring a haze of rusty grit with a roar of suspensor engines.

Garon said, "I do not like these ghola troops, but I recognize the need for them, since my efforts to recruit fighters from the prison population here have met with less success than I had hoped."

Count Fenring knew the secret antipathy Garon held toward the failed Emperor; he blamed Shaddam for the many disasters that had shamed the Sardaukar ranks and cost the life of his own son. "The single legion of Sardaukar loyalists that Muad'Dib let you keep has never, ahh, been adequate for our purposes."

"Why is it so hard to train the prisoners?" Shaddam snapped. "When I was on the throne, Salusa provided a ready pool of Sardaukar trainees, who were already hardened by survival experiences here."

Garon bit back an annoyed retort, and said with forced calm, "In those days the prison population was much greater. Kaitain sent shipload after shipload of dissidents here, political prisoners, outright traitors, and violent criminals. Only a small percentage survived, and an even smaller percentage of those became Sardaukar recruits. When the Atreides Emperor stopped sending his prisoners here, our pool dwindled considerably. And his years of terraforming work—which you wanted—have made the Salusan landscape less of a challenge to harden our available men."

When Paul-Muad'Dib gave his promise to turn this hell into a planetary garden, supposedly as a concession to the defeated Shaddam, Count Fenring had detected subtleties in his reasons: In such a difficult environment, where daily life was a brutal challenge, only the strongest, most resourceful, and most hardened prisoners survived, and thus they became perfect Sardaukar candidates. By softening the populace and dulling the edge of Salusa Secundus, Muad'Dib had hamstrung Shaddam's ability to find adequate replacements for his terror troops.

For his own plan, however, Shaddam Corrino had looked elsewhere.

When the corpse ship's hatches opened and a series of parallel ramps extended to the ground, more than six thousand new ghola soldiers marched out. Their uniforms were mismatched—the better to blend in among the planet's ragtag population. Many of them showed scars from mortal wounds. They had already been indoctrinated by the Tleilaxu, their loyalty programmed to the Padishah Emperor. Their old reflexes, muscles, and automatic responses had been reawakened.

As the last ghola soldiers emerged from the vessel, a gray-robed little Tleilaxu man scuttled toward them, crystalpad projector in hand. The Count knew the man would demand his payment now.

Shaddam looked at the new arrivals, satisfied but somewhat bored. "For the sake of humanity, and the sake of history, Hasimir—we have to get rid of these damnable Atreides monsters, and those bastard twins, too. It would be best if someone just drowned the two babies and had done with them."

Fenring smiled. "It would be truer Fremen fashion, Sire, if they could be buried alive out in the sands."

We write our own definitions of gratitude.

—Bene Gesserit axiom

Upon careful consideration, Alia decided to grant an audience to the visitor from the Bene Gesserit. It was a lone Reverend Mother, someone who obviously considered herself important and was willing to take the risk of coming here despite Alia's obvious and dangerous antipathy toward the Sisterhood.

After Alia had ordered the execution of Reverend Mother Mohiam, the Bene Gesserits had been wise to avoid her. The young Imperial Regent had long since made up her mind that she would never forgive them for conspiring against her brother. Still . . . she found this intriguing.

As the visiting Reverend Mother made her way to the Regent's private offices, Alia considered summoning her mother to join her. Jessica had no great love for the Sisterhood either; they could sit together, a powerful alliance of mother and daughter. Then again, Alia was never sure how her mother would react to particular situations. In the end, she decided she could always tell Jessica after the meeting, when she found out what the Sisterhood wanted.

A Reverend Mother named Udine entered the room with a formal bow and a proper show of respect. Genuine humility from a Bene Gesserit was an unorthodox occurrence.

Alia remained seated in her chair, hands folded in front of her on the desk. She wasted neither time nor breath on pleasantries, nor did Udine mince words. "The Sisterhood dispatched me here, Regent Alia, regarding the matter of Bronso of Ix."

Alia arched her eyebrows. "Proceed."

"We have unexpectedly come upon certain information that may help you in your efforts to capture him. We have recent knowledge of Bronso's movements, and strong evidence where he may be, even now."

"Where?" Alia had one hand ready to call for her amazon guards and dispatch a hunting team immediately, but she was also wary of tricks.

"We believe that he is here, on Arrakis."

Alia jerked with surprise. "Why would he come here again? That's a foolish risk to take."

"Perhaps he has business here."

"How do you know this?" *And why should I believe you?* she thought.

"For years, Bronso's mother was held in protective custody on Wallach IX. Tessia Vernius is a valuable specimen."

Alia frowned. "I remember something about her mental breakdown—it occurred before my birth."

"We no longer have her." Udine remained erect, still keeping her eyes slightly averted. "Bronso rescued her."

Alia laughed sharply. "*Bronso* freed a captive from the Bene Gesserit Mother School?"

Udine was not amused. "He is quite clever, and elusive, as you well know. We do not yet know his allies, nor how he spirited her away. However, you can find Bronso through Tessia—and we believe *she* is on Arrakis."

"Why do you say that? What is your evidence?"

"While Tessia was in her coma, we implanted certain diagnostics within her. One of them was a device that can be used as a locator." Udine handed over a small data plaque. "The tracker coordinates indicated Arrakis, and we have every reason to believe that Bronso is with her."

Alia could barely contain her excitement. This was the best lead she'd had in some time. "Excellent news, Reverend Mother. All Imperial subjects have been asked to assist in the hunt for Bronso of Ix. The

Regency appreciates that you have volunteered this valuable information, but I warn you, there had better not be tricks here."

Udine folded her arms across her chest. "No tricks on our part, my Lady, but the news is not all good. We tracked Sister Tessia to Arrakis, but lost the trail here . . . perhaps from one of your sandstorms. We no longer have a signal." She shook her head. "It is most frustrating, but we thought you would like to know what we learned. Though the information is not perfect, we hope that your gratitude will reflect upon the standing of the Sisterhood. We long to return to some positions of influence."

Annoyed, Alia set aside the data plaque showing the last known co-ordinates. "The information you brought me is next to worthless. Tell Harishka not to expect anything from me."

"But you promised a reward. Your announcements, your condemnations of Bronso of Ix have all made it plain that—"

"I made it plain that anyone who reported valuable information would receive the blessings of Muad'Dib." Alia raised both hands in a benedictory, but dismissive, gesture. "There, you have half a blessing. Let that be enough for you. The Bene Gesserit have done nothing but try to destroy me and my brother."

Udine looked sickened rather than outraged. "We have not made any moves against you or your Regency, Lady Alia."

The Regent rose to her feet, walked around her desk to stand by the taller Reverend Mother. "Oh? Have you forgotten how Lady Margot Fenring—*Reverend Mother* Fenring—trained and unleashed her daughter Marie upon me and Paul, hoping to assassinate us? That girl pretended to be my friend, but I killed her anyway. Shall I list more offenses?"

Udine was taken aback. "Lady Fenring acted without our knowledge! That was not a Bene Gesserit plan."

"Lady Fenring is a Bene Gesserit, therefore it was a Bene Gesserit plan. I am not interested in excuses. Now, scurry back to your Mother School, content in the knowledge that you have assisted us." When Udine continued to argue, Alia whirled the woman around and pushed her toward the doorway. "Enough! Now leave!"

The shocked Reverend Mother started to say something, then reconsidered, and hurriedly departed. The amazon guards escorted her away.

Paul-Muad'Dib did not have a historical monopoly on creating fanatics, but he perfected the art.

—from The Mind of a Killer, a pamphlet
published by Bronso of Ix

Jessica had to take extraordinary precautions when she went out to meet Bronso. Considering the mood in the Regency, she felt this might be the most dangerous thing she had ever done.

It did not prove difficult for her to arrange for transportation from Arrakeen out to Sietch Tabr. She had connections and history there, and no one questioned her request to make a personal pilgrimage, nor her desire for privacy. She had done this several times before, and as the Mother of Muad'Dib, was not to be challenged.

Each day, a certain number of offworld visitors flooded out to the famed sietch, like irritating dust blown on the wind, and transport 'thopters departed every hour, weather permitting. Before entering the crowded passenger cabin of the aircraft, Jessica had smeared her face and ragged clothing with dust and slouched her posture, so that when she stepped off, surrounded by the swirl of others, she was just another pilgrim in a press of bodies wanting to see where Muad'Dib had made his first Fremen home, where Chani had given birth to the royal twins, and where the blinded, broken man had vanished into the desert.

At the sietch, slipping away from the other pilgrims to gather the necessary items, Jessica altered her appearance to that of an ordinary village woman in a stillsuit and gray robe. When she departed an hour later, wearing yet another identity as a government inspector of weather stations, she journeyed aboard an industrial transport that flew high above the weather patterns, covering great distances to reach new terraforming stations built in a bustling base near the southern pole. From there, after assuming the identity of a man in loose desert garb, she piloted a small, unmarked ornithopter herself out into the deep Tanzerouft, following the location coordinates that Bronso had secretly provided.

"I need your help—for my mother's sake," Bronso had said.

In her small craft, she circled over a wide expanse of whiteness, a salt flat that hinted of ancient seas on this arid planet. At the eastern perimeter of the flat, in a sheltered area of rocks, she found what she was looking for: the wreck of a spice factory amid veiny orange sands. The wind picked up, making the landing difficult, but she managed it anyway, after which she locked down the struts and stilled the vibration of the articulated wings. Several small dust devils whipped around the wreckage of the spice factory, circling, gaining strength and then fading. Little storms . . . *ghibli*, the Fremen called them.

As she stepped out, a tired-looking man emerged wearing a scuffed old uniform and carrying several weapons. He looked like a smuggler, and wore a face mask, fitted in the Fremen fashion. The man stood silently, waiting for her to come to him. As she approached, Jessica became more certain of his identity, and for a long moment the two just looked at each other, before she moved forward to embrace Bronso. "It has been so many years!"

"With so many events, my Lady. I would never have imagined life might bring me to this." His eyes were sharp, as he twisted the fire jewel ring on his finger. "But I finally have good news. Come, I have to show you."

With a surprising spring in his step, Bronso led her inside the old spice factory and down a plazcrete stairway into an underground redoubt. She heard the wind whistling through the wreck above, the scour of sand like hissing whispers against the hull. "Paul had this place dug as a bolt-hole with barrier walls to keep worms out, and to prevent sounds from escaping," Bronso said.

Jessica had heard that her son had secure locations such as this one on various worlds, places where he and his family could go if necessary—but she hadn't known where any of the safe havens were.

He turned to her with a smile. "It was the perfect place for us to hide."

"Us?"

Bronso led her into an austere metal-walled chamber with mauve chairs arranged around a central metal table that once must have been a mess area for a spice crew. Holo photos shifted on the walls, a succession of desert scenes.

Tessia sat there, prim and motionless.

Jessica drew in a quick breath, and Bronso's mother raised her head to smile. "My son helped me escape from the Bene Gesserit. I knew he would come, eventually. I waited for him—and the Sisters never did understand how I defeated their guilt-casting."

With real joy, Jessica moved forward to embrace her friend. "Tessia, I'm so glad to see you safe!" She looked at Bronso. "How did you manage it?"

"I had help . . . the way I've managed everything so far." He sat down heavily in one of the mauve chairs next to his mother. "But she's not safe with me. You know the dangers I face, and I can't keep doing my work if I have to worry about her. That's why I called you here. Can you take her, find a home for her on Caladan? When I arrived at the Carthag Spaceport, I ran a scan on my mother, and found a Bene Gesserit tracking device implanted in her neck. I disabled it electronically there, and destroyed it later. Even so, the Sisterhood may know that Tessia is on Dune. There could be danger for her. I need your help."

Jessica weighed the risks, the consequences. She had come to loathe the Sisterhood and its unrelenting schemes, the way they sent tentacles everywhere. And Alia hated anyone connected to Bronso. This would not be simple . . . But honor—Atreides honor—allowed her only one answer. "Of course I'll do it. I can arrange for secret passage back to Caladan."

Tessia sounded wistful. "Caladan . . . I'd rather go to my own home."

Bronso's words were clipped. "Caladan is a far better choice. Ix isn't safe anymore, and the Sisterhood might go looking for you there."

"Yes, I liked Caladan. Rhombur and I were happy there. . . ."

Jessica immediately saw practical problems, even though she could not turn down the request. "She can't be seen with me, because Alia will know you and I have been in touch. But I can keep your mother hidden for a few days, then arrange for her to travel to Caladan under an assumed name. The Bene Gesserits must never know where she is, and neither must my daughter."

Tessia smiled at both of them.

A few tears of relief ran down Bronso cheeks, but he wiped them away. "I can't thank you enough. Caladan is the perfect place for her."

"We'll have to be very careful, Bronso. Ultimately, her identity could leak out, and we don't want to bring down the wrath of Alia—or the Bene Gesserits—on Caladan and its people. That is my priority, as Duchess. But for a while Caladan will be safe, under conditions of utmost secrecy, until we can find a long-term home for her. Give me a week to make the proper arrangements." Perhaps Gurney could help; he was due to return with Duncan in the next day or so, and he could surely find a way to slip Tessia away.

"I won't rest easily until I know for sure that my mother is safe. Take her with you, but let me know when everything has been taken care of." He told her of an identity he would assume for himself and a secure place in a slum in the city of Carthag. "That is how you can reach me. And I always know where you are. Meet me in a week? By then, we will have other matters to discuss."

Tessia had nothing to pack or carry. Jessica was already considering where she could hide the woman in Arrakeen for a few days. After Bronso hugged both of them one last time, whispering a long and heartfelt good-bye into his mother's ear, Jessica led Tessia to the exit of the wrecked spice factory, and the copper-haired man bade them farewell. He looked as if a great burden had been lifted from him.

"Please be careful, Bronso," Jessica said.

"I always am."

As night began to fall out in the desert, the two women slipped away, crossed the patch of spice sand, and boarded the ornithopter. Jessica powered up the engines and lifted off.

A FREMEN STOOD on a dune in the distance, watching through oil-lens binoculars. A veteran Fedaykin in a weathered stillsuit, Akkim had been studying sandworm migrations, one of the many scientific projects sponsored by Muad'Dib's School of Planetology. He was not certain how much longer this particular project would last, because it involved placing electronic tracking devices on the great worms of the deep desert—and the Qizarate criticized the practice, saying it tampered with the sacred domain of Shai-Hulud. However, Kynes-the-Umma—the father of terraforming Dune—had been a scientist and highly admired, even revered among the tribes.

Akkim didn't care about the politics, or the religious implications, which he considered to be minimal. Mostly, he just liked an excuse to ride the great worms and spend extended periods of time in the open desert. He was one of the best wormriders on all of Dune, the winner of numerous races and other competitions at grand convocations, whenever the members of many tribes gathered.

For nearly a month, he'd been summoning the monsters with thumpers, riding them, and implanting electronic tracking devices between their armored segments. One worm after another. He wondered how many there were, and was sure that his fellow students in the School of Planetology could use his data to come up with an estimate.

A short while ago, Akkim had been afoot on the sands, heading toward a wrecked and apparently abandoned spice factory he had spotted on his travels. He walked desert fashion, taking care not to cause vibrations that might draw a worm. His mapping experience told him that the wreckage had once been atop a fortified shelter for the Emperor Muad'Dib, and thus he considered it a sacred—and secret—site. He intended to install a signal device there, so that his comrades could confirm its geographic location. Dunes and spice sands in the Tanzerouft had a curious way of shifting, of moving over time as if they were living creatures, but this site was in a stable area, sheltered among the rocks.

While scrambling up a line of exposed rock that lay like the vertebrae of an enormous skeleton across the desert, he had gotten a view of the factory wreckage which lay like a beached beast up on the tumble of boulders and outcroppings, far from the open sands. That was how it had survived out here in the open for so long.

He was surprised to see three people emerging from the decaying mound of machinery—two women and a man. An ornithopter had landed nearby on the hardpan, and the women boarded it, surrounded by small whirlwinds of dust, while the man stayed behind in the abandoned spice factory. Akkim hurried to get out his binoculars, but the oil lenses needed adjustment, and by the time he got them set, the aircraft was already airborne and flying away in a blur of articulated wings. With his spotter imager feature on the binoculars, he took pictures of the craft, though there were no identification markings.

Smugglers, he thought.

Pointing the oil lenses at the spice factory, he studied the man watching the 'thopter leave. He wore what looked like an old smuggler uniform, and his face was partially concealed by a stillsuit mask. Using the binoculars, Akkim captured more images to add to his report. He had encountered plenty of spice smugglers out in the wilderness, hard but industrious men who refused to pay the Imperial tariffs.

Akkim took care not to be seen, feeling some trepidation. There were likely to be more smugglers inside the bolt-hole, probably using it as a base, and they would be armed, while he was just a lone researcher. Akkim did not move. Presently, the redheaded smuggler went back inside.

The Fremen waited. Just after sunset, he crept around the wreckage site, and found another 'thopter, gray and unmarked like the other one, well camouflaged. The School of Planetology did not care about the movements of smugglers, but Regent Alia would. He placed one of his spare worm-tracking devices on the undercarriage of the craft, and concealed another signal unit on the derelict spice factory. *Someone* would surely be interested.

In the falling darkness, Akkim sprinted across a rock surface, down onto the flat, and back up onto more rocks, climbing higher until he passed over a low ridge and dropped down into the open desert beyond. Safely out of view, he activated a thumper he had planted that afternoon and waited, listening to its rhythmic pounding noise.

Presently, he saw an undulating, subterranean motion out on the dunes, the approach of a great worm. With the ease of a lifetime of practice, Akkim mounted the beast, dug in his maker hooks, and set them to guide the monster. He would ride all night and another day to reach Arrakeen, taking his report back to the School.

Ultimately, trust is a matter of perception and detection, of small and large things, parts that add up to a whole. In deciding whether or not to trust, judgment is usually visceral and rarely based on strict evidence.

—DUKE LETO ATREIDES

Carthag, the second most populous city on Dune, had been called "a pustule on the skin of the planet" by Planetologist Pardot Kynes. The former Harkonnen capital boasted a population of more than two million people, though such numbers were only estimates, because many of those who lived and worked in the city eluded census takers.

Lady Jessica had her own reasons to dislike Carthag. Even after so many years, the Harkonnen stench still lingered, but she had agreed to this secret meeting. Besides, her news was good, and Bronso would be glad to hear that Tessia had been placed on a Guildship under an assumed name. By now, she was on her way to Caladan, armed with the name of someone on the Atreides homeworld, who would help her start a new life for herself under an assumed identity. Tessia was a strong woman, obviously damaged and scarred by tragedy, but greatly healed. She would have to relearn how to live as a normal person, but Caladan was the place for her to begin that effort.

During their secret discussions out in the desert, Bronso had arranged the time and place for this meeting; since then, though, Duncan and Gurney had recently returned with their supposedly triumphant news of progress with the Spacing Guild, which had imposed widespread crackdowns among the Wayku stewards. Jessica just had to trust Gurney to do his best to delay the inevitable.

After losing his Wayku allies, Bronso would no longer have an effective method of distributing his material, but his ideas would not be silenced. Over the years, his constant questions and challenges to Muad'Dib's mythology had gained their own momentum. Other critics had taken up the effort as well, raising further questions and collecting additional data on the numerous atrocities. Many people were cautious, but others less timid; they had begun to write their own analyses, targeting the errors and the lack of objectivity in Irulan's reports, especially those that had been published since Paul's death. The die had been cast. . . .

At the appointed time in late afternoon, wearing nondescript clothes, Jessica rode a small, rickety taxi through one of the city's slums. With its narrow, cluttered streets and dilapidated buildings, Carthag had grown even more tarnished and tattered since the defeat of the Harkonnens.

Her hood pulled forward to hide her face, she had removed her noseplugs to keep her senses alert. With her sense of smell, she searched the odors of the old city, absorbing her surroundings.

Many of the stained, blocky buildings—architecturally simple prefab structures erected for Harkonnen spice workers and the support industry—had grown like diseased organisms, patched and expanded with random and irregular sheets of metal and plaz. Dirty children played amidst junk and vermin.

Making a snort of either disbelief or disapproval, the escort driver stopped the small taxi. "Your destination, ma'am." While driving her along, the man had studied her on the rearview screen, trying to see through the façade of her worn clothing and her serviceable but faded stillsuit, as if he sensed Jessica might be someone more important than she was letting on. "Watch out for yourself around here. Would you like me to stay with you? I could walk you wherever you need to go—no extra charge."

"That's very generous of you, and gallant, but I can take care of myself." Her tone left no doubt that she could. She paid him a generous gratuity.

Looking up, Jessica saw a six-story building that might have toppled over from the weight of its decay, if not for adjacent structures propping it up. She stepped out onto broken pavement and walked along, seeming to ignore—yet intently aware of—shadowy figures lurking in doorways, watching her.

Bronso's instructions had told her to go through a metalloy gate on a side street. She pushed it open with a creak that sounded like a small, panicked scream, then climbed a plazcrete stairway to an upper level and turned right into a dark hallway. The odors of a poorly sealed body-reclamation still oozed into the confined space. The Fremen believed that evil smells were bad omens; at the very least, this one showed sloppy water discipline.

Before she could rap on a scarred door, it opened, and Bronso rushed her inside, out of sight. He closed the door quickly.

JUST BEFORE SUNSET, Duncan Idaho stepped out of a groundcar down the street from the target building in Carthag; Gurney followed close behind him. Uniformed men and women closed around the two men from their stakeout positions, moving from street to street. Gurney had insisted on participating in this operation, and the ghola did not seem to suspect that the two of them had entirely different agendas.

Though he knew the truth, Gurney felt trapped in a great Coriolis storm of events, and he didn't know how he could salvage the situation. Duncan and his troops were closing in.

The tracer on Bronso's 'thopter had pinpointed his location. For three days now, a ten-block radius around his dwelling had been kept under close military scrutiny. Only moments before, the hidden watchers had seen a disguised fellow conspirator hurry inside to see him, and Duncan was about to spring the trap.

Though the visitor's features had been largely concealed, Gurney felt sick, sure he knew who the woman was, though Duncan did not seem to suspect. Alia's soldiers, intent on capturing Bronso, would swarm inside, and the trap would close around Lady Jessica as well as the Ixian. Gurney worked his jaw, clenched his fists, struggled to find any possible solution, but he could think of no way to save her. If Jessica's collusion with Bronso were exposed, not only would it defeat everything she—and *Paul*—had hoped to accomplish, but she would undoubtedly face death. Without question, Alia would order the execution of her own mother.

Gurney's greatest fear was for Jessica's safety. If faced with the choice between saving her or the Ixian . . . she was more important than anything to him. *How can I protect you from this, my Lady?*

Duncan had all of his troops in place and ready.

At the forefront of the operation, the two men entered a dilapidated building across the street from the target structure. A lean military officer in a sandy camouflage uniform met them, identifying himself as Levenbrech Orik. With gestures made jerky by his excitement over the culmination of the long hunt, Orik led Gurney and Duncan past anxious soldiers to the crumbling stairwell. On the sixth floor, they crossed a littered hallway out to a wide-open room with a small balcony. Black scanlight bathed the area to prevent anyone outside from seeing them.

From there, the levenbrech pointed out the veiled window to a building across the narrow alley. "Bronso Vernius's hideout is two floors below the roof of that building. The 'thopter we've traced is on the roof, hidden by some sort of Ixian camouflage." Orik's voice held an angry sneer. "Our engineers have already dropped a riley-ramp into place, so we can cross as soon as we're ready for the assault."

Gurney peered into the deepening shadows of dusk, but saw only clutter on the flat rooftop. "Won't they see us coming?"

"We're protected by scanlight all the way, and there are noise-suppression systems in place, though sounds are harder to veil. Ixian technology against Ixian technology. He's only one man, and he can't match our resources."

Gurney was aware that to help capture the fugitive, the Ixian Confederacy had provided Alia with many new devices that used innovative technologies. Apparently, the Ixians wanted Bronso stopped as much as Alia did.

"Before we move, we should search every room over there," Gurney said. "Remove the innocents, in case there's violence." *Give Bronso more time.*

"We move now." Duncan looked at his wristchron, all business. "Let's close the net. Bronso has already eluded us too many times."

BRONSO BROUGHT SPICE coffee for himself and Jessica on a silver tray, handed her a steaming cup. He had been waiting a long time for this meeting. "Now that my mother is away from Wallach IX, I have begun to rethink my role, Lady Jessica. For the past seven years, I have done exactly what Paul asked. I did it because he convinced me of the necessity—attacking the reputation of a great man, my friend. I have planted my seeds, and we will see if Time's fertile ground allows them to grow."

He looked down at his hands, then up at Jessica. "But now the Spacing Guild has cracked down on my distribution network. Thanks to Duncan Idaho and Gurney Halleck, my Wayku friends have been arrested and my documents destroyed." His voice hitched, and he shook his head. "Oh, I shudder to think of the danger to which I've exposed my allies. My friends."

Jessica saw his pain and felt a similar sadness in her own heart. "When Paul charged you with this task, he didn't foresee that your work would still be necessary, all these years later. He's gone, Bronso."

"Then my job is finished?" The Ixian's voice took on a pleading tone. "Do I maintain my criticisms, or can I stop now? How much is enough? Paul said he didn't want to be a god, or a messiah . . . but how can I take *everything* from him? Vermillion Hells, there should be something left of his noble legacy! He was still a great man, despite what has happened."

Jessica felt torn between wanting her son to be revered and beloved and preventing the damage his memory and martyrdom could cause if left untarnished. "You think I can answer those questions? Oh, Bronso. Try to imagine how it must hurt me, as his mother." She suddenly realized what he was asking. "You want my blessing for you to stop, don't you?"

"It's exhausted my heart, my mind, and my soul. I have already said what I needed to say. I think I have accomplished the task that Paul gave me. The more Regent Alia tries to suppress my writings, the more credence she gives to my statements. Do I keep saying the same things, over and over? The doubts I have raised will thrive—with or without me." He stared down at his cup of spice coffee; he had not taken a sip. "Please tell me it's enough, my Lady. Tell me I can rest at last and make a new life with my mother. Have I accomplished what Paul wanted?"

"Of course." Her voice cracked. "You have already done all that Paul asked—and more. You built a levee against the flood of the Jihad, directing the channel of history in a different direction. Only time will tell how successful you have been." She felt a great relief growing within her. Yes, she could release him. "You eluded us for a long time when you and Paul were just boys. I suggest you vanish now, create a new future for yourself. Slip away, leave Dune, and find a place of safety on one of the outer worlds, where I can send your mother to join you one day."

His eyes were bright with a sparkle of tears. "I always make sure I have a way to escape in a matter of seconds. My 'thopter is camouflaged on the roof, and if that route is blocked, I've installed an Ixian high-speed lift tube that leads below street level and into a whole network of underground passageways the Harkonnens built. I have learned how to stay safe."

"Always having an escape is not the same thing as being safe." Jessica was unable to shake the uneasy feeling. "I don't feel safe here."

Bronso gave her a wan smile. "That is quite understandable. After all, you are an Atreides, and there are Harkonnen ghosts in this city."

WITH A FEELING of trepidation, Gurney heard chatter over a com-line as the command was relayed. He touched his earpiece. "They're reporting it's only Bronso and one other potential conspirator. Maybe it should just be the two of us, Duncan. Go in ourselves."

At the very least, if just he and Duncan went in, maybe the ghola's loyalty would let them save Jessica.

The other man shook his head firmly. "We will not underestimate him. Levenbrech, block off the closest streets, surround the building, guard every possible exit. Watch the 'thopter on the roof so he can't use it to escape."

Orik was eager to make his report. "Our engineers have cut the fuel lines and disabled the jet pods. He cannot fly away from us." With a hand signal, the grinning levenbrech led the way out onto the balcony and across the riley-ramp, which remained rigid and steady even as the men trooped across it quick-time.

Gurney said, growing more desperate, "Maybe I should go in first, try to convince him to surrender. Bronso will remember me. I don't like the potential for casualties—"

Duncan scowled. "A foolish risk to take. No, we will go in, full force. The time for half measures is past."

The assault team signaled their readiness, and Gurney felt a lump in his throat. He touched the long knife in its sheath at his waist. With their body shields activated, Duncan motioned them forward, and the net closed.

WITH HIS SENSES heightened and paranoia sharpened by living so many years on the run, Bronso detected the assault first. A change in the air, a series of faint, out-of-place sounds. He cursed and looked out a window, but saw nothing. Still, something was not right. "To the 'thopter on the rooftop—we've been tracked!"

Jessica balked. "They'll have pursuit 'thopters."

Bronso gave her a quick, sly grin. "Mine has Ixian modifications."

The sound of booted feet running in the corridor grew louder, and Jessica knew there was no time for further discussion.

AS THE TROOPS crashed through the door of Bronso's bolt-hole apartment, Gurney remained right behind Duncan. Both men had their long knives drawn and ready, but Gurney was ready to throw himself upon Jessica, to prevent her from being harmed by overzealous soldiers. He had to whisk her out by any means possible . . . if he could only find a way.

Reacting to a flicker of movement, he spotted a concealed door at the back of the room just as it closed. Before Gurney could hope that no one else would notice, before he could exclaim that Bronso wasn't there, Levenbrech Orik yelled, "They're getting away!"

Duncan smashed open the door at the back of the room. Footsteps could be heard rushing up the stairs. "To the roof!" he shouted. "Send more men to the roof!"

Gurney shouldered him aside and took the lead. Bolting up through the passage, he hoped to gain an extra second or two. He tripped intentionally on piled debris in the stairwell, stalled the men behind him, then proceeded upward with exaggerated caution.

Emerging onto the rooftop in the uncertain light of deepening dusk, Gurney spotted two shadowy figures dashing toward the faintly shimmering camo-shield that covered an ornithopter. Knowing what he knew now, one of them had to be Jessica. After a brief, heated discussion, the two figures split up, the woman running toward a different access door on the far side of the roof. *Good . . . they're apart.* If Jessica could get far enough away, perhaps she would have deniability.

Gurney knew what he had to do. *Cut losses. Focus on the objective.* Give Jessica just a little more time. "Bronso is our main target! After him!" This was a battle like so many others, and Jessica was more important to him, even given the sacrifice of the Ixian. "Duncan, I'll take the other one. Go!"

Moving like a shadow, Bronso dove under the camo-shield and vanished in a ripple of color and darkness. Gurney heard a metal 'thopter hatch being yanked open, a seat creaking, controls being activated.

With a burst of speed, Duncan bolted to the hidden aircraft as engine sounds coughed and ground together. With a disorienting flick, the ghola tore away the chameleon cloth and reached inside the cockpit to grab the figure behind the controls, hauling him out onto the hard, dusty surface of the roof. Bronso was no fighter, and the Swordmaster easily subdued him.

When she saw Bronso fall, the disguised woman eluded Gurney and ran recklessly back toward the 'thopter. She leaped into the fight, kicking and whirling with her own combat skills, hitting Duncan with repeated blows, forcing him to release his captive.

The ghola spun to face the unexpected opponent, raising his short sword. Even with her Bene Gesserit fighting methods, Gurney did not know how long Jessica could last against a seasoned Swordmaster of Ginaz. She eluded Duncan's thrusts, and kicked his weapon arm so hard that he had to shift the sword to his other hand. Her abrupt movements caused the hood to blow back and reveal her face, just a flash of skin and her eyes.

At that instant, Bronso threw himself at Duncan's legs, knocking him off balance. Gurney lunged to put himself between the ghola and Jessica, then hissed sharply, close to her ear. "My Lady! Strike me now—*hit me!* Then escape."

With a flash of understanding, Jessica drove a hard kick into the center of Gurney's chest, knocking him backward. He reeled off balance, retching, physically stunned. As he coughed and made a show of chasing her, she ducked into the roof access and plunged into another stairwell.

Levenbrech Orik and his men yelled to each other and spread out across the roof. Duncan seized Bronso and held him immobile. Strangely, the Ixian was laughing with a sound that seemed to carry a hint of relief. Duncan pushed the man roughly into the arms of two waiting soldiers. "Take him. Full shigawire bindings and restraint cuffs. If he escapes, you will explain your failure to Alia herself."

Hearing the threat, the men added enough bindings to hold a dozen Sardaukar fighters. After they had ushered the bruised Bronso away, Duncan turned his back to Gurney and shouted to the officer. "Levenbrech, take your men down the other stairway—catch the second conspirator! Gurney Halleck and I will secure the rooftop. We have it under control." The ghola's metal eyes were unreadable, but his face showed unmistakable fury.

As the soldiers rushed into the second escape stairwell, racing off to follow orders, Gurney found himself alone on the rooftop with Duncan. The ghola glowered at him, keeping his voice low. "You let her escape."

Gurney heaved exaggerated breaths, shook his head. "Gods below, Duncan, she caught me by surprise."

The ghola regarded him coldly, activated his body shield and stood in a combat-ready posture. "I have always trusted you, Gurney Halleck, but perhaps not any more. That was Lady Jessica. You let her escape, and I *will* know why." The flat face of Duncan Idaho was drawn with strain. He lifted his short sword. "You have a great deal of explaining to do."

Gurney could not deny it, didn't even try to. He activated his own shield, took a half step backward, and prepared to fight.

Each death is different, in myriad ways.

—Zensunni axiom

On the darkened rooftop, Gurney refused to volunteer any information, even to Duncan. "I serve the Lady Jessica and House Atreides—*as do you*, Duncan Idaho. Or have you forgotten your loyalties?" He stared hard at his shadowy companion, trying to detect any shards of humanity there, any remnants of his old friend and comrade in arms.

The ghola did not flinch. "I've forgotten nothing." Both men stood, their short swords drawn, body shields flickering.

"Damn it, Duncan, we've both distrusted Lady Jessica in the past. You were convinced that Jessica was the traitor to House Atreides, sure that Duke Leto himself had stopped trusting her. And you were wrong then—remember that. Just as I was wrong when I suspected her of treachery. Gods below!"

Gurney would never forget the feel of Jessica as he had grabbed her unawares in the Fremen sietch, his arm around her neck, the point of his knife at her back. His hatred for her had burned for years while he hid among the smugglers, utterly convinced that *she* was the one who had betrayed the Duke, when it had been Yueh all along. Back then, Gurney's own shame was so great that he had offered his life to Paul and to Jessica, but they had let him live. He would not fail her now.

"Duke Leto and Paul both trusted Jessica implicitly," Gurney said, "and they told us to trust her. Those are not loyalties to be taken lightly. They are *Atreides* loyalties."

Duncan remained implacable. "Alia is also Atreides—and she is my wife. I cannot question her orders."

In a sudden move, the ghola struck out, driving his blade against Gurney's body shield, causing him to parry and use the shield to its fullest advantage. Both men were skilled fighters and had trained together for countless hours on Caladan, had fought side by side on dozens of battle-fields. Gurney drove his blade forward, penetrated Duncan's shield at precisely the right speed, cutting his arm slightly. He withdrew to meet another blow from his opponent's edge and was driven backward by the ghola's anger.

Duncan seemed to have made up his mind. "I can no longer turn a blind eye to the answers that were in front of me all along. My friend-ship for you prevented me from acting on my suspicion that you were sabotaging or misdirecting our efforts to find Bronso. Why did you do it?"

Panting, Gurney eluded another thrust and then charged Duncan, putting him on the defensive. "Because Lady Jessica commanded me to!"

Duncan met blade against blade. "*Why?*" With a stiff forearm, he slammed Gurney against the ornithopter, so that the articulated metal wings creaked and flopped. He held Gurney there for a moment, pressing the blade tip against his throat. "If you refuse to answer, then your guilt is plain."

"Listen to yourself! When have we ever required explanations from the Atreides?" He pushed Duncan away, made him stumble backward. "When is your loyalty conditional on a whim?"

Hearing this, the ghola hesitated, a flicker of uncertainty. In that mo-ment, Gurney could have delivered a disabling blow, but he did not. "I wonder if you really are the old Duncan—the man who sacrificed his life so that Paul and Jessica could get away. Are you still guided by Tleilaxu programming? Or are you Alia's puppet?"

"Alia *is* House Atreides!" Duncan repeated. "Is the Lady Jessica a puppet of the Bene Gesserit? Why does she want the Ixian traitor to live? Why has she been helping him?" He pressed closer, pushing the sharp tip of the blade against Gurney's throat again. "You fight with words when your hand is weakened."

"And I see you've forgotten the things we taught Paul when he was just a pup." Gurney's gaze flicked. "Look down, and see that we'd have joined each other in death." It was a saying he'd used on occasion in practice sessions. The tip of his blade extended through the shield, touching Duncan's side where a quick and easy thrust could deliver a fatal blow through liver and kidneys.

"I have already been through death, Gurney Halleck."

"And what sort of ghola came back out? The real Duncan Idaho would never expose the Duke's Lady—whom we swore to serve—to total ruin."

Ultimately, Gurney knew he could not do this thing. He relaxed his muscles. "Do you truly believe that she would do anything against Paul? There are plans within plans here. Kill me if you must, but I will not betray her." He lowered his blade. "She is the Lady Jessica."

Duncan stood rigid, staring off into the tiny bright eyes of the Carthag city lights, then with a curse he threw down his short sword. It clattered on the rooftop. "If Jessica's involvement with Bronso is proved, there will be no stopping Alia from killing her own mother. She would never accept—or *choose* to accept—any explanation."

Gurney nodded. "I doubt Levenbrech Orik or his men will catch her if she has planned an escape. But if *you* expose her identity . . ." He clenched his hand around the hilt of the short sword. Duncan was unarmed now, and Gurney had one last chance to kill him.

The ghola remained silent for so long that Gurney feared he had fallen into one of the fabled, never-ending comatose states that flawed Mentats entered. Finally, Duncan blinked and let out a long breath. His voice was crowded with rationalizations. "Our orders were to find and capture Bronso of Ix. Accomplices are incidental, for now. Bronso has been taken into custody, as Alia requested, and I *will* ensure that he does not escape this time.

"For now, the extent of Lady Jessica's involvement—and her reasons—need not concern either of us."

Without melange, Paul-Muad'Dib could not prophesy. We know this moment of supreme power contained failure. There can be only one answer, that completely accurate and total prediction is lethal.

—*Analysis of History: Muad'Dib,* BRONSO OF IX

Bronso remained silent during the rough journey from Carthag, closing his eyes and concentrating on the vibrations of the military-transport 'thopter as it flew high above the dunes, casting moonshadows on the open sand below. The thrum of machinery reminded him of the great industries on Ix. He would never see them again . . . had not expected to for years.

Though he longed to know whether Jessica herself had escaped the trap, Bronso refused to ask questions of his captors, refused to utter a word. From now on, his manifestoes would have to speak for him. They were his words, written with a clear mind and a clear conscience. Others would spread them and keep them relevant. Others would continue to raise questions and doubts.

Bronso steeled himself: He would not let any torture-coerced confessions or distortions diminish the work he had done. Yes, he had embellished facts about Muad'Dib, extrapolated them, even spun and bent them to fit, but only to balance the equally false absurdities Alia had encouraged. No matter how vigorously the Qizarate tried to suppress his writings, copies would survive. And over the course of time, the truth would overcome all lies.

But Bronso would not be there to see it. He was certain of that.

At least he had freed his mother, and could rest easily knowing that Tessia would find a home, and peace, on Caladan. Jessica would make sure of that. . . .

BRONSO'S DEATH CELL in the deep levels beneath the fortress citadel offered no amenities, not even a pallet for a bed. One corner held a small reclamation still for bodily waste. He could tell from the lingering, wafting odor that the still had been used recently, and the seals were old. He did not need to ask what had happened to the cell's previous occupant.

He tried to sleep on the cell's hard plazcrete floor. Dim, unfiltered glowglobes provided the only light, denying him any direct awareness of the passage of hours or days, but with the implanted Ixian chronometer on the skin of his forearm, he could mark the exact passage of every interminable second.

Time no longer mattered, however.

With each stirring in the corridors outside the thick-walled cell, he sat up, remembering how Paul had come to him the last time he was here. The Emperor Paul-Muad'Dib himself had dismissed or diverted all the guards, then opened the cell door to let Bronso flee down empty corridors and dusty tunnels.

It made him smile to think of that now. Yes, even all those years after they had been boys together, Paul had remembered his promise. He had protected his Ixian companion—saved his life—by secretly setting him free. Bronso had followed the escape path out to the dark alleys of Arrakeen.

Weeks of public outrage had followed, and an unsuccessful search for traitors in the prison levels of the fortress palace. The hated Bronso of Ix had vanished from the most secure prison on Dune, like a magician, or a demon.

Not long ago, he had escaped execution again when the Face Dancer Sielto had died in Bronso's place—much to Alia's embarrassment. Now, though, the young Regent would take no chances. Her priests would interrogate and torture him, try to make him recant while she devised some particularly horrific execution for him. He had humiliated her too many times, and her animosity was personal.

He needed only to remember what Rhombur had endured in his life: the skyclipper explosion, the pain of living with cyborg replacement parts for years, the shock of watching his young son denounce him. And he thought of his mother, crushed by guilt-casting but finally finding her way back to consciousness, waiting for years to be rescued from the Bene Gesserit's clutches.

If his parents could endure all that, then surely Bronso could tolerate a few hours of pain, knowing it would be over soon enough.

He paced the perimeter of his cell, then forced himself to sit calmly, sure that hidden spy-eyes watched him. He would not slip into empty despair. He wouldn't give them the satisfaction.

The temperature in his cell increased, as if the baking sun from outside penetrated even this deep belowground. He perspired heavily. *Wasted water.* What irony.

If he had sheets of rough spice paper, he could have written his final thoughts, a masterpiece of sorts. He tried to write in the dust on the wall, but his words were unreadable and easily erased.

After his father's death, the Ixian technocrats had taken everything from House Vernius, bleeding away his family's power and influence, keeping him as a figurehead, and finally discarding even that. Bronso had given everything he'd had left to Paul Atreides, and at least he had made a difference. The legacy of "Bronso of Ix" would endure far longer than anything "Bronso Vernius" could have accomplished in the Landsraad.

He sat on the hard surface and stared directly into the glowglobe without blinking, not caring what damage it did to his eyes. Paul had been blinded in a stone-burner blast—so what difference would his own loss of sight make now? Muad'Dib's fanatics were the blind ones . . . unable to read, or understand, the messages Bronso had written. The glowglobes were far too weak to do any more than make his eyes burn.

His writings had emphasized the unvarnished facts, flaws and all, to hammer home the point that Paul was human, not a god, and just as subject to weaknesses as any man. One day, when he and Paul Atreides were joined in the dust and grit of Arrakis, it would matter little how many people knew why Bronso did what he did. The important part was that some people would heed the message.

However, when some forger—Alia, presumably—co-opted his name and spread an outrageous false manifesto, it marred the purity of Bronso's purpose. She had wanted to inflame anger against him, to drive people into the comfortable delusions of Irulan's version of history. That made him angry, but Lady Jessica knew the truth, and he trusted her to help historians navigate through the treacherous waters of fact and fiction.

My ego, he thought. *My ego lingers, but I must let it go. . . .*

He wished Alia would throw him to the crowds outside. He knew they must be shouting and chanting, demanding his blood. They would beat and trample him, but at least their fury would make the end swift.

"Shall I tell you how you're going to die?" A female voice filled the cell.

Blinking away the glare from staring into the glowglobe, Bronso turned to see that the cell door was open. He caught a glimpse of three angry-looking amazon guards outside, and young Alia standing there in all of her dark splendor. Only sixteen years of age . . . a few years older than when he and Paul had run away from Ix to join the Jongleurs. The black robe fit her closely, following the contours of her figure; the red hawk of House Atreides adorned one side of her collar. Interesting that she chose to wear the Atreides emblem, rather than the trappings of a fanatical cult.

He rose to his feet, acting aloof. "You are a poor hostess, Lady Alia. Am I to receive no food or water?"

"On Dune, we learn not to waste resources. It's the Fremen way. Your body's water will be reclaimed in a huanui deathstill."

He shrugged. "I know the Fedaykin death chant: 'Who can turn away the Angel of Death?' Are you my dark angel, Alia Atreides? On with it then. I have long been prepared to die."

He wondered how she would react if he told her now that *he* had reported to Jessica the conspiracy in the priesthood to assassinate Alia and Duncan. Bronso doubted if she would express any gratitude, though . . . and the information would only throw suspicion on her mother.

Alia remained haughty. "Don't expect pity from me, after all the pain you've caused, all your years of trying to destroy my brother's reputation."

"All my years of trying to keep him human." Bronso did not harbor any hope that she would understand, or desire to understand. "You've read my *Analysis of History* and other works, and I know you comprehend the purpose of my writings. You've even twisted them to your own ends. Isn't imitation supposed to be the highest form of flattery?"

Alia shook her head sadly, her expression filled with disappointment. "For seven years my brother and I hunted you. Now . . . you are just a dismal, uninteresting little man." Straightening, she raised her voice. "We have chosen a style of Fremen execution reserved for only the most heinous criminals. You will be put in the deathstill while still alive. We will draw out the water from your body, bit by bit, leaving your mind aware until the last."

Bronso did not let her see his expression of revulsion. Fear screamed inside him. But now, at least, he knew. He wiped sweat from his forehead in the excessively hot cell and summoned what little bravado he had left. "You'd best hurry then. At the rate I'm dehydrating in here, there won't be any moisture left to squeeze out of me."

She turned and departed, letting the amazon guards seal the cell behind her, leaving Bronso alone with his thoughts. She had wanted to intimidate him and make him fear his fate, but he knew that a cringing, whimpering death for Paul's greatest critic would only serve to weaken the impact of his writings. He could still help Paul a while longer. He vowed to himself that he would march forth proudly and face the deathstill with his head held high. He was sure Lady Jessica would be watching.

Outsiders call some of our procedures "Fremen cruelties," without understanding what we do. Consider the huanui, the deathstill that enables the tribe to recover and save moisture from those who have died. On a planet where water is the most precious of all commodities, how can this possibly be called cruel? It is practical.

—*The Stilgar Commentaries*

Bronso of Ix . . . infamous traitor . . . the man who tried to paint Muad'Dib as a man instead of a god. Though she knew the true heroism of what he had done, Jessica could not save him.

But she could not just abandon him, either.

Alone, she strode into the Arrakeen prison complex, down brightly lit corridors, tunnels, and wings protected by guards and yellow-robed priest-warriors. She had dressed herself carefully in the hooded black robe of a Fremen Sayyadina, covering the lower portion of her face with a nezhoni scarf, leaving only her eyes exposed. As she walked, the voice of Duncan Idaho came to her through a concealed earpiece. "At the next door, the entry code is 10191."

The year we arrived on Arrakis, she thought. An oddly easy number to remember. She wondered if they were hoping someone would try to break Bronso out, as had happened before. More wheels, schemes, and plots . . . more possibilities. Paul would have wanted that.

"Thank you, Duncan," she subvocalized. "Thank you for trusting me."

He did not answer. So many things going on behind the scenes, so many secret motives. . . .

During the uproar following Bronso's capture on the Carthag

rooftop, after the military teams had rushed into Arrakeen in triumph, Jessica had met Gurney and Duncan on the loud and bustling landing field outside the Citadel's perimeter. 'Thopters rose and landed, and service personnel rushed about. Firmly bound and gagged, Bronso had already been whisked into the highly secure levels of the death cells. The prisoner had put up no struggle; he had completed his mission and would no longer fight.

Jessica could tell immediately by their expressions that something had happened between Duncan and Gurney, and she wondered if the ghola had recognized her on the rooftop. When she faced the two men on the landing field, the tense silence had dragged out until finally Jessica broke it. Gurney already knew the answers, but now it seemed that Duncan held her fate in his hands.

She decided to take yet another gamble, hoping that this was more than a Tleilaxu ghola. "Duncan, if you are the real Duncan Idaho, hear me. *Paul* asked me to help Bronso if I could, in utmost secrecy." She could have used Voice to manipulate him, but she needed this to be Duncan's own, honest decision. "I can explain Paul's reasons, prove it to you. Or is my word enough?"

She saw him struggling to control the questions that reeled through his Mentat mind. He regarded her for a long moment with his metal eyes. "Your word is sufficient, my Lady." He bowed, sweeping one arm across the front. When he straightened and looked at her, his expression clear and readable, she felt convinced that this was the real *Duncan Idaho*, and he would never let his loyalty falter. . . .

Now, as she made her way through the prison levels, Jessica focused on completing what she had to do. She tapped the appropriate numbers onto the keypad of the sealed door, and a heavy barrier ground away on tracks, closing itself again after she had stepped through.

She had visited here once before, to free Irulan from her own death cell. Mohiam had also been held in a place like this before Stilgar executed her. Bronso, though, was on an even more secure level.

Duncan's voice guided her to the appropriate confinement section, but the additional security already told her that this was Bronso's cell. She let her scarf fall away and shrugged back her hood to reveal the gray-flecked bronze hair, and summoned her presence and majesty, as if she were a Jongleur performer. *I am the Lady Jessica, the Mother of Muad'Dib.*

The amazon guards and the angry-eyed Qizaras saw her, recognized her, and immediately straightened. "My Lady!"

Now she did use Voice, letting the intonations of her words as well as the commanding stance of her body push the guards and priests into cooperation. "I will speak to this man who has insulted my son. He has blasphemed against Muad'Dib, and he has much to answer for. He shall answer *to me*."

The priests seemed resistant to Voice, because four of them crowded together, blocking her access. One said, "We have strict orders that the prisoner is to be allowed no visitors before his execution. No food or water. Nothing at all."

Jessica let her anger hint that if she grew any more displeased with them, she would order their executions. All of them. "Should I wait and speak to him *after* he has been executed?" They looked as if they might all wither at once. "I demand a moment of privacy with this Bronso of Ix. I invoke the desert tradition. It is my right to face him."

The same priest said, "He is a dangerous prisoner, my Lady. We should have at least two guards accompany you—"

"I once bested Stilgar himself." Her look silenced the priest. "I have nothing to fear from this pathetic man."

At a signal from the priest, one of the amazon guards unsealed the door and allowed her inside. "Close it! I don't need an eager audience of gossipers." The woman left her alone in the death cell with Bronso.

Although the haggard, copper-haired man was clearly weak and thirsty, he sat straight, as if supported by the throne of House Vernius. It struck her what a tragic and lonely figure Bronso was. And yet he smiled as he recognized her. "I hoped we would have a chance to talk before the end, my Lady."

She silenced him with a quick hand signal, then reached into her robes and removed a small device, which she activated. The air pressure seemed to change in the room, and a subsonic thrumming vibrated at the roots of her teeth. "A blanketing field. Now we can speak in complete privacy." She smiled at the device. "It's of Ixian manufacture. Alia has many Ixian devices that have never been tested, and I've . . . borrowed some of them."

"Oh, I recognize that one," he said with a rueful smile, then looked up at her with red-shot eyes. "But even taking such precautions, you come here at great peril."

"You've risked much more over the years, Bronso. But don't worry— I have a legitimate reason to be here."

Bronso understood. "They think you have come to spit on me?"

"Ah, but on Dune, that would be no insult."

He just shook his head. "There is nothing you can do for me. I need you to be free, to remain beyond suspicion. I need you to be sure my mother is safe."

"She will be, Bronso. I promise."

He nodded. "I will not reveal our relationship, or Paul's plan, no matter how much torture they inflict upon me. If this execution makes me a martyr, well, then even more people will read my treatises. My writings will take on a life of their own . . . and some readers will believe what I say. The truth is a powerful weapon."

Jessica took a step closer. "So, Alia has told you the manner of your execution?"

"Huanui deathstill, while I'm still alive. I don't imagine it will be very pleasant."

With a sudden move, Jessica brought up one of her hands, revealing a silver needle in her grasp. "Bronso, this is the high-handed enemy, the gom jabbar. One prick of the poison on this tip and your miseries will be over—quick and painless."

He didn't flinch. "Alia has sent you as my executioner, then, just as she earlier used Stilgar? It's to be you? That needle would certainly silence me. You'd have nothing to worry about."

"*I* chose this, Bronso, as a kindness to you, and a reward for your bravery. The others will see it as the act of an outraged mother. Not even Alia would dare punish me for it." She held the needle only centimeters from his neck.

Though Bronso was obviously not afraid of the needle, he shook his head. "I thank you from the bottom of my heart, but I cannot let this happen—not only for you, but for my own legacy. Remember, I worked with the Jongleurs. What sort of finale would this be, a quiet and painless death, witnessed only by you? No, I prefer playing my part to the end. Let me finish this show and leave the audience satisfied. You must permit this, my Lady—for the Atreides name, for *Paul*." He pushed her hand away, and she lowered the gom jabbar. "Give me a last moment of dignity and worth. I am protecting Paul's legacy the way I was supposed to watch out for him when we were just boys. By holding to that promise, I honor not only him, but my father."

Jessica had not expected him to accept her offer. "Then take what comfort I can offer you." After secreting the deadly needle in a fold of her robe, she produced a small flask. "I brought water."

Trusting her completely, he drained the flask, sighed. "I won't need that after tomorrow. But thank you."

When he was off guard, she embraced him. "I'm grateful to you, Bronso. And so sorry." In doing so, she brushed the back of his neck with a different needle, leaving just a trace of potent residual chemical— another one of the new Ixian toys that the technocrats gave to Alia in hopes of impressing her. Bronso didn't even notice. As they drew apart, she thought, *I've done everything I can for you. Paul's good and loyal friend, and a true patriot of the Imperium.*

Then Bronso said, "Before you leave, slap me hard across the face. For appearances sake."

She concealed the Ixian device in her robe and switched off the blanketing field, then resurrected her infuriated demeanor. "Guards!"

The door burst open as if the amazons expected to find her under attack. Before they could step into the cell, Jessica swung her open hand, striking Bronso's face with such force that he reeled to the side. He pressed a hand against his throbbing cheek.

She sneered at Bronso and spoke for the benefit of her observers. "When you feel the pain of the deathstill, think of me. I have nothing more to say to the prisoner."

I have seen enough acrobats and dancers. I have seen amazing py-
rotechnic shows and solido-hologram illusions. I have seen audi-
ences swoon, scream, and cheer. But the greatest spectacle of all is
Life—and Death.

— RHEINVAR THE MAGNIFICENT

At the hour of Bronso's execution, Lady Jessica sat on a high observation platform, gazing down at the teeming crush of humanity in the square, the hawkers and gawkers, the unseemly carnival
atmosphere. Next to the observation dais stood the ominous deathstill, portending a slow and horrific end for the despised traitor. This
time, there was no chance that the victim was a mere Face Dancer in
disguise.

Jessica had wanted to remain out of sight, to avoid witnessing the
execution, but Alia demanded her presence. She had to play her role
in this show, just as Bronso did.

On a high seat next to her mother, Alia seemed exceedingly pleased.
Duncan sat at her side, expressionless. While he had grudgingly agreed
to trust Jessica and not expose her alliance with Bronso, Duncan would
not cooperate in any plan to free the Ixian, even if he did believe the
man was following Paul's true wishes.

To Jessica's practiced eye, Irulan appeared sickened, though the
crowd would misinterpret her expression as one of disgust. In her position as Muad'Dib's official biographer and historian, everyone assumed
the Princess was impatient to see the end of the malicious gadfly.

The crowds pressed even closer, and Jessica thought more people

had come to see the violence than had attended Paul's funeral ceremony. Watching the preparations with interest, Alia turned to her
mother and spoke in a casual tone. "You should be glad it is almost
over, Mother. By insulting Paul, Bronso insulted both of us."

Jessica could not disguise her bitter undertone. "And you think
Paul would have wanted this? Even after all Bronso has written against
him, the two were once close friends."

The crowd was getting louder, buzzing with anticipation.

Alia laughed. "Of course this is what Paul would have wanted. I
don't think you understood my brother very well at all."

Two Qizara guards escorted the condemned prisoner toward the
central dais, where the gray, slick-walled deathstill stood, its hinged
lid thrown back like the hood of a tribal robe. It reminded Jessica of a
sarcophagus for a giant. Taken from one of Arrakeen's many mortuar-
ies, the huanui was round and utilitarian, with tubes, separators, va-
porizers, and collectors. Its sides had been replaced with transparent
panels, so that the observers could see the victim's agonized
writhings.

Bronso walked toward his fate without hesitation or apparent fear,
holding his head high. *Yes, a true Jongleur show,* she thought.

When Bronso stood facing the transparent walls of the deathstill,
he looked at the workings. Although he was fully aware that he would
die inside that chamber, his back remained straight. After focusing on
the means of his execution, he turned to Alia. "Will I be allowed to
speak? Or will you silence me here, just as you tried to silence my writings?"

Alia's face darkened. "You have spouted far too many words." She
made a quick gesture, and one of the priest guards strapped a gag across
Bronso's mouth.

Jessica made no attempt to hide her disapproval. "Alia, by tradition
the accused has a right to speak."

"He is not accused—he is condemned. And he has said quite
enough, in his heretical writings. We have no need to hear more."

With a glance, Jessica tried to convey an apology to Bronso, but he
did not seem dejected, or even surprised by Alia's pronouncement. Instead, he nodded to himself and turned his gaze out to the crowd.

Before Alia could command her guards to wrestle him into the deathstill chamber, a commotion occurred out in the vast throng, accompanied by sounds of unrest and surprise. In the sea of faces, several men stood forth . . . all identical, all with reddish hair. They looked precisely like Bronso Vernius. More appeared, then dozens, then at least a hundred of the doppelgangers.

As they were recognized, a resonating gasp rippled through the packed crowd. Face Dancers, Jessica was sure—Bronso's allies. It seemed the gallant Ixian had guessed long in advance that he would someday face this fate; he must have asked the shape-shifters to deliver this last message, should he be prevented from doing so himself.

When the Bronso lookalikes spoke, their voices boomed out from artificial amplifiers, and their words—in Bronso's familiar voice—thrummed high into the yellow sky in a vibrating, convulsive harmony. "I am Bronso of Ix, and my final statement will not be silenced. I have opened your eyes and ears. I have diluted your myths with the truth. I have demonstrated that your revered Muad'Dib was *Paul Atreides* as well. And I have assured you that your emperor was only human, not anyone's messiah. By showing you who Paul Atreides really was, I have done him a greater service than all of your temples and all of the battles in your Jihad! I die without regret, for even when my body is gone, my words will remain."

Alia dispatched her guards, but the hundred or more lookalikes dispersed into the confusion of the crowd. The Face Dancers ducked and moved, altered their features. They yanked off their capes, rags and hoods, and tossed them away, discarding them into the stunned and astonished throng.

From her vantage, Jessica watched the flurry. The Face Dancers were like moths, slipping away, flitting, mingling, vanishing. Within moments, they were indistinguishable from others in the crowd, and she doubted if any of them would ever be caught. Although the spectators roared in indignation, they were clearly fascinated by the trick that had been played upon the powerful Regent and her priestly guards.

Trying to regain control of the moment, Alia raised her voice in a shrill command: "Commence the execution."

The priest guards cuffed Bronso forward, and he stumbled toward the deathstill. Jessica felt her heart burning with tears that her eyes could not shed, and decided it was time. She had her own trick that Bronso did not expect. In her conscious thoughts she triggered an activation code, then formed words, which she spoke silently deep in her throat and in her mind.

Bronso. Can you hear me? She saw the prisoner's unmistakable reaction, as his head jerked in surprise and he looked around.

Communication by nerve induction, she explained, never opening her mouth. *A prototype Ixian technology—extremely expensive, designed for espionage and surveillance. I applied the chemical to you in your cell. I wanted to be there for you. Now.*

Bronso seemed to freeze for a moment. Before him was the yawning mouth of the deathstill, behind him the howling mob. He turned his gaze toward Jessica.

"He's an arrogant one," Alia said. "Look at him glaring at us!"

Jessica concentrated, formed words inside her throat so that Bronso could hear her distinctly. *I am here. Listen carefully. I will guide you in Bene Gesserit techniques. Let me ease your suffering.* She could not teach him years of prana-bindu training in only a few thoughts, but she could help him focus.

"He is brave, Alia," Duncan said. "See the benign expression on his face."

"Gods below, I don't like this," Gurney grumbled. "Is this how we show the rest of the Imperium we are civilized?"

"It is how we *keep* the rest of the Imperium civilized," Alia retorted.

Bronso stood at the deathstill, looking inside. Jessica heard his thought via her own chemical receivers. *I feel much calmer now, my Lady. Thank you.*

The guards pushed the doomed man into the hard, smooth embrace of the deathstill, where he reclined willingly. The crowd roared, screaming insults in a babel of languages from the planets of the Imperium. For several seconds, Bronso gazed beatifically at the heavens, until the guards slammed the huanui lid shut, engaged the seals, and clamped down the heavy locks. At a nod from Alia, they activated the simple controls and began the slow extraction from Bronso's living body.

All the while, Jessica maintained a steady, reassuring contact with Bronso. *There is time for only one more thing,* she said silently. *Say the words with me.*

She knew there were monitors on his body that were linked to the deathstill, with remote technicians collecting data on the pain and nerve centers of his brain. Alia would be disappointed when she saw the flat, calm readings, very disappointed.

With enhanced concentration, aided by Jessica, Bronso detached himself from the agony of his shriveling, dehydrating body. She spoke with him through her transmitted thoughts, and in the final focus of his life, he repeated the words with her:

I must not fear. Fear is the mind-killer. Fear is the little-death that brings total obliteration. I will face my fear. I will permit it to pass over me and through me. And when it has gone past I will turn the inner eye to see its path. Where the fear has gone there will be nothing. Only I will remain.

After that, nothing remained. The deathstill completed its work, and Bronso became no more than water, chemical residue . . . and a body of writings that Jessica promised herself would not be forgotten.

He had given his life for Paul, just as so many other fanatics had . . . but for an entirely different reason. *Bronso did it for Paul,* Jessica thought.

We build our own prisons with our conscience and guilt. Exile is in the mind, not in the location, and I've come to realize that I can make my plans here on Salusa Secundus as well as anywhere else.

—COUNT HASIMIR FENRING

As a Bene Gesserit, Lady Margot Fenring had learned to *endure*. After spending years on Arrakis when her husband was Imperial Spice Minister, Margot did not see that this exile on Salusa Secundus was any worse. Now, conditions were improving by degrees as ambitious Imperial planetologists continued to work on the barren planet, resuscitating ecosystems that had been knocked flat by atomics millennia ago. Even with Muad'Dib himself gone, their work continued apace.

She and Hasimir could make do here, for now. And as soon as the ghola armies were ready, the Fenrings would be able to leave again and thrive in a new Imperial court. On Kaitain, she assumed—certainly *not* Arrakis.

Years ago, after the failure of their assassination plot using the sweet but murderous Marie, Lady Margot had expected to be summarily executed, but Paul had sent the Count and his Lady into exile instead—as Duke Leto the Just might have done. Unfortunately, the Fenrings were now forced to share the company of Shaddam IV, whom Hasimir had grown to despise.

The oblivious fallen Emperor still thought the two men were partners, working together for the restoration of Corrino glory, but Hasimir no longer regarded Shaddam as the rightful Padishah Emperor, nor even as a friend. The disgraced man was merely a tool, and Margot knew the Count would be happy to discard him at the appropriate moment. First and foremost, the Fenrings were survivors, always survivors.

Though the couple's movements were restricted on Salusa, offworld travelers could still visit them. When Margot received word that a transport had come bearing a delegate from Wallach IX, she was pleased to know that the Bene Gesserits still remembered her. Instead of a large delegation, the Sisterhood sent only one old and hard woman, the Reverend Mother Stokiah. Margot did not know her well, but she was intrigued about why she had come.

Hearing about the visitor, Hasimir raised his eyebrows. "Would you like me to join you, my dear? Hmmm?"

"I keep no secrets from you, my love, but a Reverend Mother may be uncomfortable having you participate." She knew he would listen in anyway, from a discreet hiding place.

Alone in her rooms, Margot prepared spice coffee and spread small pastries on an otherwise bare side table, an intentionally meager buffet to emphasize their frugal situation. The Reverend Mother glided in, wearing traditional black robes that made her look even older than she was.

Margot had never accepted the role of dowager witch; she preferred to maintain her beauty. Thanks to melange and Bene Gesserit biochemical control, the willowy, golden-haired Margot was still quite lovely to look at; Hasimir had certainly never tired of her. The two were compatible in all ways.

She greeted the other woman with a gentle bow—enough to show respect, but well short of deference. Margot had been so long removed from the inner politics of Wallach IX that she didn't even know if the woman outranked her. "Reverend Mother Stokiah. I've been hungry for news of the Sisterhood. We are so cut off here, so isolated."

Stokiah ignored the refreshments and refused the weak spice coffee. "The Sisterhood has been persecuted for years, stripped of power. During his reign, Muad'Dib cut us off and crippled us, and now his Abomination sister continues that policy—primarily because of your foolish attempt to kill Paul."

"Because of me?" Margot chuckled. "Come now, Reverend Mother, Paul Atreides held a grudge against the Bene Gesserit all the way back to when Mohiam tested him with the gom jabbar. When has the Sisterhood ever done anything to earn his goodwill?"

"Nevertheless, your foolish assassination attempt against him had little chance of success, and its failure had terrible repercussions. Alia still bears a personal grudge against you, and against us. You may have been exiled here for the past nine years, but the rest of the Sisterhood has been rendered impotent. The Regent seems to hate us even more than her brother did, if that's possible. We have never been so weak in ten thousand years! You, Sister Margot, may have single-handedly brought about the downfall of the Bene Gesserit order, which has endured since the end of the Butlerian Jihad."

Annoyance rose within her. "That is absurd."

When something changed in Stokiah's demeanor, Margot went instantly on guard. The old woman's voice became more resonant, her eyes flared, and tendrils of psychic force seemed to ooze from her, insinuating themselves like wet tongues into Margot's ears and around her chest.

"You must feel the guilt . . . the oppressive weight of the crime you have committed. The Sisterhood sent me here as a guilt-caster to make you *feel* the horrific consequences of your actions."

Margot raised her hands and squeezed her eyes shut as the pounding shame and guilt hammered her mind. "Stop! This serves . . . no purpose!"

"Our purpose is *punishment*, and you must crumble. Your mind will collapse into itself under the weight of what you have done . . . the *shame*. You shall live in a screaming hell of retribution, from which you will never be released. The Bene Gesserit have little left but our punishments, which we reserve for the likes of you."

In the years since she'd last had direct contact with the Sisterhood, and since the failure of little Marie's assassination attempt, Lady Margot Fenring had continued her private studies. But she did not have the same abilities as one of the fabled and highly secretive guilt-casters, did not understand what Stokiah was doing . . . Margot rallied a weak defense to silence some of the screaming voices inside her consciousness. But only temporarily.

The guilt-caster bared her teeth and continued to concentrate, slamming wave after psychic wave against Margot's mind, battering her crumbling defenses. Margot knew she would fail soon; she had neither the power nor the training to resist this for much longer. Her legs turned to water and she fell to her knees, reeling, struggling. She squeezed her eyes shut and tried to scream.

Suddenly the psychic waves crackled and skirled, and the invisible mental hammer seemed to fall to the floor, discarded. Reverend Mother Stokiah raised her hands, clutching her fingers into claws. Her eyes bulged.

Standing close behind the black-robed woman, Count Fenring drove his dagger in harder, then twisted it, withdrew, and stabbed the old woman again, plunging it deep into her heart. Not even a Reverend Mother with control over her internal chemistry could survive such extensive damage.

"Hmmm," Fenring remarked, gazing at the blood on his hand with interest rather than revulsion. "You appeared to be in a bit of difficulty, my love." He jerked out the knife, and Stokiah collapsed to the floor in a puddle of black robes and red blood.

"She caught me off guard." Margot struggled to catch her breath. "It seems the Bene Gesserit would rather turn against their own than develop an appropriate plan to regain their power and influence."

Fenring pulled a fold of black fabric from Stokiah's body, used it to rub the blood from his hand and his dagger. "So much for their vaunted skill of visualizing long-term goals. We can no longer consider the Bene Gesserits to be our staunch allies."

Margot leaned over and kissed him on the cheek. The last echoes of imposed guilt faded from her like ghosts in the wind. The couple stood together and regarded the inert body. "A pity," she said. "The Sisters could have been helpful when Shaddam finally decides to launch his ghola army."

"Aaahh, hmm. A pity." He nudged the dead Reverend Mother with his toe. "You know we will have to send a message to Wallach IX. If we hurry, we can package the body and ship it back before the Heighliner leaves again."

They decided not to waste time on any sort of embalming or fixative; instead, they wrapped Stokiah's corpse in airtight packaging. Margot then signed a note, which they affixed to the Reverend Mother's chest: "I don't need any more guilt, thank you."

Low-wage handlers came to pick up the package and deliver it to the shuttle, where Stokiah would be stored in the Heighliner's cargo hold and eventually returned to the Mother School. The roundabout delivery from Salusa Secundus would take some time, and when the Sisters on Wallach IX opened the package, they would likely be treated to quite a stench.

Had the choice been mine, I would have put Shaddam Corrino to death and Count Hasimir Fenring along with him. However, I will honor my brother's decision, though it may bring me misery later.
—ALIA ATREIDES, comment reported by Duncan Idaho

Accompanying the somber procession after Bronso's execution, Princess Irulan walked beside Jessica along a wide swath that the guards had cleared through the crowds, so they could make their way over to the deathstill. Neither she nor Jessica spoke.

Despite her initial resistance, Irulan had come to realize that the entire scheme *was* one that Paul would have devised: He *would* have set up his own nemesis in order to dismantle the massive power structure of his own legend by whatever means possible. And Bronso had taken the secret with him into the deathstill.

Alia and Duncan, the Imperial Regent and her ghola consort, ascended the steps to the dais where the deathstill sat in the sunlight. Reclaimed moisture condensed on its transparent side panels and circulated through internal vents.

Droplets of humanity, Irulan thought.

The Qizarate had announced a day of rejoicing, a ghoulish celebration, and Alia seemed quite pleased about it. The thunderous cheers grew louder as Alia, Duncan, Gurney, Jessica, and Irulan stepped up to observe what the government had done, the "justice" that had been served. Irulan tried to recall her former anger over all the things Bronso had written, the lies he had told, the bold exaggerations he had concocted. She was not sure if she would have been willing to die—at least not *that* way—to protect her version of the truth.

A group of priests formed a ring around them on the platform, surrounding the deathstill. The Regent spoke in a loud, resonant voice that carried far beyond the dais. "Princess Irulan, wife of Muad'Dib, you are now free to correct the historical record, to refute the absurd claims of Bronso of Ix, and to strengthen my brother's legacy for all time."

Irulan formed her answer with great care. "I will do what is right, Regent Alia." Jessica glanced at the Princess, but the answer seemed to satisfy Alia, as well as the crowd, judging by the exuberant response.

Though obviously disturbed, Jessica stepped forward so that she reached the deathstill before Alia. She raised her voice to the throng. "Priests, bring us goblets! This is the water of Bronso of Ix, and all of us know what he has done."

After a flurry of confusion, two Qizaras rushed forward bearing five ornate goblets. Irulan watched Jessica, struggling to understand what she was doing. Gurney Halleck held his tongue, though he seemed deeply concerned.

Alia, however, was delighted by her mother's suggestion. "Ah! Just as Count Fenring drank of his evil daughter's water after I killed her— so now we do the same to Bronso."

The priests formally distributed the goblets, and Irulan accepted hers. Despite the day's heat and the pressing crowds, the metal felt surprisingly cold in her grip.

From the deathstill's reservoir, Jessica decanted water into her cup and waited while Duncan did the same for himself and Alia. With pointed movements, Jessica also filled the goblets held by Gurney and Irulan. When the Princess hesitated, Jessica said clearly, "It is *water*, Irulan. Nothing more."

"The water of the vanquished traitor." Alia lifted her goblet. "As the enemy of Muad'Dib vanishes, his water rejuvenates us and gives us strength." She took a long sip.

"Bronso of Ix," Jessica said, then drank.

Irulan shuddered, suddenly understanding Jessica's motives. To her, it was not a condemnation, but a *toast*, a salute to acknowledge his brave, selfless actions, and the terrible sacrifice he had made for Paul and for the legacy of humankind. In a way, it was a counterpoint to the harsh but necessary thing that Jessica had done to the ten foolish rebels on Caladan, so many years ago. But this was not a goblet of poison, merely water. . . .

Irulan drove back her uncomfortable feelings. *It is water.* The liquid was warm and tasteless, distilled, filtered, pure . . . and not at all satisfying. But she drank it to honor Bronso, as Jessica had intended.

Afterward, Alia commanded that the rest of the traitor's water be distributed among the highest ranking members of the priesthood, as a sort of communion.

AS THE CROWDS began to disperse following the execution spectacle, a commotion erupted in the streets. With great fanfare, a troupe of acrobats began bounding and pirouetting, using suspensor belts to fly high in the air and perform tricks. People laughed and applauded, their good humor hard-edged and barely slaked by the blood of the man they had just seen put to death.

"Jongleurs!" someone called. Jessica watched them come, saw them use the crowd as a springboard. Agile acrobats, seemingly made of an elastic substance, pranced and danced and flew, moving closer to the dais, performing for the crowd as well as for the royal spectators.

At the front strutted an elegant man in an amazingly white outfit. He stood tall, raised one hand, and shouted: "I am Rheinvar the Magnificent, and we have come to perform for you in honor of Paul-Muad'Dib!" With a gracious gesture, he extended both hands toward the platform. "And of course, to honor the Regent Alia, the Princess Irulan, and the lovely Lady Jessica."

In the midst of polite applause, Jessica recalled something Bronso had said when telling his tale about Rheinvar: *Many things have changed . . . only appearances remain the same.*

The dignitaries remained to watch as the Jongleurs completed their show. Then Alia directed her priests to pay them handsomely.

You cannot hide forever from grief. It will find you in the wind, in your dreams, in the smallest of things. It will find you.

—The Ghola's Lament

The festivities after the execution of Bronso left Jessica's heart heavier still. Knowing that Alia expected her to be there, smiling and pleased with their "victory," Jessica put in an appearance, a brief one, for as long as she could stand. But as the hedonistic celebrations in the sprawling citadel grew louder and more raucous all around her, she could no longer bear the tension and the grim disgust she felt within her soul.

How could everyone be merry, when something inside her felt so obviously *wrong*? She needed to be alone.

The Bene Gesserits had hammered their training into her, to exert control over what they believed to be personal weakness, *human* weakness. They considered themselves such experts on humanity! But their attempts to control it—from prohibiting love to breeding for a Kwisatz Haderach—invariably fell flat. Human beings could never be controlled completely.

If they could see her now, the Sisters would likely have approved of Jessica's remarkable success at disciplining her emotions since she'd learned of Paul's death. But her very remoteness from her own feelings left her with a sense that she was incomplete, like a eunuch rendered incapable of a basic biological function.

Jessica had shielded herself for so long from any outpouring of emotions that she had successfully crushed that spark into a cold, gray ash. And to what purpose? On that night long ago, lost in the desert, when she and Paul learned of Duke Leto's death, she had wept . . . and she'd been greatly disturbed by *Paul's* inability to show his feelings. Later, during the Battle of Arrakeen, she had been upset with *Paul's* stony reaction upon hearing that Sardaukar had killed his firstborn son. Paul, the brave and victorious commander whose Fremen armies had overthrown an Empire, was unable to weep for that martyred infant.

Now Jessica had become the same type of person, unable to grieve, even for her lost son.

Now, in the Citadel, fleeing the maddening parties and the commotion, she followed an unconscious need that drew her through doorways and down corridors. To her surprise, she found herself at the entrance to the crèche. Something clarified in her mind. *My grandchildren*, she thought. *Young Leto and Ghanima—the future of Arrakis and of House Atreides*. She felt a powerful urge to see them, to look into their eyes and search for any hint of those she had lost: Paul, Chani, even her beloved Duke Leto.

By now the uniformed guards at the conservatory doorway let Jessica pass without challenge. She strode through one door seal and then another into the lush greenhouse that had been converted into a nursery. Harah was there, dutiful and loyal, like a lioness defending her cubs. She had wanted nothing to do with Bronso's execution or the celebrations afterward.

"Harah, I would like to be alone with my grandchildren for a while. Please indulge me?"

Stilgar's wife bowed, always formal around Jessica despite their years of familiarity. "Of course, Sayyadina."

The other woman slipped away, leaving Jessica to stare down at the boy and girl, only months old. These two already carried a great potential, as well as a strangeness, within them. Jessica knew that Alia had wrestled with Other Memories and unusual thoughts all her life. What else might these poor babies have to endure?

Although she had been reticent around the twins on previous visits— had only been to see them a few times—Jessica did not hesitate. She lifted one baby into the crook of each arm. "Dear Leto . . . sweet Ghanima." She leaned over and kissed each child on the forehead, and as she did so she realized it was a rebellion against how *she* had been raised, never allowed to feel any affection, never allowed to learn it.

Her vision seemed to double, echoing with memories as she recalled holding her infant son Paul for the first time. She'd been exhausted and sweat-streaked, surrounded by Suk doctors, Bene Gesserit midwives, Reverend Mothers, and even Shaddam's wife, Anirul. Paul had faced danger within hours after his birth, snatched away by a would-be assassin and rescued only later by *Mohiam*. How ironic that was!

Her words came out as a whisper. "What things must lie in store for you." She didn't know what else to say.

The babies gurgled and squirmed in her arms, as if they had established a mental synchronization. Jessica stared into their faces, and detected a ghost of Paul in the lines of their tiny jaws, the shapes of their noses, the set of their bright eyes . . . a biological déjà vu.

Vivid in her mind, Jessica imagined poor Chani lying dead in a birthing room in Sietch Tabr. Jessica knew how much Paul had loved her . . . and she knew herself how awful the pain had been when she learned that her Duke Leto was dead. But with prescience, how many times had Paul seen that same image in his dreams, knowing he could not prevent it? What must that have been like for him? Jessica could only imagine her son without his vision after the stone-burner, could not begin to comprehend how his towering confidence had been crushed by the unimaginable grief of such immense losses. Had Paul believed that he had lost everything? It must have seemed that way.

Jessica had her own part in the blame, too. She had not been there for him, had not offered her strength, sympathy, or understanding. Instead, she had remained on Caladan, turning her back on politics and on her son. Leaving him alone. She had alienated her children and distanced herself from them when they needed her most . . . just as Paul had now left his newborn twins. These two would never know the love of their father or mother.

Jessica held the babies close, and she kissed them again. "I'm sorry, so sorry." She didn't know exactly to whom she was apologizing.

Now, in the nursery, her knees felt weak. The babies looked up at her, but she could only see her imagined picture of Paul smothered by immeasurable sorrow as he faced his Fremen destiny and walked off into the dunes, never turning back, never intending to be found. "Now I am free."

There will be no shrine of his bones, she thought. *Not like my Duke.*

She hadn't even been there to say goodbye to her son . . . her beloved Paul.

Her knees gave way, and she sank slowly to the floor of the conservatory. Like a windstorm rushing across the desert, surpassing all expectations, the sadness, the realization, the *loss* swept over her, and she could not fight it. The unnatural Bene Gesserit strictures meant nothing to her. All that mattered was the grief that she had not known how to express—until now.

Jessica took a gulp of air and let it out in a low, whispered moan. She sobbed, her shoulders shaking, her back hunching. She drew the babies close to her breast, clinging to them as if they were her only anchor against the terrible buffeting storm.

My Paul . . .

The Fremen prohibition against shedding water for the dead meant no more to her now than the foolish commands of the Bene Gesserit. Jessica didn't know when her tears would ever end, but for now she let them flow as long as they needed to come.

THE REVELRY CONTINUED throughout the day at the Citadel of Muad'Dib. No matter where she went, Princess Irulan kept smelling the faint scent of death all around her, as if the seals of many deathstills had failed, letting the odors leak out.

It made her think of the rot of a decaying government. . . .

One of the Fremen women, new to the royal court, had brought a miniature vulture with her to the reception hall—and it perched on her shoulder, where it appeared to be asleep. In a tailored robe that could not hide her heavyset body, the woman drank several tankards of spice beer and cackled too much. Irulan would have found her irritating under any circumstances, and this macabre occasion made it even worse. Alia, though, seemed to like her. The entire celebratory affair was in very bad taste, a display of crudeness that never would have been permitted in her father's regime.

Had it really been necessary to overthrow the Corrino dynasty and replace it with a Fremen Imperium? Irulan had her doubts. It all seemed like a massive overreaction to the corruptions under Corrino rule.

The woman with the vulture, noticing Irulan's attention, turned to stare at her. The little carrion bird on her shoulder focused its tiny black eyes in the same direction, as if it considered Irulan prey. The Princess responded with a casual smile and wandered away, trying to disappear among people she did not know.

She filed details in her mind, already thinking of how she would por-tray the day's events in her ongoing, obligatory chronicle. Undoubtedly, Alia would insist that Irulan launch a new and vigorous campaign to re-fute Bronso's manifestoes, although many additional critical voices had begun to appear on planets scattered around the Imperium. On two iso-lated worlds, men looking like Bronso and claiming to be him had made very public appearances, denouncing the excesses of the Regency. . . . Perhaps they were Face Dancers, or just brave individuals. Rumors had continued to circulate that Paul was not really dead; no doubt, dissidents would make the same unfounded claims about Bronso of Ix. His legacy, or notoriety, would continue long after his death.

Yes, Alia would insist that Irulan write her slanted accounts, but the Princess had decided to demand a concession. Since the Regent had refused Jessica's request to take the twins back to Caladan, Irulan must become their strong foundation here. She would insist on spending more time with little Leto and Ghanima. Raising Paul's children would be her most important mission.

After Jessica departed, surely she would want familial reports of the twins' progress, objective descriptions of what was happening in Arra-keen. Perhaps the relationship of the two women could be strengthened, restoring what had once been a clear friendship. Cut off from her family, husbandless and surrounded by people who could easily turn into ene-mies, Irulan longed for someone she could trust . . . even if only through correspondence. Maybe that person was the Lady Jessica.

But Jessica was Alia's mother, too—not just Paul's. Irulan would have to walk a fine line.

On the Citadel grounds, Irulan worked her way across a square crowded with officials, priests, sycophants, merchants, uncomfortable-looking Fremen, scarred veterans from the Jihad flaunting their medals, and a few wide-eyed townspeople who did not appear to belong there at all. She looked for Jessica, but one servant informed her, "The Mother of Muad'Dib has retired to her quarters, to celebrate privately."

Irulan decided to slip away as well, to find much-needed solitude and quiet in her chambers, with the security seals engaged.

Before she could leave, a man appeared in front of her, blocking her passage. He had brightly colored clothing, a high collar, jewels on his wrists, and complex folds in his voluminous robe. "Majesty," he said in a low voice, "please accept this gift in honor of lost glory and our hopes for the future."

From the folds of fabric he produced a message cube, which he placed into her hands, activating it as he did so. Then he slipped back into the crowd.

Immediately, words began flowing across the face of the cube, from her father. She memorized them as quickly as they appeared and vanished, synchronized with her eye movements.

"It is time to make our move, my Daughter. Muad'Dib is gone, his heirs are mere infants, and the Regency flounders. At long last, House Corrino is poised to retake the Lion Throne, and we demand your assistance.

"Never forget that you are a Corrino. We are counting on you."

Stunned, she watched the words dissolve. The message cube crumbled into brittle debris in her hand. Paul was gone now, and what obligations did she truly have toward Alia—who had thrown her into a death cell? But the Corrinos could not lay sole claim to Irulan's loyalty either.

Irulan decided she would have to keep her options open.

She brushed the remnants of the message from her palm and watched the lightweight fragments flutter to the polished floor of the reception hall, where they scattered in the barely noticeable air currents.

The whisper of Caladan seas called to her, and Lady Jessica knew it was finally time to go home. When she informed Gurney that she intended to leave Dune in a matter of days, he could not have agreed more heartily.

That morning, she had informed Alia of her departure, and though the Regent encouraged her to stay longer, there was little sincerity in her voice. Jessica took the opportunity to extract a promise from her that Caladan would be permanently removed from the route of the pilgrimage and unsullied by angry veterans of the Jihad. In that, at least, she took considerable satisfaction.

Immediately after hearing her mother's announcement, Alia departed on an unscheduled week-long desert retreat with her priests and military leaders. "Matters of state are pressing. Goodbye, Mother," she said, and then apologized for not being able to see her mother off from the Arrakeen Spaceport.

Jessica knew that her daughter felt increasingly uncomfortable around her, and if she delayed returning to Caladan much longer, Alia would view her as more and more of a rival or hindrance than a support. Best to leave Dune now before any real damage was done to their relationship.

With Alia away, Jessica had a period of relative calm to collect a few mementos of the Atreides, especially keepsakes of Paul and Chani, to take back to Caladan.

Lady Jessica stood in her chamber with the familiar packing wardrobe open before her. Its sides bore the stickers and date stamps of transport authorities, showing the many planets and star systems she had visited since the time she first left Wallach IX as a young woman to become the concubine of Duke Leto Atreides. Jessica had seen a great deal since then, had experienced supreme joy and profound tragedy.

A calm feeling came over her. Caladan was her Duke's world, *her* world, and she belonged there. *My life is not over yet,* she thought. *There is still time for happiness.* And she knew Tessia would be there, needing a safe haven.

At her orders, the plaz windows in her quarters had remained opaqued following Bronso's execution. She did not want to look out at the square ever again, because it reminded her too much of the savagery to which mobs could be driven. A few glowglobes illuminated her apartment.

The wardrobe's wide doors were open to reveal bars and shelves inside for clothing, drawers for jewelry and other small articles, and a honeycomb of hidden compartments. With a fingerprint scan, she opened a secure drawer that contained special sentimental items and added an Atreides hawk insignia that the Harkonnens had cut from Duke Leto's uniform after his capture. Gurney had found it for her.

Just then, Irulan entered wearing a long dress that glittered softly golden, and pearl jewelry. "Would this be a good time to talk, my Lady?"

"I've been expecting you." She knew Irulan would never have let her leave without a final conversation.

The Princess clutched an object in her hands, as if her fingers were reluctant to part with it, though she seemed to have made up her mind what to do. She released her grip to reveal a long string of colored beads, polished stones, and small metal rings. Considering the extravagant and breathtaking jewelry she had owned as the daughter of House Corrino, this seemed a primitive necklace, a string of found objects that a magpie might have collected.

"This was—" Her voice caught. She drew a breath, straightening her long elegant neck, then began again. "The Fremen gave me this immediately after my formal marriage of state to Paul. A bond-strand, they called it. Even though they knew that Chani was Paul's love, the Council of Naibs had to recognize my marriage as a legal thing. The Fremen understood that.

"I was offended at the time and almost discarded the necklace, but for some reason, I kept it. Something in me hoped . . ." She shook her head. "Now that Paul is gone, I am giving it to you." She thrust her hands forward, offering the bond-strand to Jessica. "Take it. Place it with your other keepsakes of Paul."

Jessica accepted the strand, running it through her fingertips as if trying to read messages there. "Are you sure, Irulan?"

The Princess gave a small nod, then nodded again with more vigor. "This place is already infested with keepsakes and relics, many of them counterfeit. I want the bond-strand to remain in your possession, with other objects that are real."

"I will indeed treasure this, Irulan. Thank you so much."

The Princess's eyes lost their luster for a moment. "I need to say something to you. We haven't been the closest of friends in recent years, but you've shown that you trust me. I remember discussions we had in the gardens of my father's palace on Kaitain when I was just a young woman, before Paul was even born. I would like us to be good friends again. After you return to Caladan, I hope we can send messages to each other . . . to keep in touch."

Jessica arched her eyebrows in a mixture of amusement and alarm. "Haven't you had enough of conspiracies?"

A small smile. "I do not propose a conspiracy, just an exchange of information. Few other people in the galaxy can understand the problems we face, and I admire your courage."

Jessica sealed the secure drawer, closed part of the wardrobe. "You have proven your courage, Irulan Corrino. I know what you tried to do for Paul, and I know your loyalty to him, your supreme strength of character in defying your father when you knew he was wrong."

"I defied Paul, too, when I was complicit in a conspiracy against him. I didn't jump into it wholeheartedly, but that is no excuse."

Jessica's voice hardened. "And for that you must bear your own guilt. Still, Alia is bound by what Paul would have wanted. She thinks she has you wrapped around her finger now."

Irulan did not deny what Jessica had said. "It's good that you are leaving now, my Lady. You can see how the government is cracking down against even the most innocent dissent, and I am being watched—I sense it."

With a nod, Jessica said a great deal, wordlessly. Both of them knew that in Arrakeen the Qizarate had already begun holding public trials of purported heretics; a mere accusation seemed to be sufficient evidence in itself, and virtually all of those charged were sentenced to death.

"Perhaps you should come with me until things settle down here? As my guest on Caladan."

Irulan shook her head. "And leave Leto and Ghanima under Alia's care? A life on Caladan sounds almost as pleasant as Kaitain, but this is my fate, what I was commanded to do—by House Atreides, by House Corrino . . . and by Muad'Dib."

Jessica empathized, feeling her own duty toward Paul. Bronso's writings had successfully tarnished Muad'Dib's idealized image—at least among some historians, if not among the fanatics who had fought in the Jihad. She had heard offworld emissaries, Landsraad representatives, and even CHOAM merchants asking questions, demanding explanations from Alia, causing problems.

In the short run, the youthful Regent had tried to divert attention, reinvigorating several jihadi divisions and sending her armies out to purge populations where "necessary." But without their charismatic leader, the Fremen-led forces did not have their old fervor, their enthusiasm for fighting and killing. Many of the soldiers wanted to return home to their old ways and families, and armies had been gradually disbanding. As Regent, the girl might not realize it yet, but her rule was in trouble.

And what would be left to pass on to the twins?

"Yes, we have much in common," Jessica said. "Contact me on Caladan whenever you wish. I'd like to hear about my grandchildren, of course, and about you as well."

Irulan smiled and gave a slight bow. "I shall look forward to it, my Lady."

ON THE DAY of their departure, in a secure area of the Arrakeen Spaceport, Jessica and Gurney waited for the Imperial frigate to load.

They were accompanied by a Qizarate escort that neither of them wanted.

While waiting, Gurney set his baliset on his lap, though he did not play. In the tension of recent days, he had broken several of the old instrument's strings, but had not repaired them. "The air is too dry here, and music doesn't sound right. I'll fix it and play for you again, when we get back home."

Looking through a filtered plaz window of the terminal building, Jessica gazed at the huge citadel complex that encompassed a large portion of the city. Yes, she was sure that Paul had indeed charted a near-impossible course through hazardous waters. But he had left so much unsettled in his wake . . . including the twins. "I can't stop thinking about the two babies we are leaving behind."

"Arrakis is their destiny, my Lady, though I'm worried that under the influence of the Lady Alia—" Glancing up, he shot to his feet and set the baliset aside with a jangle.

The Regent strode toward them from the main entrance of the terminal, followed by four haughty priestess amazons in long white dresses. Their sandals clicked on the stone floor. Alia stopped in front of Jessica, and smiled. "I decided I could not let you go without saying goodbye after all, Mother."

"I'm glad, but surprised. I thought you were on retreat."

"And you are *in* retreat, going back to Caladan." Alia's hauteur was forced, her voice showing faint but distinct tonal patterns of longing, a hair-fine hint of desperation.

Jessica shook her head, answered in a mild voice, "Hardly a retreat. I have no reason to flee—and I am always available to you. As Imperial Regent, you have all the advisers you could wish for." She looked dismissively at the priestesses. "But I am your mother, and if ever you need me, if ever you require advice or just an understanding ear, I will help you." She softened her voice. "You're my daughter, as Paul was my son, and I will always love you both."

The amazon priestesses stepped over to Jessica's sealed wardrobe and began to inspect it, but Alia brusquely waved the women away. She turned back to Jessica. "I understand that you have taken valuable artifacts with you, keepsakes of my father and my brother."

Jessica stiffened. "A few personal articles, reminders of my husband

and my son. I don't want them replicated to be sold as trinkets by vendors, whether or not they are authorized by the government." Wondering why Alia would push back on such a trivial thing, Jessica was prepared to argue the point, though she didn't want her departure to end on a sour note.

The young woman smiled enigmatically, dipped a hand into a pocket of her black aba robe, and withdrew it, her fingers clenched in a tight fist. "Then there is one more thing that belongs with you on Caladan, Mother. Something that should never be copied for seekers of souvenirs."

She opened her fist, palm up, to reveal the hawk signet ring that Duke Leto had worn, and then Paul. The official ducal ring of House Atreides.

Caught off guard, Jessica fought back a wash of emotions. She took the ring, turned it over in the light to examine it, saw the signs of wear and the mark of the engraver—all as she remembered. Alia's voice was barely a whisper. "It's real, Mother."

"I don't know what to say." Memories flooded over Jessica with the swiftness of an unexpected windstorm out on the sands. "This pleases me very much."

"Only the two of us know how much you loved your noble Duke." Alia's Fremen blue eyes glistened, and Jessica reached out and hugged her, the first time she'd done so in some time. Normally, Alia would have pulled away, but not now.

"I'm overwhelmed by this, by what you've done for me." Jessica tightened her grip around the priceless ring.

Though the Imperial frigate was ready for boarding, Gurney waited in silence, giving Jessica all the time she needed. She continued to look into her daughter's face, measuring her, studying the spark of compassion she saw. She hoped it was more than a brief detour on Alia's journey in an entirely different direction.

"I'll keep your offer in mind, Mother. Will you return here in a few years perhaps, after all this turmoil has quieted?"

Jessica could only nod. In time, all things came back to Dune.